UP
ALL
NIGHT

ALSO BY LAURA SILVERMAN

Girl Out of Water
You Asked for Perfect
It's a Whole Spiel
Recommended for You

UP
ALL
NIGHT

13 STORIES BETWEEN
SUNSET AND SUNRISE

edited by LAURA SILVERMAN

Algonquin 2022

Published by Algonquin Young Readers
an imprint of Algonquin Books of Chapel Hill
Post Office Box 2225
Chapel Hill, North Carolina 27515-2225

a division of Workman Publishing
225 Varick Street
New York, New York 10014

Printed in the United States of America.
Design by Carla Weise.

Library of Congress Cataloging-in-Publication Data
Names: Silverman, Laura, editor.
Title: Up all night : 13 stories between sunset and sunrise / edited by Laura Silverman.
Description: First edition. | Chapel Hill, North Carolina : Algonquin Young
    Readers, 2021. | Audience: Ages 12 and up. | Audience: Grades 7–9. |
Summary: A collection of thirteen short stories by young adult authors,
    all revolving around the theme of staying up late into the night.
Identifiers: LCCN 2020056550 | ISBN 9781643750415 (hardcover) |
    ISBN 9781643751641 (ebook)
Subjects: LCSH: Night—Juvenile fiction. | Short stories, American. |
    CYAC: Night—Fiction. | Short stories.
Classification: LCC PZ5 .U728 2021 | DDC [Fic]—dc23
LC record available at https://lccn.loc.gov/2020056550

ISBN 978-1-64375-263-1 (PB)

10 9 8 7 6 5 4 3 2 1
First Paperback Edition

For all the night owls

CONTENTS

UP
ALL
NIGHT

NEVER HAVE I EVER

by Karen M. McManus

IF THIS WERE A NORMAL FRIDAY NIGHT, I WOULD'VE LEFT
Katie Chang's party before midnight. Curfew is nonnegotiable
in the Finch household, and I'm way past it. But my parents
are in Bermuda for their anniversary, and as Katie pointed out
when convincing me to stay, "It's not like they put a tracking
device on your phone before they left, Grace."

Probably. My father didn't become the detective with the
most arrests on the Owens Mills police force without having a
few tricks up his sleeve. It's almost two in the morning, though,
and I haven't received a *get your ass home* text yet, so I'm probably safe.

From parental ire, anyway. Not from playing what feels
like an endless Never Have I Ever card game in Katie's basement. Granted, I'm the one who suggested it, but we've barely

started and I'm already yawning. Still, this is about as exciting as nightlife gets for our band-nerd crew, even when it's well after midnight.

"Never have I ever gone skinny dipping," Malik Roy, Katie's boyfriend, reads from the card he's holding. The dozen or so people sitting in a circle on Katie's threadbare rug all take a drink, except for me.

"Liars," I say.

Malik rolls his eyes as he chugs the last of his beer. "Grace Finch, ladies and gentlemen. Oh-for-four in this game because she's allergic to fun."

"Because I'm honest," I protest. "You guys are only pretending you've done stuff so you can drink."

"Which. Is. *Fun*," Malik reminds me.

"I guess," I mutter, shifting restlessly beside him. Every party at Katie's house is exactly the same: we watch movies, we drink (but never too much), and we play some kind of game. Usually, the game is designed to let us experiment with being edgier than we actually are; last time, it was Crimes Against Humanity.

Which is fine. Obviously. I'm Detective Steve Finch's only child; mildly risqué card games and warm beer are as edgy as I'm supposed to get. I am, as my father likes to remind me, a Role Model. I used to chafe at being labeled "the boring one" in a group that's not known for excitement, but I've come to accept it. Mostly.

"Maybe you're not asking the right questions," someone says.

We all turn at the new voice, and my pulse picks up when I see who's leaning against Katie's wall near the basement stairs.

"What the hell is Caleb Manning doing here?" my friend Adita whispers in my ear. It shouldn't be any surprise that Caleb's at a late-night party—that's pretty much what he's known for, along with using his older brother's ID to buy alcohol for said parties—but he's never bothered with our crowd before. Everybody in the circle tenses, like a herd of gazelles that just realized a lion wandered into their midst during mealtime.

"I, um . . ." I whisper back, trailing off as Caleb's eyes find mine and he smirks in recognition. "I might've invited him."

Take *that*, Malik. Caleb Manning might be a lot of things, but boring isn't one of them.

"Whaaaaaat?" Adita breathes, taking a bracing sip from her cup. Of Sprite. She drove here, but even if she hadn't, she's not a drinker. "When did you . . . why would you . . ."

"It was a spur of the moment thing," I say. "We were both in the principal's office this afternoon." My friend's eyebrows arch higher as I add, "I was making copies of next week's resolution for debate team." Debate is one of the many, many extracurricular activities that Adita and I do together.

"And what was *he* doing?"

"I didn't ask. It seemed, um, discipline-related."

Adita regards me doubtfully, and I don't blame her. She's one of the most careful, methodical people I've ever met. She needs a scholarship to get out of Owens Mills, and every move she makes is part of a complex calculation where the underlying equation is always *how will this look to a college admissions officer?*

Sometimes I want to ask her if she ever gets the urge to break out of our good-girl roles and do something unexpected. But it's not a fair question; she doesn't think she has the option.

Even being in the same room as someone like Caleb is practically giving her hives.

Maybe I shouldn't have rocked the boat like this. But it's too late now.

Someone hands Caleb a beer and he takes it without looking at them, draining half of it in one gulp. His bright blue eyes rove around the room, a half-smile on his lips. Caleb is tall and lean, with shaggy, dark blond hair that frames sharp cheekbones and a strong jaw, and he would hands-down be the most sought-after guy at Owens Mills High if he ever decided to lose the attitude. And the criminal tendencies.

Adita plucks at my sleeve. "Are you *into* him?" she hisses.

"Of course not! I was just being nice."

"Not to Katie you weren't," Adita mutters. And I have to agree: Katie looks more than a little terrified as Caleb moves closer to the Never Have I Ever circle. "Have you forgotten your father arrested Caleb? Or has *he*?"

"Nobody's forgotten that." It was last summer, for trespassing in a skate park after dark. Before that, Caleb had been warned a few times by other Owens Mills cops about disturbing the peace and underage drinking, so that relatively minor crime landed him on probation. Along with a permanent spot on my father's shit list.

Which, admittedly, is part of why Caleb interests me. It's exhausting being Steve Finch's daughter for lots of reasons, not the least of which is the long list of people, places, and behaviors I'm supposed to avoid. When everything you do is scrutinized, there's something fascinating about someone who couldn't care less about rules.

"He looks twitchy," Adita says, her mouth pressed into a thin line. "I'll bet he's high."

"So are we playing or what?" Caleb asks. He doesn't sit, though—just sort of looms over Malik, who's still holding the Never Have I Ever cards.

"Uh, yeah. You know the rules, right? You just—" Malik goes to hand the deck of cards to the girl sitting next to him, but Caleb intercepts them.

"Let me guess," he says, deftly shuffling the deck with one hand. "You're playing old school. Drink if you've done whatever the card says, right?" He doesn't wait for an answer. "That's boring. We should mix it up, ultimate-challenge style."

"What does that mean?" Katie asks, her eyes on the spinning cards.

Caleb drops them into his other hand and extracts a single card from the deck, holding it against his chest. "One-on-one. I pick someone to take a turn, and they have to do whatever the card says—right now. So who should it be?" He takes his time shifting his gaze across the silent group. "Eenie . . . meenie . . . miney . . . Finch," he finally says, locking eyes with me.

"No way," I say. "That's not how you play." I turn to Adita for support, but she just shakes her head. The expression on her face couldn't be more clear: *serves you right.*

Malik, who's looked nervous ever since Caleb walked in, starts to grin. Of course he would; the last few cards all had to do with getting naked. "Change approved," he says. "Let's see what you've got, Grace."

"Absolutely not—" I start, but Caleb's already reading the card.

"Never have I ever . . ." He frowns, full lips turning down. "Spied on a neighbor. Huh. That's boring. Let's do a different one."

"You can't," I say quickly, letting a relieved smile spread across my face. "That would go against the rules *you* just established. Anyway, Katie's neighbors aren't boring. She lives across the street from a haunted house, you know."

Caleb's brow furrows. "A what now?"

"Murphy Manor!" Malik crows. When Caleb doesn't react, he adds, "Come on, you must've seen it on your way here. Giant Victorian that looks like it should be condemned? Same old dude has lived there for, like, fifty years."

Katie nods energetically, eyes wide. Her strange neighbor is one of her favorite topics. "Mr. Murphy's wife died a few years ago from *unknown causes*," she says, her voice dipping dramatically on the last two words. "Like, she wasn't sick or anything, and she wasn't even *that* old. Ever since then—and I swear to god I'm not making this up—we keep hearing weird noises, like someone's crying or moaning. And sometimes I see a figure in the window that's, like, *transparent*."

Caleb stares at her. "Are you for real right now?"

"Oh, yes." Katie smiles happily, her earlier nerves forgotten. "It's totally haunted. Mrs. Murphy had all the money, you know. She inherited that house from her family and she was super cheap. People say Mr. Murphy got rid of her so he could finally enjoy life, but it backfired because her ghost is still there and she's slowly driving him insane."

"Nothing slow about it," Malik says under his breath.

"Katie," Adita says patiently. "There's no such thing as ghosts."

"You haven't heard the noises!" Katie insists. "Or seen the *figure*."

"Well, I guess that settles it." Caleb stuffs the card into the pocket of his ratty leather jacket. "Come on, Finch. Let's go spy on a haunted house."

"Let's?" I ask. "When did this become a team effort?"

The half-smile is still on his lips. "I can't make you deal with a ghost all by yourself."

"We should all go," Malik says, rubbing his hands together. Which isn't surprising; he's the self-appointed *fun one* of our group. If something interesting is going to happen, he's not about to miss it.

Adita glances between Caleb and me with a faint frown. She looks like she can't decide whether Caleb is more likely to try to kiss me or kill me on the way to Mr. Murphy's house—or which one would be worse. "Great idea," she says drily. "We'll turn Never Have I Ever into a late-night, live-action game involving trespassing on a potentially disturbed man, because what could possibly go wrong with that?"

I avoid her glare. "The more the merrier."

She sighs. "Is that your way of saying I have to come with you?"

Malik turns to Katie. "You in, Katie Kat?"

Katie shakes her head firmly. "No thanks."

"Thought you were into ghosts?" Malik teases.

"I am. I'm also into maintaining respectful boundaries with them. Especially when they live across the street," Katie says. Caleb hands the deck of cards to her and she tries to shuffle them like he did, but only manages to spill them onto the floor. "Plus, I still have guests, so . . ."

"There are enough people going already, anyway," I say, getting to my feet before the crowd can mushroom even more. A yawn builds at the back of my throat—I almost never stay up this late—and I swallow it before shaking out my hands to wake myself up. "We'll report back once I win this round."

The four of us have barely gotten down the front steps of Katie's house when we see it—bright lights burning in half the windows of Mr. Murphy's house, shining like a beacon into the darkness that surrounds us.

"So . . . he's still up?" Adita asks, her steps slowing. I'm surprised she made it this far, to be honest; loyalty to your bestie since fifth grade only goes so far. When it comes to College Admissions Math, trespassing = no Ivy League.

"Or the ghosts are," Malik says, raising his hands and wiggling his fingers to show just how not-bothered he is. "Boooooo."

"Ha, ha." She shoves at his arm, stopping in place. "Forget it. Let's go back inside. I thought he'd be asleep."

Caleb shrugs. "Maybe he sleeps with the lights on. But if not, who cares? We're *spying*, remember?" He turns and walks backwards, arms spread out as he speaks in an exaggerated stage whisper. "The whole point is to be sneaky. He'll never know we're there."

"I don't like it," Adita says stubbornly. "This is a bad idea. I'm out." She puts her hands on her hips and cocks her head toward me. "You should be too, Grace. If Mr. Murphy is awake he'll call the police on you, and your father will *lose it*."

I pause a beat. The night is cloudy and windy, the moon a pale crescent above us. The Changs' house and Mr. Murphy's are the only two at the end of their cul-de-sac, separated from the rest of the street by a wooded area. Everything is quiet and peaceful. "Only if we get caught," I say.

Caleb puts his hands together in a silent clap. "Grace Finch, ladies and gentlemen. Turning to the dark side." He glances at Malik. "You bailing too, man?"

"Nah," Malik says, although he sounds less sure than he did a minute ago. "Come on, Adita, we're just gonna peek in the guy's window. It's not a big deal."

"It's a bad idea," Adita repeats. "I'm going inside. And I'll probably head home in like ten minutes, Grace, so you'd better be back by then if you want a ride."

"I can take you home," Caleb offers.

Adita rolls her eyes. "This night just keeps getting better and better," she says. Then she backtracks through the Changs' front door, shutting it firmly behind her.

"Never have I ever been a tightass," Caleb murmurs, and I swallow a guilty laugh. Adita's right; she always is. But I can't turn back now.

The three of us cross the darkened street toward Mr. Murphy's house. It must have been gorgeous when it was first built: graceful turrets, wide stairs leading to a stately front door, high windows with stained-glass detail, and beautiful crown molding everywhere. But years of neglect have left it decrepit and crumbling, the white paint peeling so badly that the entire house looks gray. The grass is almost knee-length, the bushes surrounding the house wild and unkempt. It's the polar opposite of my parents' neat, orderly Cape, and I have to admit: I kind of like it. There's something dramatic and forbidding about the entire scene, almost as though we're stepping into a dark fairy tale—or, like Katie said, a ghost story. An alternate reality where anything could happen.

"We should approach from the side," I whisper when we reach the edge of Mr. Murphy's lawn. "Then make our way to those bushes under the window."

We're halfway there when the wind picks up around us, causing one of the loose shutters on the bay window to rattle. Malik lets out a startled yelp, then drops to the ground with his arms over his head like he's dodging sniper fire. "Did he hear me? Is he coming?" he asks, his voice low and panicked.

Caleb and I both crouch beside him, waiting, but there's no sound except the wind and our own ragged breathing, and no movement from Mr. Murphy's house. "We're good," I whisper. "Maybe we should crawl the rest of the way, though."

"Adita might've had the right idea after all," Malik murmurs, but he follows my lead to the edge of the bushes that run across the front of the house. I wanted to slip behind them but now that I'm here I realize it's impossible; they're too close to the house. So we creep beside them, hunched over, until we reach the bay window. Then I force my way between two bushes, their stiff needles pricking my arms, and stand on my tiptoes. "I can't see inside," I whisper. "I'm too short. Can you?"

Caleb's a lot taller than me, but still a few inches shy of the window. "Here," he whispers over my shoulder, and before I realize what's happening his arms have wrapped around me, lifting me a few feet off the ground. I exhale sharply, surprised at the suddenness of the movement—and yeah, okay, maybe a little breathless at the contact, too.

But once I get my bearings, I have a clear view into the room. It's filled with clutter, floor-to-ceiling bookshelves and heavy, old-fashioned furniture. Even with the lights blazing, it's a dark and dreary space. Everything looks forlorn, from the circular rug in an outdated floral pattern to the mismatched lamps on either side of the couch.

"What do you see?" Caleb asks.

"A couch," I start, but I don't get anything else out before he grunts dismissively.

"Nobody gives a crap about the furniture, Finch. Is anyone there?"

My eyes rove around the room, flicking from one corner to the next. Even though I know Katie's ghost story is bull, the back of my neck still prickles at the way certain shadows fall. The grandfather clock looming against the far wall looks a lot like a person, and I could see how glancing through the window during a certain time of day might—

"*Finch*," Caleb says. He's starting to sound a little out of breath. "Speed up the surveillance. I don't have arms of steel over here."

"I think we're done, right? With the game?" Malik asks nervously. "I mean, we're spying. We've spied. Nothing on the card said we had to do it indefinitely."

"I don't see—wait." My whisper gets urgent as the shape I've been looking at suddenly becomes clear. "Guys. There's a foot."

"A foot of what?" Malik asks.

"A *person's* foot. On the floor, behind the couch."

Caleb is still holding me. I peer down at Malik's worried, upturned face, reflected moonlight obscuring his eyes behind his glasses. "Is someone, like, hiding?" he asks uncertainly.

"I don't think so. Put me down." Caleb drops me so quickly that I stumble when my feet hit the ground, and have to grab his arm for support. "It looks like whoever it is might've fallen or something, but I couldn't see enough to tell."

"We better check it out," Caleb says. "Maybe the old guy hurt himself. Depending on what kind of lock he has, I might be able to pick it."

"Are you out of your mind?" Malik asks. "We can't break into his house at three o'clock in the morning!"

"Malik's right," I say. "We should call an ambulance."

Malik bites his lip. "And then what? How do we explain why we're here?"

"I mean . . . probably the truth, right?" I say.

While we were talking, though, Caleb was already mounting the front steps. Now he's poised with one hand pressed against the door. "Guys," he calls in a loud whisper. "It's open."

"What?" I make my way beside him and see that he's right; there's a shadowy sliver of empty space between the door and its frame. "Why would it be open in the middle of the night?"

"I don't know," Caleb says. He pushes lightly on the door, causing it to swing fully open with a loud, prolonged creak. "But it is."

"Oh, hell. We need to leave." Malik sounds full-on panicked now. "Somebody might still be inside. Caleb, don't—*Caleb!*"

Too late. Caleb's already inside, and with a resigned look over my shoulder to Malik, I join him in Mr. Murphy's hallway.

It's dead silent inside the house, except for a loud ticking that's probably the grandfather clock I saw in the living room. I take a deep breath, and the dust that tickles my nostrils almost makes me sneeze. A large, curving staircase is in front of me and a set of double French doors is to my right. I glance at Caleb, who's standing stock-still beside me, then slip through the doors.

I blink a few times when my feet hit carpet, letting my eyes adjust to the brightness of the lights after the dimness of the hallway. I'm in the living room I'd just been looking into from outside. Same bookcases, same rug, same couch, same . . . foot.

"Right there," I breathe.

Caleb's hand grasps mine, squeezes once, and lets go. He stays beside me as I approach the sensible brown shoe. It's Mr. Murphy, the rest of him hidden behind the couch. He's face-down and perfectly still, dressed in a flannel shirt and the kind of chino pants my grandfather wears. Somehow, that's what finally sets my heart racing as I kneel beside him.

"Mr. Murphy, are you okay?" I ask, reaching for his shoulder. Caleb helps me turn him over and—oh, god. His eyes are wide open but lifeless, his face pale and slack, and the right side of his head is covered in blood. *I should scream*, I think hazily, but my throat has closed to the size of a pinprick. I can't push a single sound out. Caleb doesn't speak either, and we sit in silence until I hear heavy breathing behind me and a loud, shocked gasp.

"Holy shit," Malik says, sinking to his knees. His hands fly to his mouth and his body spasms as he retches. He manages not to throw up, but his voice is muffled by his palms as he chokes out, "He's dead. Mr. Murphy is *dead*."

"You never should have gone inside, Grace."

My dad's partner on the Owens Mills force, Detective Lisa Ramirez, rubs a hand over her face as she hands me a steaming cup of vending machine coffee. I know it's going to taste horrible, but I take a long sip anyway because it's four in the morning and I need the caffeine. "You should have called us as soon as you realized the door was open."

"I know. I just—I wasn't thinking straight," I say.

Detective Ramirez makes an exasperated noise. "Apparently not. Playing drinking games and trespassing in the middle of the night? That's not like you, Grace."

"I wasn't drinking," I protest. Detective Ramirez quirks a brow. "I *wasn't*. Give me a breathalyzer if you don't believe me."

She folds her arms and gazes at me for a few beats before relenting. "I do, actually. You seem perfectly sober. But this entire night is still a mess. I'd text your father if it weren't so late." She rubs her face again. "Or so early, I guess. Either way, he won't be pleased."

Story of my life, I almost say. Dad's relentless drive toward perfection makes him an excellent cop and an impossible-to-please father. Detective Ramirez doesn't need to hear that, though, so I stay silent and pour a healthy dose of sugar into my coffee. I look around for a spoon or a stirrer, but there's nothing, so I swirl the coffee gently in my hand.

Detective Ramirez and I are in a small conference room with the door closed, and I haven't seen or spoken to Caleb or Malik since we arrived. I understand the drill; the officers need to take our statements independently to collect as many perspectives as possible, and avoid having one person's memory morph into everyone's. Still, it's been a long time since I've seen anyone except Detective Ramirez. Or slept. I'm starting to feel the effects of both.

"Maybe it was a good thing, though?" I say. "Mr. Murphy could have been there for ages if we hadn't found him. He lives by himself, doesn't he?"

Detective Ramirez doesn't answer, and I inch my chair closer to the table. "Did someone kill him? That's what Malik thinks. Since the door was open and all. And because of the . . ." I take a gulp of my too-sweet coffee, grainy with all the sugar floating near the top. "Vase."

We found it on the floor. Malik picked the heavy bronze vase up first, dropping it in horror when he noticed the dark red stain along one side. Caleb saved it from rolling beneath the couch before I snatched it away and put it carefully on a side table. "Evidence," I reminded them. Malik just nodded, eyes wide, as Caleb continued checking Mr. Murphy's wrist and neck like he'd find a pulse eventually if he kept trying.

Detective Ramirez sighs. "You know I can't discuss that with you."

"Was he robbed?" I press.

She ignores the question. "You're here to give a statement and that's it. So let's review everything one more time, and then we can get you home."

We spend another half hour going through the night in painstaking detail. I'm so tired that when I close my eyes to remember the layout of Mr. Murphy's living room, I briefly fall asleep sitting up. Detective Ramirez raps her knuckles on the table, and I jerk awake. "All right," she says. "That seems to be a sign I've kept you here long enough. Is there anything we haven't talked about that we should? Anything you observed that surprised or confused you?"

"I mean, everything did," I say, and she gives me a wry smile.

"Touché. Listen, we're going to want fingerprints and a DNA sample from you for exclusion purposes, but you're not eighteen yet, right?" I shake my head. "So we can't do that without parental consent. We'll call your dad once it's no longer the crack of dawn, and bring you back after we've spoken to him. Also, it's possible you'll remember something new after you've gotten some sleep."

"Maybe." I slouch lower in my seat, my veins buzzing with the combination of exhaustion and caffeine. "Is Katie going to get into trouble?" I blurt out. "For, you know. Having alcohol at her party. Or will Malik, for drinking? Or all of us for trespassing, or—"

"None of that is our primary concern," Detective Ramirez interrupts. "We'll leave the disciplinary action to your parents." I swallow audibly, and her tense expression softens a little. "You're a good kid, Grace. In the scheme of things, this isn't a big deal, and I'll be sure to remind Steve of that. Same for the rest of the kids who got pulled into this mess. Except one." Her face hardens again. "This is the first time Caleb Manning has been in this station without being the cause of the problem."

"He was helpful tonight," I say.

"Mm-hmm." She regards me in silence for a few seconds, a frown creasing her forehead. Then she leans forward, elbows on the table. "Can I give you some advice?"

"Of course."

"Don't take this as an opportunity to trauma bond with Caleb Manning just because you've been through an emotional night together and he has *dreamy eyes*." I open my mouth to protest, but she holds up a hand before I can speak. "Save the denials, please. I've been doing this job for twenty years, and I can promise you this: the bad boy with a heart of gold is a myth. Caleb isn't misunderstood, and he doesn't have a tragic backstory that explains why he does the things he does. His mother is an *accountant*, for crying out loud." She shifts in her cafeteria-style chair, her frown deepening. "He's just a kid with no respect for authority who lacks a moral compass, and that's why he keeps finding himself back here."

"People can change," I say cautiously, getting exactly the eye roll I expect in return.

"They absolutely can. And yet, they rarely do." Detective Ramirez gets to her feet and gestures for me to do the same. "Come on, let's find someone to give you a ride home."

We exit the room into the hallway. Detective Ramirez wasn't the only officer called in to deal with us, and the station is a lot more full than you'd expect for five in the morning. Malik is headed for the exit with his father's arm wrapped around his shoulder. "I wonder if Mr. Roy would—" Detective Ramirez starts, clearly about to flag Malik's father down about driving me home, but he pushes through the door before she can.

"Hey." Caleb materializes in front of us, looking more rumpled and gaunt than ever. His leather jacket is draped over one arm. "You done?"

"Yeah," I say, highly conscious of Detective Ramirez's eyes on us.

"Want a ride?" Caleb asks, just as an officer sitting at a nearby desk calls, "Lisa! Bill Murphy's next of kin is on the phone."

"Shit, okay. Be right there," Detective Ramirez says. She turns as Caleb shrugs his jacket on, and a blue card flutters out of his pocket and onto the floor. I step forward, covering it with my sneaker, before Detective Ramirez pauses and looks back at us. "I can get one of the officers to take you home in five minutes," she tells me.

"Don't worry about it. Caleb can drive me," I say.

Her jaw ticks as her gaze flits between us. "Lisa," the officer calls again.

"It's fine," I say. "I promise."

She narrows her eyes at Caleb. "Drive the speed limit," she bites out before turning away. "We'll be in touch later today, Grace."

"Okay." I wait until she's crossed over to the desk to take the call, then bend over and retie my sneaker. When I finish, I slip the blue card into my hand, and then into my back pocket. "Let's go," I say to Caleb.

I murmur good-byes to the officers we pass on the way through the front door. The moon is still a pale sliver in the sky, but the glow of pending sunrise brightens the horizon. Caleb leads me to the same beat-up Datsun he used to drive us to the station earlier tonight. He unlocks the passenger door and holds it open, and I slip inside without a word. "That was—" he starts, but I slam the door closed before he can finish. He crosses to the other side of the car, slides behind the wheel, and puts the key in the ignition. "That was messed up."

"Shut up and drive," I say tersely.

"The hell?"

"Do it."

He does, and I don't speak again until the station is a mile behind us and he's stopped at a red light. Then I pull the card out of my pocket and shove it into his face. "Seriously, Caleb?"

"What? What is that?"

"This doesn't look familiar to you?" His face is a total blank as I wave it in front of him. "It's the Never Have I Ever card you pulled at Katie's house. And what does it say?" I read it slowly, for emphasis. "*Never have I ever had a one-night stand.*"

"Yeah? So?" The light turns green, but there's no one behind us. The roads are empty this early in the morning, hours before anyone needs to leave for school or for work. Caleb stays put, his eyes locked onto mine.

"So it's supposed to say, *Never have I ever spied on a neighbor.* That's what you told everyone it said at the party. Remember?" He doesn't answer, and my voice rises along with my temper. "This card is the whole reason we went to Mr. Murphy's house last night, isn't it?"

"Well, that and—"

"*Isn't it?*" I repeat.

"I guess, yeah."

"There's no *guessing* involved," I snap. "This card is why you were able to leave your fingerprints on that vase for a legitimate reason, after screwing up what should've been a simple rob-bery." Allowing Caleb—who, as I reminded him when he called me in a panic this afternoon, has fingerprints already on file with the Owens Mills police—to be excluded as a suspect. You can't rely on just wiping something clean, not with today's tech-nology. I've heard enough smug speeches from my father about overconfident criminals to know that. "This card is your *stay out of jail card*, Caleb. Unless it says something it's not supposed to. Something that doesn't match everyone's story."

Understanding finally starts to spread across Caleb's fea-tures, and I smack him on the shoulder with the card. He's lucky he's hot, because I would dump his ass otherwise. It's exhausting being the one who has to do all the thinking. "So maybe don't undo hours of *my* planning to clean up *your* mess by dropping it in front of the entire police station," I finish.

"Shit." Caleb laughs as he starts to drive again. "I didn't even know I still had that." He puts his hand on my knee and trails it upward, squeezing the inside of my thigh. "You're a genius, babe. I would've been screwed without you." His voice turns coaxing. "You know it was an accident, right? The guy surprised me. I only meant to take the money and run."

"Whatever. Where is it?"

"Woods behind Katie's house. You want to pick it up now?"

"No, leave it. We shouldn't be seen there for a while." I rip the Never Have I Ever card into tiny pieces before stuffing them back into my pocket. I'll burn them when I get home, then go to bed for a few hours of oblivion before my parents hear about what happened—about what they *think* happened—and start freaking out. But I can handle them; I know exactly how to wring my hands over all my minor transgressions so that even my father's interrogation will miss the major ones.

Detective Ramirez was right tonight about Caleb: he has no respect for authority and lacks a moral compass. I've known all of that since the first time we hooked up after my father arrested him last summer. It's what drew me to him, actually. Because the thing is, I'm exactly the same.

I'm just a lot better at hiding it.

LIKE BEFORE

by Maurene Goo

YOU ARE CORDIALLY INVITED TO THE BADDEST MOTHER-EFFING SLEEPOVER TO END ALL SLEEPOVERS.

WHEN: This Saturday, 10 p.m. (So you guys can't use dinner plans as an excuse to skip!)

WHERE: Pepper's house & various other locations

BRING: Your sleeping bag, a headlamp, running shoes, dark clothes, Britt—your inhaler, Alma—leave your mouthguard at home

WHY: Because you bitches have driven me to this

I MET ALMA AND BRITT IN KINDERGARTEN.

"You're my new wife!"

I looked up from the pile of ivy leaves and acorns I was assembling into a taco. The girl who had claimed me as her wife was sturdy but shorter than me, with curly brown hair almost the same color as her skin. Bright green eyes. Tiny turquoise studs pierced into her ears.

"What?" I asked, carefully scattering some crushed eucalyptus leaves on top of the taco. For spice.

"I said you're my new wife!"

Uneasy, I glanced around me. Any playground monitors nearby to protect me from this high-energy weirdo? "Who was your old wife?"

"*Her.*"

I followed the path from her commanding index finger to a knobby-kneed white girl doing a headstand against a springy metal frog. I knew her. We had taekwondo class together.

"Britt's your old wife?"

The girl sniffed. "Yeah. But she wouldn't let me swing first so I'm done with her."

"Who says I'll let you swing first?"

"Says me!"

"Who *are* you?"

"Alma! Who are you?"

"Pepper."

"That's not a real name."

"You're rude."

"So?!"

I shrugged. "I don't care. You have to have our babies, though."

And that's how Alma snared me. We got divorced shortly after. Like, fifteen minutes after. But you were never done with Alma. She was a force to be reckoned with. And for two shy little girls, like me and Britt, Alma was a godsend. The courage we needed to move through the world in a more significant way.

Eventually that dynamic balanced out somewhat. Alma made us stronger and we relied on her less. But the summer before senior year of high school, our friendship started to dissolve. I felt like I was about to lose one of my limbs. No, an organ. Something nestled deep inside my body, warm and reliable.

The rift started like a lot of arguments between Britt and Alma, with me trying to mediate. Then it was prolonged silences between texts in our group thread. Frantic gifs sent by me to ease the tension. And then . . . then Alma's dad died. Something really broke then. Whatever finely spun thread was holding us together snapped. You'd think tragedy might draw Alma closer to her friends, but it made her so much more distant.

And then I got busy. Between college applications and being senior class president, I just didn't have time to referee my best friends. And without me holding us together, we fell apart. Stopped being friends. I was always the glue. So it was up to me to save us.

Senior year is supposed to be full of nostalgia. When you look back on your childhood and friendships through a sepia-toned filter.

This sleepover is my Hail Mary.

The knock on my front door sends my house into chaos. Our three dogs go wild. They're three disparate mutts who, all together, look like a joke about dogs.

"Calm down, freaks!" I maneuver around them. "Mom! Can you get a handle on the dogs please?"

My mom wanders leisurely into the living room. Her dark hair is pulled up into a messy high bun tied with a scarf. Her tortoiseshell glasses askew, a dreamy expression on her face. Alma calls her the world's first Manic Pixie Korean Mom.

When I open the door, Britt and Alma are both standing on the doorstep with sleeping bags tucked under their arms, a strained air between them.

Great. Somehow they arrived at the same exact time? And from their expressions, in that very short trip from their cars to my front doorstop, something deeply petty had already been stirred.

"Hi!" The cold sweat that breaks out under my pits surprises me. Pit sweat is usually for class presentations or having a hot guy get too close to my face. Not my best friends of twelve years.

Britt gives me a tight smile and Alma kneels down to coo at the dogs. Our black Lab mix immediately wriggles his butt in front of her face, his big tail smacking her on the cheek. I don't even bother getting mad. Ed Ruscha is impossible to control, and Alma loves him.

"You're riling them up," Britt says. Our chunky dachshund mix, Frida Kahlo, is running in tight circles at her feet. Leonardo da Vinci, a shaggy dog who looks like he should be perpetually popping out of a trash can, is eating his red bandana in the corner.

I feel Alma's biting response before it comes so I look up and yell, "*Mom!*"

"Okay, okay," Mom mutters as she corrals them gently into the kitchen. "Hi girls. Sorry, Pepper's dad is out of town for work. He would have loved to see you guys. It's been a while, huh?"

Alma straightens up. "Yeah, but it's good to see you, too, Mrs. Kang."

"Alma, come on," my mom says with a laugh, standing in the kitchen doorway.

"I will not do it," Alma says with a shake of her head.

"You're almost eighteen, an adult!"

"I will not call an adult woman by her first name and that's the end of that."

I laugh at my mom's expression. "Mom, it'll never happen."

"All right, all right. Your brother's getting ready for bed, so don't be too loud." She blows us a kiss and ducks into the kitchen.

Britt and Alma stare at me expectantly. It's been weeks since the three of us were alone together.

"Why are we here, Pepper?" Alma asks. Always the first to break the silence. To punch her way through awkwardness.

"For a sleepover," I say, lifting my arms up a bit to dry the sweat.

"No shit. But what is this really?" Alma asks, watching me flap my arms. Nothing gets past her.

Britt drags her hands through her messy, long hair, its light brown dyed black this past year. "God, Alma. Can you stop being so unnecessarily aggressive for like, five seconds." She doesn't make eye contact with either of us. She towers over us height-wise, so it isn't that hard. And eye contact isn't Britt's jam.

Her conflict style is more insidious and passive—like someone who slowly poisons you over time.

"No." Alma swats at the dog fur on her black leggings. "There's no alternate mode for me."

It really shouldn't have been surprising when Britt and Alma outgrew each other. Their personalities were so mismatched since day one. But their friendship had worked anyway. It wasn't that they balanced each other out, exactly. If I'm honest with myself, it was that Britt just let Alma do whatever she wanted and then resented it. That resentment eventually boiled over, I guess.

"Well, it's not just a sleepover. I planned a scavenger hunt." I let the words hang in the air for a second. For dramatic effect.

Britt sighs and drops her sleeping bag on the floor. "Ew, why? Can we just watch a movie or something?"

Even though it kills her to agree with Britt, Alma nods. "Yeah, I'm not really down for *shenanigans* tonight." "Shenanigans" comes with an Irish accent. Ever the thespian.

This doesn't discourage me. I had already anticipated their reactions. "Nope. Sorry, my sleepover, my rules."

"Pepper—we're not little kids anymore," Britt says. Her dark eyes serious. "I know what you're trying to do and it's not going to work, okay?"

It's the first time anyone acknowledges our current state of dysfunction. In the middle of all the growing tension between Britt and Alma, Britt dropped a bomb on us—she said she wouldn't be going to college. And instead was going to work full time to save money for moving in with her twenty-year-old boyfriend, Jason. Neither Alma nor I like Jason that much—he's one of those beautiful loser types. All cigarettes and bedroom eyes and zero ambition. Britt dotes on him, though. Alma completely lost her shit and unleashed the full force of her judgy fury on her. We were disappointed and shocked at her decision—but it wasn't really the reason why the friendship was dissolving. It was just the final straw on a heap of problems. When the friendship had worked, we weren't aware of how fragile it all was.

"It's our senior year. Just one night. Please?" I do the thing, play my part. Easygoing Pepper. Mender of fences. Cheerful. Smoother of wrinkles. Best friend to all.

Both of them soften. The animosity is for each other, not for me. I'm just a casualty of it. But if it isn't the three of us anymore, would there even be a place for me in either of their lives? We come as a set. When I tried hanging out with them just one-on-one, it just wasn't the same. The easy conversation that flowed between the three of us was stilted, unnatural. Filled with gaps of silence. Laughs felt forced. I don't know if it's because we always felt the void of the missing third person or if it's because I just didn't know how to be friends with them that way. One-on-one.

Alma drops her sleeping bag, too. "Fine. Let's get this over with. Should I keep my shoes on or what?"

I smile. "Keep them on. And get out your headlamps."

"This makes zero sense."

The flatness of Alma's voice booms in the quiet hush of night. We're standing in my front yard. Someone's burning a bonfire in the neighborhood, the scent cozy in the cool October night.

Alma's staring down at the piece of paper in her hand. My headlamp's lighting it—of course Alma and Britt didn't bring any. It's the first clue. I had written it out with magazine letter cut-outs like a serial killer and shoved it high in a tree that Britt had climbed to fish out. It read:

FIND ME WHERE THE DRUMS SNARE

AND YOU SQUINT AGAINST THE GLARE

OF ALL THE NIGHT LIGHTS

WHERE GIANT BOYS TAKE FLIGHT

AND GIRLS LIKE PEPPER

CAN TAKE A FRIGHT

Scavenger hunt clues have to rhyme—that's a thing, right?

Britt mouths the words then stares into the sky thoughtfully. "Fright? I mean, Pepper's scared of everything."

I huff. "That's not true." But it is. I'm the biggest wimp of the bunch. Alma lets out a bark of laughter. The corner of Britt's mouth lifts into a half smile. That tiny interaction fills me with warmth.

"Come on, it's not that hard," I say. When I had sprained my ankle cheerleading at a football game sophomore year, both of them had run onto the field to carry me off. I'd landed badly on a stunt and it had hurt like hell, and yet it's one of my favorite memories.

One of the dogs yelps from inside the house. I turn to look at the living room windows and see Ed Ruscha's nose pressed against the glass, turning his face into a grotesque pancake with googly eyes.

Alma and Britt talk it out in hushed tones.

"Drums? Like, maybe a concert hall?"

"But what's the thing with giant boys? And Pepper taking a fright? Like what is that."

"Wait!" Britt exclaims. "It's about when Pepper broke her leg that one time! Cheerleaders! The football field? The lights on the field?" Everything ends with a question mark, but I feel her excitement. My silence is all the answer they need.

Alma pulls her car keys out of her jacket pocket. "I'll drive." Britt and I run to her BMW hybrid—a model that had been shipped to her from Europe. A perfectly normal birthday gift in Alma's world.

On the drive to school, Alma and Britt are silent. I try not to let their lack of enthusiasm sting. The night is young and I will chip away at their resistance, one clue at a time.

When we get to school, the lights on the football field are blazing.

"How are we getting in?" Alma asks, hands tucked into her pockets.

Britt stamps her feet for warmth. It's like sixty degrees. "We have to go in?"

I shake my head. "Nope. Look carefully."

We're standing at the gate near the concession stands, with a perfect view of the football field. Britt and Alma squint at it.

"Wait, is that—" Britt points.

Her question's drowned out by the sound of drums and horns. A group of people march out into the field. They aren't recognizable right away without their outfits. But they're holding instruments. Playing . . .

"What in the world?! Are they playing 'Dancing Queen'?" Alma asks, her voice pitched a little high with excitement. She looks at me with wide eyes. It's the song we had danced to at her quinceañera. "How'd you get them to do this?"

"They knew it was for Britt." She's in marching band. French horn. And she'd been the first one to run out into the field when I sprained my ankle.

Britt grins and waves at her bandmates while bopping her head along to the music. "You're such a dork," she says to me. But she keeps smiling and I start to dance along with her. We're bad dancers, jerking our limbs around with absolutely no rhythm. Bumping hips, biting down on our lower lips. We like to be extra so that Alma finally explodes and tells us to stop assaulting her eyeballs.

I wait for that reaction, but instead Alma asks impatiently, "What's the next clue?" Impatience is just part of her brand so I try not to take it negatively. I lift my chin toward the band. Alma turns to look at them, pressing her hands into the chain-link fence.

As the members of the band get closer, their clothing grows more visible. All of them are wearing dark green shirts. With writing on them.

"What in the . . ." Alma's voice trails off as the band lines up in a row, directly in front of us.

IT WAS

HERE

THAT

WE WERE

WATCHING

PEOPLE

DANCING

WITHOUT

A CARE

WHEN

ALMA HAD

WELL . . .

QUITE

THE SCARE

NEVER

COULD SHE

DRINK

AGAIN

AND NOT

PREPARE

Britt bursts out laughing. "Oh, god!"

Alma shakes her head. "You monster."

I smile. "You love it."

"Yeah," Alma says. "I love reliving peeing my pants at the movie theater."

Britt covers her mouth with her hands. The "oh shit" is muffled under her cupped hands. "What was the movie again?"

"*Magic Mike XXL*," I say smoothly.

"Of all the movies to hold my pee for," Alma says with a groan. "Like I give a crap about men dancing."

But through Alma's complaints, I feel it. A slow melting of the iciness between us. She's even tapping her foot to the song now. ABBA *was* her favorite band for most of her uncool years.

Britt shakes her head with wonder. "No, but seriously. How did you get this all set up?"

As senior class president, I have a lot of privileges. But it still took telling my advisor my friendship tale of woe to convince her to let me use the field. And then getting shirts made for everyone in the right sizes—well, it had taken a lot of time and money. Money I had been saving up for buying cute stuff for the dorm next year. But they don't need to know that, and I certainly don't want them to think about the time and effort that went into everything. I just want them to have fun.

"I have my ways." I waggle my eyebrows.

Britt turns away from the field. "So, are we going to the movie theater next?"

I point at her with double finger guns, knowing it's the worst. "You got it dude." Britt and Alma exchange a blink-and-you'll-miss-it look. It gives me a second of unease. But just a second. Because anything shared between them *has* to be good.

I turn on the radio from the passenger seat of Alma's car. I fiddle around until I hear the opening strains of "Call Me Maybe."

Britt groans. "Nooo."

I crank it up. "*Yes.*"

And because there is no force on earth that can prevent a group of girls in the presence of this song from singing along, we start belting it out.

We know our parts—each line as familiar to us as the streets we're driving through. I sing one verse, Alma the next, and then the three of us go all in during the chorus. Britt's voice is the clearest of all. She sings like she grew up isolated in the

Smoky Mountains—a young Dolly Parton somehow reborn in the hills of a Los Angeles suburb.

Our bodies move in the car, out of sync, but making sense somehow. We had long since perfected dancing while seated. The warmth I felt earlier seeps through me, slowly but surely. I will take this tiny ember of hope and fan it carefully. Make it bigger. Make it last.

The song fades and we all take a breathless moment to gather ourselves. And when we get out of the car, it almost—*almost*—feels like it used to.

At the movie theater, a girl in a burgundy vest opens the door for us.

"Hey Lisa," I say, giving her a fist bump. "Thanks for getting us in." The theater had just closed, the last showing ending at midnight.

She darts her eyes around. "Get in quick, my manager's in the back office."

I wave Alma and Britt in. Lisa's on yearbook with me and I had to bribe her with free ad space for her parents' gushing senior tribute.

She nods. "Go to theater five."

Alma winks at her. "Thanks, darlin'." In last year's production of *Cat on a Hot Tin Roof*, Alma had perfected what she called the "Southern charmer." And from the flush on Lisa's freckled cheeks, it's freaking effective.

"Don't lead her on," I whisper to Alma as we walk away through the carpeted halls.

"Who said I was?" she says in a loud, completely unmodulated voice.

We arrive at theater five without a fight and I consider that a small victory.

It's dark and empty. "Let's sit in the middle," I say, heading toward the seats.

"This is getting so elaborate," Britt says, the corner of her mouth hitching up. She props her high-tops onto the headrest in front of her.

Alma sits down next to me, the seat squeaking loudly as she throws herself into it. "What humiliation do you have in store for us now?"

Before I can respond, the screen lights up. I dig my fingernails into the seat rest.

A little girl's voice starts playing on the speakers over a video of a My Little Pony figure floating in water.

"This is a tragedy," says the voice.

Alma and Britt both sit up straight. I smile, keeping my eyes on the screen.

"Pepper . . ." Britt's voice is questioning. But she knows what's coming.

The butter-yellow pony with rainbow-colored hair bobs in the water. Then the camera pans out. The water is pale green and a stainless-steel faucet flashes in the corner for a second.

"Not all stories end happy." The little girl's voice echoes in the theater.

Alma and I start laughing. Hard.

Britt reaches over and punches both of us in the arms. "Jerks!"

"You were *so* into this," Alma says between gasps.

Another little girl voice comes in. This time with a bad

Italian accent. "Oh-my-spaghettio, what a lova-ly day this is for a swim!"

I let out a peal of laughter and Alma drags her hands down her face.

"Your first accent," Britt says with a smirk.

Alma sniffs. "I think it was pretty good for a third grader."

We watch as the poor My Little Pony, named Cassandra-Maria-Francesca, paddles about, my hand visibly moving her around the bathtub. She is blissfully unaware of the horror to come. Suddenly, my hand wrenches the stopper out of the tub, creating a whirlpool. Alma's voice is breathless as she yelps, "Help-ah me! Help me-ah!"

Britt's voiceover: "But some things could not be helped. 'Twas fated to be fated."

By the time a half-naked Ken doll splashes into the water, with a regular-sized human pencil taped to his hand, the three of us are gasping, tears running down our faces.

"Why did he need a pencil?" Britt finally wheezes.

"Because . . . because he was a reporter, remember?" Alma manages to squeak out, taking large gulps of air.

Ken attempts to save Cassandra-Maria-Francesca. "My amore!" Alma's voice booms. Her man voice is near identical to Cassandra-Maria-Francesca's, but one register lower.

"I'm gonna pee my pants," Britt cries, crossing her legs tight.

Alma groans. "The curse of this theater, apparently."

A cardboard shark fin enters from off-screen and Britt's tiny voice starts singing, "Da-la-da-la-da-la" in a weird, not-quite-right version of the *Jaws* theme.

"Your gifts sure took a while to reveal themselves," Alma says, leaning forward in her seat now, her eyes on the screen.

Suddenly Ken is dragged under and Alma's voice cries into the mic, so loud that all you can hear is muffled little-girl screeching. The water turns a bright red.

"Very good effects if I do say so myself," I say. "Just took ten bottles of food dye."

"My amore, mi amor!" Alma's pony voice screams. Like, screams. We all clutch our ears, laughing hysterically.

And then Cassandra-Maria-Francesca spins dizzily into the whirlpool—my hand whipping her around in frenzied circles.

The camera zooms in and out, in and out, making me queasy.

Baby Alma's screams fade, and baby Britt's voice speaks gravely over the bloody and chaotic images. "I told you this was a tragedy." From off-screen, you can see my hand splashing some clear liquid into the tub, hear a match being lit, and then—then the entire tub catches on fire. A second later my mom's voice shouts from off-screen, *"Son of a bi—"*

The screen cuts abruptly to black and white letters spelling out, "THE END . . . OR IS IT?"

"Genius!" Alma declares, pumping her fists into the air.

But it isn't over. The credits roll with "Music of the Night" from *The Phantom of the Opera* playing.

WRITTEN AND DIRECTED BY PEPPER KANG

GOD: **Brittany Leigh McIntosh**

CASSANDRA-MARIA-FRANCESCA/REPORTER LUIGI: **Alma Edie Ríos**

SPECIAL EFFECTS: **Pepper Kang, Brittany Leigh McIntosh, Alma Edie Ríos**

STUNTS: **Pepper Kang**

CAMERAPERSON: Brittany Leigh McIntosh

ACTING COACH: Alma Edie Ríos

Thank you to our parents and families and God for the funding and support.

The music ends abruptly, and a new image comes up on screen.

"*Mom?*" Britt's screech cuts through our laughter.

Britt's mom is standing on her front porch, squinting a little into the camera, the sun shining on her face, highlighting all the sharp angles. She looks like those old 1980s drawings of women in hair salons—all glamorous planes and defined points.

"Hi, brats." Her voice echoes in the empty theater. "Your next clue is this: *From fake ponies to real, remember when horses taught Alma how to feel? Go where she had to learn a lesson hard earned, once bitten, twice spurned.*"

The film ends and the lights turn on. I'm proud of that particular clue.

Alma scrunches her forehead. "The Topanga Stables?" She glances down at her phone. "It's like one a.m. How in the world are you getting us into all these places in the middle of the night, Pepper?"

I pull my black beanie out of my fanny pack. "You leave that to me."

Alma used to be obsessed with horses in a way that was totally off brand for her. She read all the horsey books that girls read but then took it *beyond.* She saved up allowance money for her own horse. She started wearing knee-high socks to mimic riding boots. When her parents wouldn't let her take riding lessons right away, she pretended her bike was a horse and her garage a stable. Her dad caved. It just made him too sad to watch her run a hairbrush down the metal frame of her sky-blue ten-speed.

I jiggle the lock on the entrance gate to Topanga Stables, the light on my headlamp bouncing with the movement. We can hear the soft nickering of the horses, smell the sweetness of the hay.

"Really? You thought you could open that?" Alma whispers loudly.

I stand up and sigh. "No, I'm trying it *just in case*. The reason we're all dressed like this is because we have to sneak to the side gate and climb it."

Alma whoops in excitement, but Britt shakes her head. "No way."

"Come on! No one's going to see us." I adjust my fanny pack. "I already scouted the place last week. They don't have security."

"Just how much planning was involved with all this?" Britt asks, staring at me.

The question makes me pause and I tug at my beanie. "Not that much."

Alma snorts. "Right."

"That wasn't meant to crap on her," Britt says sharply. "Not everyone speaks in thinly veiled shade."

Ugh.

Alma's head swivels to Britt. "Excuse me? I would actually *beg* to differ. You're the queen of passive-aggressive shade."

I tense, thinking Britt will stammer and back off. But if the past few months were any indicator, I should have known better.

"Whatever." Britt walks up ahead even though she has no idea where we're going.

Alma shouts at her retreating back. "For someone who's so *considerate*, you're being rude as hell to Pepper."

"You care about being considerate to your friends all of a sudden?" Britt yells back.

Before Alma can retaliate, I sprint up ahead. "Both of you just shut up and follow me, okay?" I don't give myself time to be disappointed. I think of the laughter in the theater. The car ride karaoke. That's real. I focus on those moments and our task. "The gate's right up ahead."

I had purposely picked a spot where there are no lights, and the light from my headlamp and their phone lights bounces around the murky darkness. The stables are tucked into a canyon close to the ocean and there's a blanket of mist hanging over us.

The gate is part of the wood fence running the perimeter of the stables. It isn't that high and we can scale it easily.

"I'll go first and help you guys down the other side." I shake the fence, checking on its sturdiness. The rattle echoes and a horse neighs in response. Alma makes a horsey sound back, and it responds.

"Can you stop with the chatting?" Britt whispers. "Don't rile them up. Someone might hear."

Alma mutters something rude and I grasp the fence with both hands, hoisting myself up onto the metal bar that runs low across the gate. "I'm going to fall and break my neck because you guys are distracting me and then you're going to have to live with that guilt for the rest of your lives."

They snort in unison.

After I get myself over the fence, I land hard, kicking up dirt. Another horse stirs loudly behind me.

Alma goes next, slower than me and a bit more precarious. Alma's strong but not particularly agile and I'm ready to grab her when she gets over. She falls into me, but we manage to stay on our feet. Britt hops over easily with the grace of a gymnast. Which, had her parents been able to afford it, she could have excelled at.

"Do you remember which stall Chicken lived in?" I ask Alma, turning off my headlamp so I won't blind her.

Alma's phone light stays on. "Of course I do."

Britt makes an irritated noise. My shoulders bunch up like they're being pulled tight by strings. Being aware of every annoying quality of both your friends, knowing that one might bother the other, is pretty much an exercise in torture.

I clear my throat. "Maybe we should . . . go there. To Chicken's old stall."

We follow Alma as she leads the way, the walk to her old horse's stall a permanent part of her hardwiring. She pauses a few times to run her hand over a horse's flank, its mane, its nose. Alma quit riding when her father died a couple years ago, and she never quite recovered from either loss.

The smell of hay mixes with the earthy scent of horses. Something about it implies warmth and bigness. It calms me down when we get to the stall. I look at Alma for her reaction.

The stall is lit by string lights draped around the perimeter. And in the place of a horse is a bicycle. Sky blue.

Alma blinks.

Moments pass and it's silent. Then Britt snaps her fingers in recognition. "Oh! Your old bike! The one you used to call . . . what was it . . ."

"Agatha."

The quiet volume of her voice is unsettling. And, suddenly, I realize this is a mistake.

This entire night is a mistake.

"Um, the next clue is in the basket . . ." I say as I fumble with the stall door. I step inside, my shoes crunching the hay, and stand awkwardly by the bike. I shouldn't be the one grabbing the clue. I had envisioned Alma doing that.

I had envisioned a lot of things.

And in exactly none of those scenarios did Alma's face look the way it does. It reminds me of an illustration from those old Ramona books. One where Beezus's face was crumpled and stricken after Ramona had been careless with an insult.

I feel my intestines wring themselves into a tight cord. Crap.

"Are you mad?" I manage to ask. My eyes fly to Britt's, searching for a familiar look of concern. But she's looking down at her feet, her hands shoved into her back pockets.

Alma shakes her head—short, agitated movements. "I'm not mad. I'm just . . . overwhelmed." She rubs the heels of her hands into her eyes. "This is a fucking *lot*, Pepper."

I swallow. "I'm sorry. I thought it'd be a nice memory . . ."

Britt looks up then. "You thought a lot of things about tonight." Her voice is gentle but the implication is harsh and I flinch. She sighs. "Can we just go home now?"

Something snaps. Lightning fast, my concern turns into anger. I want to scream. Tear this stable apart.

"What is *wrong* with you guys? Why can't we get through this?" My shout echoes through the stables and the horses surrounding us move restlessly.

"What's wrong with *us*? Just *us*?" Britt says, her voice loud now, too. "Are you serious?"

"*You're* the ones who hate each other now! *You're* the ones who broke up this friendship! I'm trying to do *everything* to save it! I spent fucking *days* setting all this up!" My anger is so big it fills my entire body until my extremities go numb.

"Do not put that on us. *Do. Not.*" Alma's voice is so firm, so assured. It's like each word is deeply rooted in her body. No one can budge them. But I want to. I want to drop-kick them into space. "Creating this like, catalog of memories? It feels emotionally manipulative. Trying to make us cry or something like a freaking Pixar movie."

I can't even respond. How could this all get perverted into something so shitty?

She frowns. "*No one* asked you to do this."

Britt looks at me with sad eyes. Their default setting. "Pepper. You've got to let it go."

But I refuse to believe that. I fight it with every muscle in my body. "No! We should fix this! We've been friends since *kindergarten.*"

Alma has her gaze fixed on the bike. "This isn't your memory to force on me. This was *mine*, Pepper. Not ours. Some things are just for me. Not part of some friendship nostalgia."

My anger deflates and I blink back tears. "I didn't mean to . . . it was supposed to be thoughtful."

"Sometimes your thoughtfulness is a burden."

Alma's words are a slap to my face. I hear Britt mutter "shit" under her breath. And it becomes clear, then. There's one thing they can agree on.

After tossing a murderous look at Alma, Britt says, "Pepper. I know it's hard but we're all going to separate soon, anyway. I know how you guys feel about my decision not to go to college." Alma and I are silent. And it feels damning somehow. Her skin flushes but she keeps talking. "It's just another thing that separates me from you guys. It's always been there, but I pretended it wasn't. I'm not pretending anymore—*me and Alma* aren't pretending anymore. And you have to be okay with that. Things change. Not just between Alma and me. But with you, too. All of this? It's just making it harder."

I wipe at my tears. Wow, it's complete heartbreaking shit to hear that. To realize the problem isn't just them. That maybe they're growing out of me, too. That I'm the only one who didn't get the memo.

The lights turn on. Bright and harsh. "Hey!" The shout echoes through the stables. Male and pissed. "Who's there?"

I look at my friends. Who the hell are we anyway?

The drive back to my house is silent.

In all my planning, I missed the very important fact that the owner of the stables lived just up the hill. After seeing the sad tableau in front of him, he had let us go home with a stern reprimand. Old-white-man scolding slid off our backs like water on a good day. In this current mood, it was nothing.

I open the window in the backseat. It's colder now. The air stings my face. Keeps it from collapsing like that Beezus drawing.

The apology I'm waiting for never comes. Just like the reconciliation I had imagined. Every block we drive brings me closer to something inevitable.

I had just been ignoring it this whole time.

The car ride is long. Long enough for me to realize, as I watch the passing scenery, that what Britt said is true. I panicked not just because I was sad at the friendship dissolving—but because I was scared of a future without them. It's just another uncertainty added to a pile of uncertainties about what lay ahead after graduation. And my attempts to fix it are actually pretty selfish. If they're ready to move on, I have to let it go. Even if it makes me feel like my insides are hollowed out.

When we slip inside the house, I hold my breath, waiting for the dogs to come stampeding in. I never thought we'd get home so early. I envisioned the sky pink with early morning light, the three of us exhausted when we stumbled in.

But the dogs never come, probably curled up in bed with Mom, and we stand in the entry. Ending the night like it started.

"You guys can still sleep over," I say, pointing at the sleeping bags tossed into the corner.

They look at each other. Then Britt shakes her head. "That's okay. I think I should go home."

"Same," Alma says.

I nod, my throat tight. "Okay."

But they don't move and neither do I.

"Thanks for trying, Pepper." Britt's sad eyes are the saddest I'd ever seen them. I realize then that I don't want to see her eyes that sad. That something that makes her feel that way isn't good. And she deserves to feel good.

Alma reaches for me and pulls me into a tight hug. It's a rare moment when she doesn't need words. Doesn't need to fill a room with her presence, with something to prove.

They grab their stuff and I open the front door for them. Watch them walk to their separate cars. They don't even say goodbye to each other.

And when they drive off, I sit on my front step and stare out into the dark street, lit in intervals with old-fashioned gas lamps that had been installed nearly a century ago. In the rest of the city, most of them had been replaced by modern streetlights. But I prefer the gas lamps. Intrigued by the history they'd witnessed. At the vision they conjured of a city when it was new. Not faded in sepia tones. But colorful and real and alive.

I imagine it was perfect.

OLD RIFTS AND SNOWDRIFTS

by Kayla Whaley

THE SNOW STARTED FALLING RIGHT AS SCHOOL LET OUT. An aggressive snowfall, the kind that pelts down more like frozen bullets than fluffy flakes. The news had spent days prepping us; expect half an inch, they said, maybe as much as three-quarters in spots. We were all suitably stocked on bread and bottled water, but even in Atlanta that amount of snow wasn't enough to shut the city down. You needed at least a solid inch of accumulation for that.

I made it to Prim Roses & Daffy Dills before the snow started sticking. The sidewalks leading from school to my afternoon job as salesgirl weren't in the greatest shape, but I'd driven the route enough now that the steep curb cuts and awkwardly placed manholes didn't faze me. I wouldn't want to test it on ice, though. My treads were in decent shape, but *decent* traction only gets you so far.

"Here, Mrs. Otsuki!" I called as the bell above the door chimed my entrance.

My best friend Melanie's parents ran the little florist and nursery, rated number one in the metro area eight years running, as the framed magazine clips hanging next to the door proudly proclaimed. Melanie had grown up here, surrounded by stems and thorns and bursts of blooming color. My own home was caring and warm, but utterly beige in every way. Beige walls, beige carpets, beige terrier mix named Penny. Even our food was all plain roast chicken and cornbread. In fourth grade, when I grew out of my first wheelchair, I chose fuchsia for the replacement. An artificial color that nearly matched its namesake for sheer audacity.

The store was slow today. The holiday rush had ended with New Year's and wouldn't kick up again until Valentine's. We had a few weeks of relative quiet to look forward to. The only customer was with Devi over by the bouquet buffet, as we called it: premade arrangements themed for birthdays, bereavements, congratulations, *get well soon*s, etc. The man glanced up at my arrival and stared as I maneuvered behind the counter. His eyes narrowed in confusion and his mouth puckered, arm already half-raised in my direction. I quickly pinned my nametag to my sweater and waved pointedly and familiarly at Devi. She waved back. The customer seemed satisfied (if perplexed) that I was where I should be and turned back to his conversation.

"Mrs. Otsuki? I'm clocking in!" I yelled again. It wasn't unusual for Melanie's mom to hole up in her office (dealing with customers was her least favorite part of the job), but I didn't hear the telltale synthesized sparkle of '80s pop floating out from under the door. I knocked a few times, but still nothing.

"She's not here today," Devi said from behind me. The bell above the door rang again as the man left empty-handed. Maybe he decided on chocolates instead.

"Oh no, is she okay?"

Mrs. Otsuki hadn't missed a day since she had her gallbladder removed a few years back, and even then, she'd insisted she was "on call" in case some flower-related emergency came up. In her defense, flower-related emergencies come up much more frequently than one might suppose.

"Norovirus," Devi said. She mimed vomiting, full-bodied retching and all. Devi was the distracting kind of pretty: soft jaw, dark eyes, warm brown skin that had never even heard the word *blackhead* before. Even mid-*Exorcist* reenactment, she glowed. She was also in her mid-twenties, married, and had an adorable toddler at home, which allowed my aesthetic appreciation to remain a quiet joy instead of morphing into a godforsaken *crush*. Nothing good ever came from crushes.

"Yikes," I said. "So, it's just us today?"

Devi walked over to the arranging station where she was putting the final touches on the bouquets for a wedding tomorrow. Normally it'd be all hands on-deck for wedding prep, but this was a small one, intimate. No lavish garlands or dozens of centerpieces filled with baby's breath and carnations for the reception. Just a few small gatherings of blooms for the bride and her bridesmaids. Devi chose an anemone from the spread in front of her and slipped it carefully into the nearest bundle.

"Not just us," she said. "You really think Mr. Green Thumb would let his babies go untended for the day?"

Speaking of godforsaken crushes. I glanced to the small, locked door at the back of the store that read EMPLOYEES ONLY and led to the on-site greenhouse: Owen's domain.

Melanie's twin brother had always loved flowers. Although "love" felt like too small a word for the innate connection he had to them. Mr. Green Thumb, indeed. He and I had had our own little garden, just the two of us, when we were young, but Owen was always the visionary. I would have been happy planting tomatoes or sweet peas or tulips all willy-nilly. Owen persuaded me to have patience. Even as a child, he didn't merely *plant* a garden, he *curated* one and invited me into the process.

The seasonal cycles within that small, bounded bit of land were as much temporal touchstones for me as holidays or birthdays. When I think about Melanie, nine years old and reckless, crashing her bike and dislocating her shoulder, I see the carpet of geraniums that had just begun to open. The afternoon of a near-miss tornado one spring is, in my memory, colored forsythia gold against a gunmetal sky. I've caught only glimpses of the garden over the past year, though, ever since Owen and I stopped speaking. I don't look when I pass by. I don't want to know what he's growing now. But maybe that's why time has felt so slippery lately; I've lost my sun-warmed tether.

I situated myself at the register, determined not to think about him back there, his sleeves rolled up his forearms, dirt-streaked apron tied at his waist. He abandoned me. It doesn't matter what I did or didn't feel for him. He made his own feelings explicitly clear on my last birthday. I stared out the shop's large display windows. Behind the vases of pink camellias, sweet alyssum, winter honeysuckle, and snowdrops, actual snow fell steadily in the dim afternoon light.

"I hope it lets up before I have to leave," Devi said, following my gaze. "These boots are *suede*."

I smiled. "Don't worry, this is supposed to be the worst of it."

Three hours later, the snow was halfway to the windowsill and still coming down.

"Jesus, look at this," Devi said, handing me her phone.

Helicopter footage taken over I-75, then I-85, then I-285 showed all the major highways in Atlanta were at a complete standstill. Hundreds of cars in each successive shot were parked on the interstate, snow piling up around them as their drivers hunkered down, trapped.

"They're gonna be out there all night at this rate," I said, handing Devi's phone back. I glanced at my own phone. No calls from Mom yet, but service was always spotty on construction sites. Dad had checked in an hour ago to say he was waiting at the office until the storm cleared to come get me. I had a feeling he'd be waiting quite a while. Which meant I would be, too. I tried to shrug away my irritation at being stuck here. It would do me no good to turn into Old Man Shakes Fist at Clouds. Although it did occur to me that if I had an accessible van and could actually drive myself, I'd have gone home hours ago. Teen Crip Shakes Fist at Capitalism, then.

"The local roads are even worse," Devi said, turning her screen to me again. "It's all ice. Completely impassable."

"Oh god, look at the buses," I said. A handful of school buses idled in the middle of the road, one of them having fishtailed, although it didn't appear to have hit anything. Small, shadowed bodies were visible through the dark windows. Middle schoolers, I'd guess.

Shit, had Melanie made it home? She had Latin Club after school on Wednesdays, so she probably wouldn't have headed home until the ice was starting to build. I grabbed my phone and texted her: **you okay? you make it home?**

I'm fine! she texted back seconds later. **Still at school.**

Couldn't even get out of the parking lot without my car sliding all over 🙁

at school by yourself??

No, worrywart! most of us stayed, including Mrs. Pritchett. We might end up having to spend the night here?? 🫣

whoa!

you know, i think "teens locked in school overnight" is how 80% of slasher movies start

wowwwww super helpful!

I was texting Melanie about my own snowed-in situation when Devi stood so abruptly her chair nearly tipped over. She stared at her phone in something like horror and something like anger. "Damn it! This is why you should never hire high schoolers. No offense."

"None taken."

She started gathering her things, shoving her phone and water bottle into her purse, searching around for something or other she must have misplaced. "My husband is stuck at work because half the night shift nurses couldn't make it in, which, fine. But now our babysitter's parents are demanding she come home 'right this minute' and our neighbors are stuck god knows where. Which means I have to somehow make it over a mile home on foot in a legitimate blizzard. In my *suede shoes*. Jesus fu— Wait."

She turned to me, almost in slow motion. I could practically hear her brain churning as she stared.

"What now?" I asked, wary.

"I can't just leave you, Eleanor! What if you . . ." she trailed off, eyes roving over me, as if the words she wanted were written somewhere on my person. "*Need* something? I can't just leave someone like you *alone*. What kind of monster—"

Someone cleared their throat. "Disabled."

"What?" Devi asked, turning again, this time so sharply I thought she'd break her heel.

Owen leaned against the arranging counter, arms lightly crossed at his chest, legs crossed at the ankle, like he hadn't just magically appeared out of nowhere. "You don't wanna leave someone *disabled* alone," he corrected her. "But in any case, she's not alone."

His eyes found mine and held. The room felt suddenly small and too warm for a snowstorm to be raging outside. He smiled lightly, little more than a twitch of his lips, but the expression was so familiar it hurt. I looked away.

"Right," Devi said. "Right, yes. Okay, and your mom would be cool with you looking after her?"

I sighed, but before I could tell her that I did *not* need a babysitter and I was sitting *right here*, Owen said, "You cool with staying with me, Nori?"

I flinched at the nickname. He gave it to me when we were six years old, during my brief seaweed obsession. I plowed through nori so fast Mrs. Otsuki started stocking my own dedicated container of the salty sheets in their pantry. He thought he was so clever. Eleanor, Eleanori, Nori. I hadn't heard the name in so long it felt like it belonged to some other girl.

"Sorry," he said, softly, seeing the change in my expression. "Eleanor."

I was not cool staying with him. Definitely not. Every time I was around him my stomach got all knotted up and my face got heated and I was still just so *angry* with him. Who does that? Who stands up one of their best friends on their birthday? Birthdays were our *thing*. Melanie never understood our rabid need to one-up the other. To her, birthdays were for cake and a few presents and maybe a funky hat or something. But to us, birthdays weren't a celebration. They were a competition to prove who was the better friend. We took the game seriously. Each year, a more outrageous gift, a more extravagant surprise. So, at first, I thought maybe his lateness was part of a plan. I waited. And waited. But there was no text. No call. Not even a message relayed via Melanie. Just me, telling everyone else to go get popcorn and seats, I'll come in when Owen gets here, no don't worry, at most we'll miss the trailers.

Half an hour after showtime, Melanie came out and found me still in the lobby, staring at my phone as if he might step right out of the screen and explain. *He's been so distant lately*, I said to her. *Is he mad at me?* She shrugged helplessly. *Come on*, she said, *Becca's wondering where you are.* I followed Melanie into the dark theater where I sat next to my maybe-girlfriend (we hadn't made anything official) and ignored the silent tears running down my face.

He never bothered explaining and I never bothered asking. I shouldn't have *had* to ask. It was the principle of the thing. When he passed me in the hall the next day at school, he didn't say a word. Just tipped his chin at me as if he hadn't broken our tradition without warning or even acknowledgment. The message wasn't hard to decipher. He didn't want to be friends anymore? Fine. We weren't friends.

Now, with his eyes steadily on me, waiting to hear if I was indeed "cool" with this development, I pushed away that familiar pain in my chest and gestured out the window. "Where else am I gonna go?"

"Oh, thank god," Devi said. "Okay. You kids be safe, call someone if you need anything. Not me, obviously, but your parents or whatever." She made for the door. Before she pushed it open, she took a long, steadying breath and whispered, "I'm so sorry, boots."

And then there were two.

A heavy dusting of snow blew in as Devi blew out. Enough to leave a sheen on the pale pink tile once it melted.

"We should probably mop that up," I said. "So no one slips."

As soon as the words were out, I felt ridiculous. No one was going to slip because no one else was coming in for the rest of the day. Or rather, the rest of the night. The sky was fully dark already, the sun having gone to bed early as was its custom in January.

Oh god, *bed*. If we were stuck here all night (which seemed unavoidable at this point), where the hell was I going to sleep?

"Okay," Owen said, then turned and made for the supply closet.

"I didn't mean right now!" I did mean right now, of course, but that was before I realized mopping didn't need doing at all.

He pushed the bucket over to the door. "But what if somebody slips?" he said, barely tamping down a teasing smile.

I stuck my tongue out before I could stop myself. Like perennials, old habits die hard.

He mopped methodically, moving from left to right, tile by tile. Every so often he'd dunk the mop into the warm, soapy water as carefully as you might dip a quill in ink. It'd been so long since I'd watched him work, I'd almost forgotten how magnetizing his focus was. Even something as rote as mopping a floor merited concentration, care. Soon, he was squeegeeing the last of the soapy residue away and the floor was dry once more.

"Crisis averted," he said, beaming.

I smiled despite myself, then realized this was the longest conversation we'd had in over a year. My chest clenched and I grabbed my phone, pretending to text or tweet or whatever one does when one is pretending to be busy on their phone. I didn't look up when the bucket's wheels squeaked away toward the closet, or when the greenhouse door quietly opened and closed.

I didn't look up until I was sure he wasn't coming back.

Mom finally called a while later. The ringing startled me after an hour where the only sounds were the heater periodically turning on, and the low, steady buzz of the refrigerators along the far wall.

"'Bout time," I said by way of greeting.

"What?" Mom shouted. Her end of the call was pure noise, all loud voices, clinking glasses, and blaring country music.

"Are you in a *bar*?" I asked, raising my voice to match her volume.

"No, I'm not in the car! Couldn't even get off-site! We're next door at a *bar*!"

"Oh, my god, with the yelling!" I yelled back.

"Hang on!" she said.

More shuffle and bustle as she presumably moved through the crowd before the noise blessedly dimmed.

"Sorry, I'm outside now," she said. "God, it's freezing out here."

"Well, we are in the middle of an unprecedented snowstorm."

"Dad said you're at the shop? Is Mrs. Otsuki with you? Did you eat? How are you on bathroom? What are you gonna do about sleep?"

At the back of the store, the door to the greenhouse opened. Owen stopped suddenly when I looked up.

Sorry, he mouthed, pointing to my phone. I stared at him, my ears burning and faintly ringing.

"Did you hear me?" Mom asked. "Are you with Carol? Eleanor, CAN you HEAR me?"

"Yeah, no, she was sick today," I heard myself saying.

I'm honestly surprised I managed to get that much out, because, for reasons only God herself could fathom, Owen was standing there in the doorway.

Completely shirtless.

His apron was still around his waist, but he'd undone the tie behind his neck, so the top half hung down over his khakis. Inexplicably, he wore his gardening gloves, too, thick leather affairs that looked more suited to swinging an axe than pruning some roses. Pants and apron and gloves, and nothing else.

I focused hard on the gloves. Willed myself not to look away, but my mind superimposed the other view over the top, like stubborn ink ghosting through a page. It didn't matter that I was being good and holding my gaze steady, all I could see was skin and hard planes. And all I could think was: How did gardening give you *abs*?

"You're there alone?!" Mom said, shouting again. Screeching, more like.

"What?" I pulled the phone slightly away from my ear. "No, I'm not alone." Quite against my wishes, my eyes moved: up his forearm, bicep, shoulder, from the smooth curve of his neck to his disgustingly perfect jawline, until, finally, I met his eyes.

"Owen's with me."

I could see his throat move when he swallowed, all the way from the front of the store. And was that . . . was he blushing? He grabbed a tiny pot of gardenias from the shelf nearest him and studied the petals.

I turned my attention back to Mom.

"Oh, thank god," she said. "You're in good hands then."

Great, now *I* was blushing. I did not want to think about Owen's hands. His beautiful hands.

"What was that, honey?"

I froze. "What? I didn't say anything."

"You're mumbling. Something about beautiful lands?"

Oh, my actual *god*, I had to get off this phone. "Mom, don't worry about me. I'll be fine and I'll see you tomorrow, okay? Okay. Love you!"

I hung up so fast that the phone slipped and clattered to the floor.

Owen rushed over, still holding the gardenias, and knelt. He handed me the small terracotta pot and pulled his gloves off.

"Here," he said, holding my phone out to me. With him kneeling like this, I was the slightest bit taller than him. It was nice not to have to crane my neck to look at him.

Carefully, I took my phone from him. "Thanks."

He shrugged and leaned back on his heels. "Of course."

"Why are you naked?" I blurted.

Surprise and horror and, weirdly, delight all ran across his face at once, until he seemed to settle on bemusement. "I'm not naked."

I rolled my eyes. "Half naked. Whatever. You are partially disrobed."

"Disrobed?" he asked, mouth twitching.

"Partially. Isn't this still a place of business?"

Owen raised a brow, the laughter obvious in his eyes. I'd meant to sound harsh, but he clearly wasn't intimidated. "I think it's safe to say we're closed for the night. Although, for your information, I *was* working. It gets hot back there with the heat lamps and humidity."

That was . . . annoyingly reasonable. "Okay, fine, but why are you half naked out here?"

"I heard yelling," he said. Then, softly, "I had to make sure you were okay."

Heat rushed to my face. Embarrassed heat. "Because you're stuck here being my babysitter for the night, right?" There was more venom in my voice than I expected, the words cutting more surely than shears through dried-out brush. I didn't like how satisfying that felt.

But neither did I like how Owen looked as if he'd been slapped. "Is that . . ." He trailed off, shook his head slightly, then looked at me. "Do you really think so little of me?"

I didn't answer. My silence said plenty.

He reached for the gardenias I'd forgotten I was still holding in my lap. His fingers slipped gently under mine, and I shivered. He didn't look at me as he pulled the flowers away and stood.

"I keep a stash of ramen in the back. Do you want some?"

I nodded, but his back was turned entirely away now. "Please."

"Still prefer beef over chicken?"

"Are you suggesting I might have lost my 'refried' palate?" I asked, exaggerating the final words.

He didn't notice the old inside joke, one of our mainstays. Or if he did, he didn't react. We'd been watching a Food Network marathon one summer afternoon and the chef suggested using beef broth instead of chicken for those with a more refined palate. Naturally, we rejected all chicken-based meals for weeks, citing our "refried palates." Our mispronunciation was too cute to correct, but we were made to eat the chicken regardless.

"Beef would be great," I said.

I ate my ramen alone. I'm sorry to say that it was delicious. Owen simmered it with some perfectly wilted bok choy and fresh scallions and topped the brothy noodles with a few thin slices of raw ginger, all from the little vegetable garden Mrs. Otsuki let him maintain for the store. Prim Roses & Daffy Dills wasn't in the produce business, but fresh veggies did help get customers to the farmers' market booth. From there, it was nothing to sell a bouquet or two of flowers to go along with the carrots and peppers and beets.

since when does your brother know how to cook?? I texted Melanie, mostly out of boredom.

Eleven o'clock and the snow was still falling, though gently now, more like the passing flurries we were used to. Even if it had stopped hours ago, though, there was no hope for making it home. The roads would be frozen at least until early tomorrow afternoon, the news said. We were well and truly snowed in.

My pulse skipped as reality finally hit. Fuck, what was I going to do? If I was being honest, I'd been avoiding thinking about the whole sleeping situation. None of us who were stranded were likely to get much sleep tonight, but Melanie and Dad and Mom and even Owen could all stretch out on the floor, bunch their jackets up as pillows and pretend they were comfortable. I had no such options. I'd have to tilt back in my chair and try to rest, but this thing was not made to be sat in for twenty-four hours. It would hurt. It was already starting to hurt, frankly. My hips, my back, my neck. I'd live, but this was gonna suck.

lol, as mom likes to say, he doesn't "cook" so much as "heat up"

well his ramen is heavenly

WAIT

W A I T

Owen's with you at the shop? And you're talking??

well

"talking" might be a little extreme

Melanie had been pestering me to talk to Owen and make amends for months now. I think she thought things would blow over at the beginning. Now that it had become clear that wasn't about to happen, she'd been dying for me to budge. I knew it was weird for her to have her best friend and twin brother on such bad terms, but it's not like any of this was *my* fault. I wouldn't be the one to cave.

Ugggggh Mrs. Pritchett says it's "lights out" 😑

Talk to Owen, you goober! Love youuuu!

love you too. sleep well.

I glanced at the time again (11:25) and decided to try to get comfy. At least I was dry and warm, which was probably more than Devi's suede boots could say. I turned the lights off and tucked myself into the corner behind the front desk, right under the heater vent. With the press of a button, my chair reclined, stretching my grateful spine and hips. I used my jacket, long since dry from the walk over, like a blanket. Outside, all was black and white, the world's usual shapes and shadings erased for now. I'd never really understood the breathless fascination with snow, but watching the hushed drifts slowly layering themselves into existence as my muscles relaxed and my eyes grew heavy, I could finally see the appeal.

And then, right as I was about to tumble into sleep, the power cut out.

I sat in front of the greenhouse door, imagining I could already feel the warmth of the heavy-duty gas heater. Behind that door was an oasis. Eighty degrees and gentle humidity, 365 days a year. I raised my fist and let it hover.

The store *might* not get too cold. But Mrs. Otsuki always kept the thermostat at sixty-eight degrees, so there wasn't much warmth stored up to begin with, and a quick look at my weather app said we'd be dipping into the teens before long. A chill raced through me at the thought of spending the rest of the night without heat—immediately chased by another chill at the alternative.

I couldn't remember the last time I'd been in the greenhouse. Even before the rift, I didn't spend a ton of time back there. The aisles were cramped and there were always hoses or tools or trays of this and that lying around, making the floor near unnavigable for me. I didn't mind, though. Even when we were kids working in the garden, me handing Owen seeds or pointing out weeds for him to pull or just making friends with the ladybugs, I was never as interested in the growing process as he was. I was only in it for the end product.

Well. And the company.

Pull your shit together, Eleanor. Knock on the damn door.

The door swung open after just one knock, like he'd been waiting for me. He stood aside and gestured me in with the sweep of an arm. Thankfully, he was fully robed this time.

A blast of warmth greeted me as I entered. I hadn't realized how chilly I'd been, even before the power went out. Hours of sitting next to the front window, cold seeping steadily through the glass, had turned my skin cool as marble. I shivered and moved toward the heat.

"You redecorated," I said, my gaze roving over the room's strange new configuration.

Wooden benches that acted as nurseries for all the dozens of plants normally stretched the length of the structure in six long rows. Now, they were shoved awkwardly toward the edges of the room, a pile-up three benches deep on both sides, leaving a narrow open space in the center. There, Owen had placed an overstuffed chair draped with at least four blankets and a low, round coffee table topped with a steaming teapot—and two teacups. Next to it, an old-school lantern glowed, its soft flame defiant under a glassed-in, moonless midnight.

Owen slipped past me, letting the door close behind us. "I told you I was working earlier."

He bent over the gas heater, adjusting some setting or other, either for the plants' sake or ours. My money was on the former. Plants are surprisingly hardy, he always said, but just because they can endure a lot doesn't mean they should have to.

While he tinkered, I stared at the little tableau in front of me. A clear path led from the door. No tools lying haphazardly around or spilled soil waiting to gum up my treads. The concrete floor looked dewy, recently mopped. And at the end of this runway, he'd placed one chair next to a table next to a perfectly wheelchair-sized empty space. He'd done all of this for me. What, in case the power went out? Or did he think I'd come back here just because? Did he *want* me to? I imagined him in here earlier, shirtless and sweaty as he moved every piece of furniture in this room, as he picked up the mess that always littered the floor, as he found a charming little teapot and an absurd gas lantern of all things—and I felt anger coil deep in my gut.

He sat down, sinking comically deep in his plushy armchair, and started pouring what smelled suspiciously like peppermint tea.

"Drink?" he said, holding the tiny cup out to me.

I was still loitering near the doorway, tucked into the shadowed border of the room. "You hate peppermint tea," I said.

He set the cup down and picked up his own. "I don't *hate* it."

"You don't *like* it."

"So?" he sighed, mild irritation creeping into the word.

"*So*, you know it's my favorite," I snapped, unable and unwilling to sugar my voice. "*So*, what the fuck, Owen?"

He stared at me for a minute, an expression I couldn't quite read. He grabbed the cup and crossed the twenty feet between us in a few long strides, eyes never leaving mine.

"Drink the tea, Eleanor," he said, thrusting the cup in front of me so forcefully some of the hot liquid sloshed out and over his fingers. He didn't seem to notice. "Or don't. I don't care."

It was the strangest standoff I'd ever experienced. The two of us glaring at each other over the rim of a floral-printed teacup, steam drifting up between us. If the air hadn't felt so charged, I would have laughed.

I took the cup. Owen stalked back over to the improvised seating area, and I followed.

We sat in silence, each of us nursing our tea, which was—like the ramen—delicious. Hot enough to feel all the way to your belly, but not enough to burn, and steeped to perfection. Strong, no hedging. The scent of peppermint wreathed me and created a surprising harmony with the myriad garden smells: wet soil, rose and jasmine, the crisp of clear water. And all around us, snowfall.

If I ignored the boy across from me, it was almost peaceful.

"I'm not stuck here, you know," he said, mildly.

"What?"

"Earlier. You said I was stuck here with you, but I could leave anytime. The house isn't all that far. Maybe a mile? It'd suck, but I could make it."

All hints of peacefulness evaporated. "Fuck you, Owen."

He leaned forward, elbows pressed into his knees, hands clasped tight together. "Why don't I leave, Nori?" His voice was soft, almost curious, as if he'd asked nothing more offensive than how the weatherman had gotten the forecast so wrong.

My eyes prickled. I willed them dry. "I don't know," I said, my voice shockingly steady. "It's not like it'd be the first time you bailed on me."

A spark of something flashed in his eyes. Again, I couldn't read him. When had he lost his legibility? When he'd cut me off? Or maybe before, when he'd first started pulling away.

He took a breath, but I interrupted him before he could speak. "Go home, Owen. You want to go? Go. Nobody's stopping you."

He threw his hands up. "You're not listening. I don't want to leave you."

"Of course not," I spat. "Can't possibly leave the little crippled girl alone."

He growled. Like, honest to god, *growled*. Something flipped low in my stomach at the sound.

"I. Don't. Want. To. Leave. You," he said, enunciating each word so hard he practically chewed them up.

Without warning, he slipped from his chair and knelt before me, just like he'd done earlier. I only realized my hands were shaking when he cupped them and slid the trembling teacup gently out of my grasp.

He wrapped his hands around mine again, his skin warm and rough to the touch. My breath hitched. "I'm saying I *want* to be here, Nori. I'm not staying because of the snow or because I feel obligated to. I know you don't need me. You've made that abundantly clear over the past year. I'm here because I want to be."

Abundantly clear, he'd said. *You've made that abundantly . . . over the past—*

I snatched my hands away.

"Don't you dare. *You* were the one who left *me*. Or do you not remember standing me up *on my birthday* of all days."

He stood sharply. He was so close it hurt to look up at him. I glared anyway, neck be damned.

"Why are you so impossible?" He punctuated the final word by spinning on his heel and pacing away from me.

I shouted after him, "You don't get to be angry, Owen. I didn't start this. You're the one who left me crying and alone in that theater."

He leaned over one of the benches, head down, back to me.

He exhaled long and slow. As the air left him, he looked more and more . . . defeated.

"What about Becca?" he asked quietly, almost pleadingly.

The question threw me, confusion edging out the earlier anger. "My ex? What about her?"

"Wasn't she there? On your birthday?"

"What does that have to do with anything?"

He was quiet for a long moment, leaning over his plants in the dark. When he finally spoke, his voice had a strange, thin quality that, for some reason, brought to mind the dandelions Melanie and I used to braid into crowns and pile onto Owen's head, like birds building a nest.

"I never meant for us to stop being friends," he said. "I needed some distance, and I didn't go about it the right way, I know. I didn't mean to hurt you. I didn't think you'd even notice. I'm sorry, Nori."

I took the opportunity to study him. His shoulder blades arced toward each other over his spine, as if trying to hold him up. The hair at the nape of his neck was curled slightly from the humidity. He didn't move, seemed barely even to breathe. I imagined, somewhat wildly, that if I kept my silence, we might stay this way forever. His plants would grow, and our bodies would age, and the sun would twirl its way around and around these glass walls, but we would remain cemented in place, figurines in a terrarium.

"What did I do?" I couldn't keep the shake out of my voice this time. "What did I do wrong?"

He turned, brow furrowed. "Nothing. You did nothing wrong."

"I had to have done something wrong. Because if I didn't, then that means you just got tired of me." I felt the tears coming again. I didn't try to stop them this time; we were past that now, for better or worse. "You just didn't like me anymore and tossed me aside."

Owen crossed the room almost before the last word left my mouth. For the third time that night, he got on his knees in front of me. My heartbeat thrummed way up in my throat. He lifted a hand—tentatively, slowly enough that I could stop him if I wanted—and wiped the few spilled tears from my cheek.

"Is that what you've thought this whole time? No wonder you stopped speaking to me."

"What the hell else was I supposed to think?"

He laughed lightly. "Fair point." Owen pulled his hand away. I flushed hard when I realized I had leaned forward, following his retreating touch.

"Do you remember when we were little," he said, "how I rubbed dirt all over me before we played in the garden?"

I laughed. "All over your arms, your legs, your face." I smiled as the image of little Owen came back to me. "You looked ridiculous."

"Mom would get so mad. 'Now you're gonna have to shower *again*. Are *you* gonna pay the water bill this month?'" His impression was scarily spot-on. "Do you remember why I did it?"

I searched back through the haze of memory for the exacting toddler logic he'd used. "You said you wanted to be a part *of* them, not apart *from* them."

"Prepositional wordplay. So precocious," he said, rolling his eyes at his younger self.

When he looked at me again, something changed. The air between us warmed from more than the gas heater, and I realized how truly little space there was between us. He licked his bottom lip. My breath caught.

"When you started dating Becca, it was like . . . Not like a light switching on. That's not it at all." He glanced around, frustrated, before his face lit up in triumph. "You know what it was like? It was like the day after an unheard-of snowstorm. There's been nothing but gray, gray clouds all day, right? But the sun comes up the next morning and the sky is so blue and the ground is so white and the light reflects off of absolutely everything. The entire world is sunlight, and it's so brilliant it burns, but if you look away you worry you might never see sun like this again."

"Owen, you're making less than zero sense right now."

He took a breath, then reached out and took my hand. None of this made any *sense*.

"When you started dating Becca, I realized I didn't want to be apart from you. I wanted us to be together. But you didn't want that, and I didn't know how to be a good friend to you with all of this . . . sunlight in my eyes. I'm mixing metaphors, I'm sorry."

My chest hurt. Literally. It took a second to realize the sharp burn behind my ribs was my lungs demanding air. I'd stopped breathing sometime during his speech. Air deprivation wasn't exactly helping me process. I closed my eyes and pulled a deep, slow breath through my nose. Owen, ever patient, didn't ask what I was doing or repeat himself or demand I respond. He simply waited with me.

"How did you know?" I finally asked, my eyes still closed.

When I opened them, his head was tilted in question.

"How did you know I didn't want to be together?" I clarified. "That I didn't want you?"

Owen blinked a few times, then a few more. It was satisfying to see him look as flustered as I felt. His hand was still holding mine, and I squeezed gently, pulling him back to me.

"Becca and I weren't ever official, but I did officially break it off the week after my birthday. Did you know that?"

"I did, but—"

"I broke it off because sitting in the dark in that theater, I had never felt more alone. I was heartbroken, Owen, and I hadn't even realized I'd given my heart to you in the first place." I paused and felt my blood pulsing in my wrist, right under Owen's thumb. "It was a lot to process all at once, honestly."

He looked up at me with the most hope and fear I've ever seen mixed into one gaze before.

"And then you didn't say a word. Not one, Owen."

"I know, I'm—"

"No," I said. "It's my turn to talk."

He looked up at me sheepishly. "Yes, ma'am."

I ignored the way my body reacted to that and kept on. "You shouldn't have assumed. You should have talked to me." The words rang false even to my own ears. I blew out a heavy sigh. "But I did the exact same thing to you. I assumed you hated me, and I flat-out refused to talk to you. You started this but I made damn sure it continued. Why didn't we just *talk* to each other?"

"We're talking now," he said reasonably. His fingers dragged along my palm, almost absently, but the way his eyes lit up at my sudden inhale proved he knew exactly what he was doing.

"I think . . ." I swallowed hard and tried again. "I think we've done enough talking. For now. Maybe."

He nodded solemnly and raised himself higher on his knees. Our eyes held as he ran his knuckles lightly under my jaw and leaned forward. "Is this okay?" he said. "I mean, can I . . . ? I don't want to assume."

"Owen Otsuki, if you don't kiss me right this second, I swear—"

He kissed me. No more hesitating. He tasted like peppermint and ginger. He felt like home. I parted my lips and he pressed harder, harder than I think he meant. My head snapped back from the force and I gasped in panic. Owen caught me, his hand firm on the back of my neck, bracing me.

"Did I hurt you?" he asked. "Are you okay?"

He held me steady, his fingers on my scalp a promise.

"I'm more than okay."

I was safe. I ignored my body's instincts and relaxed into his palm, letting my head fall back toward the slanted glass roof. Snow was still falling. I nearly opened my mouth to catch the flakes. I felt delirious, unreal. But then Owen's mouth feathered along the side of my exposed throat and I snapped back to myself. I was real, this was real. Here in this body in this room in this moment with this boy I'd loved in one way or another my entire life.

He gently tilted my head upright and kissed me proper again. I stopped thinking altogether at that point.

When we finally broke apart, he rested his forehead on mine. We sat there for a long moment, just breathing, his hand in my hair and mine on his forearm.

I pulled away first. "Wait a minute," I said. "Is this why Melanie's been on my case about talking to you? Did she know?"

Owen shrugged. "I don't think so, but maybe she suspected? Did she know about you?"

"Absolutely not. No way." I thought back to the movie theater lobby, when she had held me while I cried over her brother and realized maybe not everyone was as oblivious to my own feelings as I was. "Okay, it's *possible* she had figured it out."

He laughed, the sound ringing through the room. "So my sister is a terrible wingwoman. Noted. The good news is neither of us should be needing her services any time soon." A pause, a flash of doubt. "Right?"

I leaned in and kissed him again. I could do that now, I thought. Kiss him. So I did it one more time before saying, "Right."

In the morning, the sun came up and the sky was so blue and the ground was so white and the light reflected off of absolutely everything.

Neither one of us looked away.

CON NIGHTS, PARALLEL HEARTS

by Marieke Nijkamp

1.

> ALESSIA: When you're faced with endless universes, how do you know which choice to make and which to unmake? How do you know what the right outcome is?
>
> CONNOR: We don't. Every choice we make has consequences, good and bad. We can only hope the good outweighs the bad.
>
> *Parallel Hearts* S01E03: Concrete Jungle

THE CONCRETE IS COLD AND HARD UNDERNEATH OUR sleeping bags. My backpack, which I'm using as a pillow, is anything but comfortable. And to make things worse, it's starting to drizzle. Not a whole lot, just enough that if it continues through the night, we'll be soaked by the time the doors open.

"Isn't this *exciting*, Quinn?" Clara whispers, lying on her back, staring up at the con center.

"It's wet," I reply.

"It's *cold*," McKenna mutters, drawing their coat up higher.

"It's worth it." Clara beams.

She clearly has a very different understanding of exciting than either McKenna or me. But to be fair, I know where she's coming from. I'm not looking forward to tonight, but tomorrow *is* going to make it all worth it. Tomorrow, I'm finally going to cross paths with the highly elusive Jocelyn Cheng, creator of *Parallel Hearts*. Just me, her, and five thousand of my closest friends.

And McKenna, of course. We'll lose Clara to her friends in Artist Alley the moment we're inside—she warned us about that when we booked the tickets—but McKenna is sticking by my side. For *Parallel Hearts*, for Jocelyn Cheng. For me, perhaps? It's our thing, after all.

Parallel Hearts is a pretty niche show. I wouldn't have even known about it if McKenna hadn't come crashing into my room one night, when they were staying over because their parents were traveling again. Stumbling over the words, they told me about this show their cousin in Scotland watches, with time travel and parallel universes and superpowered teens, and they didn't know if we could stream it somewhere, but there had to be a way, because it sounded right up my alley.

Turned out, it was.

My mom wasn't home, and my brother was out doing whatever it was he was doing, so we sat on my bed, cross-legged, knees ever so slightly touching, and binged the entire first season. A week later, we'd caught up to the current season three. A week after that, I had fan art and fanfic bookmarked *for days*.

Of course, I also found a lot of people online who claimed the production value was low and the special effects were outdated, and honestly? Maybe that's true. But the *acting*. The *writing*. The *emotions*. There are plenty of series out there with high production value, and that's cool, but I don't just watch shows because the SFX are shiny. I watch them to be moved.

So when, by the end of the first episode, one of the main characters—Alessia—had to choose between going back home to her normal life and leaving it all behind to travel, McKenna and I were ready to leave everything behind too. And sure, maybe that feeling wasn't *entirely* because of the show either, but it was absolutely one of those right time, right place things.

"So what will you do once you have an autograph?" Clara asks us. She's tossing and turning, and I wonder if she plans to sleep at all tonight. "And what are you even going to say to her?"

"Um." Honestly I don't have the first clue what I'm going to say to *Jocelyn Cheng*. I've been going over this meeting half a million times in my head since the con announced she was coming, but I come up blank every time I try to form the right words. We're overnighting to make sure McKenna and I get autograph tickets, because apparently they're only releasing fifty. But let's face it, I'm probably just going to stand there and gawk. What are we going to do *after* meeting Jocelyn Cheng? Get in line for the *Parallel Hearts* panel that isn't until the end of the day, maybe. Do people get in line early for that sort of thing too?

I'm normally an absolutely Type-A personality in all other aspects of my life. I have three different bullet journals, for school, sports, and free time. Yes, I plan my free time. I start studying for tests the moment I learn of their existence. I make flashcards for all of my fencing opponents' strategies.

But this is too personal for strategy.

McKenna nudges me and draws me back to Clara's question. "Depending on how long it takes, we'll find you in Artist Alley," they say. "I want to buy more pins."

"Your entire jacket is pins."

"So?"

"Fair point."

"Plus, maybe we can find some cool *Hearts* fan art," I put in.

Clara laughs. "You and your obsessions. You know not everything is *Parallel Hearts*, right?"

I feel a touch of heat curl up my cheeks. I know it isn't, but at the same time . . . isn't it? I love that Alessia, Lyra, and Connor can travel through time to undo mistakes and right wrongs. Test theories and change universes. That there's nothing broken that can't be fixed, and nothing so irreparably damaged that it can't be given a second chance. That they can survive. If history functioned like that, we'd all be a lot better off.

I throw a look in McKenna's direction. "You get it, right? You were the one to introduce me to the show. You're here for Jocelyn Cheng too."

"I *like* the show, sure," McKenna starts, and off the bat it sounds like a breakup conversation. My shoulders tighten. "The concept is really cool and some of the characters appeal to me. And even though Lyra's and my experiences aren't the same, it matters a lot seeing a trans main character in a show like this. So it absolutely holds a special place in my heart. But I'm here for a thousand other things too. And I'm mostly here for Jocelyn Cheng because *you* are."

"Oh." Um. I'm not entirely sure how to respond. It's the sweetest worst thing anyone has ever said to me.

A hint of the terror I feel must be visible on my face, because McKenna winces.

"Quinn, I'm just messing with you," Clara says gently. She reaches out and squeezes my hand. "The first time I was here, it was purely for *Tortall Heroes* and I didn't notice anything else. I was overwhelmed and bright eyed and very nearly missed the second day because I completely forgot to eat or drink. So maybe don't do what I did? But also, I get it, and so does everyone here." She motions around her, at the dozens of sleeping bags and backpacks and whispered conversations and suitcases full of cosplay and the group right at the front who are playing filk songs on a ukulele and the girls behind us who are invested in some kind of midnight RPG. "It's *okay.*"

I bite my lip. Nod.

"I mean, there are far too many people here, but that's also kind of beautiful, isn't it?" McKenna says. They glance at me. "Especially if all of them are here for different things. Even though I *know*, I still didn't realize there were so many fandoms out there."

"Oh you sweet summer child." Clara smiles. "We're infinite." She yawns once and turns onto her side, her head resting in the crook of her elbow. With her free hand, she pulls her crutches close and almost cradles them as she falls asleep immediately.

McKenna *stares.* "Screw parallel universes and time travel. That's a superpower I want to have."

"I know, right?" I fake a yawn. The concrete is still unrelenting and the backpack pokes my face. Let's face it, there's no way I'm actually falling asleep anytime soon. I have a hard enough time with that on normal nights, in a comfortable bed, in a quiet, darkened room.

Tonight, I don't have to count the shadows, but my brain is a mess of nerves, anticipation, worry, *what-if-I-said-the-wrong-thing-will-they-still-like-me*.

We both lie in silence for a bit, listening to the girls and their roleplaying. It apparently involves bikes, mysteries, and a particle accelerator loop or something. They don't seem to mind the rain, though I hope they're not using paper character sheets.

At least it's nothing more than drizzle, and whatever smog comes from the city at night. Though somehow, that's the thing I *don't* mind. There's something magical about being here, quite a ways away from our suburban, WASPy home, complete with its meticulously kept front lawn (courtesy of my brother saving up for a new BMX bike) and extremely kitschy lawn gnomes.

The night isn't so dark in the city and it even *smells* different. All hot concrete, exhaust fumes, yesterday's garbage, and hell, whatever possibility smells like. Sure, the air is probably a whole lot less healthy, but I can breathe here.

Perhaps that's what I love most about *Parallel Hearts*. Possibility.

And knowing that the choices we make—the choices that *matter*—aren't just the big, sweeping ones. Sometimes a meaningful choice is a simple choice, as simple as five words.

I take a breath and say, "It's not just *Parallel Hearts*."

2.

Or, Option A

> ALESSIA: Aren't you tempted sometimes to flee from all the horror? Let history run its course without us meddling?
>
> LYRA: All the time.
>
> ALESSIA: Then why don't you?
>
> LYRA: Because every time I imagine being the girl who runs away, I can't help but think someone else will have to run into danger instead.
>
> *Parallel Hearts* S01E07: Choose Your Own Adventure

There was a scene in the penultimate episode of the first season when Alessia talked about being an abuse survivor, and I'd never felt so seen before. I had never told anyone about being abused, but I wanted to tell McKenna, there and then. I'd rehearsed the words over and over again.

But then Nate walked in, and—

"What's not just *Parallel Hearts*?" McKenna asks. They prop themself up on an elbow and tilt their head.

Behind us, the particle accelerator RPG is ramping up again, with whispered arguments and uncontrollable laughter. The ukulele music has faded away, though someone, somewhere, still seems to be singing. We're way past midnight now.

I swallow.

"It's not just *Parallel Hearts*," I repeat. I keep my voice down, so as not to wake Clara. My mind scrambles for what to say next. "It's never just been about the show."

McKenna pushes themself up farther. "I know. Do you want to tell me about it?"

I do, I do, I do. I wanted to that first night. I've wanted to so many times. I can't.

I am breathless, and even though I gulp in air, it doesn't feel refreshing. I never told anyone and now the words won't come. I've committed to another story, another Quinn. I've committed to lies so many times, and once lies have their teeth in you, it's so hard to shake them loose.

"I love that it's ours." As soon as the words are out, my heartrate calms and I feel my jaw unclench. I don't feel better, I don't feel lighter, but it's the truth—too. "I know it wasn't always easy to stay at our place. We were, and maybe even are, a mess."

McKenna was almost twelve the first time they stayed with us, their parents off to do research in a war zone, and sometimes it felt like our house was a war zone, too. Mom set up a cot in my room, because we didn't know what a permanent fixture this would be yet.

It was the first time someone had stayed over since Dad left and I didn't know how to deal with it, so I was awake all night and kept stealing glances at this strange neighborhood kid whose parents needed them to have a relatively safe place to stay. I made sure McKenna didn't see me, of course. I hid under the covers and only a mop of brown hair peeked out.

They looked lost that whole week, ill and homesick. But it wasn't so bad, the second time. Not for either of us.

A year in, no one but me remembered a time when McKenna wasn't staying at our house. When my mother worked late nights, they helped out with chores and meals. When my brother Nate and I fought—often—they were the one to broker peace. They made us feel like a family again, when we couldn't figure it out ourselves.

Three years in, they were as comfortable to me as breathing and I still trust McKenna more than I do myself. So I give them as much truth as I can. "When you shared *Parallel Hearts* with me," I continue, "it felt like so much possibility. Like we could lose ourselves in this world, and it would be just ours. Everything is better there, when the real world is scary, you know? I'm tired of the hate and the anger and the fascism and the fact that the planet may not even be habitable anymore by the time we grow up. I don't want people to hate me for who I love or you for who you are. This. You and me. *Parallel Hearts* feels like safety."

McKenna tilts their head. Their dark brown eyes stare right through me. Tiny drops of rain cling to their green hair. "Oh."

The moment they look away, I think what I can't add. *"It— you—helped me survive. I can't lose you."*

McKenna looks at their fingernails, a faint blush on their cheeks. Almost as though they heard me. Then they say, "When I first stayed over, I wanted to be anywhere but there. I was worried about my parents, you just *stared* at me, and I . . . don't know, I didn't feel welcome. I felt like all of you wanted me to be somewhere else, and I felt like all of you wanted one another to be somewhere else too. It felt like there was something I didn't know about"—they glance at me—"and sometimes it still feels that way."

It's such a perfect opening. But the moment passes in the

murmurs around us and the pitter-pattering of raindrops on a plastic bag.

"It got better once we found those knight comics," McKenna continues. "Remember those? *KnightTime* or something? The one Nate liked, too? I felt like that was something we could bond over, even if he mostly cared about the fights, and I mostly cared about the art and figuring out the page layouts, and you mostly cared about that one character who only showed up in the first three issues and then disappeared. What was her name again? I can't even remember. But the point is, I get it. Sharing that, with the two of you, it made me feel like I could find a way to belong in your home too." There's a crack in their voice and a shadow in their eyes. They brush a strand of hair out of their face, and this time, they purposefully don't look at me. "It always seemed like it was more than that for you though. You'll probably hate me for saying this, but ever since *Parallel Hearts*, you seem . . . lighter. Happier."

They glance at me through their lashes, and it's another opening. Another chance.

I could try. I could take it.

But I'm scared, and it would break this moment between us, and besides, I can't stop thinking about Nate with his comics. I bite my lip. "It's nice to be here together."

They smile at that, and if they want to say anything more, I'm saved by the dice.

"Hey!" we hear from behind us. The girls have apparently reached the climax of their game, and they're very awake, despite the shushing and complaining from others within earshot. "You mean there were actual monsters underneath the lake?"

I have no idea what's happening in their game, but it seems important.

More than that, it's enticing—I look at McKenna, who opens up their sleeping bag and pushes themself up to their knees.

It's an escape. "Do you think we can watch?" I ask. *This is another something we could do, together.*

They pull their hoodie closer and move in the girls' direction. "D'you mind if we stay and watch for a bit?"

The girls immediately shuffle around to make room for us. I watch McKenna as they absorb it all. Their face lit up the moment the girls made room for us, and they are so completely in thrall. They respect the game enough to not interrupt, but I can see all the questions and wonderment on their face.

It's somewhere around two a.m. when the game finally ends, and McKenna and I crawl our way back to our sleeping bags. We're both shivering in the near constant drizzle, but they're grinning. "That was fun. We should try it sometime."

"We'll pick up a copy of the rulebook once we're done buying you pins," I promise immediately.

"Deal."

We snuggle up again, facing each other. Inside my sleeping bag, I wrap my arms around my chest, but my hands are ice cold. McKenna twists and turns to find a comfortable position.

Once they have, they whisper, "Thanks for telling me, Q. About *Hearts*, I mean."

I feel a pang of guilt, but I push it away with a vengeance. "I'm glad you're here with me tonight."

"Me too." The words are almost a slur, and McKenna falls asleep a moment later.

And I can't help but think I should've told them the truth. I owed it to them. But I didn't have the words—and if I didn't have them, how could I speak them?

And it's so much safer to keep my mouth shut. Some secrets are best kept close to the heart, where they can't hurt anyone but me. I've been hurt before. I can take it.

This friendship is worth all of me.

Besides, every word I spoke *was* the truth. Not the whole truth, but nothing but the truth. If I repeat that often enough in the silence that stretches out around us, I might believe it by the time the sun rises.

3.
Or, Option B

LYRA: They say we're the ones with superpowers.

CONNOR: We're just genetically lucky.

Parallel Hearts S02E09: Where the Wild Things Go

Truth isn't a binary, even though it often feels that way. Tell your truth or don't tell your truth, there is no in-between. Once you're convinced that's how it works, you simply don't think about sharing anymore. Because the walls you build around yourself get higher and higher, until you don't know if they keep the world out or keep you in.

"What's not just *Parallel Hearts*?" McKenna asks. They prop themself up on an elbow and tilt their head.

The particle accelerator RPG behind us is ramping up again, with whispered arguments and uncontrollable laughter.

The ukulele music has faded away, though someone, somewhere, still seems to be singing. We're way past midnight now.

"It's not just *Parallel Hearts*," I repeat. The moment those words leave my mouth, I regret them. "It's never just been about the show."

McKenna pushes themself up farther. "I know. Do you want to tell me about it?"

I do want to. I can't tell.

I was never supposed to.

McKenna edges a little closer, making the world around us a little smaller—and I could never lie to them. They make my world feel safer.

"Would you like to give it a try?" they ask.

"Yes? No?" I laugh awkwardly. "I've been thinking about this since we booked our tickets and even before that." But every time I get too close, I walk into that wall again. Or perhaps *I* pull it closer, every time I see it in the distance. "It's a bit like falling in love, but it's also not like that at all."

McKenna tilts their head. Their dark brown eyes stare right through me. Tiny drops of rain cling to their green hair, but the way they've turned to me it's as if they're keeping the rest of the world—and even the rain itself—at bay. "I thought as much. It *seems* like it's more to you than that. I've seen you fall in love with books and movies and series before—I've done it too—but those were always moments. Lightning strikes. Do you remember that time we both got into that haunted house show? Or *Summer Camp Witches*, those books I loved? This . . . it goes deeper?"

It does, in good ways and in more difficult ones.

They reach out a hand to me. They steal themself before they continue and their voice drops. "I'm not sure if you want to hear this, but this series . . . I don't think I've ever seen you this happy."

Oh.

Ouch.

McKenna looks at our intertwined fingers, a faint blush on their cheeks. "I'm not entirely sure that's the right word, but *happier*, at least."

I stare at our hands too. In the years since McKenna came to sometimes live with us, we've grown close and closer. Not at first; I think they hated being left alone and I think they were scared for their parents, which made it hard for them to connect with anyone. And besides, I hated being saddled with a surprise sibling.

But as time passed and we both realized this was our new normal, we adapted. My brother and I found ourselves with a third sibling, who shared our home and our hearts—but not our history. And maybe because of that, some days, they were the glue that kept Nate and me together.

In a way, that's why I love this show, too. Because it's a reminder of that.

"I don't know if happy is the right word either," I say. "Lighter, maybe?"

"In what way?"

"It makes me think about the mistakes I made." The words terrify me, as I let them escape.

McKenna frowns. "What kind of mistakes?"

The first time they stayed overnight, it was all I could do to stare at the cot through the night. I knew why they couldn't stay home alone, but I hated having someone else in my room. Every time I would doze off, I'd hear McKenna's breathing, or the creak of the other bed, and I'd startle awake again. It'd been well over a year since I stayed up all night to listen. I'd grown complacent—and exhausted.

"Mistakes I wish I could go back in time to fix," I reply. And I latch onto that part, because it's easier than the other fragments of truth hiding away in my brain. "It's the first thing I loved about *Parallel Hearts*. The idea that we can mess up, but that's not the end of it. That we can go back and fix what went wrong, rebuild what was broken."

"What mistakes, Quinn?" they press, gently.

I open my mouth and close it.

Again.

Again.

I want to trust them. I do, I do, I do.

"Hey!" we hear from behind us. The girls have apparently reached the climax of their game, and they're very awake, despite the shushing and complaining from others within earshot. "You mean there were actual monsters underneath the lake?"

I have no idea what's happening, but it seems important.

McKenna glances in their direction. "Do you think they even notice they're in line anymore?"

I see the escape that's there. "If you want to go watch . . ."

In response, they pull their sleeping bag up to their ears. The drops of rain are even louder on the fabric. "I want to stay here," they say.

"This was a terrible idea." I glance up at the sky. "Why did our moms agree to this?"

"Because making mistakes is part of being human?"

McKenna's persistence is powerful, but shame and regret are more powerful still. If I could go back in time, I'd protect my brother. If I could go back in time, I'd tell my mother. If I could go back in time, I'd not be bad.

I open my mouth and close it.

I want to trust them. I do, I do, I do.

I want to *tell* them.

McKenna tilts their head. "You can tell me. You can trust me."

"I know, but . . ." I don't trust myself.

"Some things are too hard to put into words?" they suggest.

I nod. And some secrets have been buried for so long, I don't know how to go about digging them up. Because right now, I'm Quinn. Fencer with a bit of talent. Straight-B student. Well, minus the straight part. McKenna's best friend and regular roommate and oftentimes fellow fan. I love peas and I love carrot cake and I hate frosting and I could live off of Diet Coke and time-travel series. I am perfectly average with a few quirks for good measure, and if I can just stay like that, I can stay safe.

Parallel Hearts isn't real. I can't change the mistakes I carry with me.

But I *can* change my actions now.

I take a deep breath and let the words stumble out. "I'm not doing okay."

McKenna waits to see if I say anything more, and when I don't, they nod. "I'm sorry. Is there anything I can do?"

I clench my jaw. "I don't know, I'm . . ." I try on the various words, but I can't find the right one. Not okay. Broken. It's as far as I can go.

"Hurting?" McKenna offers, instead.

Oh.

Huh.

"Yes, that."

I stare at them, and they shrug. "I know that feeling. Not now. Not anymore. Just . . . I've been there, and I didn't like it."

It reassures me, frightens me, and makes me want to protect them, all at the same time.

"Is there anything you need?" they ask.

It's such a simple, well-meant question, but I have so little to offer in return. I wince. "I don't know. I just . . . don't run when I tell you, okay? If I find the words."

They nod. "I'm here. I'm not going anywhere. Promise."

Those few words nearly break me down entirely, but my walls are stronger and I haven't cried in so long. I don't know if this is better than telling or not telling. I don't know if there is such a thing as better when you're laying parts of your soul bare. But they're here, and so am I.

Maybe, for now, this is enough.

McKenna pushes a hand out of their sleeping bag and squeezes my shoulder. "Don't let the secrets devour you, Q."

"I'll try not to?" It's all I can give them. "I want to trust you. I do."

"I know." They let themself fall on their back, and they stare up at the concrete buildings. "Tell me when you're ready. I'll wait as long as it takes."

I stare up at the large square shadows too. "I'm here too. If there's anything you want to talk about."

"I know."

The silence is almost comfortable around us, now, even though the rain is doing its best to make us uncomfortable. I burrow deeper into my sleeping bag, but I keep looking at

McKenna, nothing but hair and eyes peeking out into the night.

McKenna stares right back at me. And perhaps we could fall asleep like that, but eventually they push themself up on an elbow again. "And for what it's worth, give yourself a second chance."

I understand the reference. I don't know what to say to that, and I'm not sure they expect a response either. Instead, we both wait for the night to pass.

Sleep soon claims McKenna, and I'm left with my thoughts, their quiet breathing, and five new words to mull over.

Maybe I can tear down my walls stone by stone if I have to.

Even small choices can change the world, after all.

4.
Or, Option C

CONNOR: Was it worth it? All of this?

LYRA: If it wasn't, lie to me.

ALESSIA: It was. You once told me that every choice we make has good and bad consequences, and that we can only hope the good outweighs the bad. I don't think that's all of it. Every choice we make creates a new opportunity for a better world. We're not changing the world ourselves, and we don't have to. We just have to keep giving it a second chance. We just have to keep giving ourselves second chances too.

Parallel Hearts S03E13: Wild Roses

Endless universes, and endless possibilities. I can't help but wonder who I could be if I had the world at my fingertips. If the me's of parallel universes are different. Brave. Whole.

If maybe *I* can be different. If I can be brave. If I can feel whole.

"What's not just *Parallel Hearts*?" McKenna asks. They prop themself up on an elbow and tilt their head.

The particle accelerator RPG behind us is ramping up again, with whispered arguments and uncontrollable laughter. The ukulele music has faded away, though someone, somewhere, still seems to be singing. We're way past midnight now.

"It's not just *Parallel Hearts*," I repeat. "It's never just been about the show."

McKenna pushes themself up farther. "I know. Do you want to tell me about it?"

I don't—I want to survive and be safe.

I do—out of everyone around me, McKenna deserves the answer most. Because they are here. Because they have been here for the past five years.

Because I think they'll still be here if I don't tell them.

Because I think they'll still be here if I do tell them.

I open my mouth and I close it.

Again.

McKenna reaches out a hand to me. "You don't have to talk about it if you don't want to, it's just—"

"I know."

But I want to tell them. But sometimes it's easier to keep silent. Sometimes it's safer to keep silent, because I don't know what's on the other side of my walls. But if I don't tell them now, then when? It's easier here than at home. We're shielded by anonymity. And I want to talk about it. I *have* to talk about it. I want them to know before tomorrow. I—

Take a deep breath, and say, "You never met my dad, did you?"

They shake their head, and I somehow manage a smile. "That's probably a good thing. He wasn't a nice person. He certainly wasn't a good dad."

McKenna's face falls, almost as if they can see where this is going, and not for the first time I wonder how many of us have stories like this, hidden away between the words we speak and the silences we keep. Stories we never talk about because they're too big to share, even as they devour us.

"He used to come into my room at night." Even those few words threaten to take my breath away.

"Quinn . . ."

I silence McKenna with a hand gesture. If I stop talking now, I won't start again. Not tonight, at least. Maybe not ever. "He told me I could never tell anyone about it, because if I did, he would get angry. He could get so angry sometimes that I think even my mother was scared of him. He told me he didn't want to, he didn't like being angry, that he didn't like hurting any of us, but if I wasn't a good girl . . ." I pull my knees up to my chest and wrap my arms around them. "One night, I resisted. I tried to cry out. The next day he took a belt to Nate."

McKenna pales. "Oh Quinn. I'm sorry."

"Yeah."

"I didn't know."

"No one does—did."

I don't even know now, looking back, if he realized how effective a threat it was, because I *wanted* to tell, but every time I even thought about telling anyone, my throat would just close up. I wanted to protect my brother. I needed to protect my brother. I wanted to protect my mother. And I had already failed once, so I wasn't about to do it again.

Even after he moved out, I couldn't tell. I didn't know how to. I just let the shame and the guilt become a part of me, because I was sure it should be.

"When—when did it stop?" McKenna asks.

"When he left. Mom stood up to him and gave him an ultimatum. Get his act together or get out. She didn't even know. But she saw Nate's scars. She bore her own. And somehow, she managed to break us free. He tried to get control back, but she wouldn't let him. He tried to sabotage her by having an affair, which was awful for the other woman too. He hurt us. When nothing moved her, I think he lost interest. He packed his bags and left. Found a job out of state."

I didn't believe it, at first. I lay awake for days on end, because I was sure he'd find his way back. Because I was sure he would get angry and that, even though he didn't want to, he would hurt us.

"I was eight when he left. And you know what the worst thing is?" I stare at my patterned sleeping bag. "I missed him. Some days, I still do."

"He's your father. No matter what happened, that doesn't change."

I tell myself that too. But it doesn't make me feel better. "I don't even know where he is now, or if he's still alive. We haven't spoken to that side of the family in years, and I don't particularly want to."

"It's ironic." McKenna shakes their head. "My parents always go on about how perfect your home seems."

"Hey!" A sudden shout behind us makes me tense all over, and I curl up and make myself even smaller.

The girls have apparently reached the climax of their game, and they're very awake, despite the shushing and complaining from others within earshot. I only catch part of what they say, and it's all I can do to repeat it to McKenna.

"Sometimes, there are actual monsters underneath the lake."

McKenna grimaces. "Yeah. There are."

We fall silent and the night around us grows silent too. The only sound is the soft pitter-pattering of the rain on our sleeping bags.

McKenna is so quiet, and it's only because I can see them staring at me that I know they haven't fallen asleep.

I stare back at them, and I don't feel . . . better, necessarily. But I feel lighter. And at the same time I feel dreadfully tired and sick to my stomach. I feel like I'm bursting. Like even sharing a bit of truth is enough to open a dam and now everything comes flooding out. "I don't know how to live with this, Mac."

"I'll be at your side. We'll find a way."

I take a deep breath and with a trembling voice I give them all the truth I have left in me. "I tell everyone that I love *Parallel Hearts* because it reminded me that there's nothing broken that can't be fixed, and nothing so irreparably damaged that it can't be given a second chance. But mostly, it reminded me that there's *no one* broken who can't be fixed, and I'm not so irreparably damaged that I can't be given a second chance."

"You're not broken nor damaged," McKenna says, with determination. They barely manage to keep their voice to a whisper.

"I know that. I think I know that. Most of the time. At least some of the time."

"You're not responsible for what your father did—to you *or* to Nate."

On some sort of rational level, I knew I wasn't responsible for what my father did to us, but I could still count every scar on my brother's arms and trace it back to me. "If I'd just been good, he—"

"*No.*" They wiggle closer. "No. He made those choices. He threatened you into submission. He *abused* you. He was responsible for every single step, not you. You were just a kid, Quinn."

I wince, and I pull back, so they can't touch me. McKenna realizes and immediately puts some distance between us. But they don't let up. "You were just a kid and if I have to remind you a thousand times that you're not responsible for any of this, I will. If I have to tell you a thousand times that you deserved better and that you *still* deserve better, I will."

They stare at me so intently that somehow those words are bigger than all the secrets I ever kept. I don't know if I can believe them forever, I don't even know if I believe them now. But right here and now, on the concrete floor underneath a rainy night sky, I *want* to.

I want people to see me. I want people to hear me. I want my mother to know what happened, and maybe even Nate too, so it isn't just McKenna that's the glue between us anymore.

And maybe I want to believe—not just in second chances, but in the idea that, despite the choices and the scars and horrors we carry with us, there's something worth fighting for.

Maybe that's why *Parallel Hearts* means so much to me, too. Because I *want* to believe in all of those things. Without Connor and Lyra and Alessia and McKenna, I wouldn't have found that one word: hope.

I breathe. I feel so much lighter.

"Another truth is," I tell McKenna, "*Parallel Hearts* reminds me of you, too. It's ours. It's safe. It's home." I brave a smile. "Soon, we're going to meet Jocelyn Cheng. And we're going to find you all the pins you want. And we're going to do it together, right?"

Better worlds.

Endless worlds.

And one of them is right here. Me. A hundred strangers. A hundred more secrets and stories. And my best friend by my side. Always.

LYRA: You can talk to me.

ALESSIA: Can I be silent with you instead? I'm afraid I wouldn't tell the truth, and I know how much you hate that.

LYRA: You can be anything you want to be with me. I just want you to be you. Be safe. Be here.

ALESSIA: I will be. Always.

Parallel Hearts S01E12: Bright Young Things

KISS THE BOY

by Amanda Joy

"Don't panic," Jada repeats for the tenth time since we gathered in her bathroom to get ready for tonight. She lives in one of the new developments of McMansions on the edge of town, and because she's an only child she has an entire Jack-and-Jill suite to herself. Much better than the bathroom I share with my younger brother. Currently the counter is laden with eye shadow palettes, foundation bottles, many pots of loose glitter, and a five-pound bag of sour gummy bears.

It's hungry work, preparing for our last school-sanctioned event at Hoffman High. And the last one I'm responsible for conducting as president of student council. Every year after the last day of high school, the graduating class returns to campus for Senior Game Night, the most anticipated event of the year.

It's legendary enough to draw most kids back to campus after their final day of classes.

"The plan is perfect," Malcolm, my other best friend, adds as he glides a fluffy brush across the top of my cheekbone. The resulting slash of golden highlighter looks like he's somehow sewn sunlight into my skin.

"Of course you two think so. Y'all aren't the ones who have to execute it."

Jada whips her head toward me, a few strands of her perfectly pressed hair clinging to her lip gloss as she protests, "Uh-uh, Ayana, I seem to remember I play a key role in phase one."

I open my mouth, prepared to call off the whole thing, but Mal cuts me a look—one that says *don't you even think about backing out of this*—and my mouth falls shut instead.

I already know what they'll say: A Promise is a Promise.

It's one of the main tenets of our friendship: keep your promises, always text back, and snap a picture of your outfit before every party.

And since we spent every afternoon of the last week planning for tonight, the only way I'd get out of this now is probably death. The plan is to get me to fulfill one of our sacred promises.

As freshmen, Mal, Jada, and I swore to pick out one boy each and kiss him by graduation. Jada chose Mark Hill and made good on her promise four weeks later at homecoming. Malcolm picked Detroit, who was the best basketball player at our middle school and came out in seventh grade by getting a rainbow etched into his fade. At the start of high school, Detroit was already popular enough for it to seem like him and Mal hooking up was a pipe dream. Still it only took Mal two years to make it happen and the two have been together ever since.

I chose Khalil Moore because we slow danced at the eighth-grade spring dance and his big brown eyes and long, fluttery lashes made my heartbeat stutter every time our eyes met. We live on the same cul-de-sac and after years of watching him walk his kid sister home every day, I'd decided he was sweet and a bit shy. I thought it would be easy to find a way to kiss him, sure that by the end of the year I would have acquired the skills necessary for a boy to kiss me. (I've long since learned taking the reins myself is a better option.)

When we'd made the promise, Khalil played ball but Detroit was the one college coaches had scouted. If Mal was shooting for the stars, I was aiming for my perfect fit. Or so I thought, until Khalil grew six inches between sophomore and junior year and kept growing until he towered over every boy in our class, except for Detroit. The short, awkward locs he'd had freshman year now hung, perfectly, just past his shoulders. In three short years, he'd ascended to a level of popularity and beauty that was beyond me.

In the years since the promise, I've gone from barely being able to speak to Khalil to holding a conversation without making a complete fool of myself. Considering my track record, this would be decent progress, if not for the fact that our best friends are dating and I see Khalil all the time.

"I still think there are aspects of the plan we can rework," I say. Jada and Malcolm are still working in tandem on my face and hair and I'm sure if I threaten to leave, they'll tie me to the chair.

I don't just have Khalil and the Plan to worry about, I also have to make sure tonight's event goes smoothly. I've already planned all the details for SGN and delegated most of the night-of responsibilities to my copresident, Jaxon, so I can devote the night to my friends. But I'm pretty sure eight missed calls are an indication that my carefully laid plans are already falling apart. A bad omen.

Both Jada and Mal are already dressed and only have finishing touches on their looks left. Mal wears a green utility jumpsuit he distressed himself, which suits his freckles and auburn coils well. Jada and I are wearing cutoffs and matching Beyoncé-inspired cropped, goldenrod hoodies with our names bedazzled across the shoulders. Her eye shadow is an even brighter yellow and is perfect against her luminous dark skin.

Malcolm, holding a blush brush between his teeth, and a curling wand in hand, makes a noise of annoyance. "Like what could we possibly change?"

"Too much depends on me talking to Khalil. How about, instead, you two—"

Jada straightens, the lipstick tube in her hand, once on a trajectory to coat my lips, falls into the sink, forgotten. "Hold on a second, Ayana, you're saying you want to *kiss* Khalil tonight, but talking to him is going to be a problem?"

"Remember what happened last time?" I ask with a shudder.

A week ago, I was in the courtyard with Jaxon, handing out the permission slips for Senior Game Night. Detroit was there—all flash as usual, in a throwback Raptors jersey and a red kilt, paired with Jordan 1s that matched the gold threads in the plaid. His hair was faded in the back and long on top, and dyed several shades of green, from neon to forest.

At his side was Khalil, looking very much his opposite in a sleeveless white T-shirt, black denim shorts, and highlighter-yellow Air Maxes. His locs, usually tied back, hung past his shoulders, bleached golden at the ends.

Struck by a rare flash of bravery, I pulled two sheets from my Day-Glo orange clipboard and walked toward them. Detroit saw me first and smiled, flashing his teeth as he bent down to murmur something to Khalil. Eyes locked on his phone, it took Khalil a second to react. When he did, he looked right up at me.

My thoughts stalled, turning to mush as our eyes locked. Dully, distantly, I thought about how his skin looked copper in the sun.

Off balance, one foot raised, someone bumped into me and all I saw was Khalil's look of horror before I went sprawling onto the concrete. The flyers pinned to my clipboard went rogue, flitting in every direction.

Pure disaster.

Malcolm has already covered the scrape on my chin that I'd acquired in the fall with several layers of concealer and powder. And Jada has already parted and pinned my curls creatively to hide the fading green-gray bruise on my forehead.

"I'm not panicking," I say. "I'm just saying we should consider me a chaos agent—liable to ruin even the simplest of well-laid plans!"

When I fell, Detroit and Khalil were the first to react and pulled me to my feet before I could become even more of a spectacle. Khalil's hand dwarfed mine as he dragged me to my feet. But I was too surprised to relish the feel of his warm skin. And then Khalil flinched when I looked up at him. "Your chin is bleeding," he murmured, glancing away. "Sorry, Ayana, I'm, uh, not good with blood."

I suspected that was an understatement by the green flush rising in his cheeks. I opened and closed my mouth a few times, but no words came to mind as he turned away. I've been avoiding him in the hallways ever since, hoping he'll forget the whole thing happened.

"You are not a chaos agent! You're perfectly capable of keeping it together when it matters," Malcolm says, tipping my chin up with a finger and squinting at his and Jada's handiwork. "And we're finished. Your makeup is perfect. Perfectly . . . perfect."

I let them put me in green lipstick with a glossy metallic finish, fill my eyebrows, and liberally dust bright yellow gold highlight on my cheeks. It's not the look I'd usually go for—I like my clothes colorful and my face bare—but the dress code tonight is school spirit. And since this is the last time I'll be in Hoffman green and yellow, it's only right I let them paint my face.

"Did Detroit ever tell you what he said to Khalil last week?" I ask.

"Yes, he was telling Khalil you've been in love with him for years," Mal deadpans, prompting me to kick him in the shin. "Oof, I don't know, Ayana. They probably weren't even talking about you. Detroit promised! He won't betray you."

Last month Malcolm decided to tell Detroit about our pact. Who better to help with my *objective* than Khalil's best friend?

Thing is, Detroit can't hold water, let alone a secret. If he got it in his head to play matchmaker . . .

"Besides," Jada adds. She stands a bare inch away from the mirror as she applies layer after layer of liquid eyeliner. "What's the point of kissing Khalil if you can't *talk* to him?"

Fair point, but worry still crawls around my stomach like a million-legged insect.

"Why don't we just . . . call it? The promise was silly. This whole thing is silly. I just want to have a good time with you two tonight."

"And you will. We'll make sure of it," Mal says, meeting my eyes through the mirror. "Don't back down now, Ayana. You promised. Besides you haven't kissed a boy since sophomore year."

"Oh so we're back to pretending last summer doesn't count?" I ask.

Last summer I tried beer for the first time and discovered it smoothed my awkward edges enough for me to successfully make out with four different guys in three months. Though the memory of their drunken pawing is enough to put me off drinking until college.

Jada arches her perfectly attenuated eyebrows. "Correction: you haven't kissed a boy you *liked* since sophomore year."

"Yes, and look how well that went." Leon Perry was my seatmate in pre-calc for half the school year. In lieu of doing actual work, we traded doodles and played games on our phones. Within weeks I was deep in the throes of infatuation. Jada and Mal took every opportunity to tell me that Leon's head was too long and his eyes far too close together, but I didn't care. The gap between his front teeth, his chocolate skin and dimples, were enough for me to overlook the fact that he barely looked in my direction outside of class. When I did finally kiss him at a party two suburbs over, he ghosted me all summer. Since then Mal and Jada have refused to speak his name.

Thing is though, as much as I liked Leon, that was a flame that burned hot and quick. The way I feel about Khalil is entirely different. My crush on him has been simmering in the back of my mind for years.

Mal scoots into the chair I'm occupying, nearly hip-checking me onto the floor. "Khalil isn't like Leon. Detroit wouldn't be friends with a fuckboy. And I can't believe we have to convince Ayana Gets-Shit-Done Parker to do something as simple as kiss one boy."

"You do want to kiss him, right?" Jada asks. "We're not peer pressuring you into something you don't want?"

"Oh, I definitely want to kiss him," I say, glancing at my phone again. I'll be late if I stay any longer, but I reach for their hands anyway. "Let's go over the plan then. One last time."

"One last time," Malcolm hums as he scrolls through his summer playlist in search of the song. When Ariana blares through the speaker, we fall against each other, whispering as if we're discussing something sacred.

11:02 p.m., Hoffman Football Stadium

The first time I see Khalil, there's a hotdog wedged between my teeth while Malcolm hoists me onto Detroit's back.

I can't quite manage it on my own, since Detroit's a good foot and a half taller than I am. Plus I'm afraid of flashing everyone. Mal shoves me again and I nearly tumble over Detroit's shoulders and onto the hard track around the football field.

"All good, Ay?" Detroit asks as he steadies me, hands loosely curled around my ankles. I scan the crowd for Jada and spot her immediately, because she's towing Khalil by the arm and talking a mile a minute. People part around them easily, because of Khalil's height and Jada's propensity to throw her shoulder into anyone in her path.

Twenty minutes ago, we decided we'd spent enough time at the buffet in the cafeteria. We moved with the tide of people outside to the football field, where stadium lights give the impression that it's midday despite the encroaching darkness.

Six teachers and Jaxon, megaphone in hand, are gathered at the fifty-yard line, preparing to explain the rules of the mini golf course set up on the field.

I hop down from Detroit's back and try to calm the butterflies dive-bombing around my stomach. "They're headed our way," I say, grinning.

By the time Jada and Khalil reach us, Jaxon has begun explaining that all of the students on the field will be split into teams of up to eight and each team will start at a different hole on the course. At least a hundred students mill around the field, and a couple dozen more sit in the bleachers, eating walking tacos and pizza from the concession stands. At the edge of the football field, neon signs painted by the senior cheerleaders point to the tennis courts, where carnival games are set up, and the field house turned board game hall.

"Whoever completes all eighteen holes first wins . . . something that the PTA won't tell me." He laughs awkwardly, pulling the megaphone away from his face when it crackles and whines. "And one last thing: if your team gets stuck at one hole for over ten minutes, the team behind you gets to pass you."

Jada pays Jaxon no mind as she stops in front of us, Khalil's arm in an iron grip. "Sorry guys, I got distracted and then you were gone, but look who I found! Ayana said we needed one more team member for mini golf."

Her eye twitches, and so far that's the only sign that this whole thing is a farce. Jada *got lost* on purpose and didn't find Khalil by any coincidence. This is phase one of the plan, the only part that doesn't require my involvement.

"Anyway," Jada tells Khalil. "We're doing the scavenger hunt together and walking to Brady's for breakfast at sunrise if you want to come." She lays it on so thick I'm afraid Khalil will think she's the one with a crush the size of the Milky Way galaxy.

But for some reason, Khalil's eyes slide to me. I manage a smile that feels entirely too wide—are my molars showing, what about my tonsils?—and blurt, "I promise, no blood this time!"

When Khalil's eyebrows draw together, perplexed, I point at the now mostly hidden scab on my chin and add, "You know, like last week."

Classic Ayana fumble.

"I remember, Ayana," Khalil says, smiling down at his sneakers. I decide to count it as a win.

Detroit, Jada, and Malcolm lead us to the fifty-yard line. And somehow I end up next to Khalil, who stares at a twenty-foot papier-mâché windmill in the end zone.

"You planned all this?" Khalil asks. He's the only one of us who didn't bother dressing up for tonight. The only sign of his school spirit is the camo bandana tying back his locs.

It takes me a second to pull his voice out from the sounds of people all around us.

Sensing my confusion, Khalil bends down, and repeats his question a mere six inches from my face. Cinnamon freckles march across the bridge of his nose and his eyelashes cast long shadows down his cheeks. He speaks with a calm that makes me wish he'd keep talking until the morning.

"Not exactly," I answer. "We asked all the clubs to sponsor a different game. The Theater Club and Engineering Club put this together." I shrug, hoping he can't see my cheeks redden in this artificial twilight. "The PTA takes care of a lot of it too. I just had to coordinate between them, the principal, and the different clubs."

Really it hadn't been all that much work compared to prom and homecoming. The PTA hosted Senior Game Night for the past ten years. They'd done a murder mystery theme, held movie marathons, and had even had an overnight swim party, which I was strongly cautioned against.

Khalil whistles. Our gazes meet and hold. "That's still impressive."

"Thanks," I say and when I smile, he returns it.

We fall into silence, listening instead to Jada, Mal, and Detroit bicker over who's going first in the rotation. Our first hole, complete with a mini-castle and about five dozen tiny evergreen trees arranged in imitation of an enchanted forest, is no simple task.

Mal and Jada are sure they're the best at mini golf, so they go first. I'm in the middle. And Detroit and Khalil are the tail. When Mal completes the first hole in three shots, Detroit swears he'll beat him by taking only two.

Turns out, Detroit and Khalil are both terrible. They overshoot every time. We have to chase down the colorful golf balls that go flying across the field. One particularly horrible shot from Khalil lands in the miniature pond on the fourth hole, which is actually a large kiddie pool. I valiantly rescue the ball by wading in. The water, thankfully, only comes up to my ankles. When I return the ball to Khalil, he bows and says, "My hero. Is it against the rules if you take my next three turns?"

Yes, a small voice in my head whispers.

Maybe it's because he's grinning at me, but right now only a small part of me still cares about the rules. He holds out his club like a sword, but I don't take it. "What if I help you instead?" I offer.

Khalil's grin widens. "By all means."

I catch a glimpse of Mal, Detroit, and Jada smiling, tongues practically hanging out of their mouths. This is very much not a part of the plan—I'm meant to break the physical-touch barrier in phase three—so I try not to think about what happened last time I went off script.

First I position Khalil's hands on the club, one on top of the other, and then I crouch down to pull his legs until he's standing with them shoulder width apart. He's in the same bright Air Maxes as the other day and he smells like chocolate chip cookies and boy sweat—not a bad combination.

My palms are damp by the time I stand up. As soon as I

prompt Khalil to give it a try, Jada asks, "What about his swing, Ayana? That's the main problem."

Her smile is pure innocence.

Rolling my eyes, I walk behind Khalil and mime reaching around his back for the golf club. It's no good; Khalil's arms are so much longer than mine. With an exasperated sigh, Jada stalks forward, snatches the club out of Khalil's hands, and yanks me in front of him. "Try like this. Just this once."

"Just so you know, I'm plotting your murder!" I whisper as she backs away.

Jada returns to Malcolm and Detroit, who are both vibrating with barely suppressed laughter.

"This okay?"

"Sure," I say.

It isn't though. It is much, much better than okay. I have to remind myself to breathe when Khalil's arms come around me to grasp the handle. His hands completely cover mine. I'm certain I'm either going to burst into flames or melt into a puddle.

His body is taut and warm, but he gives me plenty of space to breathe. And wonder what would happen if I closed the distance between us.

I let out a breath through clenched teeth. *Focus, Parker.*

I swing, just a soft putt that sends the pink ball slowly rolling uphill, then down right into the castle's mouth. "See, it's as simple as that."

"Whoa," Khalil breathes, still close enough that I shiver. When I look over my shoulder at him, I can't decide if it's my imagination or if there really is a flush to his cheeks.

The moment between us is cut short when Detroit crows, "What! Hole in one!"

Even though we're still basically dead last, Detroit and Khalil lift me onto their shoulders while Jada and Mal cheer, "Parker, Parker!"

Our high is short lived though and two more teams pass us at the next hole. When Detroit fires another ball clean across the field, sending people scattering like pigeons, we decide to bail.

It's nearly one in the morning, but I feel wide awake, electric. Jada and I walk arm in arm down the path back to Hoffman's main campus. It's lined with twinkling lights. The moon hides behind the clouds and willows cast hulking shadows that bend and twist in the breeze. If I hadn't walked this path a thousand times, it might have been spooky. Instead it's almost cozy in the dark.

Khalil, Detroit, and Mal walk a few feet ahead of us, their heads bent together, whispering. Shameless gossips, those boys. Khalil looks back at us over his shoulder, and I reflexively look away.

Jada pinches my side and whispers, "Go talk to him!"

I pinch her back. "Phase three doesn't begin until we start the scavenger hunt, remember?"

"We're already far from the plan, Ayana. What could it hurt?" She waggles her fingers at his back. "It's not difficult for me to translate awkward staring, because I've been watching you since we were twelve. He likes you, or at least thinks you're cute. Just go talk to him."

Earlier we lapsed into silence almost as soon as our conversation began. I honestly liked that Khalil didn't feel any need to fill the quiet. "And what exactly am I supposed to talk to him about?"

Jada takes on a contemplative expression, her black eyes dancing with laughter. "Hmm, maybe start with how you want to shove your tongue down his throat?"

I reach for my backpack, with plans to take out my clipboard and beat her over the head with it, but it isn't there. Because I'm off-duty tonight.

With a groan, Jada tugs me forward until we catch up with the boys. Detroit and Malcolm are making eyes at each other, while Khalil watches with a small smile on his face.

They're talking about next year and the end of an era, one I will welcome with open arms. As soon as August hits, I'll be on a plane headed far west of the Midwest and will only return for holidays and weddings thereafter.

I can't wait to start over. And I feel guilty for thinking that, when my friends are terrified of college and leaving everyone behind. But at college I can reinvent myself, finally hang up my event-planning hat, and be known for more than just a clipboard and can-do attitude. A year from now, I hope to be unrecognizable—California carefree, instead of Midwestern girl with big plans—and bold enough to kiss the boy I like without a multistep plan in place.

Jada pinches me, drawing my attention ahead of us. We're coming around the bend in the path that leads back to Hoffman's main campus. About three dozen seniors crowd around the doors beneath an arch of green and gold balloons, taking pictures.

I check my phone; it's five minutes to one, meaning we've got five minutes to make it to the auditorium or phase three of the plan will be ruined before it can begin.

Detroit and Khalil lead the way, cutting through the clumps of people who apparently like the boys enough to let our group pass by them. We make it inside and even though I've walked these halls a thousand times, the twinkling lights in the windows and hundreds of pictures hanging from the ceiling on gold streamers make it an entirely new place. Which was an accomplishment considering Mal, Jada, and I had walked through this hallway arm in arm thousands of times by now. It was hard to believe that was all over now. A small part of me hoped that if I couldn't fulfill my promise, time would just reset and give us another four years.

We make it to the gym just in time for the scavenger hunt, and someone passes me our list. Everyone cringes at the sharp crackle from a microphone and turns their attention to the stage where Jaxon, bless him, is grinning ear to ear. He's always reminded me of a golden retriever, with his bleached curls, tawny skin, and spaced-out expression. I'm forever indebted to him for agreeing to host tonight. My gratitude only deepens when Khalil slings an arm over my shoulders to closer inspect the items on the list.

Jaxon yanks the mic away from his mouth, waiting for the feedback to quiet, before explaining the rules: get as many items on the list as you can and don't steal another group's items.

He forgets to add that we're not allowed to go into any classrooms and that there will be a prize, but I'm too busy worrying about phase three to consider correcting him.

Phase three in which our team splits up. Phase three in which I kiss Khalil.

I'm pretty sure Khalil notices my building panic, because he drops his arm and straightens. He doesn't step away, which is what I'm expecting, dreading, and longing for so I can breathe around the joy that's going off like fireworks in my chest.

"You all right, Ayana?" Khalil asks, tucking a few escaped locs behind his ears.

Get it together, Parker.

"Yeah—sure—I—we should split up!" Words bubble up and out of my mouth like a shaken bottle of Coke, which is exactly how my stomach feels right now. I swallow, my tongue gone dry as a cat's, and try again, "We'll be able to check more off the list if we split it in half. Divide and conquer, you know?"

Jada and Mal, their heads bent together, are whispering, but they seem pleased.

Detroit and Khalil stare at each other, holding a silent conversation. They've been close forever. Their friendship has a secret language, just like the one I share with Jada and Mal.

Before I can give any input as to which of us should pair up, Khalil plucks the list from my hands, folds it down the middle and rips the paper in two. He hands one to Detroit and tucks the other half into his back pocket.

Detroit extends his hands to Jada and Malcolm. "Come on, dream team. Meet you back here in two hours?"

I'm saved from answering by Khalil, who puts both hands on my shoulders and steers us toward the exit.

"So what should we start with first?" Khalil asks once we're outside the gym.

"Uh," I manage. The sound is long and drawn out because my brain is a stalled engine. My heart offers no help, my pulse beating hard against my skin. *Shit.*

Khalil pulls out the list, scans it once, and hands it to me. Immediately I know where we can find four items. We're only supposed to search the halls or outdoors, and if classrooms are off limits, surely this place will be too. Staring at the cupid's bow of his lips, I decide now is the perfect time to break the rules.

Summoning all the boldness the Ayana one year from now will surely possess, I smile. "I know exactly where to go."

Breaking into the front office takes my mind off kissing Khalil.

I dig through the rocks and not-soil in the huge, fake ficus tree next to the office doors. The hall is dark, lit only by string lights above, and the office looks abandoned. Finally my hand closes around a small, cool metal key.

I hold up the key and grin at Khalil who keeps looking both ways down the hallway, like we're going to be caught any minute, which may very well be true. But I'm pretty confident in my ability to talk us out of any trouble.

"You're full of secrets," he murmurs, impressed.

I shrug. "No secrets. I've been spending my free periods in this office since freshman year. The secretaries trust me."

I'd seen our principal's assistant looking for the spare office key on more than a few occasions. Mr. Huerta would never expect me to attempt a break-in, and before this moment, I wouldn't have either.

We slip inside and when the door clicks shut behind us, it's dead silent but for the sound of our breathing. Khalil gropes the wall for the light switch, but I shake my head—that one turns on every fluorescent bulb within a fifty-foot radius. I pull him deeper inside, past a few deserted cubicles, and into Dr. Fleishman's office.

Lit only by the moonlight filtering through the window, everything looks blue and silver.

Khalil breaks the silence. "I hope you're not trying to get me expelled, Parker."

"Don't worry. I'll keep us out of trouble," I say, walking farther into the office. In the back, there's an unmarked door.

I gesture for Khalil to open it. When he does, a low whistle escapes his mouth. "Jackpot."

The closet attached to Dr. Fleishman's office is large enough to store all his furniture, Tetris style, but even so it's difficult for both of us to step inside. Its floor-to-ceiling shelves are crammed with dusty Hoffman memorabilia: a box of green foam fingers with the Hoffman Eagle emblazoned in gold; little plush footballs the cheerleaders give out at games; the headpiece for a vintage Eagle mascot; and so, so much more.

We check six items off the list and liberate a few more priceless finds from this dust-ridden prison of a closet. I check my watch again, amazed that it's already half past two a.m. According to my plan, we should be locking lips right about now.

Almost like he heard my thought, Khalil sits down and pats the floor beside him. I take a deep breath and join him. "We should get going soon," I say, since self-sabotage seems to be one of my strengths.

Through the closet door, a sliver of moonlight illuminates half of Khalil's face, lining his lips in silver. "You sure? I doubt Detroit, Jada, and Malcolm have found anything yet."

I shake my head. "No, you're right, I just thought . . ."

My voice trails off. I'm not sure how to explain my instinct to flee during uncomfortable situations. But then again, that was why we came up with a plan. So I could rely on clear directives instead of slowly descending into a panic spiral. But we'd kept this part vague, Jada and Mal promising me that I would know when it was the right moment for The Kiss.

"Detroit told you, didn't he?" Khalil asks, voice as soft as a whisper. "I swear he can't keep a secret to save his life."

"Huh?"

Khalil doesn't seem to hear me as he goes on. "I made him swear on his shoe collection, swear he wouldn't even tell Malcolm, but I should've known he wouldn't be able to help himself. Detroit *loves* playing matchmaker."

This can't be serious. "Matchmaker?" I squeak, and it's this that finally stops him.

Khalil's eyebrows knit together. "Oh. Uh. So he didn't tell you?"

"Tell me *what*?" I ask.

My entire body goes warm as Khalil's gaze settles on mine. "I told him last week I've had a thing for you since him and Malcolm hooked up. You just always seemed so busy, so I never said anything."

My pulse thunders in my ears as I lean forward. Jada and Mal were right. I would know the moment, and the moment is—

But then the lights turn on, the fluorescents painfully bright, and I jerk backwards into the overstuffed shelves. A box full of mini-footballs falls, pelting us. Half go bouncing into Dr. Fleishman's now well-lit office.

"Crapcrapcrap," I mutter, jumping to my feet. More boxes fall as Khalil stands up and part of me wants them all to collapse on top of me and bury me beneath a mountain of school spirit. My thoughts are a scattered mess. Khalil has a thing *for me*? Did I really hear him right?

Likely drawn by the sound of the boxes falling, the door to the principal's office swings open. I nearly collapse when, instead of Dr. Fleishman, Mr. Huerta walks in drinking a Big Gulp and swinging a massive key ring around his wrist.

"Ms. Parker?" he says, slowly taking in the scene. "Mr. . . . Moore? Well now, this is unexpected."

"This is not what it looks like!" I say. "We were just looking for stuff for the scavenger hunt, Mr. Huerta, I swear."

He shrugs. "Uh-huh, well it looks like trespassing, young lady. You'd better go hunting elsewhere."

When Khalil retrieves our box of treasures, Mr. Huerta gives him a sharp look. "I think not, Mr. Moore. Now you two get out of here before someone else sees you. If an administrator catches you two, I won't be making any excuses."

We give sheepish apologies and practically sprint from the office. We don't stop running until we're back to the auditorium. Khalil's hand is in mine and I can't remember who grabbed onto whom, but neither of us lets go at first.

His hand only slips away when our eyes meet and we dissolve into near hysterical laughter. Khalil gives a flawless impersonation of Mr. Huerta's expression when we stepped out of the closet. Wiping tears from my eyes, I check my phone. "At least we still have an hour left to search."

"What's next, boss?" Khalil asks.

I pat my back pockets and groan, "Crap. I left the list back in the office."

"I'm guessing he won't let us back inside to find it?"

"Oh, definitely not. I guess we just have to hope Detroit, Mal, and Jada have better luck than we do."

He shrugs. "I say we're pretty lucky. We're not booted from graduation Sunday and I learned you're fearless."

I start to protest—unlike most humans, who are seventy-five percent water, I'm seventy-five percent fear—but Khalil reaches for my hand again. It's like an electric shock goes through me as I suddenly remember what he said before we were interrupted. When I blink, I can still see his face etched in darkness and moonlight, and a half-second later, his disappointment as all the lights flashed on.

I was so close, but I can barely spare a thought for the missed opportunity when Khalil's fingers lace through mine. When he suggests we go to the cafeteria instead of waiting for our friends to return, I manage a nod.

I try to smother the giddy butterflies careening around my stomach, but it's no use. Khalil seems completely oblivious to the furtive looks from the other seniors and only lets go of my hand while we load up bags of Fritos with taco fixings.

We finally sit down at one of the long cafeteria tables and Khalil immediately digs into his walking taco. Now that I'm not touching him, my thoughts return to coherence. No way is he getting away with dropping that bomb earlier without any explanation.

I may as well keep pretending to be fearless since it's working well so far. "So what you said back in Fleishman's office?"

Khalil pauses mid-chew, eyes widening. He takes a swig of Coke and smirks, dimples flashing, "Yeah?"

Before I can reply, I recognize a peal of laughter that can only belong to Jada and look up to find them ten feet away from our table. Detroit has a mesh bag slung over his shoulder, full of random things. There's a broken trophy, two volleyballs, a rolled-up poster, and a math textbook with the cover torn off.

"These," Detroit announces, "are the items we found."

"And not a single one of them," Jada finishes, "is actually on our list."

"What can I say?" Detroit shrugs. "It's hard to stay on task without you, Ayana."

They look near to falling asleep, but as Mal and Detroit begin to explain their random assortment, I realize we all probably look the same. But the buzz of this final night at Hoffman with friends that will be hundreds of miles apart in August is keeping us wide awake. When Jada asks about our lack of scavenged items, Khalil and I tell them about Dr. Fleishman's office, leaving out the near kiss. Unfortunately neither Jada nor Mal seem to pick up on my brain waves telling them to give us more time alone.

It's a bit past four a.m. and the darkness through the cafeteria windows is only just beginning to soften. Clumps of seniors, eyes red with the lack of sleep but bright with excitement, trail in with their findings.

We find our sleeping bags amid the mountain in the cafeteria. And instead of bedding down inside them, Malcolm and Detroit make a fort using two of the cafeteria tables. We crawl beneath the blanket canopy and everyone but me falls asleep, or so I think until Khalil's eyes pop open as I'm in the midst of studying his face.

I emit a squeak and jump, banging my head against the table.

Jada's between us, snoring faintly. Khalil crawls around her with surprising adroitness for someone so lanky, but the space is so cramped that my legs end up on top of his.

"Not exactly ideal," I whisper, laughing even though my palms have begun to sweat.

"I wouldn't say that. Are you all good? I think my heart's still trying to beat its way out of my chest. I swore Dr. Fleishman was going to storm in and kick us both out of graduation." Despite the darkness, this close I could trace the pattern of his freckles if I dared.

But I don't. "Same. I'm not very good at relaxing under normal circumstances."

"And these aren't normal?" His smile is not as easy as Jaxon's, as sly as Mal's, or as broad as Detroit's. It's softer, makes his eyes crinkle, and is radiant like the faint predawn light.

He makes me feel like a jangly bag of nerves, but maybe that isn't the worst thing. "*No, I'm basically sitting in your lap.*"

He wipes a hand across his face. "After I confessed my longtime crush. You can cringe, I won't be embarrassed."

"I didn't get a chance to tell you earlier, but I've liked *you* since freshman year," I whisper. "We can cringe together."

Oops. I decide it's the sleep deprivation loosening my tongue, and not his breath, warm against my neck. Or his hand balanced lightly on my knee.

"Word? Freshman year? My hair was terrible back then." He laughs so loudly, I'm afraid it'll wake Jada.

"It was," I agree. "And you were still fine. So unfair."

The smile on his face makes me feel warm down to my toes. He leans forward and closes the small amount of space left between us. His warm lips press right against mine and his hand curls around the back of my neck, drawing me in. His lips are insistent and soft and taste like strawberry Carmex.

A cleared throat sends us both careening apart. I land on top of Jada who wakes with a snore turned snarl. As soon as I can extricate myself from her flailing limbs and squeeze between her and Khalil, I look up and see Detroit and Malcolm.

"Right before our eyes, can you believe it, Mal?" Detroit grins and pantomimes applause.

They dissolve into laughter. Maybe I am fearless because I flip them off with one hand and grab Khalil's neck with the other before kissing him again.

"We did it. We really did," Mal says, practically swooning.

"We should really open a matchmaking service," Detroit agrees, eyes shining with genuine glee.

"You two didn't do anything!" I groan, but I can't hold back my grin either.

"Gonna have to agree with Ayana," Khalil says. "This was all us two."

I'm afraid for a split second that they'll tell him about the plan, but Jada rolls over and bares her teeth. "Will y'all hush? Some of us are trying to sleep!"

But we can already see that the sun is up and hear the scrape of tables and chairs that means it's time to leave.

I climb out of the fort and check my phone for the time. It's 6:05. I need to thank Jaxon about a dozen times and hand out thank-you gifts to the PTA and make sure everything gets cleaned up, but that can all wait until later.

For now, we set off for breakfast at Brady's.

Detroit, Malcolm, and Jada walk hand in hand in front of us. Khalil and I are just a few steps behind, trading smiles.

CREATURE CAPTURE

by Laura Silverman

11:50 P.M.

"Ow!" Curtis yelps.

I spin around, eyes searching for injury, but all five-foot-ten of him and his muscled thighs and his gangly arms and his *I Am Groot* T-shirt look entirely unscathed. "You okay?" I ask.

"Abby, a fly bit me!" he moans.

"You giant baby. C'mon."

"Fine."

We make our way through the shadowy woods, my heavy-duty flashlight illuminating the trail. The hunt is about to begin. Creature Capture said the Loch Ness would be released tonight, for the second time ever, between midnight and sunrise, available at different lakes all over the world. My index is packed with fairies and ogres and so many unicorns I now hate those common as heck one-horned ponies, but there's only one question mark, residing on index box 473, the last creature missing from my collection.

"I'm going to sell mine." Curtis takes a giant step forward so we're side by side. "How much you think I can get for it?"

I shrug. "A hundred? Depends how many are captured tonight."

Selling creatures is *technically* illegal. But, of course, that doesn't stop anyone. The game has a massive black market, people trading digital creatures and items for cold hard cash, or you know, bitcoin.

For me, Creature Capture is about the hunt. Paying for a creature ruins the experience. Also, I don't have that kind of money to waste. Which is why I don't judge Curtis for selling. He doesn't have that kind of money to waste either, so if he can get twenty bucks for selling a white griffin he caught at the top of Kennesaw Mountain last summer, then go Curtis.

But I'd never sell a creature, especially not a Loch Ness.

My pulse races as I hold my flashlight steady with one hand and scroll through my item inventory with the other. I've been hoarding items ever since the Loch Ness event was announced last month. You can earn items from leveling up, catching special creatures, and discovering hidden caches. I have a virtual backpack full of nets, fruits, and even two lures. Will it be enough? Anxiety knots my stomach. It wasn't last time. A year ago, I spent every single item trying to capture a Loch Ness from Lake Carlisle and still went home empty-netted. But I was younger then, both in age and player level.

"What now?" Curtis asks, as we make it out of the woods and to the lake.

Crickets chirp around us. The air is warm and sticky, summer humidity pressing in, even with the sun long since tucked away. Expensive houses surround the lake. Their security lights cut swaths of brightness through dark backyards and shine across the water. The lake is a public area, yet it feels like we could be arrested for trespassing.

"Um, hold on," I say.

I check the Creature Capture app, eyes scanning the screen. My heart jumps at the mere thought of a Loch Ness appearing. But no luck yet. A lone werewolf prowls the perimeter of the woods. A single water sprite buzzes above the lake's opaque surface. "No Loch Ness," I say. "Not sure if I should activate a lure. I only have two, and there are five lakes to hit tonight . . ."

A lure draws out creatures otherwise hidden. The app will use its random algorithm to populate certain lakes with Loch Ness monsters tonight. A Loch Ness could appear without the help of a lure, activated simply by our GPS presence in their zone, but some will only show themselves with that extra magical boost.

"Wait—I have a lure!" Curtis pulls out his phone. Of course he has a lure and didn't tell me. He doesn't care about Creature Capture like I do. "Yep! Got it when that dragon flew away last month."

Dragons are notoriously difficult to catch, but often they'll escape and leave behind guarded treasure, like lures and berries. Sometimes I'll throw a weak net on purpose hoping the dragon gets away but leaves good items behind.

"Okay," Curtis says. "And go." Blue dust swirls on my screen the second he taps the lure. I stare, pulse thudding in my ears, waiting for a Loch Ness to emerge. Nothing. But the lure lasts ten minutes, so we need to wait.

We sit on a crooked wooden bench. One side has sunk half a foot into the mud, the other only a couple of inches. Curtis and I slide into each other. He smells a little sweaty and a little citrusy, his body wash from this morning almost faded into nothing, but it's a familiar scent, comforting.

Curtis and I have been best friends since fifth grade when our teacher assigned us to the same math group. Spoiler alert number one: it wasn't the advanced group. We spent the session writing an alien story together instead of doing our worksheets. We then went on to spend almost all of middle school together: sci-fi movie marathons, board game marathons, reading marathons—there were a lot of marathons. Everyone assumed we'd end up dating. Spoiler alert number two: it is possible for a guy and a girl to be just friends. And Curtis does like girls. And I do like guys. And I also like girls. But it's just not like that between us. It'd be like dating my brother, which would be both disgusting and illegal.

But things changed in high school. Curtis joined the soccer team freshman year, and then he made varsity sophomore year. And suddenly he wasn't just my Curtis—he belonged to so many people, people who call him Feldman (his last name) or Seventy-five (his jersey number), people who high-five him in the hallway and invite him to parties with alcohol and parents who say *I'd rather you break the law under my roof.*

Curtis doesn't ignore me now. My life isn't some stereotypical teen movie where one friend gets cooler than another and then drops the loser like a common green fairy. Curtis isn't like that. It's just, I can feel the space, the gap widening between us.

And it's not only Curtis.

I used to have other friends, lots of them, in middle school, but then high school happened. My old friends entered freshman year with new clothes (grown-up clothes, tight clothes) and new hobbies (Instagram, followed by making out, followed by drinking) and new topics of conversation (who is dating who and do we approve). Which makes them sound shallow and me sound like a judgmental jerk. They're not. And I'm not. My old friends still study and get good grades and read books and are good people—but they added these adult things to their lives— adult things I don't understand.

I don't judge them. I just don't get them.

And I wish I could. I wish I could be like everyone else. I wish I wasn't the only one left who'd rather spend the weekend marathoning *X-Files* or working on a craft project instead of *just chilling*.

Then Creature Capture launched. Junior year. Everyone was playing it. Like, the entire world. You'd see people running toward the same fountain in a park, cheering and yelling, people sharing their screens in the hallway, showing off the weekend's haul. One teacher even got caught playing *during class* when he screamed, "OH MY GOD A PEGASUS!"

For the first time since middle school, I belonged. Creature Capture had us all coexisting in the same world again. Emma Fairfield even traded creatures with me in history class when she asked if anyone had a fire fairy, and I had three sitting in my inventory.

But then a month passed. And people got bored. And another month passed. And everyone got bored. And then I was the only one at school left playing, well, except for Curtis when I dragged him along. Creature Capture is no longer cool. So now I hide my screen from not-prying eyes and pretend to text when I'm really throwing nets to catch gnomes and particularly pesky leprechauns—those guys take ages to catch but usually come with a gold pot of fruit.

And I'm glad Curtis had a lure to use tonight but upset he didn't mention it earlier. He has a life outside of this game, so of course he wouldn't think to mention his lure when I've been cultivating my inventory for weeks. Embarrassment crawls across my skin. If I can just catch a Loch Ness tonight, I'll have a complete index. And then maybe I can be done with Creature Capture forever. Next year we'll be off to college, and I can move on to normal teenage stuff. Next year I can be like everyone else.

Suddenly, a screech blasts out from our phones, the iconic sound of a creature appearance. My heart jumps in my throat, and I scramble to get a firm grip so I can—

And it's another freaking werewolf. Of course it is.

"Must have lured it out from the woods," Curtis says. "Those guys breed like werebunnies. I have like thirty of them in my index."

I sigh as I watch the werewolf sniff around my screen. Werewolves are one of the most common creatures, not worth the cost of a single net to catch them.

Curtis gives me a sympathetic smile. "Nessy could still come, right?"

"Yeah," I say, but my mood dips even lower than before. Suddenly I'm convinced this whole hunt will be a failure. I won't catch a Loch Ness. I won't complete my index. And I'll have wasted Curtis's entire night on this loser game. I just want to be done with this. It's so embarrassing—

A noise breaks the silence. But it's not from our phones. It's footsteps, quick ones, crashing through the woods, and mingled voices. "Hurry up!" one voice says.

"I'm wearing flip-flops!" another replies.

My stomach clenches as two people emerge from the woods, barreling toward us at a full-fledged run. Curtis yelps, scared— because of course—but then he stands up and narrows his eyes. "Is that you Twenty-two?"

"Seventy-five!" Emily shouts. Emily Clifton, star soccer player, classmate who hasn't said more than five words to me since middle school. She tightens her ponytail as she asks, "Y'all set the lure, huh?"

"Sure did," Curtis replies.

Wait.

Wait.

What?

Emily Clifton plays Creature Capture?

No, that can't be right. It doesn't make sense.

"Cool! This is my sister, Gracie," Emily says. "She loves this game, got the parental permission to hunt after midnight and everything. Any luck yet?"

Ah, there it is. Emily doesn't play, not really. Her little sister is dragging her around like I'm dragging around Curtis because Creature Capture is a game for cute little kids and nerds.

Real nerds. Not Marvel-movies-and-marathon-the-new-season-of–*Stranger Things* nerds. Embarrassment clings to my cheeks. Gracie looks at least a few years younger than us. Her hair is braided into two buns, in a Princess Leia way I could never pull off. Even this middle schooler is cooler than me. Of course she is.

"No luck yet," Curtis says. "Think the lure has a minute left though."

All four of us turn to our screens, watching as the final seconds tick down. Unease tightens my muscles. I wanted to have fun tonight, catch a Loch Ness with my best friend. But now I feel like I can't let my enthusiasm for the game show.

"And . . . time!" Gracie bounces on her feet. "Where to next?"

"Abby mapped out a route. Y'all can join us!" Curtis offers.

Mapped out a route. I want to kill him, but I really don't see myself adjusting well to prison life.

"Cool, thanks," Emily replies. "I have a few lures if you guys need more."

At that, my eyes flick up and meet hers. I have two lures, so if she has a *few*, that will cover all four lakes, greatly increasing our chances of catching a Loch Ness. I bet they've been collecting dust in her inventory for years. "Oh." My voice feels stuck in my throat. "Cool."

Emily grins, then tilts her head. "Abby, right? I think we have calc together."

"Um, history. I think."

I know it's history.

As we all walk back through the woods together, I tell myself it's okay. I shouldn't care what anyone thinks of me playing this game, especially not someone who can't remember what class we share. I have a better chance of catching a Loch Ness now. This is a good thing. An objectively good thing.

My hand tightens around my flashlight.

Objectivity is bullshit.

1:24 a.m.

"I like the music," Emily says as we pull into the parking lot of the second lake. It's tiny, more pond than lake, and only a dozen feet from the parking lot. The entire zone can be activated from one spot, so we can hunt from the car. It took us thirty minutes to get here, thirty minutes of Emily, Curtis, and Gracie chatting and me silent, charging my fully charged phone.

"It's Abby's Spotify mix," Curtis replies. "She's a wizard with playlists."

I stare intently at my phone, cheeks burning red. I love putting together playlists. It's awesome—like assigning a soundtrack to my life—but it's nerve-racking to have people other than Curtis listen. I rack my brain and try to remember if there are any embarrassing tracks on *We're Here Tonight, Part II.*

"Very cool," Emily replies.

"Thanks," I say so softly she definitely doesn't hear me.

"Y'all see anything?" Gracie asks, eyes on her screen.

"I'll drop a lure," Emily offers.

Should I volunteer to drop one instead? Am I greedy for hoarding mine? I'll use them when I need to, but Emily and Gracie might decide to ditch this hunting party early, and then

I'll only have one left. Before I can reply, Emily taps her screen, and the blue dust swirls on mine.

And then, a cacophony of screeching invades the car.

"Whoa!" Emily says.

"A horde!" Gracie screams with glee.

Every now and then a lure activates an entire horde of creatures. Pixies and griffins cloud the sky. Mermaids and kelpies consume the lake. My pulse ricochets as I rotate the screen, eyes hunting in *Where's Waldo* desperation for a Loch Ness somewhere in the melee. The sounds amplify as people capture creatures. I don't want to waste any nets on commons, but I need to clear my screen to see if a Loch Ness is here. Crap. What do I do? My palms sweat.

Crap, crap, crap.

I could ask if anyone else sees a Loch Ness. But does that sound too desperate? If I weren't so into this game, I'd be tossing nets left and right like a casual player, like Curtis. Desire for a Loch Ness versus desire to not seem like a freak battle against each other. Eventually, I muster up the courage to ask, "Um, anyone see a Loch Ness?"

But no one hears me in the melee.

"FUCK YOU, KELPIE!" Curtis screams, then looks up with a sheepish grin. "Sorry, dude is pissing me off."

"Throw a net from left corner for better odds to catch a kelpie," Gracie says.

"Wait. Really?" I ask and crane back to glance at her. I had no idea, and I've spent an unspeakable amount of time creeping on the Creature Capture Reddit.

"Yep!" Gracie smiles. "Works every time."

"Hey, that did work," Curtis says. "Thanks! No Loch Ness, though."

My shoulders slump.

"What if it's all a prank?" Emily asks. "Like, the app won't actually release a Loch Ness ever again. They just want to see how many people they can get out here playing all night long."

"They wouldn't do that," I say, voice firm.

I'm sure they wouldn't. If Creature Capture says there will be Loch Ness monsters, then there will be. The thing I love most about this game is that I can depend on it. There are rules. Creature Capture's random appearance algorithm is still that—an algorithm. Real life has too many variables, too many unknowns, too many actions that make no sense.

Curtis leans back and glances at Gracie. "Sorry for the cursing, by the way."

She rolls her eyes. "I'm *thirteen*."

Emily laughs. I do too.

A few minutes later, the lure finishes, and no Loch Ness appears. I check the time and see we're already nearing two in the morning. Anxiety knots my stomach as I manage to say, "So maybe onto the next lake?"

"My thoughts exactly," Emily agrees.

2:05 a.m.

I will not say something like an impatient loser. I will not say something like an impatient loser. I will not—

I basically have to bite my tongue as we pull into the gas station parking lot. Curtis wants a Mountain Dew and Gracie has to pee. I refrain from telling Curtis we packed snacks and drinks so we wouldn't have to stop at a gas station because I *really* can't tell Gracie to hold her biological urge to urinate. Because that would be ridiculous.

But . . . I *do* want to tell her that.

We only have four hours until sunrise, and we're wasting precious minutes. My fingers clutch my phone tightly as we lock up the car and walk into the fluorescent-lit gas station. Curtis grabs his Mountain Dew and makes small talk with the cashier—within seconds, they're both laughing. My fingers twist together. Who even is Curtis? How does he make friends with a gas station attendant in the middle of the night when I can barely string a sentence together in front of my classmates?

I decide to use the restroom, because might as well, and awkwardly stand in silence while Gracie, and then Emily, finish up. As Emily walks out, she says, "Heads up, it's next-level gross in there."

"I'd expect nothing less from a gas station bathroom at two in the morning," I reply.

Emily laughs. Her green eyes light up as she again tightens her ponytail. I'm thinking she needs to buy stronger holders. "You want me to grab you anything? I know we're both itching to get back on the road."

My brain freezes because I said something funny, and she laughed, and then she offered to grab me something, which is really nice, even if she asks me to pay her back later, and then she said *we're both* itching to get back on the road. She's itching to get back on the road. Emily Clifton, star soccer player, must be itching to find this Loch Ness just like I am. It's almost impossible to believe.

"You like doughnuts?" she asks. My brain must have frozen for too long. "I'm going to get a doughnut. Those glazed ones are hollering my name, and I won't deny them."

"Yeah." I clear my throat. "Thanks."

"Sure thing!"

The bathroom is indeed next-level gross, but you know, it's okay.

3:28 a.m.

My stomach hurts—both because lake number three is a total bust and because of the two doughnuts, cheese puffs, and Mountain Dew I scarfed and guzzled down respectively. There are two lakes left, and we're inching quickly toward sunrise. If I do find a Loch Ness, I could keep playing Creature Capture after, find the same creatures I already have, just with stronger powers, and wait for the app to release a new generation of mythicals. But I hope the Loch Ness will be enough for me, will allow me to move on and do normal teenage things like *just chilling.*

We zip down the highway. Curtis's hands stay at the proper ten and two. He always drives like he's taking the test for his license, adjusting side-view mirrors a millimeter before starting the engine, waiting a full one, two, three Mississippi at stop signs. I might be the shy one, but he's always been the careful one. When we went to the water park in sixth grade, he insisted on talking to the lifeguard about all the *Mega Burst Tycoon!* safety measures and watching five other kids slide down before we could get on. I still have a picture of us from that day, dripping wet, mustard from our corn dogs smeared at the corners of our mouths, smiles so wide they made our cheeks hurt.

I know we're not little kids anymore. But I miss that. Pure happiness. No self-consciousness. The thought of having that again is euphoric.

But we won't have it again. Next year, Curtis will be off hours away at college with his soccer scholarship, and I'll be here, at a local college, because I was too scared to apply anywhere else.

As we pull into the lot for Lake Wendy, another car pulls out. Gracie rolls down her window and waves for them to stop, but they zip off into the night. Did they just catch a Loch Ness? Is this, finally, the right spot?

As we get out of the car, Emily and Curtis elbow each other, laughing over some inside joke. In elementary school, we always had to hand out Valentine's Day cards to the entire class so no kid got left out. But real life isn't like that at all. No one in the real world is forcing others to *share with the rest of the class.*

"Look at my new avatar!" Gracie says. She skips ahead and tugs Emily's hand.

Curtis falls back to me, almost like an afterthought. "Hey." He shoots me a grin. "How's it going?" My jaw aches I'm clenching it so tight. I don't know how to explain what I'm feeling, and I'm scared if I attempt it, I might start crying. Curtis persists. "Abigail Kleinman, what's going on?"

I roll my eyes. "My name is *not* Abigail."

"Oh, but it is," Curtis replies. "I've seen the birth certificate."

"Traitorous parents."

"Aw, I love Beth and Aaron." We trudge through the woods. It's a clear-cut, mile-long path to the lake. The trees are growing back their coats after a long winter. Leaves rustle without enthusiasm in the tepid wind. Our flashlights cut through the shadows and guide the way. "Seriously." Curtis glances at me again. "What's up?"

I look down at my screen. Elves and unicorns and even a lone centaur roam the woods. I focus on the centaur. They usually travel in packs, but not this one. I wonder why. If something is wrong with him. My finger hovers over the screen, tempted to catch him, see if there's something different with him, see if there's a reason *why*.

"Abby," Curtis prods.

Emily and Gracie have taken the lead now, far enough ahead to not overhear our conversation. "It's nothing," I say. "It's just—" I put my phone down and glance at Curtis. "I don't know what I'm going to do without you next year." As predicted, my throat tightens, and my eyes threaten to water.

Curtis's gaze softens. He knocks into my shoulder. "I don't know what I'll do without you either. You're my best friend, Abby."

"I know. But it's different." I swallow hard and return my eyes to the woods in front of us, the real ones, focusing on twigs and leaves as I walk. "You're going to college on a soccer scholarship. You'll make friends with a bunch of people on the team, just like you make friends in school. You'll fit in and have a great time. And I'll still be here, the same Abby. But without Curtis."

Without anyone.

There's a long stretch of silence. Too long. Twigs crunch beneath our feet. Creatures, real-life ones, rustle in the woods.

"Abby—" Curtis starts, and I expect him to say *everything is going to be great, you're stressing out too much, you're awesome,* but instead he says, "You can make friends. You just have to try."

My shoulders tighten. I keep my eyes trained on the forest floor.

"I feel like you go around thinking people won't like you, but that's not true. They just don't *know you.* And you're amazing. If you don't want to be social, that's okay. If you're good on your own, that's awesome. But if you want friends, then you have to make an effort."

The comment stings, hard, and a few tears slide down my cheeks. I pray he can't see them in the darkness. "You don't get it." My voice wobbles. "It's easy for you. You like the right stuff, and I don't."

"You're probably right," Curtis agrees. "It probably is easier for me. But plenty of people like what you like. You have to put yourself out there to find them. I know it's scary, but you can do it."

I don't respond.

We keep walking.

I still don't respond.

"You're mad at me," Curtis says.

I shake my head. "No."

And I'm not. I'm not mad at Curtis.

I'm mad at myself. Maybe I'm too different and that's why I don't have friends. Or maybe I'm not putting myself out there and that's why I don't have friends.

But the thing is, either way, it's my fault.

4:54 a.m.

There's no Loch Ness at lake number four. By the time we make it back to the car, we're all sticky with sweat from the collective two-mile hike, and it's almost five in the morning. The sun lurks under the horizon, threatening us.

I want to give up. We're not going to find a Loch Ness. Everything about this night has gone wrong, and instead of being a cherished memory, it will haunt me for years.

"Can I sit up front?" Gracie asks. "I'm feeling carsick."

"Sure," I say, grateful not to sit next to Curtis. I think he's right—about me. About needing to try. Which means I really don't want to speak to him.

We don't talk on the drive to lake number five. We listen to my *Prowl* playlist. I mixed it last year as a hunting soundtrack. Emily stares out the window. Highway lights flick by. Lake Carlisle sits in a little foothill of mountains, up a long winding road, shrouded by trees. I found a Loch Ness at this same lake last year and lost it. It's far away and one probably won't show up to the same place twice, which is why I put it at the end of the route, a last-ditch effort.

Curtis turns off the highway, and we take back roads up the small mountain. I direct from my phone, my voice the only sound other than the music. Eventually we pull into the alcove lot. Curtis clears his throat as he cuts the engine. We all sit in silence for a long moment until Gracie says, "Come on! Only thirty minutes left! What are you people waiting for?"

We climb out of the car. The sky is lightening already, the earliest sign of dawn. The lake is beautiful and whisper-quiet.

My skin prickles as we walk, feet crunching down the dewy grass. Our screens are quiet as well, not a single creature in sight. It's by far the largest lake on the list, so we have to walk the full perimeter to activate the area.

Over halfway through the walk, Gracie stills, and we all stop with her. "What is it?" Curtis asks. "See something?"

She chews her lip. "Not yet."

"C'mon." Emily nods ahead of us. "Let's check out the rest."

Gracie shakes her head. "The Loch Ness is going to be right here. I know it. I'm going to drop a lure."

It doesn't make sense to stay in the same spot. We've got to walk the full perimeter. This is our last chance, and the sun will be up any minute.

Curtis glances at me, probably catching my unease. "I can stay with—" He yawns, loudly. "—stay with Gracie if you two want to check out the rest."

"Great! We'll drop a lure on the other side," Emily says, then tugs my hand, and I'm stumbling forward with her. She drops my hand shortly after, but we walk side by side through the damp grass. *You have to at least try*, Curtis said.

I glance at Emily. Her eyes are pinned on her screen, her mouth set in a furtive line. She seems nice. She got me a dough-nut. *Two doughnuts.* She hangs out with her kid sister. She likes Creature Capture, at least enough to care about the Loch Ness.

Am I that scared to try? I used to be good at this. I used to not think about it. I think I could try. I can try.

"So, you play a lot?" I ask. "Um, Creature Capture. Do you play Creature Capture a lot?" Bonus points to me for making that question way more complicated than necessary.

"Pretty often! It's addictive, right? My friends are always

complaining that there's nothing to do, and *I'm like look, right here! Literally something to do!*" She laughs. "What about you?"

Ah, yes, well my friends . . . do not exist . . .

"I like it," I say. "It's fun. Curtis plays with me sometimes, but you know, I might stop soon. After I catch a Loch Ness."

We've made it to the other side of the lake now. I tap my last lure as Emily tilts her head. "Why would you stop?" she asks.

"Um, you know, it's kind of embarrassing . . . how much I play . . ."

She grins. "You saying I should be embarrassed too?"

"No!" My cheeks flame red. "Of course not. I'm sure you don't play as much as me." And you do other stuff, like soccer, and go to parties, and have more friends than a single one you met in elementary school, I think.

"You sure about that?" Emily raises an eyebrow and shows me her screen. "Level fifty-six." She pretends to brush dust off her shoulders. "Not bad, huh?"

Level fifty-six. That's *my* level. That's a serious amount of playing level.

"Yeah," I say, a smile edging into my tone. "Not bad."

"Look." Emily leans toward me, eyes conspiratorial, voice lowered. "I'll let you in on a little secret. No one really cares about you—"

My stomach drops. Wait? What—

"—and no one really cares about me, and no one really cares about anyone all that much except for themselves. We're all too focused being worried about what people think of us to spend time judging others, you know? So, like screw it. Be who you are."

No one really cares.

Huh.

"That's, um, weirdly comforting."

Emily grins. "I know, right?"

I've spent so much of high school worried what other people will think of me, worried that I'm not like them, but maybe Emily is right. Maybe no one cares that I play Creature Capture or like knitting glow-in-the-dark scarves or think a wild Saturday night involves a Scrabble tournament with my parents. Maybe I should say *screw it* and just be me. And maybe, maybe then if someone does care, it'll be in a good way.

I take a short breath and suck up all my courage. "So. Um." I dig my foot into the grass. "What are your favorite creatures?"

Emily's face lights up. "Oh my god! I went skiing over winter break and caught my first yeti! I'm freaking obsessed with her. She's the cutest. Here, look."

The yeti is the cutest. I show Emily my gold basilisk next, and she shows me her collection of rare fairies as she says, "We should play together sometime!"

"Yeah!" I say. "I mean, maybe. Like I said, I was going to give up after the Loch Ness . . ."

"You have fun, right?" Emily asks. "You like the app?"

I nod.

"So why would you stop? C'mon. I could use a partner in Creature Capture crime. Don't let me down, Abby!"

Her eyes are bright, and my stomach flutters. "Okay, I'll think about it. Promise." I pause. "Actually, yes. Definitely yes. I'm in."

"OH MY GOD A FUCKING LOCH NESS!" Gracie screeches.

"Language!" Emily shouts.

But then what Gracie said hits us, and then Emily and I are racing back around the lake to Gracie and Curtis, and Gracie is screaming, "I'M FUCKING THIRTEEN!" as she messes with her screen, and Curtis is hopping from foot to foot and shouting, "LOCKING DOWN THE LOCH NESS, COME ON NOW!"

And then Emily and I are with them, and I look at my screen, and there it is, magnificent and massive in the water. Absolutely perfect. I want this so bad. Even though I know better, I start throwing nets with too much fervor. Slow down. Okay, use some berries to make the Loch Ness happy and easier to catch. Focus on the throw. I can do this. I aim carefully, and the net flies over the creature. He struggles, back and forth, back and forth. Stay. Just stay. And—

"I CAUGHT ONE!" I scream.

"ME TOO!" Curtis screams.

And then we've all caught one, and we're jumping up and down and cheering, and it's such an incredible feeling. I did it. I caught a Loch Ness. I go to my index, and there it is. Complete. I screenshot it for posterity. Then I tap over to my Loch Ness and feed him extra berries just because I'm so happy to see him.

"So," Emily says to me a bit later. We're sitting around the lake now, watching the sunrise, warm colors streaking across the water. "Are we hunting next week? I need my own gold basilisk."

"I want a gold basilisk!" Curtis says.

"Hmm." I tilt my head. "Did we invite you?"

He smiles, a smile as wide as our day at the water park. "No, you did not."

SHARK BAIT
by Tiffany D. Jackson

MY MOTHER'S PAIN IS BEAUTIFUL. YOU CAN SEE IT IN THE stitching of her Hermès bag, the gold in her Prada sunglasses, the way the sun sparkles off her new diamond tennis bracelet on Katama Beach. One would say Dad's adultery is the best mistake that could have ever happened to us. Royalty could never be shadowed by scandal.

"Wasn't it amazing how easy it was to register you for school," Mom said, adjusting her chair to face the sun. "If this was private, we'd have to shell out thousands and call in dozens of favors."

I didn't glance up from my copy of *Finding Martha's Vineyard*, stories about the African Americans who summered on the island. The longer we stayed, the more fascinated I've become with the history.

"Well maybe not dozens. Maybe one or two."

Waves crashed against the shore, the sun burning off the morning fog. Mom laughed, pouring more champagne into a travel mug. It wasn't even noon.

"Life is just so much simpler here," she said, taking a sip. "We can change, be new people. I think I'm . . . going to be a painter. Or maybe an art collector. Open up a gallery, perhaps?"

This is the longest we've ever stayed on the island. Two solid months. Although I was happy, the fall was fast approaching and I worried about practical things, like where I would get my hair done or buy McDonald's chicken nuggets. Martha's Vineyard isn't as standardized as the rest of the country. And in one week, I would begin my junior year at a new public high school, far different from any private school I'd ever attended. Everyone could use a fresh start, a change in pace, but something kept gnawing at my insides. Something that made me look out at the horizon, at the ferries floating to the dock, shuttling passengers to and from the mainland, and wonder if I should be on that boat, too.

Mom focused on her crossword. Since we decided to move here, she'd taken up a variety of new hobbies. Without Dad, she was determined to be a new woman. This week, it's puzzle magazines. Last week, it was knitting. I worried what would happen when we'd run out of things to do.

"You feel like going out to dinner tonight? It's getting chilly," Mom said, brightening. "We can make a reservation at the Oyster Bar! Have some clam chowder."

"Not tonight," I said, slipping a cover-up over my red two-piece bathing suit. "I have plans with Hunter, remember?"

Mom made googly eyes while sipping her drink.

Mom seemed fine when we'd first arrived at the house that summer. During the day, we soaked up sun on the beach, shopped in boutiques, admired the old, colorful gingerbread houses, and ate lobster rolls. But at night, she cried her way through bottles of red wine before passing out drunk on the sofa. By her first snore, I'd make my escape, walking the pitch-black roads into town, strolling down Circus Avenue in Oak Bluffs and ending the night with a hot donut. Better conditions, away from the tears and fog of pain that leaked through the vents into my room. I'd pass the closed ferry port to circle around the Flying Horse, a super old merry-go-round from the 1800s. So old the wooden horses' faces were faded, frozen in agony from carrying thousands of children over the years. The lights always flickered and it sounded like a music box on its last leg.

That's where I first saw him. Or, ran into him. Captivated by the millions of stars in the sky, I bumped right into his chest as he attempted to lock up for the night.

"Ooof, sorry, I—"

The chain he had been holding fell to the ground like a wind chime and his eyes widened. I don't believe in love at first sight. Or lust for that matter. But in that moment, I could almost hear fireworks explode overhead, stars bursting around us.

Then there was silence.

Followed by more silence.

"Um, hi," he'd said, with a raspy voice, his hand making an awkward waving gesture.

My mouth parted, but nothing came out.

"You lost?" he asked, chuckling.

"I . . . uh, no. Just going to get a donut."

It sounded completely ridiculous and yet I couldn't figure out what else to say.

He nods. "Um, can I join you?"

We stood in the long line at Backdoor Donuts, a popular afterhours spot that served fresh, hot donuts until one a.m. On any given night, the line is around the corner. But I didn't notice the crowd. I only noticed him.

He had gray-blue eyes and a crisp French crème complexion, with drops of vanilla extract on his nose. He even smelled sweet, like sugar cookies or a waffle ice cream cone. His hair was thick, a tight curly mop of dusty blond tangles. For a long while, we didn't say anything, just taking pleasure in the electric moment.

"You're, like, the most beautiful girl I've ever seen," he said out of nowhere.

My face engulfed in flames as I waited, and waited, and waited for a comment to follow. Because the last time a boy called me pretty, it ended with "for a Black girl" and I never wanted to feel like I was an exception again.

But this boy said nothing, only offering a crooked grin.

"Thank you," I whispered, kicking a pebble with my sandal.

"I'm Hunter."

"Candice."

"Nice to meet you."

His thick New England accent made me smile.

Just as Mom and I walked in the house, legs still covered in sand, my cell phone buzzed. Dad.

"Hey Candy! How's my beautiful, smart girl?"

"I'm . . . fine," I mumbled. Mom's eyes locked on me. She knew it was him. Her back straightened as if preparing for an attack, but then she drifted to the wine closet, in search of a salve.

I stepped out on the porch to regain my voice. As much as I tried not to hate him, I couldn't stand these perfunctory calls.

"What's up, Dad?"

"You," he said, plainly. "And this decision your mother has made about moving up there."

"Dad, I'm not a baby," I snapped. "It was my decision, too."

"You're right. You're not a baby," he said. "You're more mature than your mother in most ways. So here's the deal, you are not going to school in MV. This is your junior year, your most important year. Colleges will be looking at everything, including your extracurricular activities. Juilliard-level piano and dance lessons, national winning debate club, museum internships, art fellowships . . . none of those things can be offered for you there. You still want to go to Yale, right?"

My tongue stuck to the roof of my mouth. The word Yale sparking a flame snuffed out by his infidelity.

"Of course you do," he said. "And you also know you're not a trust fund kid or an affirmative action charity case. You earned every merit, fair and square. You want to continue showing them that, right?"

"Them," meaning white people. If I inherited nothing else from Dad, I got his hunger to prove people wrong.

"I've booked you a nine-thirty a.m. ferry back," Dad said. "A car will be waiting for you at Woods Hole to bring you home."

What home? Not my home, our home. The new one he moved into. Will that woman move in with my new sibling, too? My heart flared at the idea of standing up to the one person I looked up to most.

"Dad, I—"

"School started last week but I talked to the dean. He's aware of our recent family issues. Your mother can stay there if she chooses. But you . . . you're bigger than that island. I know you see it too."

A silver pickup truck pulled up to the end of the driveway with two honks. Hunter turned off the ignition and climbed out.

"Dad, I gotta go." I didn't wait for his response before stuffing the phone into my back pocket.

"Hello gorgeous," Hunter said, wrapping me in his warm arms, smelling like the sea. "Ready to roll?"

Hunter was at least three inches taller than Dad and had exceptional southern-like manners. Not a hint of a wandering eye. How could I feel so safe in the arms of someone I've known only a few weeks, versus a man I've known my whole life?

"Uh, yup, let me just grab . . . um, my bag."

I ran inside, up to my room. My bookbag was already prepped, but I triple checked to make sure I packed condoms. Hunter said he would bring them but I was too nervous to remind him. I stopped to glance at myself in the foyer mirror, wondering if I'd look different once the evening was over. Will anyone see the change?

Mom sat on the living room sofa, surrounded by family

photos dating back generations, uncorking a fresh wine bottle, the first bottle already empty.

"I see Hunter's here," she said. "Charming as ever."

There was a bite in her voice that made me shift to face her. "Going to a bonfire tonight so don't wait up."

Mom nodded. "I know you like Hunter and I like him, too. But he doesn't . . . I mean, you should . . . want to date someone that can really give you the world."

Like Dad, I almost shot back but stopped myself, catching a photo of him and Great-Grandmother by the fireplace. Great-Grandma must have bought this home for the same reasons other African Americans of her time did, to escape the Jim Crow South, to flee the racism, to be wholly free. And since it stayed in our family all these years, maybe it was meant to be our refuge, too. I didn't want the world like Mom did, just the humble slice Hunter offered.

But then I spotted another picture—Dad with his Yale diploma—and my stomach clenched.

Outside, I hopped into Hunter's truck, wild thoughts buzzing in my ear. Dad had a point; my dream was Yale. The dream kids at school said would be given to me to fill a minority quota. Nothing but a handout. A charity case. Not something I worked just as hard for.

"What's wrong?" Hunter asked, picking up on my silence.

"Dad," I sighed, slouching in my seat.

He nodded and slid an arm around my shoulders, brushing a braid out of my eye.

"We don't have to do this tonight. We can just stay here, just like this, forever if you want."

That" was all I wanted. To spend the rest of my life staring into the tender parts of his eyes and forget that I'm the strange lone Black girl in a white fancy school. The token in every extra-curricular activity and on every dance stage. Here with Hunter, on Martha's Vineyard, I could be free to really be . . . free.

"No, I want to," I insisted, buckling my seat belt. "Let's go."

Still, my mind betrayed us as I checked the time on Hunter's dashboard. Fifteen hours until the ferry.

In the early days of that summer, Hunter made it his mission to pull me into the folds of New England life.

"Lobster . . . ice cream?"

"It's delicious!" Hunter insisted as we walked hand in hand down Menemsha Beach, waiting for the sunset.

"No way! No fishy ice cream for me."

"Lobstah's a shellfish," he laughed, stopping to pick up a rock smoothed over by ocean waves.

I loved his thick New England accent that made all his words end on an upswing. I loved his beat-up truck that smelled like mulch, the holes in his mismatched socks, and the tan on his broad shoulders from fishing with his dad.

I also loved his silence. He never asked intrusive questions. And he never showboated like the boys at school, talking about all the money they had or how famous their parents were. He was peace wrapped in warm skin.

"Do they put butter on top of that ice cream or whipped cream?" I asked as I tripped over a rock with a yelp.

Hunter caught my arm before I could faceplant into the

sand and stood me upright. He smirked, tilting my chin up to his, arms wrapping around my waist.

"You know what? Bet you by the end of the summer, I'll make you fall in love."

I gulped. "With you?"

"Yeah . . . and with lobstah ice cream."

He was right. I did both.

Hunter had plans for us. We were going to go to college together in Boston. Have a Vineyard wedding. Buy a house in Oak Bluffs. He'd become a cop and I could write historical fiction, facing the very sea our people were taken across, maybe travel the world giving speeches. He had it all figured out.

Then, Dad called and reminded me of a finish line no one thought I could reach. The one those boys thought would be handed to me. And how desperately I needed to prove them wrong.

When the rumors first started to brew, they were easy for Dad to blow off. A woman here or there, no big deal. Folks just trying to trap a Black man, Dad had assured us. But when his assistant started to show at six months, Dad's recycled paper-thin excuses didn't hold up weight.

On the day Dad's scandal hit the Upper East Side grapevine, Mom had a craving for blueberry pancakes and suntan lotion. We packed our bags and by the next morning, we were sitting at Right Fork Diner in Edgartown, Martha's Vineyard, watching the old aviator planes make smooth landings in the tall grass. The butter on my toast hadn't even melted when the idea hit her.

"You know what? Let's move here! For good."

Mom presented the idea with the simplest of reasons: a chance for a fresh start in a familiar setting.

Black people have been coming to Martha's Vineyard, specifically Oak Bluffs, since running for freedom. It was a safe place to shelter, until it became a tourist destination for upper-class Black people. Dad inherited my great-grandmother's Victorian home and we've spent no less than two weeks every summer here since the day I was born. With so many Black families owning property and working in tandem with white families without incident, it was considered the first place where Black people were thriving, not just surviving, and could have a reprieve from the racism in the rest of the country. Here, for a change, we could let our guard down.

Hunter stopped at the entrance of Katama Beach.

"I was just here," I laughed. "I thought you said we were going to some special beach."

He gave me a sly grin. "We are. Hang tight."

He revved his engine and drove right over a sand bank.

"Whoa!" I screamed.

"Hold on!"

I gripped the ceiling handle as he drove, up and over the first sand dune, then another dune, like a roller coaster. Hunter clicked gears as the wheels kicked sand behind us. For a moment, it looked as if we were in the middle of some desert, the moon lighting our way across the Middle East.

"Reminds me of Dubai," I shouted over the roaring engine.

Hunter turned, perplexed. "What's that?"

I smiled and shook my head, remembering Hunter had never left the state, let alone the country, in his entire life.

"Never mind."

Mom's words echoed. *You want someone who can give you the world.* How could he give me something he knows nothing about?

"I'm real excited about you meeting my friends," Hunter said. "Been waiting all summer to do this."

It's not that I didn't want to meet his friends. I was sure his friends were just like him—gentle and tender thinkers who'd rather look up at the stars than down at their phones. But I just loved living in our own tight bubble and didn't want to relinquish it yet.

A few minutes later we came to a downward clearing, the beach nearly empty except for a small group of trucks, the beds facing the ocean, and kids gathered around a large bonfire.

Hunter parked the car, grinning. "Ready? Let's do it!"

A group of white faces were waiting for us, five guys and three girls. I ignored the pinch of disappointment in my throat. I thought I would see more . . . color. Color that reflected all the people on the island.

"Hey everybody," Hunter shouted, opening the truck bed.

"Hey Hunter!" the group cheered. "What up dawg!"

I don't know what they were playing before we arrived, but someone quickly switched the music to Jay-Z and I wanted to pretend I didn't notice. Their heads bob, singing along the wrong lyrics. Hunter introduced me to everyone individually, his hand never leaving the small of my back, and even though I'm always a little uncomfortable around new people, I felt safe with him.

"And this is my best friend Jake."

Jake yoked me into a tight hug. "What's up boo? Good to finally meet you, after all this hiding."

The slang sounded as off-beat in his mouth as his rhythm.

"Hi," I croaked out, trying to relax, sliding out of Jake's grip.

"Dawg, she's real pretty," Jake said, as if I wasn't standing there. "Prettiest Black girl I've ever seen! Told you you'd find someone of your kind soon."

The comment landed with a thud against my chest.

I waited for Hunter to say something, but he just unloaded the beers in silence.

Twelve hours until the ferry.

"Wait? You're BLACK?"

Hunter wiped the sticky donut glaze off his mouth as we sat on wooden horses in the carousel, closed for the night.

"Well, I prefer biracial."

I narrowed my eyes. "So, you're Black?"

He sighed, shaking his head. "It's not a big deal."

Hunter's father was a Black man from Georgia who met his mother working on the island one summer. They fell in love, then parted ways. A few months later, Hunter came into this world and his father gave up law school and moved back to the island to be with the ones he loved most.

In awe, I took in his features, again. I thought the golden crisp of his skin was from being in the sun too long. He could pass as a white boy.

"We've been seeing each other every day for the last three weeks and you're just mentioning this now?"

He shrugged, avoiding my stare. "Guess I wanted someone to like me for just being . . . me."

"These stupid fucking tourists are paying crazy money to Airbnb Old Man Johnny's house," Jake said, laughing, a gold beer can in his hand. "What a bunch of idiots!"

Hunter's friends talked about the tourists that swarm the island every summer, bringing their so-called ignorance, inflating prices on just about everything. They bragged about the rich girls' virginity they took and the rich boys they convinced to throw parties at their parents' rental houses. Their pandering was painfully familiar. Change the setting, and we could've been back in New York with the very people I wanted to run from. Is this what awaits me at school here?

I glanced at my phone. Ten hours until the ferry.

"Jesus, imagine if tourists found this spot," one of the girls said, poking the fire. "I'd be sick!"

"Only locals know the spots to avoid."

I'm so caught up in the conversation that I didn't notice Hunter sneaking behind me to tickle my sides. We chase after each other, dancing under the starlight, floating through space, our own world once more. How could I ever board a ferry back to who I was, leaving who I really am behind?

"Aye! Get a room you two," Jake said from somewhere, his voice like nails on chalk.

Hunter smiled at me. "Come on, let's join the party."

We walked hand in hand back to our spot. More people had showed up, more kids I would see in the halls of my new school next week. *Didn't he have any Black friends?*

I tuned into a debate Hunter and a few of the other guys were having.

"No bro, the best rapper out of all of them was Mac Miller! RIP!"

Hunter shook his head. "Bro, you're nuts. Best rapper dead or alive is Jay-Z!"

Jake cackled. "HA! Yeah! See, that's why you my nigga for real bro. Always got my back!"

I slipped on my shoes, preparing myself, unsure what could go down.

But Hunter just stood there, the same smile on his face. They tapped their beer cans together and continued on as if nothing had happened. I blinked at Hunter. Surely we weren't staying after this white boy dropped the N-word.

"Something wrong?" Hunter asked, measuring my face. I could only stare back.

"Hey Candice," Jake said. "Are you gonna let my bro smash tonight or what?"

With the blazing sun on my back, I ran through a group of seagulls before I'm yoked back.

"Gotcha!" Hunter wrapped his arms around my bare stomach and lifted, carrying me closer to the sparkling shore. Hunter knew all the best beach spots where it could just be the two of us. On our own island, in the middle of the sea.

"Ah!" I giggled, snuggling into his chest. "Put me down!"

He set me down right at the water's edge, kissing the back of my neck. I blushed, squirming, but never wanting him to stop.

"Hey, hey! Look! Out there. You see that black shape coming out the water?"

I followed his finger pointing out to the dark ocean, a shadow popping up then disappearing.

"Whoa, yeah! What is that?"

"That's a seal. Around here, we call them shark bait."

I gulped. "Sharks?"

His dusty blond curls flew in the wind. "Yeah. Especially seals that hang out alone. That's an easy TV dinner for a great white. You know that movie *Jaws*? It was based here. My great-uncle worked on the film."

I swallowed, biting the inside of my cheek. "Really?"

He laughed. "It's okay babe. We're safe. Just stay out of the water during their dinnertime and you'll be fine."

I stared at the boundless sea. "I thought sharks liked to eat all the time."

The hours passed by with more crude jokes about tourist conquest and Hunter didn't seem to notice that I hadn't uttered a word. Just sat beside him, stewing. Somewhere after midnight, Hunter packed up our chairs and cooler, saying goodbye to his friends, the fire now a roaring blaze, casting an orange glow on their pale faces as the anger sizzled inside me.

We drove in the dark through the sand dunes, the other side of Katama Beach empty and black.

"Okay, here's the fun part," Hunter said, driving fast, his headlights only going so far in the blackness. He turned up another road to another sand dune.

"Okay, everyone off the ride!"

Hunter lifted me out of the truck and set me down in the dark sand.

"Sheesh, you're so tiny." He laughed then straightened. "Hey, something wrong?"

I shook my head.

Hunter shrugged and didn't push it, and I quickly realized he never pushed anything. He seemed so insistent upon always catching me before I fell, how did I not notice his missing spine?

Hunter grabbed the blankets from the truck bed and led the way. We climbed up the sand dunes, through the brush, my eyes adjusting to the dark, until we reached another clearing.

"We'll be out of sight here," Hunter said as he laid out the blankets. I stood frozen, listening to the waves crash on the shore and thinking about all the great whites ripping seals apart, blood bleeding into the dark water. I wanted to save them, but it's impossible. No matter where they go, the sharks will always circle.

Hunter sat on the blanket and offered his hand. "Hey, come here."

I joined him, looking up at the sky, and it felt as if we were hiding under a blanket of stars.

"Okay, so there's the North Star, and the Little Dipper . . ."

Hunter loved studying the galaxy as much as he loved the sea. He continued, trying to point out all the constellations, playing with my hair, kissing my temple, and I tried to pay attention, but all I could hear was Dad's warning and the N-word ringing in my ears.

Hunter sat up, staring down at me. "What's wrong?"

"Huh? Nothing."

"You've been quiet. What's going on? Are you having second thoughts?"

I sat up, hugging my knees. "You . . . just let him call you that?"

"What? Who?"

"Jake." I paused, hoping I wouldn't have to elaborate further but he only frowned. He really had no clue. "He called you . . . he called you the N-word. Did you not hear him?"

Hunter cocked his head to the side then laughed. "Oh, he was just messing around."

"You think the N-word is funny?"

Hunter straightened. "Hey, it's no big deal. He was joking."

"No big deal? Are you kidding me?"

"Black people say it all the time! He's just copying what he hears in rap songs."

"That doesn't make it okay! And that's not his music to copy."

"Music is music! It's color-blind."

I snort. "Did he tell you that?"

We argued. Well, I yelled, words cutting but not cruel, while he rolled his eyes. We had gone an entire summer not seeing each other's dark sides, making us almost unrecognizable in this moment. I never expected Hunter to be so flippant and unbothered. If I were in his shoes, I'd make them sorry for ever thinking they could call me the N-word. I'd make them pay!

Hunter rubbed his face, exasperated, then held his hands up to surrender. "Okay, I'm sorry. Can we move on?"

"Do you even know what you're sorry about? You have nothing to be sorry for! He should be apologizing to you!"

"He doesn't have to apologize. He's my best friend. We're like brothers."

I looked at the time. Two a.m. Seven and a half hours until the ferry leaves.

"Can you take me back home now, please?"

Hunter's shoulders slumped. "Hey, let's not let stupid shit ruin our night."

"It's just late, and I have stuff to do tomorrow," I said, my voice cold.

"Stuff? What stuff?"

Since we started, we knew each other's every move. I wouldn't be able to hide it for long so I had to just come clean.

"I'm heading back to New York. For good."

Hunter stared at me for ten painful seconds.

"I thought you said . . . you were moving here?"

There was a devastation in his voice I wasn't prepared for with my last-minute decision. I wasn't even sure if it was the right decision or a fleeting thought fueled by anger. But I couldn't let him know that.

"I was, but . . . things have changed."

"Your dad?"

I wrapped my arms around myself. "Yeah. And other things."

"Oh god, tell me this isn't about Jake."

"It's . . . part of it."

He rubbed his face again. "When?"

"Tomorrow."

"Tomorrow!"

More arguing. More aggression. More . . . more.

"Okay, fine. Well, we can just . . . do long-distance," he offered.

"How can we do distance when we have trouble when we're together?"

He shook his head. "I thought we were happy."

My heart tugged in both directions, body splitting in two at the crack in his voice. Happy, yes, I was happy. Never been happier. But fantasies aren't dreams.

I sighed. "Yes, happy pretending the real world doesn't exist. But it does. Once we go to school, I'll be the lone Black girl again, and you'll go back to passing just to make your life easier."

Hunter was silent. He stood away from me, his back turned. I flopped back on the blankets to stare up at the sky.

"Okay. I'll take you home, if that's what you really want."

We piled into the truck. The night had drained us both dry.

"I'm . . . sorry," I whispered as he started the ignition. He didn't say anything. We remained silent, the truck rumbling beneath us. He revved the engine and took off, shifting gears, catching air over the high sand dunes.

"Slow down!" I shouted, but Hunter didn't listen.

At the next incline, the truck engine choked, and Hunter jerked the clutch. The wheels spun, spitting up sand like a tornado before the truck tipped violently to the left, and we lost gravity.

"Oh shit!"

The truck flipped. Once, twice, three times.

When I came to, my head rang and I tasted copper on my lip, blood dripping in my eye. The windshield was shattered, headlights pointing into white sand. The truck had landed on its side, leaving me suspended in the air.

"Hunter," I cried. "Are you okay?"

"Yeah," Hunter groaned with a cough. "You okay?"

The seat belt squeezed into my rib cage, pinching my lungs, and I struggled to breathe.

"I can't move. I'm stuck!"

"Can you reach your phone?"

I wiggled around, patting my pockets. All empty.

"No, I don't know where it is! Can you?"

"I can't move my arm," he hissed through clenched teeth.

Hunter made a gurgling noise. He looked bad. My neck hurt from hanging sideways but if I tried to free myself, I'd land right on him, crushing him even more.

Panic made a home in my chest as a sob bubbled up. I glanced at the time on the dashboard. Two thirty-five. No one knew we were out here. Eventually, people would start coming to the beach. But morning was light-years away.

"It's okay. It's okay," Hunter said, pushing at the horn, the sound an ant's cry in the abyss.

"No one's coming," I cried, my head throbbing.

Hunter let off the horn and coughed.

"Okay. Just stay calm. Night patrol will hopefully see the headlights when they make their rounds. Just . . . try to relax for now. Relax and listen for a car or anything."

We fell silent with only the sounds of waves to comfort us.

"Do you . . . really want to go back to New York? I thought you hated it there."

"Now's not the time for this!"

"Only time I got and I'm going to take it," he said, sounding winded. "You don't want to go back there."

"I . . . I want to go to Yale," I shoot back.

"Yeah, but that's not your dream and you know it. You just want to go to say you went. To prove someone wrong."

I licked my lips, thankful he couldn't see the bubbling tears. "That's . . . that's not true."

"You said it yourself, 'Gotta get into Yale so they know Black girls are smart.' But aside from proving a point, then what? What happens then? You find another point to prove? When does it end?"

I bit the inside of my cheek. My own words sounded ugly in his mouth. "What do you know about what I want?"

"I've seen you come alive here. When's the last time you did something just for fun in New York? Meaningless fun?"

I blinked then blinked again. Longer. Three forty-five. I jumped and a shock of pain blasted through me.

"Gah," I gasped, taking in my injuries again. "Hunter? Hunter?"

Hunter was quiet and I prayed he'd just passed out like I did. The chilly breeze swept through the broken windows. The smell familiar and homelike. That's what I loved most about Martha's Vineyard. The crisp ocean waters that reminded me of when I was a kid. Playing in the backyard with Dad, going to Inkwell Beach, standing in line for donuts. All the moments I loved . . . most of them being with Hunter.

The thought of Dad made my ribs throb. If I didn't show up to the ferry in the morning, would he give up on me, just like he'd given up on Mom? Mom didn't fit into his plan so she was easily disposable. Was that me? Was that why I was able to tell Hunter I'm leaving in the morning without a proper goodbye? Was I that heartless? What would happen if I let go of the mission to be right and just be free?

"Candice?"

On instinct, I reached for him, clawing at the air. "Hunter! Are you okay?"

"Candice?" he whispered.

"Yes! Yes, I'm here," I cried, relieved to hear his voice. "I'm here!"

His eyes were closed, skin pale and gray. "Don't leave, okay?"

Four twenty-one a.m. An hour or so before sunrise and we still hadn't heard a single car or a human. It was as if we'd fallen off the planet. I wasn't sure if I was ready to see Hunter in the light of day when he looked so terrible in the glow of the dashboard.

"Hey, try honking the horn again," I suggested.

Hunter pushed with his one good arm. Over and over, fifteen minutes straight. Nothing. Hunter started to cry, banging on the horn, screaming.

"Hey, hey, hey. It's okay it's okay. Just . . . relax," I said, reaching for his shoulder. "Try to relax. Just . . . listen to the water."

Hunter gave the horn a break and we fell silent, the waves seeming closer.

"Candice . . . I want you to know . . ."

"Nope! Don't you dare give me some kind of goodbye-I-love-you bullshit speech."

He chuckled. "No, although I do love you. I was just . . . thinking about what you said. About Jake. There is stuff he says that bothers me. Lots of stuff. But . . . he's my friend."

"Friends don't hurt each other."

He sighed. "It wasn't until you came, that I really saw that . . . I guess. You don't run. You stay and fight."

The sky began to lighten, the sun nearby. I listened to the waves, my teeth chattering, the morning fog enveloping the car.

"Don't . . . don't . . . go," Hunter mumbled. "You are home. My home."

Tears crawled down my face. Hunter wasn't making sense anymore, he needed help. I pushed at the horn, then at the door. Stuck. I screamed and yelled. Wasn't there anyone on the beach?

"Don't run," Hunter mumbled again.

Why *should* I run away from an island that brings me so much joy? Why should I let one stupid white boy run me off?

You're bigger than that island.

Even if I am, the island can handle my weight.

"Hunter, you . . ."

There was a noise in the distance, like a bark. A dog . . . no, much sharper. I gasped.

"Hunter, do you hear that? Seals!"

Silence.

"Hunter? Hunter!"

Hunter didn't answer.

A PLACE TO START

by Nina LaCour

A FEW HOURS AGO, THE SUN SETTING AND THE SKY A purple-pink behind her, my mother took my face in her hands and kissed me on the lips. "Goodbye, my sweet," she said to me. Her hair was swept in a bun, a style she never wore, and even though her dress was mauve instead of white it was still unmistakably a wedding dress, all tight and lacy. There was a new ring on her hand, the hand I'd held forever, and I had to blink back tears because it felt like she was saying goodbye for good.

Behind us people whooped and clapped from the front steps of a stranger's fancy house. It was all marble stairs and manicured lawn, alarmingly perfect. I smiled, pretending I was just so happy.

"I'm excited for you, Mom," I said.

"My beautiful daughter. You'll always be the love of my life," she told me, but that just made it worse.

And then she was in the car with Macey, my stepmom as of that afternoon, and our station wagon got farther and farther away with pink-and-white streamers waving behind it, the words *Here come the brides!* painted across the rear window, and I stood there as everyone cheered, tears streaming down my cheeks like a little kid even though I'm going into my junior year of high school and generally have a decent level of control over my displays of emotion.

I still don't know who decorated the car. *Our* car. My mom's and mine.

I turned and found the crowd dispersed. Most of the people were probably back inside the house eating tiny bites of fancy snacks. I followed because I didn't know what else to do.

"Claude!" said the stranger who lived there. "Did you get enough to eat? How are you holding up?" Her arm squeezed my shoulders a little too tightly.

"I'm good," I told her.

She wiped a spot under my eyes and I remembered that I'd put on mascara earlier in the morning. It was probably all over my face now.

"Sweetie, you can talk to me," the stranger said. "We're practically family now."

Across the sprawling kitchen, its surfaces so shiny they hurt my eyes, I saw Jamie look at me and then look away.

"I'm just tired," I said. "I think I'll go home now. Unless you need help cleaning."

"Oh, no, nobody's going to lift a finger tonight. Tomorrow morning a service is coming and it will be like there never was a wedding at all."

"Perfect," I said.

I thought about my yellow front door and my soft bed, the rack where I'd place my shoes before stepping onto the carpet. And then I remembered that the cabin was gone now. It was rented to someone else. So, I slid out of the stranger's hug and crossed to Jamie. They turned to me and didn't look away this time.

"You have makeup all over your face," they said, but not in a mean way.

"I know," I said. "And you look miserable."

Jamie shrugged with one of their shoulders and the rise and fall of it made me smile for some reason. Like they were just too tired to shrug with both their shoulders.

"I want to go home," I said.

Jamie nodded. "Yeah, let's go then."

On our way out, another one of the strangers called for us to stop.

"Let's get a picture of the new stepsiblings!" he said. He lifted some fancy camera, totally unnecessary given the presence of an actual paid photographer. If he noticed that we didn't even smile he chose not to let on.

Flash-click! and then we were free.

Jamie unlocked their car and we slid onto the leather seats. I didn't know why our mothers took the car they did when Jamie and Macey's cars were both nicer. It made me feel good for a moment, like not *everything* would change. Maybe I should have felt happy that I was going to be rich now, but it was just another thing to get used to, a change I had no say in.

Our doors closed and I could feel how it was the two of us now. Neither of us were only children anymore. Not exactly, anyway.

"Straight to the house?" Jamie asked. The time on the dash read 10:23.

"I guess," I said.

Jamie drove us away from the stranger's house and into San Rafael, to a neighborhood where all the houses were similar, all one story and set back from the street, the neighborhood our mothers had chosen for all of us, the house that was neither Jamie's nor mine. We parked in the driveway and sat there for a full minute, engine idling, like Jamie was considering going somewhere else after all. The lights shone under the eaves. The gable in the middle rose before us, flanked by long, flat roofs on either side.

Jamie cut the engine. Silence. "I'm suddenly starving," they said.

I nodded. I was starving, too.

And now we are out of the car, standing in the driveway in the glow of the eaves.

It is a beautiful house.

Even tonight, I can be objective enough to admit this. A beautiful house, a special house, built in a neighborhood conceptualized by a developer named Joseph Eichler in the 1960s. Jamie and I walk through the front door, which is mostly glass set against more glass, and into the living room, where Jamie drops the keys into a small ceramic dish perfect for key-holding, under the exposed beams of the bright white ceiling. Across from us is another glass wall that opens into an atrium. We've only spent a few nights here but everything is in place, thanks to the movers and decorator Macey hired. "You know," she'd said, waving a hand, stacked bracelets dangling. "With the wedding and everything, no one wants to be living out of boxes." But I saw Jamie's face when she said it, the skepticism, and I felt it, too. I don't think Macey would *ever* live out of boxes. The excuse was for me.

"I'll see what's in the refrigerator," Jamie says, and I follow.

They open it and I peer in and both of us sigh at the sight of barely anything.

"Sol Food delivery?" Jamie asks.

"*Yes.*"

We scroll through the menu and order way too much food—a whole chicken, two kinds of beans, rice and plantains, and then Jamie declares the fried shrimp as their favorite thing in the entire world and I haven't ever tried it so we add that, too.

I realize how expensive it will be and a low-key panic sets in. As Jamie reads their credit card aloud, I grab my phone.

"Venmo?" I ask when they hang up.

"What are you doing?"

"Paying you back for my half."

"It's not my money, it's my mom's," they say. "But it's all the same now anyway. It's yours, too."

My cheeks get hot. I want to tell Jamie that I don't need their money. We live across the Golden Gate Bridge from San Francisco, in one of the most expensive counties in the country, but Mom and I have always gotten by just fine. We lived in an in-law unit in Mill Valley with a view of the ocean when I was a baby, and then a tiny guest house in Larkspur surrounded by redwoods all through elementary school. The summer after fifth grade, we moved into our cute two-bedroom cabin way up in the hills of Fairfax. We had to walk up sixty stairs to the front door but it looked over the whole town and the hills in the distance. It was a little rundown, a little musty, but it was the most perfect house I'd ever seen.

"The food will be here in half an hour," Jamie says.

"Thank god," I say. "I couldn't eat any of the dinner."

"Yeah, me neither." Jamie runs a hand through their blond hair and looks down at the kitchen floor. Our mothers had the kitchen remodeled before moving in and the floor tile was their most difficult decision. For weeks the two of them had studied samples, laid out the possibilities. They decided on rectangular ceramic tiles, arranged in an intricate herringbone, the color of a grassy field. As Jamie looks at them now, I notice for the first time that their eyelashes are so light they disappear at the tips.

All I really knew about Jamie before our mothers started dating was that they played clarinet in the school band and hung out with mostly other band kids. And I'd also heard people say Jamie was a snob. Not because they were rich—almost everyone I went to school with had a lot of money—but in a queer way. "Jamie judges *everything*," I heard this girl Sienna say once. "We went out a few times but they didn't like anything I liked. They kept saying how heteronormative everything was. It was exhausting!"

I want to know what Jamie thinks of all of *this*. How fast our mothers fell in love—from just met to married in less than a year. How sudden the wedding was. Do they sometimes forget their life is changing, like I do, and then feel the wind knocked out of them when they remember?

I want to know all of it. And I want to know what Jamie thinks of *me*.

"I'm gonna get changed," they say.

"Yeah," I say. "Right. Me, too."

I suddenly feel the soreness in my feet from the high heels I've been wearing all afternoon and night. And the waistband on my dress is tight, and I think of my old sweats folded in a new dresser drawer in my new room. Of my T-shirts and my slippers. All the small things that are still mine. Jamie and I have rooms across the hall from each other and we each shut ourselves into them now. Once my dress is thrown onto my bed I take a moment to look at everything. It will only be my third night sleeping here. I've been spending a lot of time at my best friend's house lately. Mom says she understands.

The framed posters and photographs that used to be in our cabin are now arranged on the walls of my room. The quilt my grandmother made covers my bed. Our old kitchen table is now my desk, and atop it sits the light that used to be in our living room. All around the house are new things to look at. New furniture and art and rugs and pottery. New curtains. New appliances. New tiled floors. But my room is a time capsule of our old life. My mom worked on it with the designer as a surprise. The walls look like something out of a magazine, not the sleek kind Macey reads but the kind Mom and I love, where you get glimpses into the worn and comfortable places people have lived in for a long time.

I know Mom meant well. I know it's a refuge for me. But I can't help but feel like she took all these things we used to love together and left me to love them on my own.

Across the hall, Jamie's door opens and I hear them walk toward the living room. I don't know what Jamie's room looks like. I haven't been inside of it yet.

I'm not ready to go back out. I lie down on my bed and stare at the exposed-beam ceiling and transom window. The mattress is so comfortable, unlike anything I've ever slept on. On a normal night, I would be falling asleep at this time, and I guess we might crash right after eating. But we might not. We barely talked all day, both of us swept up in the festivities, whether we wanted to be or not. I don't yet know when Jamie sleeps and rises. I don't know if there is some initiation process for new stepsiblings that we're supposed to take part in. I wish there were *something*. A vow to profess platonic familial entanglement, maybe, so that I could know who we're supposed to be to each other—siblings or friends, or still almost-strangers—but if there is, it's a mystery to me.

I close my eyes, just for a little while, and here is the afternoon, playing back in my head. *I do,* Macey said. *I do,* Mom said. And then they kissed. I could see how much they love each other. I am happy for them. Truly. I don't fault Macey for being different from us. She's always been kind to me. She's always been generous. She asks me questions about myself and really listens when I answer.

I do.

I do.

The doorbell rings. I hear Jamie talking to the delivery person before I can get up. Then the door shuts.

"*Claude,*" Jamie calls. "*Time to feast!*"

"Where should we eat?" Jamie asks.

The dining table with its matching chairs sits right off the kitchen, the obvious choice. But the sofas and the coffee table look more welcoming. Jamie follows my gaze and heads there with the plates and silverware. I follow with the boxes of food, sure that both our mothers would disapprove.

"Let's be very careful," I say, eyeing the Persian rug and the pale gray wool sofa upholstery.

Jamie heaps black beans onto their plate. "I'm pretty sure we can manage to eat without destroying anything."

I almost don't respond. But then I do. "And if we get black beans on this sofa and it gets stained, then what? We just buy a new one?"

Jamie pauses and looks at me. "You think I'm careless."

"No." I shake my head. "That's not what I'm saying."

"Then what *are* you saying?"

"I'm saying that . . ." I sigh, the boxes of too much food scattered on the coffee table now. "I'm just saying that you might take all of this for granted."

Jamie takes a bite of plantain and chews slowly. I can see them thinking and I hope I haven't said too much.

"It isn't the way I'd choose to live," they say once they swallow. "This is my mom's shit. *Our moms'* shit. I'm just using it while I'm here. It's their call if they want to spend an ungodly amount of money on furniture. We should be able to eat dinner on the couch if we want to."

"Okay," I say. "All right." Jamie has a point. This is where I'm going to live for at least two more years of my life, so I guess I should make myself comfortable. I won't start taking it for granted, but I don't need to be afraid of it either. At long last, I fill my plate with a little bit of everything we ordered, relieved that Jamie isn't offended, proud of myself for being honest. It doesn't feel like a bad start.

As we eat, I look around at everything, considering what Jamie said. I could see how excited our moms were when they were picking things out, but that doesn't mean I have to like what they chose. The kitchen tile is incredible. The dining set too sleek for me. I love this rug we're sitting on, its soft colors. It's in near-perfect condition but it's also very old and I like that. The sofas are soft and special and I would feel genuine remorse if I stained them. I slip onto the rug so that I can eat right over my plate on the coffee table.

"Isn't this the best shrimp you've ever had?" Jamie says. "Here, try the sauce."

I agree that it's delicious. Maybe not the *very* best of my life, but I don't say so. It feels good when my hunger lessens. "I can't believe we didn't eat all day," I say.

"I know. The food looked really good, too, I just couldn't."

"Are you . . ." I say.

"What?"

"I don't know," I say. "Never mind."

I can't think of any good way to ask if Jamie's as conflicted about all of this as I am. I can't think of a single way of phrasing the question and I'm relieved when they let it go. I turn back to the room we're in. This time I look at the giant piece of art that covers the main living room wall: bold lines in blacks and reds and yellows.

"I hate this painting," I say.

Jamie's mouth opens in shock. "You aren't serious."

"I'm completely serious."

"I *love* this painting. It's my favorite thing we own. I wish it could hang in my room."

"It isn't new?"

"No. We've had it for years. It's by Val Jones. Her stuff is in SFMOMA and the Louvre."

I cover my face with my hands. "I'm so sorry," I say.

"Whatever," Jamie says with a smirk. "It's fine if you like posters better."

I'm confused for a moment and then I realize. "You've been in my *room*?"

Jamie's fork hovers mid-bite. "Shit."

"I feel violated."

"I was curious! I didn't go through your stuff or anything; I just looked. You didn't look in mine?"

I shake my head. "I respect people's space," I tease.

"Ouch. Well, okay. I'll show it to you now." They set down their fork without taking the bite. "Come on."

Jamie's room is the mirror of mine in layout, but the vibe is totally different. Minimal and monochrome.

"Is blue your favorite color?" I ask.

"No. My mom and the designer thought it would be soothing."

I lean against the wall, taking in all the shades of blue, from indigo to the palest blue-gray. "Do you often need to be soothed?"

"Apparently my mother thinks so."

"What did your old room look like?"

"Like a human person actually existed in it."

"You should do yours over," I say. "Make it your own."

"Yeah, eventually. But I don't know. Part of me feels like it isn't even worth it. I'll only be here for another year."

Jamie's a senior, one year ahead of me. Mom and I have been planning for college for a while. We started in the beginning of the summer and drafted a list of California state colleges to visit. We talked about saving money with community college for the first two years in case I wanted to transfer to a UC later. But then suddenly, about a month ago, brochures from places like Pitzer and NYU started coming. Mom left them on the kitchen table for me.

"What is this?" I asked her, holding up the stack.

"I looked up the top writing schools," she said.

I narrowed my eyes, confused. *Top schools* had never entered our conversations. We'd talked about places I'd enjoy living, about course offerings, about responsible choices, about graduating with the least amount of debt as possible.

"These are so expensive," I said.

"Just . . . Let's not rule anything out, okay?"

And then she came home with a diamond on her finger and I understood. Now my choices are wide open and I don't know where to start. Something about those first schools we talked about—Cal State Long Beach, San Francisco State—sound comforting, but I don't quite know why. Jamie's so much closer to having to make actual decisions.

"Still," I say. "You have a whole *year* to spend in this room. And then summers and holidays. I think it's worth it. You should feel good when you're home."

Jamie gives me their half shrug, the same one from the stranger's kitchen earlier, and it's hard to believe this is still the same night. I follow them back to the living room and we both heap seconds onto our plates. I check my phone. Nothing from

Mom. It's past midnight already. Maybe it's foolish to think she'd check in when she already kissed me goodbye. They're on their honeymoon, after all. They shouldn't be thinking about their children. Jamie and I can handle ourselves.

When I've finished everything on my plate, I lean back against the sofa and look at the painting again. The *Louvre*? I really don't understand art.

"I think we should move this painting into your room," I say.

"Wow. You hate it *that* much."

"No. I mean, yeah, I do hate it, but that's not the reason. Who wants a blue monochrome room? It's ridiculous!"

"I agree."

"And you love this. You said you wanted it. And I got all the stuff from my old house in my room. Why shouldn't you have this in yours?"

"My mom wouldn't be able to show it off."

"She could buy something new. My mom could help choose it."

"She'd kill me."

"We can get away with anything right now," I say. "I'm pretty sure. We're *adjusting*."

Jamie stands up, hands on their hips, facing the painting. "Would it even fit in my room?"

"I think so. We can measure."

They nod. "Okay, let's measure."

A bolt of adrenaline goes straight to my heart. I had this outlandish idea, this bold idea, and Jamie likes it. We venture into the garage where, of course, everything we could ever need is stored and labeled on shelves along the perimeter. Measuring tape in hand, Jamie leads us back to the living room. We measure ten by twelve feet—truly massive—and I begin to have doubts that it will fit, but when we measure the one windowless and doorwayless wall in Jamie's room, we see that it will. It will take up the entire thing—the rooms are modestly sized—but Jamie grins and I grin back.

Thankfully, it's just canvas on wood, and we lift it from the wall fairly easily. We remove the hardware from where it hung in the living room, and after taking down the artwork from Jamie's wall (three long pieces of driftwood painted various shades of blue), mark where to drill on their wall.

I go back to the garage to retrieve the drill and find Jamie laughing when I return.

"I can't believe we're doing this," they say. "It's two a.m. We're about to drill four holes into the wall of a newly restored Eichler in order to hang a Val Jones in a teenager's bedroom."

"Sounds pretty awesome to me," I say.

"I'm totally blaming you when my mom comes home and loses her shit."

"Not fair. It was my idea but *your* decision to do it tonight without asking. We get equal blame for this."

"Maybe we'll get grounded together."

"Sounds fun. I've never been grounded before."

Jamie's eyebrow raises. "Interesting. Very different parenting styles, our mothers. But, yeah, sure, equal blame. You drill the holes, though."

I laugh and get started. I'm good at it. I line everything up carefully. We briefly panic when we realize the painting might not fit through Jamie's doorway, but once we angle it diagonally, we get it through. When it's time for us to lift the canvas, it rests perfectly on the hardware. We step into the middle of Jamie's room. Taking it all in is almost impossible—it's so big for the small space. Jamie backs up onto their bed.

"Every morning I get to wake up to this. In the living room, it was just a decoration. In here, it's the entire room." Their eyes fill with wonder.

"Are you happy with it?"

"Yeah," Jamie says. "It transforms everything. You are a genius."

"My work here is done, then," I say.

"No, it isn't! What should we change next?"

"What do you *mean*?" I ask.

It's past three a.m. now. I thought for sure we'd say goodnight. I'd leave Jamie to bask in the glow of their favorite painting while I crawled back into my bed.

"I *mean* that we can do more," they say.

But I don't want to go too far. This place only feels a tiny bit mine. My mother's money didn't pay for any of it. "Let's sleep on it," I say. "We might wake up in the morning full of regret."

"It basically *is* the morning. Okay, look: Nothing else needs to be this extreme. But there are small things we could do. Some of those boxes in the garage have stuff from my old house. I want to find a vase I've been missing. And I'm sure you have a secret vision you could fulfill."

Ultimately, this is what gets me: That Jamie thinks I'm the kind of person with secret visions, that I wait around until the right moment to bring them to fruition. And as soon as I

consider it, I realize it might be true. I know exactly what I want
to do next in this house.

"Okay," I say. "If we've come this far we might as well see
it through."

Jamie clasps their hands together and pumps them in the
air in a silent cheer. "I'll make coffee," they say. "Do you like
coffee?"

"I like it. Yes."

"Or do you prefer tea?"

"Either one."

"A flexible genius. A rebel of décor," Jamie says on their way
to the kitchen.

I eye the driftwood on the floor and stack it in my arms.
The living room wall is now bare, save for the holes where the
hardware once was. I hold a piece of driftwood up where the
painting hung to see how it would look.

"Hey, Jamie. What if we stacked these vertically right here?"

Jamie pops their head out from the kitchen. "It looks pretty
good there, actually."

I agree. They look airy and floaty and calm—and it might
be less shocking to our mothers if, when they arrive home, they
don't see an empty wall where the painting used to be. I get to
work with the hardware and I've already finished hanging the
first piece when Jamie comes out with my mug of coffee.

"Want my help?"

"I'm okay," I say. "Go see about your vase."

I've hung the second piece of driftwood by the time Jamie
appears again, holding a box spilling over with objects. "I found
a lot," Jamie said. "Our old salt and pepper shakers. A sculpture

I made in eighth grade that I *distinctly* remember her promising she'd keep on display forever."

"Let's see it."

They hold it up for me.

"Is it a horse? It's actually pretty good."

"Yeah. I made it at an art camp. I worked on it for an entire week."

"It deserves a place of prominence."

Later, I see they've placed it in the center of one of the exposed kitchen shelves, stacks of neutrally toned plates on either side of it, and the sight of it there is so perfect I feel like I could cry. It's a vignette from a family's house, and somehow this is my family now, even though it doesn't feel that way yet.

The clock reads four-fifteen a.m. Along the dining space's wall is a bank of white shelves and I discover what I want to do next. I choose one of the framed photographs from my room and carry it out there. Heavy art books rest on the shelves in curated stacks. I notice the vase Jamie added, which doesn't look all that different from a couple of vases the designer chose, but to them it means something. I shift everything over a little bit to make room for the photograph of my mom and me. It was just the two of us for my whole life, at least all of my life that I can remember. Sure, a girlfriend now and then, but mostly just us. In the photograph, we're standing by the small secret waterfall we often hike to in Mill Valley. I'm probably about six. My pants are soaked to the knee and we're smiling huge, matching smiles. I want it to be here, in the living room, where everyone will remember. We had a whole life before this one.

Jamie and I move around each other, past each other, placing our old objects on shelves and in corners. Jamie sets a woven basket on the floor. I take my grandmother's quilt and toss it over an arm of the sofa. I unplug the lamp on my nightstand and turn the knob of Mom and Macey's door. Their room is really lovely. The same exposed rafter ceilings, the same transom windows, but larger. A handmade wood chair sits in a corner. And flanking the bed are matching lamps atop matching bedside tables. It's too perfect. I find which side is my mother's—I can tell by the stack of books waiting to be read—and, gently, I take her lamp off the table and replace it with our old one. When I turn to take a look from the doorway, Jamie joins me.

"Surprisingly, it really works," Jamie says. And it does. The lights are different but they complement each other, and with so much symmetry this one difference transforms the room. *We're together but we're not the same*, it seems to say. I hope Mom likes it. I carry the other light into my room and plug it in. It's shinier than our old things, but I feel that it belongs.

We've finished. Jamie collapses onto the living room rug. I curl up on the sofa with my grandmother's quilt over my feet.

"My mom drives me insane. Doesn't yours?" Jamie asks out of nowhere.

My eyes tear over and I'm too tired to even try holding them back. "No. I really love my mom."

"I mean, I *love* mine, too. Now I feel like a terrible person."

I laugh, wipe my eyes. "*No, I get it.* I get it. Of course, you love her. I'm the weird one. My mom and me . . . She's always let me be exactly who I want to be. She's just special, I guess. But Macey seems great, too. It's good, I guess, that they found each other."

It's Jamie's turn to laugh. "'It's good *I guess.*' Such conviction."

"Whatever. You looked miserable the whole wedding. Or bored."

"My mom, she just, like, she can't let anything be about me."

I'm confused. "I mean, it was their wedding. It wasn't supposed to be about us."

"That's not what I mean."

I sit back. The driftwood hovers above us and I like the look of it there more and more. "I have time."

"I don't really know how to say it. It's just—I came out, you know, and she was all over-the-top accepting, wanting to go to all these family support meetings, and then just a month later she came home and came out to *me.* After being married to my dad until just a few years ago and only ever dating men."

"Wow," I say. "Yeah. That must have felt weird." Jamie doesn't say anything. "It must have been hard," I add, wanting more. I'm ready to listen to whatever they say next.

But Jamie squirms. "It's gotten *very* late, you know," they say.

I laugh. "Okay, got it. No more on the subject." But it really is so late and I'm beginning to feel it in a new way. My scalp tingles; my eyes are heavy. "I've never stayed up all night before," I say.

"I think I'm actually sleeping right now. Right this moment." Jamie stretches their arms out and yawns, closes their eyes.

I smile at the way their short blond hair, carefully styled this afternoon, now sticks up on one side. I want to know more but I guess we have time. A lot of it. I can wait until they know I'm the kind of person who can listen well. Maybe some kind of trust will form between us when we've spent more time in this house together than we have as two high school students just passing each other in the halls, hearing snippets of gossip about the other, some surface-level judgments or opinions.

"Do you think we're ever going to feel like real siblings?" I ask.

It comes out before I can think better of the question. Part of me wishes I could unsay it, but the other part, the up-at-six-in-the-morning part, the all-bets-are-off part, the we-just-tore-apart-the-house part of me lets it hover in the air without apology.

Jamie's expression changes just the very slightest bit. A softening around their mouth and eyes. I try to breathe through the waiting—this moment of suspension—this fear of *did I reveal too much?*

They open one eye to peer at me. "Well, I *do* like you," they say, with half a smile. "Even though you have shitty taste in art."

Half shrugs, half smiles. How many more of Jamie's quirks will I discover? How many little things about me have they noticed without letting on? Maybe one day we'll talk about tonight, how new we were to each other, and how strange. How much our lives were changing in ways we couldn't even fathom yet.

"Let's go to the atrium," I say suddenly. "I want to be outside."

We open the sliding door from the living room. I'm still getting used to it, the open sky, surrounded by walls on all sides. We sit out there on the aesthetically perfect patio furniture, wishing it were more comfortable. We're sitting out there still when the first light touches the sky. And I want to say, "Jamie, the sun is rising on our new house." I want to say it simply without the ache of memory of soft light through my cabin's window. I'm not there yet, but I might be, someday. I hope I will be. For now, I'll leave it at this: We sit outside together, Jamie and me, on the morning after our mothers' wedding day. We sit without speaking. I am only slightly thinking about the silence and wondering if it means anything. It's almost comfortable. It's a start. And the sun rises and warms us.

WHEN YOU BRING A DOG TO PROM

by Anna Meriano

Jayla wakes me by calling four times in a row. When I finally answer, she says, "Start your shower, I'll be at your place in half an hour for mani-pedis."

I hang up and roll over, only for my phone to buzz thirty seconds later. Jayla has texted.

And don't you dare go back to bed.

I'm not worried, though, because the one bright side of my ill-conceived haircut is that my showers (like my hair) are eighty percent shorter now. I bury my head under my pillow.

The phone wakes me again.

"No-eh-MI, if you cannot swear to me that you are currently upright, I will seriously disown you."

"Okay, okay, ya voy, geez."

Don't ask me how I can hear Jayla's smug grin over the phone, but I definitely can when she says, "Thanks bestie. I just want everything to be perfect tonight."

"Yeah, the Perfect Prom. You may have mentioned something about that eighty-five times a day since January." Prom has eaten my best friend's brain, basically. We haven't been into school dances since freshman year (Jayla has definitely called them "heteronormative bullshit"), so I'm not sure why she's buying into this one so hard, but I've given up trying to resist.

I sit up, wiping sleep out of my eyes, and gain enough consciousness to ask, "Is Jayden coming for mani-pedis too?"

I can't decide what I want her answer to be, which is just part of the fun roller-coaster ride of being in love with your best friend's twin, who is also your other best friend. If he comes over for prom prep, I won't get the chance to wow him with my glamorous transformation that lets him see me in a totally new (make-out worthy) way. But if he *isn't* here, I'm going to spend the whole day wondering what he's up to and why he didn't come.

"Do not even talk about my brother right now, please." Jayla sighs in my ear as I shuffle to the bathroom and squeeze out the last dregs of toothpaste. "He would have been invited, but he's currently dead to me."

"Just because he didn't invite someone? You have to let that go. He said he'd pay you back for the unused ticket." Jayla has been moaning and groaning about Jayden's lack of prom date for weeks now, saying that it will ruin all the pictures and that he's doing this just to spite her. I support her sparkly prom dreams, but secretly I love that Jayden has passed on the chance for a romantic night with someone who might try to kiss him or dance on him or who knows what else. He's such a human cinnamon roll that I'm sure he would give his date his full attention, and I want his attention for myself because I am greedy for his goofy jokes and easy banter and solid taste in memes.

I do have a prom date, but it hardly counts because it's Austin Kim, my stand partner from orchestra (where we both slack our way through the easier second-violin part), and his parents are making him go with a girl instead of his boyfriend because they are terrible.

"Um, keep up," Jayla says. "He did ask someone."

It's a good thing I'm standing over the sink, because my mouth falls open so fast a stream of toothpaste foam spills out.

So much for the Perfect Prom.

"Who?"

Hour 6: Noon

Dodge Jenkins. The name repeats in my head while Jayla slathers some kind of cream into my wet hair that's supposed to keep the curls curly instead of Medusa-esque. He invited Dodge Jenkins to prom, and he didn't even text me about it. Dodge Jenkins, who has blue hair and brings their dog to school and once organized a courtyard lie-in to protest gun violence, who seems to exist on a separate plane from the normal high school bullshit the rest of our five-hundred-person senior class participates in. Confidence (or apathy or something) keeps them above it all. I'm not trying to put people in boxes, but I would've pegged them to attend the queer anti-prom instead.

"I think that works!" Jayla declares, spinning me so I can see the effects of the Perfect Curl Styling Cream. Her dark hair is shiny smooth, so the only expertise she has here is all the googling she did to be supportive of the haircut. Baffling as her prom obsession may be, I appreciate the type-A structure she brings to my life, and I know she always has my back.

My hair does not have my back. I should've kept my aesthetic experimentation in my pants until college.

Maybe I just need to own the dandelion look. After all, Dodge Jenkins sports what can only be described as a turquoise fluff undercut, and they seem to be doing quite well for themself in terms of date-catching.

We take a break to let my hair dry and pick up lunch from Whataburger. Jayla warns me to fill up because once she applies my makeup, she does not want me ruining it by eating. I obediently dip my chicken fingers in creamy gravy and scowl as Mom bustles in to take another round of preparation photos "for posterity."

Dodge Jenkins. How does Jayden even know them? Where exactly was I when this friendship was developing? I guess it doesn't have to be a friendship. I guess people can be *interested in* people they aren't friends with (haha, can't relate).

"Hello, Noemi." Jayla waves her hand in front of my face. "Are you listening? We have so many eyeliner decisions to make."

I blink at her. "Is Dodge going to bring their dog?" We're all used to the emotional support golden retriever at school. It's a little weird, but no weirder than Dodge's whole "Luna Lovegood meets Bilbo Baggins" vibe. But I don't love dogs, especially big ones. Growing up in a neighborhood that takes leash laws as an unrealistic suggestion will have that effect.

Jayla blows out a long breath. "That's a good question. That would make a super cute photo op, actually. I might be able to work with that."

Hour 12: 6 p.m.

Austin Kim is ditching me to take his boyfriend to queer anti-prom.

I would take the news harder, but I already put my dress on, and it turns out my curves look too good in tulle to be disappointed by this development. Also, good for Austin Kim and his boyfriend.

Jayla's type-A personality didn't react well.

"We made plans for a reason! How dare he stand up my best friend! Why does everybody think this is like, some casual group hang that you can duck into or out of last minute? I made a playlist curated to the specific members of the group! Why are you not more upset about this?"

I offered to help her rework the playlist, but she basically hissed at me so now I'm hiding in the bathroom admiring myself—from the neck down at least. My hair is still a disaster that I'm only making worse by fiddling with it. We have at least a half hour to kill before Jayla's date shows up for pictures. And Jayden. And his date, which he has now.

If Austin had bailed twenty-four hours earlier, things could have been different. Twenty-four hours ago, Jayden didn't have a prom date either. We could have commiserated and made a

pact to go alone together. We would have watched Jayla and
Roger Donovan exchange their corsage and boutonniere and
take photos. And then Mom or Mrs. Dajao would have said *we*
should take a photo together, and Jayden would have positioned
his arms around me . . . and then fallen in love with me forever.

But now that moment belongs to Dodge Jenkins.

I tug another curl that will never be coaxed back into place.

My phone buzzes because I've been texting Jayden. I mean,
I'm always texting Jayden in a rambling stream of conversation that has no beginnings or endings, just pauses and threads
that get picked up or passed over. I'm complaining about Jayla
and Austin and my hair, and he's sending pics of his extremely
wonky pocket square. Neither of us mentions Dodge Jenkins.

Jayla knocks. "My brother says I have to apologize or he'll
show up in swim trunks."

I smile against the door. Jayla's high-strung perfectionism
and Jayden's people-pleasing chill don't seem like a good combination for sibling friendship, but they balance each other out
nicely. "I thought you weren't talking to him."

"Nah, I'm over that. Dodge seems cool. I always wanted to
get to know them better. And queer folks have to stick together."
Jayla's bi and I'm still trying to figure out what I am (other than
inconveniently in love with one particular boy). "I just don't like
surprises. Not that you've noticed, I'm sure."

I laugh and open the door. Jayla hops onto the bathroom
counter, smoothing the skirt of her two-piece midnight blue
dress. "I'm sorry I yelled. And I'm sorry about Austin."

I shrug. "I'm sorry I wasn't taking it seriously. I'm not trying
to ruin your night, I just think it's good that he and Omar are
together."

"Yeah, the anti-prom sounds fun."

I chew my lip. I don't want to upset Jayla, but this seems like a good opening to ask the question she's been avoiding all semester. "I kind of wondered why you didn't want to go to it. Or why you're so into the prom phenomenon."

Jayla grimaces. "Yeah, I'm not usually in favor of compulsory heterosexuality, but . . ." She flips her complicated braid over her shoulder and leans against the mirror. "You're going to think this is silly."

"Will not. I think it's silly that you waited this long to talk about it."

"It's just . . . Mom's been talking about prom since I was a freshman. She got so excited picking the dress. You know how she is."

Mrs. Dajao is trying her best, but her reaction when Jayla came out last year was not immediate and uncomplicated acceptance. It's not Jayla's responsibility to fix that by being perfect, but it's not really my job to tell Jayla how to handle her family either. Still, I can't help pointing out, "Austin Kim had the same idea."

"I'm not ditching my significant other and hiding my real life, though. I'm just . . . presenting a certain version of myself. I want to prove I can do traditional milestone things. Like, if I can give Mom a nice-looking prom photo to show to her church friends, she won't worry that I'm on the wrong track. She'll realize I'm doing okay."

We both let out a long breath. Jayla dabs a finger against her lower lid eyeliner. "Okay, pause, no emotions until the pictures are done. It's not all that deep. I also think dressing up and being fancy is fun. Plus, prom movies are the best."

I laugh and think better of mentioning *Carrie*. Jayla's more into rom-coms; Jayden's the one who'll do horror marathons with me (often curled up on one of our couches, often sharing a blanket, always resulting in very confusing in-love-with-best-friend feels). "Okay, fine, Perfect Prom. You already know I'm on board."

"Thanks," Jayla says. "But it's your night too. What's your perfect prom?"

I open my mouth, then close it. My perfect prom is the one Dodge Jenkins got, because I didn't even try for it.

Prom is such a weird concept. My family wants a million pictures. Pop culture wants me to lose my virginity (ew). Austin wants to make a declaration. Jayla wants the night to prove something.

My perfect prom is not a safe snapshot of us as we are. My perfect prom would set the tone for the next four years: something different. Our high school is big and public and at least a hundred of our classmates are going to the same big public university, the one my mom and older brothers all attended, and I can already see how the transition will be smoothed by familiar faces and experiences.

But I don't want more of the same. I want something risky and untested, and I want to face it unafraid.

Hour 13: 7 p.m.

Mom starts flashing her camera the second the doorbell rings. *Click*. Me and Jayla running to the door. *Click*. Pausing and primping with one hand on the knob. *Click*. Jayla rolling her eyes from two different angles, shooing Mrs. Dajao and her camera away from the door so Jayden can come in.

"I thought it was going to be someone real," Jayla complains, making a face at her brother. He retaliates by tugging the end of her braid.

"Good to see you too," he tells her. "You look fancy." He steps past her and looks at me, and I think I see his eyes flick up and down for one stomach-fluttering second. "Hey. I'm glad you survived a day with the Prom Police. Cool dress." And then his eyes flick over me again, this time I'm sure of it.

He's wearing a suit. A *nice* one that didn't come out of the orchestra storage closet. A tux, maybe? I don't know the difference. His dark hair is freshly washed and combed back out of his face, and his pocket square turned out perfectly and I can't remember whatever casual thing I had planned to say while lounging seductively against the side table.

Click, probably. Me ogling Jayden right in front of both of our families, embarrassingly enshrined in the scrapbooks for the rest of eternity.

I've only had one other major crush, and it lasted through all of middle school and most of freshman year. What I remember about liking Bennet is how bad it felt. Every time he passed me in the hall without saying hello, every time he gave a confused shrug in response to one of my jokes, I'd spend days dwelling on all the things that were wrong with me. Back then, Jayden was the one who listened to my insecure ramblings and joked me out of my bad moods (Jayla told me three times in no uncertain terms that Bennet wasn't worth it and then refused to indulge me any further). I'm still full of insecurity now, but

I'm going on my third year of crushing on Jayden, and he never makes me feel like I'm weird, or boring, or annoying. He's nice to everyone, and he's specifically nice to me, and that's the part I actually care about. The way he looks in a tux is just a bonus.

I'm going to say that he looks nice. I'm working up to it, giving him eye-flicks of my own and smiling, which makes him smile at me, which makes me smile even more, but then Jayla throws the front door open again and my face falls. A tiny green car has just pulled up to the curb, and out hops a medium-sized person in suspenders and a bowtie accompanied by a very large golden retriever.

I feel the pang of missed opportunity again, and even though I know it's not Dodge Jenkins's fault, I can't help but wish they hadn't shown up just yet.

Jayden greets Dodge Jenkins and their dad. Mrs. Dajao makes Jayla spin and lets out an excited burst of Tagalog. We take more "candid" pictures. Eventually Mom offers Mrs. Dajao and Mr. Jenkins some of her superfood juices and leads them inside while we all gather on the porch to catch our breath off camera. I smile at Suka, Dodge's dog, who is extremely polite about wagging her tail at everyone but not jumping or slobbering or doing any of the other things that make me wary of big dogs. I don't quite have it in me to smile at Dodge, but it's a start.

"Do you have a dog?" Dodge asks. They're holding the leash short and standing in the doorway. "Suka's great at school but she can get kind of reactive around other animals. We're working on it."

I shake my head, eyeing the golden retriever suspiciously. What exactly does "reactive" mean?

"Great," Dodge nods. "And nobody has allergies?"

If I say I'm allergic, maybe Dodge and Suka will stay outside, miss the posed photos, and I'll get my chance to be oh-so-unwillingly forced into a picture with Jayden.

It's not a nice thought, especially when Dodge looks slightly nervous, twisting the extra length of the leash around their hand. Which is more than understandable; I would probably die before I'd show up almost unannounced to a prom group of virtual strangers.

"Nope!" Jayla answers before I can. "We're all ready for you. And you too," she coos at Suka, patting the dog's head as she enters. "You both look great."

Dodge adjusts their floral bowtie and mumbles something as they bury their head in Suka's silky fur.

And then, finally, Roger arrives on a bike, suit jacket draped on a hanger over his shoulder. He's a lacrosse player, the whitest and nerdiest group of jocks, and he kind of looks like pre-serum Captain America, but he's nice enough and he'll definitely look good on Jayla's arm, and vice versa.

The parents swarm again, cameras capturing Roger's ascent onto the porch.

"So B-Dog's house is on for the after party," he tells Jayla, slipping his jacket on. "And I told him we'd all be there." He high-fives Dodge, claps Jayden on the shoulder, and gives me a thumbs-up.

"Do you mean Brandon Wasserstein?" Jayden asks.

"Yeah, B-Dog!"

I cover a snort by cautiously patting Suka. Her fur is as soft as it looks. I accidentally catch Dodge's eye and notice that they're also hiding a smile.

"I want to go to the official afterprom," Jayla says. "But I guess we can go after that, right Ma?"

"His parents are supervising," Jayden adds. "It won't be anything wild."

"As long as you stay together and answer your phones," Mrs. Dajao says. "Now get together so we can do a whole group."

I'm an uneven fifth wheel, and Mom positions me in the center of the photo, like the eye of a hurricane of cuteness. *Click.* Poor Noemi, all alone. *Click.* Maybe if you all put your arms around her she'll look less out of place. *Click.* Have her hold the dog.

"Mom, this is humiliating," I mutter at that last suggestion.

"It's not," Jayden says softly behind me. "They're just having fun. Nobody cares if you go with someone or not. And you look amazing."

Did he just say "amazing"? *Click.* One picture ruined because I'm staring back at him instead of looking at the camera.

"Yeah I love that color on you," Dodge adds, which makes me feel like an extreme jerk for still kind of wishing they weren't here and I could stare at Jayden in peace.

Hour 17: 11 p.m.

Prom might not be perfect, but a couple hours in, I have to admit it's not terrible. Sure, Roger hasn't stopped trying to convince Jayla to skip the school-sanctioned afterprom entirely to spend more time at "B-Dog's" house party, and Dodge keeps pulling Jayden onto the dance floor with a level of energy and enthusiasm I wasn't expecting, but the music is decent, the buffet is good, and I like seeing how people dressed up. Gabby DiMarco ditched her combat boots and black lipstick and went full pink sequins, while super-shy Helene from chem rocks fishnets and lace. Dodge gets a bunch of compliments on their bowtie from other drama kids with candy-colored hair and statement accessories. And Jayden . . . well, I continue enjoying his suit.

I wonder what people think of my look. I wanted to surprise everyone (well, mostly one person), but it's hard to tell if I accomplished it.

Jayla pulls me out of my seat, and we all dance in a ring of flailing limbs. Even Suka joins, trotting around the circle while we applaud her fabulous bowtie collar. The music is cheesy and a critical mass of our classmates are drunk and everyone is sweating through their nice clothes. I like this more than I expected to.

Jayla ducks away for a water break, and Roger's lacrosse friends lure him off to chant something incomprehensible at full volume. I lose track of Dodge as the circle disintegrates, and moving bodies push me closer to Jayden, who's dancing his heart out: hair flopping over closed eyes and serious duck face. I step back to avoid crashing into him, and spin around into a surprise hug from Helene from chem, who is very happy to see me and also might have gotten someone to share their flask. Then the song ends and the dance floor stalls as we all hear the slower softer beat of the new music, and people turn to each other or book it back to the tables as fast as possible.

Slow dance.

I'm planning to flee. But there's Jayden, standing with his back to me now, one hand in his hair. My mouth goes dry because, well, this could be it. A chance for things to be different. A chance to make things different.

At our first official high school dance, back when I was moping over Bennet, I remember Jayden turned to me, face red, and stammered something that sounded like half a question. I was too surprised to process it, and when he reached out I flinched away, and that was that. He never tried to ask me to dance again.

A year later, when I went to the Dajaos' house for a movie marathon instead of going to another official high school dance, Jayla fell asleep early and Jayden and I got into a popcorn fight that turned into a scramble to clean the couch, a mess of grappling hands and whispered laughter. It was comfortable and exciting and my stomach dropped with disappointment when there were no more spilled kernels to fight over. That's when I got punched in the face with the realization that I was in love with him.

I push through a few dancers, reaching for Jayden's shoulder. It's a familiar touch, but my face heats at the warmth of it. Everything feels slow and important in the dim crush of the dance floor. Jayden turns, his eyes meet mine, the tiniest tilt of his head asks what's up. And I'm staring deer-in-headlights back at him, watching his face change in slow motion from casual to focused curiosity, and he's leaning closer, eyes still locked on mine, and he's shouting above the music, "Did you want to—?"

"There you are!"

Dodge crashes between us, panting a little. "Do you mind if we head out? I need to take Suka for a walk, and Jayla says the buses to afterprom are only running for another half hour."

It's probably not cool to say this about someone who got bullied out of their old school—*but*—I seriously want to smack Dodge Jenkins.

Jayden looks from me to them and back. "Uh, what?"

"Yeah, sure," I say. "Let's go."

We follow Dodge back to the table where Jayla offers cupped handfuls of water to Suka, who splatters the Perfect Prom dress with droplets from her lolling tongue.

"Oh good, you found them," Jayla says, wiping her hands on the stained silver tablecloth. "Hurry up. We need to find Roger too."

The slow song fades away, and couples morph back into individual dancers, and we all traipse off toward the chanting of the lacrosse team. Jayla's determined to get the rest of her perfect night. I'm still mourning mine.

Hour 18: Midnight

"This will be the FINAL bus to the bowling alley!" a frazzled PTA mom with a megaphone screams for the fifth time. "Please make a LINE so that we will be ready to load when it arrives!"

In spite of her reasonable instructions, the mass of students in the parking lot ignores her. There's a general current toward the curb where the last bus should be pulling up any minute, but nobody's in any hurry.

"We could just miss it," Roger suggests. He's the main reason we haven't left yet, as it turns out that he's as bad at leaving his jock friends as my mom is at leaving her chismosa friends after mass. "Catch a Lyft to B-Dog's house instead."

"Afterprom is part of the whole experience," Jayla says. "My mom was on the planning committee. There's supposed to be a photo booth. We can leave once we've gotten pictures."

Roger shrugs. He's been a good sport, but I recognize the tight smile he gives Jayla because it's the same one I gave her all morning.

My toes are raw from hours in heels and my nerves are raw from the slow-dance-that-wasn't. I lean against a cylindrical stone parking barrier. In the bushes behind me, something furry with light-reflecting eyes peeks out, and I debate the pros and cons of getting rabies (might get a hospital-bedside love confession from Jayden; would ruin Jayla's plans pretty definitively; also possible death). The group mills near the curb, Jayla talking soothingly to Roger while Dodge stands on tiptoes to whisper something into Jayden's ear that makes him laugh.

That laugh is enough to pull me forward. "What's up?" I ask, limping to retake my spot at Jayden's elbow. He just shakes his head, and Dodge smiles an infuriating smile. "Didn't Suka need to pee a while ago?" I snap. "There's grass right over there."

"Oh, thanks, yeah." Dodge slaps their forehead and then shoves the leash into my hand for some reason. "Do you mind? Call me if I need to bring a bag."

I'm too caught off guard to argue, and pretty soon Suka and I are wandering back toward the bushes alone while Dodge and their stupid undone bowtie and unbuttoned collar lean in closer to Jayden.

The last bus pulls up, a nice one with individual seats, which means you can't squeeze three people into a row, which means I'm going to be the odd one out again. Suka strains at the edge of her leash, sniffing at the bushes.

I slip my phone out of my pocket (Best. Dress. Ever.) and hover my thumb over my messages. It's too desperate to text Jayden right now, even though that's who I want to talk to whenever the world gets quiet and my thoughts get loud. I steal a glance over my shoulder and startle because he's looking right at me. I clutch the phone and the leash in one hand, leaving my other hand free to comb through my hair. And then my phone buzzes and Jayden's name lights up the screen, and as I fumble in my eagerness to read it, the leash falls to the ground. Suka seizes her moment and darts toward the bushes, yapping loudly as the cat-or-opossum-or-whatever streaks away.

"Suka!" I stumble forward, tripping on my skirt as I try to grab the dog or the leash.

Behind me I hear Dodge scream. I spin around, look at my friends' frozen expressions of horror, and then, while the rest of our classmates file onto the last bus to afterprom, we all take off running after the rapidly disappearing yellow dog.

Hour 19: 1 a.m.

I should have brought some damn flats. My sparkly heels dangle heavy from my fingertips as we all scurry toward Rice Avenue. The balls of my feet burn like the sidewalk is made of hot coals, while my ankles ache at the stretch of being angled normally again. Every step feels a little bit like penance, but it doesn't make the guilt lessen at all.

"Can y'all slow down?" Roger complains. He's lagging half a block behind me, which doesn't seem right since he's the athlete and the one wearing shoes. Jayden hangs back with him, while Dodge strides almost a full block ahead, hands shoved in their pockets and head tucked to the ground.

"At least she didn't head toward the freeway," Jayla huffs, tugging Dodge's rolled-up sleeve. Dodge slows down and nods gratefully when Jayla puts a hand on their elbow.

"I think we should call a Lyft," Roger says for the twentieth time. "This doesn't make any sense. And didn't you want to make it to afterprom?"

"Shut up, Roger," Jayla calls. "This is more important."

I frown over my shoulder until my eyes meet Jayden's. He shakes his head and rolls his eyes, then lengthens his stride to leave Roger behind.

"What's his problem?" I ask when Jayden falls in step with me. I'm more annoyed than I need to be, just because it feels good to be mad at someone besides myself. "Nobody forced him to come with us."

"Right?" Jayden snorts and suddenly my chest doesn't feel so tight. "I was just about to give him the brotherly seal of approval too." He shakes his head.

"I don't think Jayla particularly wants to date him anyway, she just picked the most photogenic person she could tolerate for the night."

"Well, still, he's acting like complete . . ."

"Basura," we say in unison, sharing an *our people were colonized by the same assholes* smile.

"I guess you can't trust someone just because they're fun at a party." Jayden sighs.

"Yeah, you should withhold approval until you really know how someone will react to a crisis," I say. "Like, for example, will they panic and hide under a blanket instead of helping their friend babysit their crying infant sister?"

Jayden laughs at the memory and bumps my shoulder with his. "Janelle is almost eight now; you have to let that go. I did apologize, several times. And she was *so loud.*" I snort and shake my head. "And by the way, I am an excellent babysitter these days. How do you think I paid for this sweet suit?"

"Clearance aisle?" I guess, earning another shoulder bump. "What? That's where I got my dress. Are you being classist about savvy shopping?"

"I'm just trying to point out that I'm not an incompetent man-baby in a domestic crisis," Jayden says. ". . . Anymore."

"Good to know."

"Hey so about earlier," Jayden starts, but then I step on a twig and double over in pain. I hop on one foot for a minute and lean on Jayden to put my horrible shoes back on. Whatever he was going to say gets lost as he instead points to Roger. "I think he's calling that Lyft." Roger has stopped walking, and his phone screen illuminates his furrowed brow. "Should we tell Jayla?"

"Nah," I shrug, "bigger worries." Jayla is talking softly to Dodge, rubbing small circles into their back. I gulp. "This is all my fault."

"Don't," he says. "You didn't do anything wrong."

I did several things wrong, actually, starting this morning when I put serious evil eye vibes on Dodge Jenkins and ending when I endangered their dog and ruined their night. Why isn't Jayden mad at me? Why is he walking back here with me while

Jayla comforts his date? All I wanted was to spend this night with Jayden, and now the bite of guilt is ruining it.

"You okay in those heels?" Jayden asks. "We can switch shoes."

"I'm fine," I reply. And to prove this obvious lie, I set off quickly and confidently, leaving Roger behind and closing the gap with Jayla and Dodge. Jayden follows, and politely stays quiet when I trip on a sidewalk seam and have to grab him to keep myself from pitching forward.

Hour 20: 2 a.m.

Walking is so much slower than driving. Texas was not designed with pedestrians in mind. I'm tired and thirsty and it's been ages since we last spotted Suka.

Dodge stops at the end of the block. "We could be getting farther away," they groan. "There's no guarantee she headed straight." They snort a choked-up laugh. "You wouldn't really expect her to, considering her owner."

Jayla bites a perfectly painted nail. "Do you want to split up?" She holds her phone in her hand, which buzzes with text messages every twenty seconds or so. "We can keep going straight, and Jayden and Noemi can look down side streets."

My heart does a somersault, but Dodge is already saying, "No, no. It's hopeless." They pat their pockets absently. "I should have brought treats with me—I always bring treats. And she should never have pulled away like that."

"There was a cat or something," I say. Guilt forms a lump in my throat.

"Oh my god," Jayla grumbles as her phone buzzes again. I see a screen full of texts from Roger asking her to come to the house party, sending Brandon's address and strings of emojis that I interpret to mean "B-*Dog*'s (dog emoji) *house party* (house and confetti popper) is *number one!* (gold medals and more party poppers)."

Dodge buries their face in their hands.

"It's going to be okay," Jayden says. "If we don't find her tonight, we can try again in the morning. Put up signs, post on that neighborhood app for old racist busybodies. Somebody will find her."

"She's not wearing a tag," Dodge whispers. "I thought the bowtie was cute and I didn't want to mess up the aesthetic and—I'm the worst. I'm the worst and she's lost and I'm sorry I ruined y'all's night. I knew this was too much for her. But you invited the emotional support animal kid, so I assumed you wanted the emotional support animal."

"Shh," Jayla tries to stop Dodge's spiraling. "Hang on a second. Breathe."

Jayden steps forward. "I didn't invite 'the emotional support animal kid.' I invited you because you're cool."

I recognize an anxiety attack when I see one, but I'm too busy drowning in my own thoughts to throw out lifelines to anyone else. It's strange. I always thought of Dodge Jenkins as cool and alternative, and it's surprising to see them self-conscious, beating themselves up for making decisions based on what other people will think. Acting like me.

"It's okay," Jayla croons.

"It was an accident," Jayden says.

They both look at me, waiting for me to say something, and all that comes out is, "I let go of the leash."

Dodge Jenkins goes through a whole face journey starting at surprise, taking a long pitstop in blazing anger, and ending somewhere alongside resignation. It's kind of like a time-lapse recording of my day.

"I'm so sorry," I whisper.

Dodge nods at the ground. I don't know how I can hope for forgiveness when I've been hanging onto my grudge for a lot longer with less provocation.

Jayla cuts the silence. "Let's go home. I'll call a ride."

"I'll do it," Jayden says. "Babysitting money."

Before they can work it out, Jayla's phone rings. She taps the screen with a frustrated sigh.

"Hello?" Roger asks over speakerphone. "Is that you? Are you coming?"

Jayla sighs. "Actually, I think we're going to get a ride . . ."

"Yes!" Roger shouts. "Okay good, how far away are you? I think you can find it, but I'll wait outside so you won't miss it—" Jayla taps the screen again. "Oops," she deadpans. "My finger slipped."

Jayden looks at his phone. "Huh. We're actually walking distance from Brandon's house."

"We should go," Dodge says. We all protest, but they shake their head. "If we're not finding Suka until tomorrow anyway . . ." Jayla puts a hand on their shoulder. They smile crookedly. "Thank you for trying. Really. You missed afterprom for me . . . Uh, all of you. Y'all didn't have to do that."

"Obviously we did," Jayla says, and I tilt my head at her because I know why I had to help Dodge and I know why

Jayden had to, but Jayla has basically no reason to drop her plans like this.

Dodge shrugs. "We should go to the party."

We start walking, quiet and tired. I fall behind in my heels, and to my surprise Dodge hangs back with me. I wait for them to say something, but they don't, and pretty soon I'm too uncomfortable to maintain the silence.

"You can scream at me if you want. I deserve it."

"Oh, ha, no." Dodge fiddles with the cuff of their sleeve. "I was going to see if . . . uh, you seemed kind of upset earlier. At me? I know I kind of showed up out of nowhere, but—"

"God, no," I stop them. "You're good. You're awesome, actually. I'm . . ." I suck in a breath. "I'm kind of jealous of you." Dodge's eyebrows jump, and I quickly change my mind about being brave and honest. "I mean, jealous of how you're just out here doing the 'be yourself' thing like it's no big deal. I've been ruining my own life with overthinking since I left the womb."

Dodge snorts. "Noemi, I am the royal sovereign of overthinking. That's why I don't talk to anyone! That's why it takes me three years to so much as interact tangentially with my crush!"

I blink. "But . . . you have blue hair." Which is a ridiculous response, but how does an overthinker work up the nerve to dye their hair blue?

"I also bring a badly trained therapy dog to school. Does that say 'stable' to you?"

"I mean . . . I guess it just says Dodge?"

It's their turn to blink at me. "Well. Um. Thanks for that."

I take another deep breath. "Listen," I say as fast as I can, "it's not my business but if you have a crush on Jayden I'm happy for you and—"

"I don't have a crush on Jayden," Dodge says with a slight smile. "You can drop the jealousy hackles."

"Wait, what?" My heart pounds in my ears. I'm probably going through a whole face journey.

"*Dodge!*" Jayla's voice, half a block ahead, squeaks, and then there's a loud yap, and then Dodge has forgotten about me because they're booking it toward the front yard of what must be Brandon's house, where Roger stands, one arm waving above his head and the other holding a very familiar leash.

I do my best to catch up while Dodge sinks to the ground and Suka licks their face and hands.

"What took y'all so long?" Roger asks. "I've been texting you that I found her! I told you it made more sense to search in a car!"

Jayden groans something about ambiguous emojis, and Jayla laughs hysterically and throws her arms around Dodge, who might be crying as they stand up, but they play it off as dog slobber. I stand on the sidewalk, relief hitting so hard I'm afraid I might collapse if I try to take a single step.

I didn't ruin everything. I messed up, but my mistakes aren't permanent. And, Dodge Jenkins and I might actually get along?

Roger gestures toward the house, and Dodge slings an arm around him and another around Jayla and they all head inside, Suka tangling them up in her leash.

Jayden walks over to me on the sidewalk. "You good?"

"I'm . . ." About to faint. So goddamn happy that dog is okay. In love with you. ". . . Sorry. It's been a weird night."

"Tell me about it," he says.

I smile. "At least Jayla got her pictures before things got all sweaty and teary."

"I hate to admit she was right, but . . ." He shrugs. "Well, it worked out in the end. Everything can go back to normal now."

I turn to meet his eyes, which is always dangerous territory. "Is that what you want?" God, where did that come from? It sounded way too dramatic. "I mean, uh, is the goal for everything to stay the way it is?"

"Yeah, why wouldn't it be?" His head tilts and his eyes bore into mine and he's so goddamn cute, but his response crushes me. He *wants* things to stay the same. He doesn't have heart-eyes feelings for me.

"We should go in," I mutter. I spin and run up the walkway toward the music and the light and hope no one notices my suddenly sniffling nose and red eyes.

There's a huge pile of shoes just inside the door, mostly heels. I happily kick mine off and then wander farther inside before Jayden can catch up with me. Brandon's house is big, a mix of dark polished wood and beige fabric. The kind of house that screams, "We love to entertain and we never leave our dirty dishes in the sink for a week and a half." The vibe inside isn't that different from prom, just a larger percentage of folks I recognize in a smaller area. There's music but no dancing. There are people in the pool outside and people dozing on couches in their prom clothes or in towels and T-shirts. There's a TV set up for Mario Kart, and a ping-pong table that's being used for actual ping-pong (I guess Brandon's parents really are supervising).

I want to find my people. Jayla. And I guess Dodge now, too. I check the living room and kitchen with no luck, but I catch sight of turquoise hair winking from the end of an empty hallway. When I get closer I also see the midnight of Jayla's dress. Then I notice that their faces are really close together. Then a second later the gap closes as they kiss, and like a second after that they're making out, which, okay, that escalated quickly.

Well, Dodge said they didn't have a crush on *Jayden*.

Suka barks and jumps to join in the fun, breaking the kiss into a mess of giggles and red faces, and then of course they both see me.

"Glahhhh sorry," I mumble, "I was just . . ."

"Called it!" Roger's voice behind me is loud and triumphant. "Called it like six hours ago! I am so good." He pushes past me and high-fives both startled parties. Then he points over my shoulder. "You owe me Takis on Monday."

I glance behind me. Jayden stands looking slightly bewildered, eyes darting from me to the clump of people and dog.

Jayla cocks a hand on her hip. "You bet against me?" she asks indignantly.

"He also got me in position to make my move, so give him some credit," Dodge says softly. Jayla smiles a bright goofy smile. If Dodge makes her lose her ability to scold, I firmly approve this pairing.

We all pour back out into the main body of the party, congregating around a table of chips and dips. Jayla gets close enough to whisper "perfect prom" in my ear, her hand tangled with Dodge's.

"I'm happy for you, but don't pretend this was your vision all along," I tease.

Jayla shrugs. "I'm not saying I was wrong, but I might be saying that Austin Kim was right."

Dodge rolls their eyes and whispers something I miss, but it makes Jayla laugh. My heart twists with love and just a tinge of wistful jealousy.

"Noemi!" Helene from chem appears holding a bottle of water, their eyes a little less glassy now. "You made it! Isn't this so fun?"

"Yeah it's been quite a night," I say. "I love your dress by the way. I don't know if I said that."

"Thanks." They bite their lip and smile. "I wanted to try something dramatic. And speaking of which, I'm in love with your haircut."

"Yeah?" I touch my head, eyes finding my reflection in the dark window across the room. The curls have long escaped their prison of holding cream, but they're sticking together better than they do when I panic and run a brush through them. Now that it's not such a shock to see my earlobes, the cut actually looks . . . kind of good. It looks like me.

Maybe I should trust myself a little more.

"I'll be right back," I say. Helene has already turned back to the chips anyway. I adjust my dress, shake out my curls, and then muster every drop of confidence I have. I need to find Jayden.

Hour 21: 3 a.m.

He's sitting on the edge of the pool next to his shoes and socks, pants rolled up and feet distorted in the green-tinged water.

"Hey." I hike up my skirt and sink down next to him. It's quiet out here, and the water feels amazing on my poor feet. But my blood pounds like ocean waves.

"Hey." He dips a finger into the pool to make a current that sends a tiny leaf floating toward me. "Hectic night. I feel like I keep missing things."

Oh. Of course. I'm so focused on making my confession, I totally forgot his sister just made out with his prom date. "I'm sorry. Are you really upset?"

"About Dodge? No! That's the whole reason I invited them."

"Oh." I try not to feel too pleased by this information. "Then what . . . ?"

"I don't know. Never mind." He kicks his feet and rubs the back of his neck.

"I came out here to tell you . . ." I start.

Jayden's voice overlaps mine. "Earlier at the dance, you came up and it seemed like you wanted to . . ."

I need him to stop talking. I can't focus when he's talking. I want to listen when he's talking, because he always has something interesting or funny or nice to tell me, and I can't handle that right now because I need to stay focused on what I came here to say.

"No, don't worry about that," I interrupt him. "Whatever that was it wasn't . . . it was nothing. You were saying before how you want things to go back to normal. But we're all going to college, so . . ." Jayden is staring at me. Of course he's staring at me; I'm making zero sense. "It could easily be, you know, another four years of the same thing, but that's not what I want."

"Oh." Jayden looks into the pool. I can't read his closed-off expression as anything other than discomfort. I'm making him uncomfortable. "Yeah, sorry, I didn't mean it like that," he says after a long pause. "You can obviously reinvent yourself in college if you want to. I won't cramp your style. I just meant that things could go back to normal for tonight. For the rest of the year or whatever."

I don't totally follow, and I'm tempted to leave the conversation at that, but I've already started, and you can't stop a haircut halfway through. "I don't want that either."

"Wow, okay. So you just, what, don't want to be friends or something?" Jayden laughs, but his voice is strained.

"Um, obviously I want to be friends." He's not getting it, and I need him to get it. We talk all the time—why are we so bad at communicating? "I just don't want to be like, 'Yep here we are, two parts of a friend group, such excellent pals.'"

"And . . . that's different from saying you don't want to be friends? Or you don't want to spend as much time together?"

"Yes, it's different! I'm saying I want to spend *more* time together! I'm saying I want to be your friend and also date you!"

Dead silence. It's like I'm holding my chopped-off ponytail in my hand all over again, the breeze on my neck freezing cold.

"You don't have to say anything! I just wanted to tell you!"

"No that's . . . I want to say something."

"Well you don't have to."

"Well I want to."

"Okay. Go ahead."

Jayden grunts, kicks his feet in the water. He lifts his hand off the lip of the pool, first moves it toward my face, then pulls it down so it settles where the tips of his fingers barely touch my hand. "Um, yes?"

The touch already stopped my heart. Nothing else can surprise me. "Yes what?"

"Yes I want to date you?"

"Oh." *Oh.* "Yes. Good." Jayden wants to date me. It makes
no sense and also it's the only thing that makes any sense. I
should probably say something with more syllables, but I can't
find the right words, so I flip my hand palm-up and curl my fingers tightly around Jayden's. This works even better than texting
him as a way to calm my spinning brain. Finally, I can speak.
"Why didn't you say anything? Or invite me to prom?"

"I was afraid you'd say no."

There's a lot I could say, but it all feels extremely unimpor-
tant compared to the brown of Jayden's eyes and the flop of his
hair and the electric touch of his fingers on my palm. The yard
feels like a snow globe, air thick and liquid and swirling.

"We're, uh, we're not going to make out at Brandon's house
party, are we?" I ask breathlessly.

Jayden laughs. "No, uh, not unless . . . we definitely don't
have to."

"Just because there are windows everywhere." I gesture
with my free hand.

"Yeah." He pulls his hand away, and I shift to get it back.

"And I'm not super into PDA."

"Yeah." He grins at me, squeezes my fingers.

"And, no offense to Jayla and Dodge, but I'd rather *tell*
them about us than show them."

Jayden snorts, leans to bump my shoulder.

There's a lot more I could say, but instead we sit in silence
and it's the perfect kind of different.

Hour 26: 8 a.m.

My eyes blur staring out the car window. I'm so tired. We spent the night playing ping-pong, Mario Kart, and one frustrating half attempt at Monopoly with twelve people. I'm not usually a fan of all-nighters, and Jayla even less so, but nobody wanted this experience to end. Thankfully, one jolt from Jayden's coffee-brown eyes is better than any real source of caffeine.

The party got a second wind at dawn when everyone stood at the windows cheering that we made it, which was when Brandon's dad woke up and made waffles and very politely suggested that people take their breakfasts to go. We weren't sure how a Lyft driver would react to Suka, so Roger woke up his younger brother and convinced him to come pick us all up. Jayden carried my heels out onto the street because I refused to put them back on.

"How long have we been awake?" I ask, watching stop signs speed past, catching the morning light. I only meant for Jayden to hear me, but my sense of a whisper has been destroyed by loud music and lack of sleep.

We told Jayla. And Dodge and Roger, earning another round of high fives. Everyone was less surprised than we were. Which means we can now hold hands in the car, which is a new and exciting development that I will more fully appreciate when I am less sleep deprived.

"You were up really early, right?" Dodge asks. "So more than twenty-four hours."

Jayden squints into the air, a crease wrinkling his nose and the dark hollows under his eyes. "It's got to be close to thirty hours."

"Oh my god." Roger twists around from the passenger seat to stare at us. His eyes are wide. "How are you still alive? That's like, three days!"

In the pause that follows, Suka stretches across the back seat, her paws snagging on the fabric of my skirt. Then Jayla says, "Wait . . ." and the whole car bursts into bubbling laughter, the sound as golden as the slanted sunlight and as warm as the puppy head snuggled in my lap and Jayden's hand in mine. And as the car moves forward, I catch a glimpse of how we might be over the next four years, and it's different and exciting and perfectly unexpected.

MISSING

by Kathleen Glasgow

IN THE BEGINNING, THERE WERE FOUR: DORSEY, ANGIE, Kate, and Kim. They all attended Wellington High, an unassuming brick building in the middle of an unassuming town that bled crisp red and orange leaves in the fall, delivered postcard-perfect snow in the winter, warm and soft rain in the spring, and summers filled with lemonade and lakes and broken hearts at the county fair.

Oh, and Lissy. Lissy was there, too, but it was easy to forget Lissy. Everyone always forgot about Lissy. *Mouse*, the girls whispered at Lissy's school. *Freaky little mouse.*

When Kate opened her front door, backpack slung over her shoulders, she wore an irritated expression.

"Lissy's coming," she told her friends.

The three girls peered at Kate's little sister, who was shrinking against the wall of the tiny apartment. The apartment smelled like unwashed clothes and over-boiled pasta noodles, the kind that come in a cardboard box.

Dorsey held up a finger, the nail as bright as blood. "Absolutely not."

Angie said, "We can't take a little *kid*."

Kate said, in that same flat voice she'd been using for the past year, "My dad got called into a shift. I have to take her."

Kim said, "Why can't your mom—ow!"

Dorsey had elbowed her sharply. Kim looked at the ground, realizing her mistake. No wonder the apartment smelled bad, but still: Kate's dad should have stepped up by now. It had been a *year*. She looked around Kate to Lissy. Lissy's pants were frayed at the hems and too short, showing her knobby ankles. Her hair was choppy, like something done in a kitchen with sewing shears. Kim frowned. A girl's life was hard enough and Lissy's dad was sending her out looking like *that*?

"Okay, then," Dorsey said, and sighed. Dorsey was big on sighs. "But I'm not watching out for her."

"*Fine*," Kate answered. She snapped her fingers.

Lissy pushed herself off the wall and squeezed by her sister and went to stand with the older girls in the hallway.

It's funny, Kate thought, as she locked the door to the apartment, how quickly everyone forgets when a mother has died.

Dorsey's car rattled on the old road. They were heading to the outskirts of town, where hills rose and fell like breath and the trees stretched out like hands with very long fingers. Dorsey cracked her window and lit a cigarette.

"That's so disgusting," Kim said, rolling down her window.

"I can't go home smelling like smoke," Angie said, cracking her own window. "My mom will kill me."

"Calm down," Dorsey said. "Let me live my life."

"You won't have one if you keep smoking," Kate warned.

Lissy said, "I saw a commercial on television and the woman smoked and her cancer spread all through her face skin and they had to take it all off. She's lopsided now."

Lissy was sitting on Kate's lap. Kate dug her nails into Lissy's thighs, pressing through her thin jeans, and it hurt, but Lissy refused to let her sister know it.

Dorsey took a deep drag on the cigarette and threw it out the window. In the rearview mirror, her eyes were glossy and dark. Lissy looked away from them. She found Dorsey mean and eerie, with those eyes that seemed to see you and not see you at the same time.

"Fun fact," Dorsey said cheerfully. "The place we're going? They put women in there just for smoking. Punished a whole lifetime just for a moment of pleasure. Can you imagine?"

No one wanted to.

They sat in the car. The Bedford Lunatic Asylum for Women loomed before them, a vast, ornate gray building, like something out of a book about castles. It seemed to glow against the bleakness of the night sky. It was September. Rain drizzled slowly down the windshield.

"The night is dark and full of terrors," Dorsey whispered.

She turned abruptly in her seat and shouted, *"Boo!"* The girls jumped. Lissy whimpered but stopped when she felt the sharpness of Kate's nails again.

"Why is it so *big*?" Kim asked. "I mean, how many crazy women could there *have been* back then?"

Dorsey was all business, checking her backpack for supplies. "That's the thing," she said. "Most of them *weren't* crazy. They put you here for the stupidest, most sexist reasons. Like not wanting to do your husband. Or reading. A woman was put in here for reading *novels*. Her husband thought books were giving her too many ideas! So he called a doctor and the doctor was, like, why are you reading all the time? And the woman got angry, because whose business is it if she reads a damn book, so in she goes, never to come out. The records called it *intellectual aggression*, whatever that means."

Angie sucked in her breath. She'd finished four books just this week. "I'd be in here, for sure," she murmured.

Dorsey looked around the car at all of them.

"All of us would," she said. "Angie for getting big ideas from books, me for complaining about my bad periods, which, by the way, was called being 'menstrually deranged,' and Kate for excessive grief."

Kate flinched.

Kim said, "What about me?"

Dorsey thought for a moment. "Probably for liking sports too much. As in, not being ladylike."

Kim shrugged. "You have a point." She looked down at her nails, painted a glossy pink, a color that made her inexplicably happy. She liked pink nails and she liked to run *fast* and she wondered why those things weren't allowed to coexist.

"What about me?" asked Lissy.

"No one cares about you," Kate said, opening the car door and shoving her sister off her lap and out into the dark.

The ground was cold and wet, seeping through Lissy's thin shoes, and she shivered.

Dorsey got out of the car and slung her backpack over her shoulder. Her voice was determined. "Let's go."

She started walking, then stopped when she realized they weren't following. She turned to face them.

"Come *on*," she urged. "Stop being such babies. It's midnight and the GhostConnector only has six hours of battery life."

Dorsey's smile was a shiny, electric thing that made Lissy's spine shiver.

Dorsey . . . was Dorsey. A planner. An idea-haver. A schemer. When they were ten, it was a lemonade stand, only the lemonade had a little extra kick courtesy of Dorsey's parents' liquor cabinet. "They won't miss it," she'd promised the girls. "My dad has me mix his drinks all the time. It makes people goofy."

But Dorsey must have poured too much in by accident—or maybe not, who could know with Dorsey—because they soon had quite a crowd of older kids lining up. It was kind of funny until a neighbor noticed a bunch of teens stumbling around in the street and the vomit splattered in her rosebushes.

When they were twelve, it was selling a contraption she called "The Bust-Master," a thick rubber strap guaranteed to increase your breast size within three weeks. She made quite a bit of money at first, and then a lot of enemies when customers' chests remained stubbornly uninspired after weeks of exercises. On and on, until this.

"We'll be famous," she'd said in her room one night, telling them about the GhostConnector, a strange device she'd ordered online. "We'll go find some ghosts, record them, tell their stories, and splash it everywhere."

They were sitting on their sleeping bags, pumped full of Cheetos and Sprite and several hours of *Real Housewives* on the giant flat-screen in Dorsey's room.

"But *why*?" Angie had asked.

"Why not?" Dorsey answered. "It's wrong that women were locked up for life for the worst reasons. Most of them weren't even *ill*. They just weren't acting the way men thought they should act. Also, it will be fun. And cool. Let's do something. We never *do* anything."

"Do you even believe in ghosts?" Kim had asked her. She was doing scissor kicks. She was the fastest sprinter on the Wellington track team and determined to sprint her way out of their town to a good college.

"I do," Dorsey had answered proudly. "My grandmother came to me once. Out at her old place by Pelican Lake two summers ago. I woke up and saw this weird shape at the foot of my bed."

"Oh my god," Kim said. "That's scary."

"Did your grandma *say* anything?" Angie asked. She felt a little sick.

"Yep," Dorsey answered. "She told me to goddamn stand up straight. That's how I knew it was really her. Old bat." She was sitting on her windowsill, blowing smoke out into the night.

Kate had felt anger surging within her, listening to Dorsey. It wasn't fair that Dorsey would get a visit from her grandmother, a woman she claimed to despise, when Kate's own mother, whom she missed so much it made her bones ache, remained resolutely silent. Once, a few weeks after the funeral, Kate had even tried a Ouija board, her fingers trembling as she placed them gently on the wooden planchette, whispering and waiting, her heart like a bird with a broken wing in her chest.

Where are you? she'd whispered. *Come back.*

Nothing had happened. Kate threw the board against the bedroom wall, which roused her father from his chair in the living room, where he watched television late into the night. In the dark room, he picked up the cracked board and looked at Kate, his face shifting into something that made the fluttering bird inside her go still.

"Stop," he'd said. "Please stop. She's not there."

He didn't notice Lissy, hidden in her blankets on the bed on the other side of the room, watching.

Kate heard him drop the board in the trashcan in the kitchen. He went back to his chair and the sound on the television got louder. Kate went to bed and cried.

It had been a whole year without her mother and still the wound inside her would not heal.

At Dorsey's, Kate had jammed herself in her sleeping bag, pressing her face against her pillow. Death was unfair in so many ways.

"I don't care," she'd told them, her voice muffled. "Whatever. I'm in."

They stood in front of Bedford. The sign said *PROVIDING SUCCOR FOR GOD'S HELPLESS CHILDREN* and was in remarkably good shape, only a few letters worn and faded. The asylum had been

closed a decade earlier, Dorsey had told them, and they'd trans-
ferred the last fifteen or so patients out of state.

"Why isn't this place boarded up?" Angie asked. The glass
on Bedford's windows was mostly intact, though dirty, save for
a few broken panes.

"They're starting development in a few weeks and will probably put up fencing then," Dorsey said. "Turning it into condos.
It does have a great view of the lake."

They all turned to look at Cascade Lake. The moon gleamed
on the surface.

Lissy watched the water ripple. She found it transfixing.
She and her mother had taken a paddle-boat ride once, on
another lake outside of town, on a day when Lissy had a doctor's appointment. She was always quieter than usual after the
doctor, because they asked her so many questions, and made
her do strange things, like draw a house, or play with small plastic dolls, and her mother always took her somewhere nice after,
like for ice cream, or a movie. On the paddle-boat day, they had
a few hours before Kate would be home from school. "Just us,"
her mother had said, conspiratorially. "No fussy Kate. Just me
and you and the water."

Before it fell out, her mother's hair had been smooth and
soft, a dark brown cape that tickled Lissy's cheeks when she
bent to kiss her.

Lissy watched the lake, a hot feeling spreading in her chest.
They'd had a good day, that day. Maybe one of the last ones,
before her mother had to stay in bed all the time.

Dorsey continued in her raspy voice. "My dad says the fear
of ghosts is probably what keeps most people out, so there isn't

really a need for security. They'll lock it up soon, though, so we need to do this now."

Dorsey's father worked for the city. None of the girls knew exactly what he did, only that Dorsey had excellent clothes, a big two-story house, and a kidney-shaped swimming pool with a slide.

"Look," Kate said, pointing.

To the right of the hospital was a spindly-looking iron fence with a gate that hung off its hinges. Headstones and crosses poked out of brush and weeds.

"Oh," Angie said nervously. "I guess . . . they buried them here."

"It doesn't look very big," Kim said. "I mean, should it be bigger? When did this place open?"

Dorsey frowned. "1918. That's . . . not a lot of gravestones, for the amount of women that were here."

"Maybe their families came to get them, after they died? Buried them at home or something?" Kate had a weird feeling in her chest. She'd seen the bill for her mother's funeral and burials weren't cheap.

Dorsey said, "Maybe they buried them somewhere else?" But her voice was unsure.

The girls were quiet.

"Onward," Dorsey finally said. "We're on a mission."

They were at the front doors when Kate looked around. "Lissy," she hissed.

Lissy jumped. She'd walked to the edge of the lake without realizing it. Her shoes were inches from the water.

"Come *on*, or we're leaving you outside," Kate said.

Lissy ran toward the girls. Dorsey took a breath, reached her hand out, and grasped a handle on one of the immense double doors. The door stuck and she grunted, pulling harder. It finally opened with a musty creak. Something skittered up the door and disappeared inside a crack.

"Holy . . ." said Angie.

As they slowly walked inside, Lissy looked back at the shimmering, dark lake.

Ever so slightly, in the middle, the water surged, as though something had pushed it from beneath.

Lissy ran inside.

Inside it smelled like dust, wood, and urine. Above them, the ceiling rose to a tall, octagon-shaped tower of windows, moonlight beating down through the cracked and dirty glass.

Kate was glad for the windows, because the room wasn't completely dark. Dorsey dug in her backpack, handing each of them flashlights. "You can use your phones, too," she said. "These are just for an emergency." She handed Angie a camcorder.

"You're the cinematographer," she said.

"Why me and why can't we just use our phones?" Angie asked.

Dorsey shrugged. "This makes it more old school. Like we're making a real film. And you have the steadiest hands."

Angie was an artist, creating amazing pots out of mounds of clay on a spinning wheel. Angie would go to art school in a big city someday, and live in a cute loft, and make her pots, and fall in love with people in disheveled clothes who could recite poetry from memory and sleep on bare mattresses and spend all their money seeing drowsy-eyed bands in tiny clubs. All of the girls would envy her for it, even Dorsey.

Angie took the camcorder.

Lissy looked around. The room was cavernous, splintering off into hallways that went in different directions. It was like being inside a spider, like each hallway was a leg. Her fingers crept for Kate's.

Kate jerked away. "Stop it," she said. "You know I don't like that."

Lissy folded her hands together. The thing she missed about their mother most was the warmth of her mother's hand in hers, leading her into school every morning, straight to her classroom door, her head held high. The rest of the day, without her mother, was filled with whispers of *Mouse* and spitballs in her hair.

Her father didn't walk Lissy into school, after her mother died. He said he had to get to work and she needed to be brave.

"Time to grow up," he'd said.

Lissy's body suddenly felt very small and empty.

Dorsey glanced around. "We need to find a good spot farther in," she said, turning on her flashlight. The long beams swept the entries to the hallways. "Somewhere deeper, where they lived more. This is just the lobby. Or waiting room? What do they call it in a psych hospital, anyway?" She turned the beam on Kate. "Kate, you should know."

The girls looked everywhere but at Kate.

Kate glared at Dorsey.

"Just a little loony bin humor," Dorsey said. "Don't be so sensitive."

Kate wondered what would happen if she cracked her flashlight against the side of Dorsey's beautiful head. What then? Would she get put away again for *excessive grief*? Sometimes she was so angry she felt her whole body might split apart.

Dorsey angled her flashlight around the room, catching the gleam of broken glass, shards of wood, a lopsided couch with stuffing spilling out like white guts.

She started walking and they followed.

Kim whispered, "I'm not sure I'm feeling this, anymore." But she didn't turn back.

The hallway Dorsey had chosen was long and there were benches against the whole length of wall.

"Seems like a pretty big waiting area," Angie said, turning in a circle, panning the hallway with the camcorder.

Dorsey said, "Not many people came to visit. If you were put here, it was because your family didn't want anything more to do with you. I read somewhere that they brought the patients out at six o'clock in the morning and put them on the benches and kept them there until six at night."

"Wait," Kate said. "They just sat here, all *day*?"

Kate thought back to last year, when she'd had to go to a hospital for a few weeks. Her mother's death had been slow and agonizing and it seemed when she finally died, she took most of Kate's heart with her. All Kate did was stay in bed, wordless. Her boyfriend Mick had come by and sat on the edge of the bed, texting and watching YouTube videos.

She'd watched him not watching her, all the words she

wanted to say piling up inside her like nails, needful and sharp.

Finally, he'd looked up and said, "How much longer is this going to go on?" and the pain that rose up in her sent her hands to Mick's face, the face she'd once loved so deeply she could imagine it, perfectly, with her eyes closed. Her fingers were claws on his skin.

After that, her father drove her to a hospital in another town, where she stayed with other sad-eyed kids and painted and wrote in a journal and sat in a circle and listened to everyone's sadness. It wasn't bad, and she felt better when it was done, but she still had darkness inside, and she knew it would never go away.

Kate looked at the benches. The hospital she went to wasn't fancy, but it wasn't horrible, and there were rules, but at least they never made you sit on benches all day, just staring into nothingness. Imagine, having to wake up only to be told to sit for twelve hours until it was time to go to bed again? Were the women here even allowed to talk to each other? Kate had liked most of the other kids at the hospital. After a while, it seemed like they all belonged to the same club, one made of sadness and hurt, and she could tell them things she could never tell these girls.

Dorsey held the flashlight under her chin. She was so pretty, all round cheeks and snub nose and dark eyes.

"It was supposed to be therapeutic." She pointed to the windows opposite the benches. "See, they could look outside all day and ruminate on why they excessively masturbated or read novels all day. Really, it was just a way to keep them in line. If they fell asleep or talked, they got hit with a baton."

Kate frowned. It sounded more like a prison than a hospital.

"That would drive *anyone* loopy," Kim said.

"Exactamundo," Dorsey said. "If you weren't loopy when you came in, you were by the time you died here."

They came to an area where it was darker, and colder, and they could no longer see the octagon-shaped room they'd walked from, or the moonlight from any windows. Something scuttled in the corner and Kim jumped. "*Jesus,*" she muttered.

"Mice," Dorsey said. "Always underfoot."

Lissy frowned.

"Well," Dorsey said, "we might as well get the GhostConnector up and running." She fished in her backpack.

Kim said, "I just lost service. Anybody else?" She tapped her phone.

"Yep," Angie said, holding the camcorder in one hand and peering at her phone in the other.

Kate beamed her flashlight down the corridor. There were some framed photographs hanging on the walls and she walked closer to look at them. One was of an unsmiling old man with comically bushy eyebrows, but his eyes weren't happy, or kind. They simply stared out of the frame, as though at something only he could see. "Dr. Irving Braithwaite," she read out loud. "Well, you are a creepster, Dr. Braithwaite, that's for sure."

Kate walked to a doorway and shined her flashlight in.

There were sinks along the back wall and, in the middle of the room, what looked like a dentist's chair attached to a machine by a series of plastic-looking tubes. She shined the flashlight on the floor. Scattered among papers and rectangular trays, like the kind they give you at the doctor's office to vomit in, were odd metal objects, things that looked like pliers or wire-cutters.

"Dorsey," she called. "What else did they do here? What is this room?"

Dorsey walked in. Her flashlight picked up the dull, faded green color of the walls, the paint peeling like sunburned skin.

"Some places did experiments, like lobotomies. You know, the old icepick in the eyeball to calm your brain down. Other things, probably, too. Who would know unless they kept records? You had all these women basically at the mercy of a bunch of male doctors who didn't have degrees in psychiatry."

"This is getting creepy," Angie said, sweeping the camera around the room, the little red light like an eye. She stepped gingerly over pieces of broken glass.

Dorsey smiled. "Voilà," she said, holding something up.

The GhostConnector was hardly bigger than a game console, and looked like one, with a screen, dials, and buttons. It looked like a toy and Kim said so, a hand on her hip.

Dorsey said, "A thousand-dollar toy, then, I guess, complete with an electromagnetic frequency reader, data storage, a thermal flashlight that changes color when the temperature dips or rises, and an application that turns environmental readings into real words, also known as making sense of phonetic activity."

She sounded like she'd memorized the pamphlet.

The girls stared at her.

Dorsey sighed. "In dipshit language, that means if a ghost is near, the temperature will change and this thing will alert us. If the ghost makes a sound—*ooohhh!*—this machine has a mechanism to recognize the speech pattern and turn it into a word we can understand."

Kate looked at the GhostConnector. "Do you honestly think that thing is legitimate?"

Dorsey's face closed in a way Kate didn't like. "Why, Kate? What are you afraid of? A bunch of dead lady ghosts? Afraid this might work better than your Ouija board?"

She chucked Kate under the chin with a finger. Kate ducked away, sorry she'd ever told Dorsey about the Ouija board. She didn't like Dorsey all that much, truthfully. She wasn't planning to keep in touch when Dorsey went away in a year to whatever pretty college she chose and Kate had to stay home, working at a call center or something. That would be her life: sitting in a cubicle listening to strangers complain about dishwashers not washing and recliners not reclining.

Dorsey and the other girls left the room. When Kate went to follow, her shoe crunched on something. She shined her flashlight down. Tiny, yellowy-white stones were strewn across the floor. She bent down to get a closer look, but Lissy scooped them up and held them close to Kate's face.

"Teeth," Lissy said. "Like me." She opened her mouth, exposing the gaps. She was nine, and the teeth she did have hung like mini-stalactites.

Kate's stomach heaved and she pushed Lissy's hand away, hurrying after the others.

Dorsey stopped at another room. "Hold on," she said. She held the GhostConnector up. A faint blue, blinking line.

"The temperature is dropping." Dorsey sounded excited.

Kate rubbed her arms. "It's getting cold."

"Yes," Dorsey said. "Spirits suck the energy, as in heat, from an area, when they're close."

She held the GhostConnector up to the doorway. It pinged faintly and the blue line got bluer.

Angie said, "If you're pranking us, I will kill you. No joke."

Dorsey licked her lips and stepped into the room. The GhostConnector whirred.

Kate followed nervously. She thought of Dorsey's grandmother visiting her. If ghosts could return to a place, then surely it *was* possible they were here. Or maybe Dorsey had been lying about her grandmother. Dorsey lied about a lot of things.

There were metal tables and file cabinets, sinks and a strange chair mounted to a pole with a lever in the middle of the room. The chair had straps and metal cuffs.

Dorsey whistled.

"I didn't think I'd see one of these," she said. "So, one thing they did was put patients in this chair and strap them in and then raise them up," Dorsey said, pointing to the lever. "And then spin it." She walked around the chair to a machine with knobs and buttons. She pressed some of the buttons. Nothing happened.

"Spin it?" Kate asked.

"Yes, really fast. It was supposed to clear the bad thoughts from your head."

Angie circled the chair with the camera. "Someone should get in," she said, grinning. "I mean, it's for posterity."

Lissy said, "It's freezing," but no one heard her. She had

slipped the teeth into the pocket of her pants and she felt for them now, jiggling them in her fingers to comfort herself.

Dorsey said, "Kim. Get in."

"No *way*." Kim backed away. "I have a meet next week and I'm not getting hurt for this crap."

"It doesn't work. There's no electricity here. See?" Dorsey made a big show of pressing buttons, turning knobs.

Kim shook her head.

"I'll give you fifty bucks. Here." Dorsey dug in her backpack and handed Kim the cash.

Kim held the money in her hand. She hated that Dorsey bribed them all the time. Kim once accepted twenty bucks from Dorsey to walk up to Dean Cooper at a party and kiss him and sure, she did it, she'd had a beer or two, and Dean was extremely cute, but the kiss made him think they'd be doing more, and it took her some time to get out of that. That's why boys sucked. Nothing could ever be fun. It always had to be *more*.

Kim handed Dorsey the money. "Nope."

Dorsey turned to Angie. "You do it."

Angie hesitated. She could always use money for art supplies. It could be interesting, being in the chair. Artists were always testing limits, after all. She watched a video once of an artist who sat in a store window for twelve days straight, naked in a chair, staring at the strangers gathered on the sidewalk to watch. Her expression never changed. She didn't eat, she didn't sleep. "I'm on display," the artist had said in a statement. "Women are always on display."

Angie had watched as much of the video as she could, keeping it on real time on her laptop, looking away for homework or to go to school or to sleep and always, when she came back, there was the woman, looking at her. In time, her body stopped being naked, stopped being boobs and bush, and more of a thing, a rooted, strange, immovable object. Kind of like the women on the benches must have felt, Angie thought suddenly.

"Fifty more when we get out of here and I'll do it," Angie told Dorsey.

Dorsey nodded. Angie handed Kim the camcorder and climbed onto the chair. Puffs of dust erupted around her, creamy in the beam of Dorsey's flashlight. Kate strapped Angie in.

"*Don't* put the cuffs on," Angie warned. She tried to steel herself. This was for *art*, after all.

Lissy's teeth began to chatter.

"Happy now?" Angie asked, as Kim filmed her. She tugged at the straps. "Okay, I'm getting off. Help me. Are these tangled or something?"

"Your machine's making a noise," Kate said to Dorsey.

Dorsey held the GhostConnector to her ear. "No, quiet as a kitten."

But they all heard the whirring. The chair began to rise.

Dorsey's mouth opened in a perfect O, but it was Angie who began to scream as she was lifted in the air. *Stop it, let me down, you said it didn't work, this isn't funny.*

We didn't touch it.

Kate and Dorsey tried the buttons and knobs but nothing worked. They jumped for the chair, but it kept rising, Angie struggling in the straps that criss-crossed her body.

And then, with a violent bump that shook Angie's body, it stopped.

"Get me down!" Angie cried.

The chair began to spin, slowly at first, with a great, creaking groan, throwing Angie's cries around the room, and then faster, garbling her words. She spun like a top.

Dorsey's GhostConnector gurgled, but only Lissy noticed. She stepped closer to Dorsey as Angie's cries intensified. Kim finally threw down the camera and ran under the chair, trying to find something to stop it.

Angie vomited from up high, spraying chicken noodle soup around the room.

Make it stop, thought Lissy, pressing her hands to her ears. Make it *stop*.

The chair stilled.

Angie slumped forward. Kate and Kim got hold of the bottom of the chair and wrenched it to the ground. Angie's face was bloated. Tiny chicken pieces clung to her cheeks.

Kate undid the straps. They weren't tangled at all, like Angie had said.

"I'm so sorry," Dorsey whispered. She tried to wipe off Angie's face, but Angie shoved her, hard, knocking Dorsey to the ground, and got out of the chair. She wobbled, her legs buckling for a second before she straightened herself.

"I hate you so much right now," she whispered to Dorsey. She reached into her pocket and threw the money on the glass-littered ground.

And then she ran.

The girls stood, stunned, until Kim finally spoke. "I think we should go," she said. "This is too weird."

"No," Dorsey said. "This is exactly what we came for. I

mean, what *was* that? What did that? She'll be fine. She'll wait in the car."

Lissy pulled on the sleeve of Dorsey's pink hoodie. "What is it, Mouse? You scared? This is an adventure."

Lissy pointed to the GhostConnector. "Voice."

Dorsey sucked in her breath. She pressed a button, replaying the gurgle.

Kim bent down and grabbed her knees. "Oh, god, I'm so freaked out right now." But she picked up the camera, anyway, and turned it back on.

Dorsey said, "So then, we press this . . ." She pressed a tiny green button. "And the GC searches a database of vocal patterns to find . . ." She turned a dial.

Kate felt like she might faint. Angie had been like a ride at the fair, spinning and spinning. Lissy stepped closer to her. Her body was ice cold and Kate flinched. "For god's sake, I told you to bring a jacket, you *jerk*."

Kim frowned. "You don't need to be so mean, Kate."

"Shut up, Kim. You don't know—"

Dorsey held up her hand. "Listen."

The sound from the GhostConnector was muffled, like a voice coming through cloth.

Hurts.

Hurts.

The next thing they heard was the camcorder hitting the ground, Kim's head smacking the tile next to it.

Lissy fanned Kim with paper she found on the floor. Kate splashed drops of water from a bottle onto Kim's face. Dorsey tried to piece the camcorder back together.

Kim's eyes fluttered.

"Hurts," she said.

They all flinched, even Dorsey. Kim's eyes were glassy.

"We should go," Kate whispered. "This has gone far enough."

"I'm not going," Dorsey said firmly. "If you guys want to wait out by the car, in the dark, until I'm done, that's fine. But we have something and I think we can get more. Someone *spoke.*"

"Probably just your stupid machine," Kim said haltingly. "Piece of crap somebody uploaded with voices to fool you."

"Doesn't explain the chair, though," Kate said quietly.

"It's busted," Dorsey sighed, shoving the camcorder in her backpack. "But we have the GhostConnector and the data is saved and we can use our phones to film. I'm going to keep going. Anyone with me?"

Kate helped Kim up. There was a thin trickle of blood at Kim's temple and Kate tried to wipe it away. Kim pushed her hand down.

Dorsey shined her flashlight on them. "Agreed?"

They nodded, following her to the door.

Lissy trailed after them. She looked back at the chair and for an instant, she saw a woman in a loose gown, her head lolled to the side, her eyes wide and frightened.

Lissy's heart jumped. She rubbed her eyes. When she looked again, the woman was gone.

They walked the corridor in silence, their shoes shuffling. Some rooms were filled with beds, the empty metal frames like webby carcasses. Bedpans piled in corners. Lissy found a hairbrush and petted the hairs that hung from it. That was the thing that made her parents send her to the doctor. The hair thing. The girls at school in the bathroom, always brushing their hair, leaving tendrils in the sink, which Lissy wrapped in paper towels and put in her pocket. Sometimes, when she couldn't help herself, when a girl with particularly pretty hair, soft and silky, was near, she would reach out and gently tug some strands away. She had a sewing kit she kept in her closet and that's where she made the dolls. Cut out patterned fabric for dresses, built bodies out of cotton balls and twine, buttons and yarn for eyes and mouths. Then she sewed the hair on and that was it. Instant friends with real hair she could pet. It made her mother cry when she found them. She was sorry when her father threw the dolls away.

Kate took the brush from Lissy and threw it down the hall. Something yowled.

Two eyes gleamed at them. The girls screamed. Dorsey laughed.

A gray, matted cat hissed and ran at them, the teeth it still had bared and sharp. Kim tucked Lissy behind her. Dorsey's GhostConnecter emitted a soft *ping*. The cat turned right and disappeared down another long, dark corridor.

Dorsey fiddled with the GhostConnector.

Can't have it.

Kim frowned. "Can't have what?"

Dorsey shrugged.

The machine whirred. *Hurts.*

"Just one more room, okay?" Kate asked. The cat had spooked her, but she had other feelings, too, like something that was not Lissy had been touching her. The air was weird in this part of the asylum, thicker, and when she walked, it felt like moving through spiderwebs, sticky and unsettling. She said this out loud.

Dorsey nodded. "I felt that. The GC was making noises, registering heat. I mean, ghosts are supposed to draw energy from people. Maybe there are . . . more in this part? Moving around us."

"I cannot believe you aren't scared," Kim said. "I feel like I'm going to pee myself."

"Think about it," Dorsey said. "People die everywhere. They probably died in the house you live in now, way back when. They're everywhere. Why wouldn't they be? We just choose not to listen."

She looked at the GhostConnector. "It's going crazy."

Indeed, the toylike machine was emitting beeps and clicks at a rapid rate. Dorsey held it in front of her, and turned into another room.

Lissy's hand slipped into Kim's and Kim let her. She felt sorry for the kid, really. All that messed-up stuff at school and her and Kate's mom dying. She had no idea what she'd do if her mother died. Her mother meant home-baked cookies, a heating pad when Kim's periods were awful, Bollywood movies on Friday night. It had always been just the two of them. If she lost her, what then? She hoped her mother would come back to her, maybe say something about where she was and what was happening there. She'd like that.

Lissy's hand in Kim's was warm. Kim gave it a squeeze. Kate didn't need to be so mean to her sister.

Lissy held tighter, her fingers growing hotter. Kim shook her hand free. "Let go, kiddo," she said. "Too tight." Her hand was burning up, the skin stinging in an awful way.

But Lissy was across the room, standing in front of a series of shelves with glass jars, and Kim's hand was empty.

Kim's heart flailed. She held her hand in front of her face. Blisters bubbled on her palm.

Angie had run so fast and so blindly that when she stumbled, she slid halfway across the floor on her stomach, her body raking broken glass. She had pushed herself up, glass grinding into her palms, and tried to remember which way the front doors were. When she finally found them, she gasped in the cool night air, soft rain falling on her face. She slammed the doors shut.

Dorsey hadn't locked the car and Angie sat in the driver's seat, breathing heavily, staring at Bedford. She tried to send a text to her mother, but there was still no service. She tried to calm her breathing, but every sound, even her own body moving, startled her.

Just calm down, she told herself.

She started to cry, great heaving sobs that echoed in the small car.

When she finally looked up, the windows of Bedford were alive with movement.

Angie screamed into her hands and closed her eyes.

When she opened them, the window movement had stopped, but she heard screaming from the building. "Please stop," she whispered. "Please just stop."

It was Kim screaming, flinging open the big double doors and running toward the car with her strong sprinter's legs, her eyes wide. She slipped and fell in the rain.

Angie's body drained in a cold way. There was something following Kim from the building, a cloud-like wave pouring from the doors that undulated and shuddered.

Angie had always thought ghosts, or whatever spirits were, would be white, but this wasn't that and there wasn't just one cloud, it was a series of them, pinkish and long, rippling like the lake's water.

"Get up," Angie whispered. "Get the hell up and shut the doors, Kim."

But Kim couldn't hear her. She stumbled up and ran for the car again, the pink waves swimming around her. She yanked open the passenger-side door and slammed it shut. Her face was caked with mud and blood.

"My hand," Kim stuttered. "My hand. Burning."

The blisters were the size of quarters. Some of them had burst, the gooey liquid pouring down Kim's palm and onto her wrist. Angie grabbed Kim's backpack, where she always kept creams and bandages for track practice. Kim said, "Gotta get out."

Angie stared at her. The voice that came from Kim didn't sound like Kim.

The voice repeated *gotta get out, gotta get out* in a low growl.

Angie slapped Kim's face.

"Help me," Kim whispered, in her own voice now.

Hands shaking, Angie spread cream on the blisters as Kim cried.

The car began to rock, at first gently, and then hard.

Dorsey shook her head. "Two down. Only the brave remain."

She had a file cabinet drawer open and was reading from a medical record. Lissy and Kate stared at the rows of specimen jars and the objects that floated within.

"'Beatrice S. complained of stomach ailment. Appendix removed, found healthy. Refer organ for further testing. BS deceased, infection of wound.'"

Kate looked at a blob in a jar, her flashlight catching the porous pinkness of it. It was perfectly preserved, floating in a netherworld.

Dorsey made a strange sound. "Oh, wow. Listen to this: 'Annabelle Carpenter, seventeen, received April twenty-second, 1921. Extreme mania, refuses nourishment. Mania resulted from broken engagement and refusal to return ring. Patient'—"

Dorsey stopped. Kate looked over at her.

Dorsey's face was pale and she was blinking fast. The GhostConnector began to beep, a soft sound trickling from it.

Kate said, "What?"

Dorsey cleared her throat. "'Patient secured medical shearing device and removed hand at wrist during unmonitored activity. Hand located in lower level of institution several days after severing. Patient deceased April twenty-second, 1962.' She cut it *off*, my god, she cut it off."

Dorsey didn't have to press a button this time, because clear as day, the GhostConnector said

Give it back

Dorsey dropped the file. Kate dropped her flashlight.

The room erupted.

Angie and Kim were soldered together in the front seat of the car when Dorsey and Kate ran from Bedford, Kate helping Dorsey in the muddy grass. Dorsey was screaming, which scared Kim, because Dorsey was always cool as a cucumber. The car had stopped rocking, but the windows of Bedford were alive with lights of all different colors.

Dorsey shoved Angie out of the driver's seat and into the back. She started the car with Angie's feet still half in the front, over the gearshift. The car lurched, and Angie's head hit the back passenger window. Kate pulled her to a sitting position.

From the corner of her eye, Kate saw movement on the lake.

It was no longer still, like it had been earlier in the night. It was roiling, waves undulating in pinkish bursts, and when she looked to the doors of Bedford, what she saw made her heart stop.

Angie was screaming at Kim. *You let them out. You let them goddamn out.*

Dorsey peeled across the grass and down the dirt road, Angie's screams shattering her ears.

They were flying down the road, parallel to the lake, rain plastering the windshield, Dorsey swearing, Kim crying, and Angie moaning, when Kate felt it.

An absence.

She patted around the backseat, looked at the floorboards. Her heart calved in two.

"Stop," she said. "We have to go back. We forgot Lissy."

Dorsey said, "No."

Kate felt the car heave forward as Dorsey pressed the gas. She said Dorsey's name.

When Dorsey didn't answer, Kate lunged forward and grabbed the steering wheel, turning the car to the right.

The car flew through the trees toward the gleaming, hungry lake.

In the specimen room, Lissy picked up the GhostConnector.

Home

Hurts

Give it back

Hurts

She didn't mind the voice, or voices. Maybe there were several, she couldn't tell. The room wasn't dark, anymore, like when Dorsey and her sister, Kate, ran away. There were a lot of lights now and they were very pretty, pink and purplish and white, like the watercolors she made at the doctor's office. She put the GhostConnector back on the floor, the words floating around her.

The jars were full of liquid and fleshy objects. Round things. Twisted fleshy tubes. The objects hung in the liquid, still and perfect.

Home

Soon, Lissy answered. She didn't say it out loud. She knew they could hear her. It felt kind of nice this way. Talking without opening your mouth. The way her dolls talked to her.

At the far end of the wall, she found it.

The hand, suspended, the fingers tipped upward toward the top of the jar, as though reaching for it. A gold ring circled one finger. The hand looked soft and delicate, like her mother's.

Her mother lotioned her hands every night and sometimes she put just a spot of lotion on Lissy's nose, rubbing it in gently.

Lissy could almost feel that now, the sweet press of her mother's finger on her nose.

She put her hand on the glass jar, matching her fingers against the fingers inside, like pat-a-cake. She wasn't frightened at all when the fingers inside the jar twitched.

"I know," she said, softly. "I know."

Hurts

Home

The glass of the jar was growing warmer beneath Lissy's palm. She closed her eyes. She liked the voices. She wished she could keep them.

Hurts

When the jar shattered, spilling the hand on the floor, Lissy didn't startle or scream. She just looked at her palm, and her arm, now dotted with flecks of glass and blood. She looked around for something to wipe the blood away with, but it didn't matter.

She could feel them, other hands, patting her clean and safe.

Good girl

She picked up Dorsey's backpack and rooted around inside, throwing out the cigarettes and makeup pouch and sparkly phone case. She dropped the GhostConnector inside and stood up.

Home

The hand lay on the floor at her feet.

Very slowly, the forefinger touched the toe of Lissy's thin shoe.

"Okay," she said. "Home."

Outside, the rain had gone away. The lake was rippling, releasing pinkish-white and violet shadows that hovered over the surface of the water. Over the soft hills, the glow of the sunrise was beginning, and Lissy watched the women of the hospital step carefully on the dewy grass, holding their gowns up over their ankles. Some of them couldn't walk very well, so others helped them. Were they smiling? She thought so.

Lissy thought a long walk would be fine. She wasn't afraid. She would follow the road and perhaps someone would stop for her, or Kate might remember her, and come back, or not, and that was fine, too. She wasn't alone. She'd tucked the hand inside her sleeve, so her wrist matched Annabelle's wrist and Annabelle's fingers were firmly clasped in her own. Lissy wasn't worried about what would happen to her, anymore.

WHAT ABOUT YOUR FRIENDS

by Brandy Colbert

MICHAELA HADN'T COUNTED ON BEING DRENCHED IN sweat the next time she saw her best friend.

Former best friend.

Was that right? *Former* seemed too proper.

Ex–best friend?

No. That sounded too official, like there'd been a breakup. Like they were mad at each other, when in fact, they had simply grown apart.

And now here they were, both freshmen at Brockert College, both participating in the school's annual dance marathon with entirely separate groups.

Technically, Michaela wasn't supposed to be there. She was supposed to be on a trip halfway around the world, exploring other cultures and customs and expanding her mind before she started her first year of college, according to her parents. A *gap year*, her high school guidance counselor had called it.

Michaela had thought it all sounded pretentious, and she'd tried to shut down the idea when her parents first brought it up. Her mom and dad had exchanged amused looks.

"Isn't it supposed to be the other way around?" her father had said, laughing. "Aren't *you* supposed to be the one begging us to go away and *we're* supposed to be the ones you have to convince?"

It wasn't that Michaela didn't want to see the world. She did . . . someday. But she wasn't sure about traveling alone for months, and what if starting school a whole year later than her friends messed up the whole trajectory of her college career?

But once her parents had started leaving pamphlets around the house and sending her links about cities, museums, and other places they thought she might like to see abroad, she began to soften. And, soon, she was excited to go. Maybe her dad was right—what kind of eighteen-year-old would turn down the trip of a lifetime? Especially one funded entirely by her parents.

Still, Michaela had told almost everyone but Eleanor that she was simply "taking time off" before she started school.

"Who are you staring at?"

Next to her, Harper was doing a two-step that barely qualified as dancing. Michaela pretended not to notice as she said, "No one. Just zoning out."

"Well, make sure you keep moving," Harper said, holding her brown hair in a makeshift ponytail as she fanned her neck with her other hand. "We've got another fifteen minutes before we can swap out."

Michaela nodded and did a little spin that moved her away from Harper. They didn't have partners, not official ones, but Harper had made it her job to look after Michaela for reasons Michaela didn't entirely understand. They weren't much more than acquaintances. Michaela hadn't planned to join the team when Harper shoved the sign-up sheet in front of her before their bio lab. Not until she saw the marathon was raising money for the local children's hospital. Something she wouldn't feel connected to if it weren't for Eleanor.

Michaela peeked back at Eleanor, but it didn't seem like Eleanor had seen her. Which was absurd, because as two of the only Black kids in their high school, it seemed as if Eleanor had been the only one who seemed to really *see* her for years.

The last time they'd hung out was the night before Michaela had left for the airport. Last summer. Michaela's parents had wanted to host a proper farewell party for her, but Michaela refused. Wasn't it already sort of embarrassing that she was leaving to travel throughout Europe for months while her friends were buying textbooks and bedding for their dorm rooms?

So Eleanor had come over for dinner with Michaela and her parents, then the two of them sat on a blanket in her backyard like they often did throughout high school. Not saying much of anything, which was also normal for them. There was so much performing at school; on the cheer team, yes, but being two of the few Black students meant they were aware that everyone was always watching. Eleanor knew exactly how she felt and so when they sat in silence, it felt like comfort, not moments to be filled with needless chatter.

"I can't believe you're leaving," Eleanor had said, staring up at the dark night sky.

"Only for a few months." Michaela followed her gaze. There should have been stars, but the sky was almost impossibly black that night. Only a sliver of moon peeked out at them.

"What if it's worse than high school?"

Michaela looked at her friend. "College?"

"Yeah. I mean, what if it's just us again, Micky? What if it's four more years of the same bullshit?"

They'd both chosen Brockert College because they wanted to go to a liberal arts school; it was only a few hours away by car or train, close to home but not too close. And the school promised a diverse student population with organizations that supported them. The school even had a Black Student Union.

But Eleanor had looked genuinely worried, and Michaela understood in her own way. She wasn't worried about the Black (or lack of) thing—they'd survived high school, after all. Michaela was worried about college in general.

She knew it was expected of her, but she wasn't all that excited about college. She didn't know what she wanted to do, and she didn't think sitting in classrooms with a bunch of people who were paying way too much for an "experience" was the way to find out.

"It'll be all right," Michaela said, forcing comfort into her voice.

Eleanor picked at a blade of grass. "I'm still kind of mad at you for leaving me. I thought we were going to do this together."

"I know. I just . . ." She'd shrugged, unsure how to finish. She'd wished Eleanor could go with her, but the truth was, she wasn't sad about leaving. Her initial apathy about the trip had transformed into full-blown excitement since her parents had first presented the idea. Michaela felt guilty for leaving

Eleanor—but not for leaving. "But I'll be back with you next year, and if it sucks, we can be miserable together."

Eleanor had given her a brief smile, but it wasn't the kind of smile that made Michaela think she would be okay.

Now Eleanor was doing a complicated-looking dance routine with her teammates, and Michaela openly stared when it was clear they weren't paying attention to anyone around them. She'd never seen Eleanor move like that, and they'd gone to every single high school dance and mixer.

There was a confidence in her rhythm that hadn't been there before. Not even in the years they'd spent cheerleading. Like Eleanor suddenly knew what to do with every part of her body, and how to make it look like she'd always known. The other girls on her team moved with similar swagger, and eventually a crowd of dancers gathered around, whooping and cheering them on, until Michaela couldn't see them without getting closer.

She danced around her other teammates, but she didn't know them any better than Harper. One guy, Duncan, was in her world literature class, but they'd never spoken. When they made accidental eye contact, she sensed he didn't recognize her at all.

Michaela was beginning to see all the drawbacks she'd suspected about starting school in the spring. Maybe she should have just ridden out the semester at home, working in her old job at the grocery store and spending the rest of her time as far away from her parents as possible. She'd been working at the grocery since she was sixteen, and even though she didn't really need the spending money with most of her friends away at college, it was a place to go, to keep her busy. Because ever since she'd cut her trip short, her parents were more attentive than ever. Annoyingly attentive, like they were worried she might just break one day.

Eventually, Harper tapped her on the arm, signaling the beginning of their hourlong break. The rules allowed them to trade off with other teammates, as long as a certain number of people were still dancing. They were supposed to use the time to go to the bathroom, recharge, and rehydrate, but overall, Michaela was free to do what she wanted with the break: grab some food, join one of the games taking place on the perimeter of the gym, text people. Nap.

The marathon lasted twenty-four hours. It had started at noon, and the big clock on the basketball scoreboard had just changed to 9:01 p.m.

Michaela hadn't imagined she'd last this long. She was out of shape now that she no longer had daily cheerleading practice. Before she joined the high school cheer team, she'd been at the gymnastic center several times a week. She couldn't remember a time she had been so inactive—even during her trip abroad, she'd logged tens of thousands of steps a day, walking around to the different museums and landmarks—and she had to admit the marathon felt good. Pushing her body like she used to every day. It felt so good she had the urge to drop down where she was and stretch her muscles until she felt that familiar lengthening sensation.

Instead she downed a cup of water, then started on another as her eyes scanned the center of the gym. She couldn't see Eleanor or any of her teammates. Their T-shirts were a soft lavender—Eleanor's favorite color, and Michaela wondered if she'd had something to do with choosing them.

After she filled her water cup for the third time, Michaela wandered over to the food tables. Trucks serving all different kinds of cuisine were parked outside, but the dancers weren't allowed to leave the gym; anything they needed from outside had to be brought in from a nondancer. Her stomach rumbled as someone walked by with a container of tacos. They were the best thing she'd ever smelled.

"Michaela?"

She spun around so quickly, water sloshed out of her cup and onto the chest of the person who'd tapped her shoulder.

"Oh my god, I'm so sor—" she started, then stopped when she looked up.

Eleanor.

"Wow," her old friend breathed, ignoring the water that now soaked the upper half of her shirt. Maybe it didn't matter since she was already so sweaty. Or maybe she was so shocked to see Michaela, the spill hadn't even registered. "I thought that was you."

Michaela tried to smile, but she was pretty sure it came out as more of a grimace. "It's me. Surprise."

"What . . . what are you doing here?" Eleanor stepped closer to her, eyebrows pinched together. Not with anger. Hurt. Michaela still knew all her expressions. That wasn't something you could just unlearn about a person. Especially not someone she'd known as well as Eleanor.

"I go here," Michaela said simply. Dumbly. Of course she went there. Only students were allowed to join a dance marathon team.

Eleanor's frown persisted. "Since when?"

"Just last month. I started this semester." Michaela tipped back her cup for a drink, but most of the water had already landed on Eleanor's shirt.

"Were you going to tell me?"

Michaela cleared her throat. She was suddenly parched. She wanted one of those huge gallon water jugs the football players used to carry around back in high school.

"I'm sorry," Michaela said.

"You didn't answer my question." Eleanor tugged on one of the two French braids that framed the side of her head. "I thought you were still in Europe, Micky."

It warmed her to hear her old nickname. But Eleanor's sharp intake of breath made it clear it wasn't intentional. It had been a reflex, left over from years of spending so much time together.

"I came home early," Michaela said. "Before Christmas. It wasn't exactly what I thought it would be."

Eleanor cocked her head to the side. "You didn't love it?"

That wasn't true. She'd loved the food, all the crusty breads and fresh vegetables and cheeses. And how easy it was to get around to so many different cities by train. And how the older the building in Europe, the more respected it seemed rather than something to be torn down and replaced with new.

But she'd missed so much about home: knowing how to get to and from places instinctually, waking up in the same bed every day, and her parents, who were supposed to meet her in the South of France for Christmas. She'd missed Eleanor, too, but she didn't want to say it. Not after Eleanor had been the one who was worried about the new chapter in their lives and Michaela had been so confident that leaving was the right thing to do.

And then there was the fact that she'd been terrible about texting Eleanor while she'd been gone. She was never able to keep the time difference straight, and she was so distracted by all the newness of her trip that sometimes she just . . . forgot. And once Eleanor stopped reaching out, Michaela had felt weird about telling her she'd come home early. So she hadn't told her at all.

"It's complicated."

Eleanor nodded, but Michaela didn't expand on that, and Eleanor didn't ask her to. Michaela was glad. After all they'd gone through in school, both together and separately, she didn't know how to tell Eleanor that one bigoted interaction had sent her off the rails.

Eleanor's dark brown skin was gleaming, and she wiped her forehead with the back of her arm. "Do you like it here?"

"Yeah, it's fine." Michaela shrugged. "It's good."

"Honestly, Michaela, I'm pretty surprised to see you here."

"Why?" Michaela swallowed. "You knew I just deferred. We got our acceptance letters the same day."

Eleanor had actually called her that evening, something they rarely did, because if they weren't texting, they were usually together. They'd been in their respective houses, still wearing their cheer team uniforms after a game, squealing about being accepted to Brockert, where they both wanted to go. That seemed like years ago, not months.

"Yeah, but just because you said you were coming, that didn't mean you actually seemed excited about it. Deep down, I mean. It seemed like . . ." Eleanor trailed off, shaking her head.

Normally, Michaela would've asked what she meant. Pressed until her friend said what was on her mind. But they weren't friends anymore, were they? It didn't seem like the old rules applied, especially the way Eleanor had so quickly switched from calling her Micky.

"How's Owen?"

Something passed through Eleanor's gaze, then her expression quickly righted itself. "He's good. Doing better. Daddy thinks he might be able to go back to school this year."

"Really?" Michaela broke out into a genuine grin for the first time since she'd arrived at the marathon.

She'd always liked Eleanor's little brother. Owen had been a surprise baby, born the year Michaela and Eleanor turned twelve. He was well aware that he could get away with murder; partly because he was the baby and his parents were tired, and partly because he'd been sick for most of his life.

"Yeah, you know Daddy. Always the optimist." Eleanor rolled her eyes good-naturedly, but Michaela knew she had to be happy about Owen.

Apparently out of things to say, they turned to the food table to inspect the spread. One of Eleanor's teammates walked by as they were loading up their plates. She nudged Eleanor in the side, whispered something that made them both crack up, and moved on practically before Michaela could register she'd been there. It was strange seeing Eleanor so comfortable with people Michaela had never met, and Michaela felt a jolt of—she wasn't quite sure what. Annoyance? Jealousy?

"I can't believe you joined a sorority," she said, looking at the Greek letters displayed on the back of Eleanor's T-shirt.

Eleanor shrugged, dropping a small bunch of green grapes onto her paper plate. "It's more of a sisterhood, you know?"

"A sisterhood you have to pay for," Michaela mumbled under her breath.

The words came out before she could stop them, but she hadn't thought Eleanor would hear her. She'd thought the pulsing music and boisterous DJ and nonstop chatter around them would cover up the thought that had come tumbling out of her mouth at record speed.

Eleanor whipped around to glare at her. "You shouldn't talk about things you don't know anything about, Michaela."

She should've stopped there. Apologized. But her mouth just kept moving. "I know that sororities pay dues, and you can't go to meetings or parties, or like, take part in car washes or whatever if you don't pay your dues."

"*Car washes?*" Eleanor's light brown eyes were flashing. "You think that's what we're all about? Partying and soaping up cars? You should stop getting all your information from bad movies."

Michaela just looked at her. They'd talked about sororities when they were looking at school websites together. They'd laughed at them. Made fun of the groups of girls with their matching colors and identical haircuts and overdone smiles. They had been in agreement that they had no plans to pay for their friends.

"We give back to the community. We have to complete a certain number of service projects each year or the national chapter will put us on probation."

"You could do community service on your own."

Eleanor's mouth dropped open. "Are *you* doing community service, Michaela?"

"That's not the point. You're still—"

"You don't have to like the Greek system," Eleanor said, her voice lower. She was looking at Michaela's chin. "It's not for everyone. But don't shame me for being part of it. It's a *Black* sorority. Is it so bad that I wanted to make Black friends? That I didn't want to go through the next four years repeating what we went through in high school? Being the only ones?"

Her eyes met Michaela's on this last sentence, and then Michaela looked away. But Eleanor wasn't finished.

"You left," she said, throwing her hands in the air. "And you stopped answering my texts. And my emails. The only reason I even knew you were still alive is because of your posts."

Michaela stared at the picked-over cheese plate on the table. She knew what she wanted to say to Eleanor, but she wasn't sure how her throat would form the words. Or what if she did manage to get them out and Eleanor didn't believe she could be so affected by something so seemingly tiny?

"So, I don't even get an explanation?" Eleanor shook her head. "Typical. You know, Michaela, I thought we were going to be friends forever. You . . . you came along *exactly* when I needed you. You were the only person who didn't act like I was diseased when I told you Owen was sick."

Michaela swallowed, remembering how nervous Eleanor had been when she explained her little brother had been diagnosed with leukemia. She felt tears pricking at her eyes, so she shrugged, blinked them back, and said, "Well, nothing lasts forever."

Eleanor's face changed from hurt to shock to pure anger. With each shift of her expression, Michaela thought about all the different ways she could explain:

Actually, I wanted to call you every single day, but I worried you were too busy for me now.

You're the only person I wanted to talk to, but I was afraid you'd think I got what I deserved for flitting off to Europe instead of starting college with you.

I'm terrified that I can't get through regular life without you, and I don't know what to do about it.

But her mouth remained closed. And Eleanor just stared at her, eyes shooting straight venom. "You're being really shitty," she huffed, then stalked away, leaving her plate on the table.

Michaela bent at the waist, hands pressed to her knees.

If the gym had been stifling before, with the thick, sweaty air and all the marathon's rules and strangers brushing and bouncing against her every few seconds, the next few hours felt like being underwater.

Michaela kept replaying her conversation with Eleanor. Wondering how she could be so mean to her old friend. Wondering how Eleanor couldn't see that something in her had broken in a new way.

She lost herself in the dancing. It was the only way she'd be able to make it through the night. Harper was still running point, but Michaela moved so quickly and constantly that she scooted away each time Harper tried to talk to her. She even gave up one of her breaks, not wanting to get caught in the same space as Eleanor.

"Hey, all my Brockert College dancers! It's midnight, which means you're exactly *halfway* through this thing!" the DJ shouted from his booth, turning the music down for once. "How ya feeling?"

The dancers let out a collectively halfhearted *whooo*, and the sadness of it made Michaela laugh. Their cheer captain would've reamed them out if they'd ever cheered for anything like that, on or off the field.

"Awww, come on, dancers!" the DJ pleaded, his eyes moving wildly over the crowd. "That all you got for me?"

Properly shamed, they ratcheted up their response, trying to match his exuberance.

Tired as she was, as exhausted as she was from not just the dancing but her interaction with Eleanor, Michaela felt alive. In a way she hadn't felt since she'd first set foot in London, her very first stop on the trip, when everything had been fresh and exciting.

She bumped into her teammate Duncan, who, in a move that seemed to surprise both of them, reached for her hand and twirled her away from him and then back a couple of times, eventually releasing her into the crowd as they both laughed from exhilaration.

Michaela hardly knew anyone at Brockert College, but she still felt like part of something. And that felt good.

For a brief moment, she wondered if this was how Eleanor felt being part of the sorority. But then she pushed away the thought. This wasn't the same thing.

Michaela watched the DJ, wondering if he was on something stronger than the energy drinks he'd been pounding all night. Actually, as she looked around, she wondered if any of

the teams were partaking. Drugs and alcohol were strictly for-
bidden, and Harper had reminded them of this ferociously in
the lead-up to the big day. But someone was always sneaking
something in where it wasn't supposed to be, and Michaela
couldn't imagine an all-night fundraiser was any different.

At one a.m., Harper finally made Michaela take a break.
She fell asleep on the toilet, only waking when a loud group
of girls came bounding into the bathroom, slamming stall
doors and wondering loudly if anyone ever hooked up at these
things.

When she came out of the stall, two girls were standing by
the sinks. They must have been Eleanor's sorority sisters because
they were wearing the same lavender shirts. They looked tired,
but not unhappy.

"Girl, stand still," one of them said as she fussed with the
other one's bun.

"I'm trying," the other girl said, "but I'm afraid I'm going to
fall asleep if I don't keep moving."

"You know I won't let you fall asleep," her friend said, tucking stray strands of hair back into the bun. "I got you, girl."

Michaela felt a lump inexplicably rise in her throat. She
quickly turned away from them and moved to another sink to
wash her hands. Why did she feel on the verge of tears? The
moment wasn't *that* sentimental. She didn't even know them.

But deep down, she knew it was because they reminded her
of how she used to be with Eleanor. And she missed that. She
missed *her*. And she'd probably ruined things between them
forever with the way she'd dismissed her earlier. Eleanor was
right—she'd been shitty to her.

An hour later, Michaela felt . . . Well, she didn't know how she felt. Exhausted wasn't the word. It was almost as if she were detached from her body. She kept looking down, and once, when she bumped into Duncan again, he asked what she was doing.

"Making sure I'm still moving," she shouted over the music.

The sentence sounded weird when she said it aloud, but Duncan just nodded and gave her a thumbs-up as he bopped away.

Michaela's brain was fuzzy, probably wondering why she was still awake and why it had been tricked into making her body move like that for so many hours. She blinked a few times when she caught sight of Eleanor around three thirty in the morning. Had it only been a few hours since they'd talked?

Eleanor gave her a hard look before she turned her back, trying to make her way as far from Michaela as possible. Michaela's words came rushing back to her: *Well, nothing lasts forever.*

God, she had been *really* shitty to her old friend.

Michaela was trying to figure out how she was going to get Eleanor to talk to her again when the opening strains of the song made its way to her ears. The DJ had been on a tear of nineties rap, a definite crowd-pleaser, but recently switched it up to more current songs. And as soon as this one came on, Michaela was back in her high school gym, performing with the cheer team.

The school had a dance team, and they'd sneered every time the cheerleaders used music in their routines. As if anything to do with rhythm belonged to them alone. It's true, the cheer team would never be mistaken for dancers, but every year they learned a routine at camp that they performed at least once, even if only at an assembly. And this song—by Rihanna, their favorite—was the one they'd danced to last year.

Her eyes automatically looked for Eleanor. She hadn't moved too far away from Michaela, but her back was still turned. Michaela felt the routine in her bones, it was so deeply embedded in her from days of practice at camp and then weeks of rehearsal once they were back home. She could've done it in her sleep. And soon, she was doing it involuntarily.

As if she sensed it, Eleanor turned at that moment. She locked eyes with Michaela and, from yards away, their bodies began to move in sync. They were executing the moves perfectly, without even counting out the beats before they began. Without even discussing it.

Plenty of teams had line-danced together at the marathon, and Eleanor and her sorority sisters seemed to have some kind of routine they'd put together that they repeated throughout the night. But this was different. This was just Michaela and Eleanor—the only students in this room who knew this particular routine. Their hips swerved, their arms shooting out and up on the beat. And as they moved together, starting from the top, they danced closer to each other, parting the crowd surrounding them until they were face to face, as if they were dancing in a mirror.

They didn't stop, just performed the routine over and over again for the length of the song. People watched, and some tried to join in, but Michaela and Eleanor danced as if they were the only two people in the room. Michaela felt sweat dripping into her bra and down the small of her back. She knew it must be time to reapply deodorant, but she didn't care. She was dancing with Eleanor, and they were in perfect rhythm, exactly as they'd been for the past five years. It felt better than familiar. It felt like home.

When the song ended, so did their routine, and they just stepped from side to side, staring at each other. Eleanor glared at her, wiping sweat from her brow. Michaela tried to frown, if only so she wouldn't cry. She wanted her friend back. But she was right here, and Michaela didn't know what to say to her.

Eleanor danced closer, and Michaela held her breath, wondering, for a moment, if she might be angry enough to punch her. But then her friend's arms were reaching out, not in anger but acceptance. She wrapped her arms around Michaela, and Michaela leaned into her instantly.

"I'm sorry," she murmured into Eleanor's shoulder as they swayed on the dance floor. "I'm sorry I said that to you. And that I disappeared. I'm sorry. I'm really sorry, Eleanor."

"Shhhh," Eleanor said, squeezing her tight.

Five o'clock in the morning.

Michaela wasn't sure how she'd get through the next seven hours. Her body was busted. Energy completely zapped. She'd never run a marathon, but she wondered if it was better than this. She couldn't imagine it would take anyone twenty-four hours to get through it, even with breaks.

But a part of her felt energized. *Truly* alive. Because she was sitting next to Eleanor. And the tension that had been there before—well, it hadn't totally evaporated. There was still *something* between them that hadn't been there before Europe and

Eleanor joining the sorority. But things were better between them. Almost normal.

They'd found a corner of the gym that was relatively empty, with just a couple of napping people and others who might be dozing with their eyes open, they were so still. Up in the booth, the DJ was still going strong, and Michaela thought some of the participants *must* have broken the no-substances rule with the urgent way they were still gyrating on the dance floor, their bodies positively elastic.

"So," Eleanor said, a shy smile passing over her face. "My sisters will probably never let me live that down."

"Oh, please," Michaela said, grinning. "Who doesn't love an impromptu high school cheer routine? Weren't sororities built for things like that?"

Eleanor tugged at the shoelace on her right sneaker. "You know, it's too late for this semester, but you could pledge in the fall. Everyone would love you."

Michaela's grin faltered. "Oh. I . . . I don't think so. I mean, thanks. But it's not really me. Greek life."

"I didn't think it was for me, either, but I don't know. It's been nice. Being around so many other Black girls."

Michaela nodded, thinking of the girls she'd seen in the bathroom. Thinking of how she and Eleanor had always discussed what it would be like to not be the only ones. If Eleanor liked being in a sorority, maybe it wasn't so bad. She wasn't sure she'd ever find out, but she could be a little more open-minded if it made Eleanor happy.

"I really am sorry for being so shitty about it earlier," Michaela said. "It's just that we'd talked about how we'd never do that, and then here you are doing it, and I *knew* that already from your posts, but it's different seeing it in person."

"It *is* different," Eleanor said, shrugging. "Or at least different from what I thought it was. I don't love everyone in it or everything we do, but overall, it's good for me. It was . . . It was really hard starting here without you, Micky. I was scared. Like, what if I couldn't make it without you?"

Michaela nodded. She took two deep breaths, in through her nose and out through her mouth. The more Eleanor talked, the more she thought she should just be honest with her about why she'd pulled away. Even if it seemed childish. Even if it didn't quite make sense to her now.

But just as she was about to open her mouth, Eleanor spoke. "Owen's not okay."

Michaela's lips parted. "What?"

"What I said earlier, about him doing good and maybe going back to school soon . . . That's what Daddy says when people ask. But I think he's in denial. The cancer came back, and the doctor is trying to be optimistic, but I can tell he doesn't think it looks so good. Owen . . . he doesn't look so good."

"Oh, Eleanor." Michaela touched her friend's arm. She hated to think about it, but Owen had been so sick for so long, she'd been surprised to hear that he was getting better. "I'm so sorry. He's . . . Owen is strong. If he's held on this long—"

"But what if this is the time he doesn't?" Eleanor let out a long breath. "My sorority sisters don't even know about him."

Michaela's eyebrows shot up. "At all?"

Eleanor shook her head. "They know I have a little brother, but they don't know he's sick. It was weird, listening to them talk about the marathon and raising money. Most of them haven't even seen a sick kid in person, and I've probably spent more holidays at the children's hospital than in my own home."

"You don't think they'd understand?"

"I just don't think it's their business." Eleanor shrugged. "Not yet. I know, I know—how can I call them my sisters when I haven't told them everything about my life? I can't explain it, it's just . . . different."

Michaela's heart squeezed. Eleanor had always had trouble talking about Owen, but she'd never realized just how much her friend had trusted her with the pain her brother and family were going through. Until now.

"Is there anything I can do?"

Eleanor smiled at her, shaking her head. "This is perfect. Just you being here. Listening."

"Good." Michaela smiled back at her. "I'm glad."

"So, are you going to tell me why Europe was complicated? I just can't believe you'd come home so early. Were you lonely? Scared?"

Michaela sighed. "It was great, mostly. Traveling alone, I felt so different. So . . . like a grown-up version of me, I guess."

"You *look* a little more grown-up," Eleanor teased, tilting her head to peer at Michaela.

"But then, it—god, this is so stupid."

"What?" Eleanor frowned. "Did something happen?"

"No, no. I mean, not really. I mean." Michaela took a deep breath. "You know how sometimes you're minding your own business and then someone says or does something racist that just throws off your, like, whole day or week?"

Eleanor rolled her eyes in commiseration. "You know I do."

"I was in Paris, really excited to try this new restaurant, and I walked in and . . . they wouldn't seat me."

Eleanor's eyes popped. "Wait, what?"

Michaela looked down at the floor. She knew she hadn't done anything wrong, but she still felt embarrassed anytime she thought of what had happened.

"Yeah. I thought it was a mistake at first. Like the hostess didn't see me? But then she was talking to everyone else but me—seating people, answering questions. None of them were Black. She never once looked me in the eye. And it's like I was invisible and I just—I know worse things have happened to me over here. To both of us. But the fact that I couldn't sit down and get a meal because people didn't want to look at me or didn't think I was good enough or whatever was . . . It was mortifying."

Eleanor took Michaela's hands in hers, her expression radiating fury. "What the *fuck*? They seriously refused to seat you?"

Michaela nodded.

"Micky, you have no reason to be embarrassed. This is on them. And fuck them! You should call them out online. Everywhere you can, post the name of the restaurant and all the details. They can't get away with this!"

"No," Michaela said, shaking her head.

She'd thought about doing that. As she'd finally turned away from the hostess stand after many minutes of being ignored and watching people who'd come in after her immediately being seated and served, her own anger had burned white-hot through her veins.

"Why not? They deserve to be called out."

"I know, but I honestly don't even remember the name of it now. And I didn't do it then because I just felt so alone. Like no one would believe me. Or care. And then." Michaela swallowed. "I kind of broke. I went back to my room and I didn't leave for days and all I could think about was how maybe I deserved that. So I left. Came home."

"*What?*" Eleanor stared at her, mouth open. "You blamed yourself for some asshole's racism?"

"I blamed myself for taking a gap year, and for going to Europe and . . . for being so proud of myself for traveling. For getting *life* education instead of just starting school and being a college student like everyone else. And then breaking down the minute I ran into a real-life problem."

"Okay, but I still don't get it," Eleanor said, still grasping Michaela's hands. "I mean, I do, but . . . Why are you mad at yourself for wanting something different? For getting out to see the world?"

Michaela shrugged. "Because I feel guilty that my parents could afford to give me that? Or that I can even question not going to college when it wasn't even an option for so many Black people not that long ago?"

"Honestly, Micky, sometimes I feel weird that Owen's medical care isn't a bigger deal for us." Eleanor paused. "That sounds horrible, I know. But so many people go bankrupt or, like, *die* because they can't afford health care. And we've had some help, but we're lucky my parents have good jobs and we're not struggling and . . . I get it."

"Is it dumb that we feel this way?" Michaela said. "Shouldn't we just be grateful for what we have?"

"Yeah, but I don't think it's that simple. Not without history . . . and context."

"Yeah." Michaela sighed, resting her head on Eleanor's shoulder. They sat like that through a mix of soul-shaking songs, but even then, Michaela forgot where she was or what time it was. For a moment, it was just her and Eleanor, and everything was okay. Because even if it wasn't okay in the broader sense, even if she knew she'd probably have to deal with what she'd faced in Paris for the rest of her life in some form, she felt better having confided in Eleanor. She felt better knowing that even if how she'd handled things with her friend wasn't okay, that Eleanor understood her. And she was still right by her side, telling her that what had happened to her wasn't okay. That she didn't deserve it.

"Hey, teammate!"

Michaela groaned. She didn't have to look up to know it was Harper.

"I've been looking for you everywhere!" she said, tossing back her cup of water. "It's almost time to start up again. We're practically in the home stretch!"

Michaela didn't consider almost six more hours the home stretch, but in her short experience with Harper, being agreeable seemed the best way to get rid of her. "I'll meet you out there in a minute," Michaela said.

"Ten minutes," Harper said, pointing toward the clock as she walked away.

Eleanor yawned as Michaela lifted her head from her shoulder. She stretched her arms to the ceiling. "Can I just say something?" Eleanor said, staring at Michaela.

"Um, yeah. Sure."

"I'm so glad you're here. I'm so glad we're still the same, you know? You can be a real asshole when you want to be, but I missed the shit out of you, Micky."

Eleanor stood and brushed off her shorts. She held her hand out to help Michaela up.

Michaela took her friend's hand and stood. Looked into her eyes and felt that trusting, familiar warmth they'd shared for years now. The warmth that had always been there, even when she wasn't willing to lean into it.

"I missed you, too. And I'm sorry for being an asshole. Really."

"I know." Eleanor began steering them in the direction of the bathroom. "Come on. Only six more hours."

Michaela followed, holding tightly to Eleanor's hand.

UNDER OUR MASKS
by Julian Winters

REASON NUMBER SIXTEEN WHY BEING A VIGILANTE SUCKS—
you're always late to everything.

Three more flights. Twenty-four more stairs.

I'm breathless. It's nearly pitch-black in here. He *would* choose an abandoned building with thirteen floors, a broken elevator, and barely functional halogen lights flickering every three seconds, casting shadows against the walls of the stairwell like something out of a horror film.

If I were as fast as Streamline, this wouldn't be a problem.

But I'm not. I'm only slightly above human fast. Actually, all of my metahuman powers are only slightly above human standards.

Two more flights of stairs. Sixteen steps between me and the rooftop door. I can see it. An angry red EXIT sign glares at me in the cascade of shadows.

Honestly, I wouldn't be late if this city's delinquents would respect the laws of proper criminal-activity hours. Why can't they at least wait until after I've finished my Algebra II worksheets? At least until I've had an after-school snack.

I'm starving. The mouthful of coppery blood and broken glass I swallowed after stopping that last rookie attempt at robbing a gas station isn't exactly what I call dinner.

Luckily, my body heals slightly above human too.

One more flight. Eight stairs. My backpack smacks against my spine. My lungs stretch for more air. My open blue hoodie flaps like a cape behind me.

The door's handle is right there, but—

I stop short.

My hoodie. Damn it. Between evading the police and interviewers crowding up the gas station after the robbery and stopping by *another* gas station for the supplies I needed, I forgot to ditch my costume. Panting, I peer down. The artificial flame from the EXIT sign shines against my skintight black costume, the upper half exposed while the lower part is hidden behind a pair of loose joggers. The light beams against the midnight blue bird, wings outstretched, at the center of my chest, tinting it almost indigo.

"Yeah, that'll be hard to explain," I say to no one.

Quickly, I zip my hoodie all the way up, hiding the rest of my costume.

I don't have a choice about these powers or the responsibilities that come with them. At thirteen, I figured out puberty wasn't the only thing going on with my body, and the rules were made very clear.

Nana's Number One Rule to Being a Hero: "Never tell them who you are."

I inhale deeply. This is my secret. One of many.

Slowly, I nudge open the rooftop door with my shoulder and step into Tristan Jackson's world and out of Raven's cage.

From a distance, I watch him for a second.

He's leaning on the small brick parapet surrounding the rooftop, observing the city below. To his left, the sun is shrinking, a smear of blood orange against a pink-stained sky. At the edges, purple is clawing its way through the clouds. His outline is softened by the sunset. In normal lighting, he's all angles and hair. Now, he's curves and a sloped spine and the red of his hoodie is a sharp, knife-like contrast to his brown skin.

A messenger bag sits at his feet. He checks his phone, like he's waiting.

"Hey," I say, folding a casual tone around my nervous voice. "Sorry I'm late."

He glances over his shoulder, smiling. "It's cool."

It's not, though. Arshdeep Bhatt is punctual to everything. Every class, every club meeting, every pep rally. He's the kind of guy who never misses the previews for a movie. Not that I've been to the movies with Arash. We've never hung out, on purpose, outside of school grounds. Yes, we've orbited each other's social thermosphere since elementary school. But Arash is slightly closer to the nerds and economically gifted kids while I stick to the outliers. The ones that aren't into asking too many personal questions.

The problem is, I *like* when Arash asks me questions.

"I didn't mean to—"

Arash cuts me off with a laugh. "Seriously, Tris. It's no biggie." He turns back to the city, shoulders relaxing. "You're doing me a favor, remember?"

"Yeah," I whisper.

But that's not true, either. I'm doing myself a favor by meeting him on this rooftop on a Friday night. I'm also quite possibly making the biggest mistake of my life.

I stride over to him, resting my elbows on the parapet.

Sunlight dies quietly beyond the horizon. The city rises in front of us, waking up like a restless lion. Dark towers blink with cracks of false lighting through office windows as custodians clean cubicles and boardrooms. Glittery signs sit like fallen stars across the grid, advertising shady bars and clubs we're too young to enter. Cars jerk in stop-and-go traffic.

Atlanta feels like an old, hooded sweatshirt. One size too small from constant washing; a hole in the sleeve; the drawstrings uneven. But it's always comfortable and warm. Even with all the chaos, this city's comfortable and warm.

I wish I knew how to protect it better. I wish I was a few degrees better than slightly above average.

"So." Arash twists in my direction. "Did you bring the supplies?"

I roll my eyes, smirking. Shrugging off my backpack, I unzip it and reveal the contents to him. Inside, four energy drink cans lie sideways on a mound of rainbow plastic bags. I bought five different kinds of sour candies since Arash didn't specify which kinds he likes.

Though, maybe I should know?

We sit at the same lunch table every day. I've seen Arash pop handfuls of sour gummy worms in his mouth more than I've witnessed him eat normal food. But maybe knowing his favorite brand would be level-ten stalkerish.

As if watching Arash eat isn't creepy enough.

But I've always noticed things about Arash. I've always noticed *him*.

His tall, thick hair that never sits right, a few strands always falling into a curl against his forehead. The kind of brown eyes that look like there's fireflies hidden behind them. His square jaw and angular cheeks are quite opposite from the softness of the rest of his body. He's shorter than me, five-foot-eight-ish to my six-foot-one.

He plucks a bag of sour hard candies from my backpack. "You're a legend, Tris."

I nudge his shoulder. "What about you? Tell me you came through for me."

Arash leans back, grinning smugly. "You doubt my skills?"

"I doubt everything about you, Arash."

"Wow," he says, hand to his chest, faking a pained expression. "That hurts. Total foul."

I nudge him again, laughing.

This is Arash inside the cafeteria, in the halls. He's the type of person you naturally cling to. Make jokes with. Even on this rooftop, it feels so easy to be around him.

Arash toes his messenger bag aside to reveal a giant plastic bag with two Styrofoam takeout cartons inside. I smell the heat and spice and euphoria before he opens the bag.

"As promised."

The first takeout container is from my favorite wing spot two blocks from Juniper Road High School. The scent of buffalo hot chicken wings tickles my nostrils. I almost drool all over them.

"It's not that serious," Arash deadpans.

"Oh, my dear little Arash," I say with wide eyes matching the stretch of my mouth. "It is. I almost never get to drop by that wing joint anymore."

Because I'm always on the run after school, I want to add.

Arash shakes his head. "If you really want something spicy, you should try my dādī's Chettinad chicken. You won't survive."

"Is that a challenge?"

The second takeout carton is the real gift. Inside, leftover basmati rice, still slightly warm, greets me. As part of our negotiations for tonight's plan, I requested Arash bring me some of the glorious cuisine I catch him eating once or twice a week at our lunch table when he's not demolishing a bag of Sour Patch Kids. The smell is always so intoxicating, and the basmati rice doesn't disappoint. Its spicy aroma hits me like the glass bottle that robber smashed into my jaw at the gas station an hour ago. Except, this time, my stomach yearns for its flavor instead of clenching at the taste of my own blood.

"Homecooked," Arash says, proudly.

"By you?" I ask.

He nods, a shy curl to his lips. "My parents helped, a little."

"Nice."

"You're welcome."

I can't wrap my mouth around a "thank you," not with the

way Arash's eyes squint when he smiles at me. I nod, hoping it expresses my gratitude.

We unpack our food and drink supply on the parapet. It's wide enough, but the slightest clumsy movement—most likely by me since coordination isn't a metahuman gift that runs in the family—could send everything crashing onto the road below.

Arash pops his first energy drink, chugging half of it.

I sip at mine. I know we're going to need the caffeine rush to stay up all night for this.

"So, this is an assignment for what class again?" I wave one hand around the rooftop while shoveling rice and chicken into my mouth with my other hand.

"Journalism."

"Seems a bit deep for a class," I say after swallowing. "Dangerous too."

Arash shrugs. "Not really? It's not like he's a supervillain or something."

"No," I say, almost choking. *Nothing super about me.* "Just a regular, average hero." In my peripheral, he's watching me, head tilted. "He's just . . ."

"The Raven," he says.

"It's just Raven," I correct him with a bit too much bite.

Arash stares at me.

"No, seriously. Raven. One word."

"I think it's interchangeable? Like the Batman. Or the Superman."

Actually, it's not. Just Raven, unfortunately.

Note to future teen vigilantes or potential superheroes— don't choose your name while binge-watching movies made in the nineties after spending two weeks reading Edgar Allan Poe for an English essay.

Don't choose your alter ego after watching *anything* on Netflix.

"Uh." I pick at the rice. "I think it's *the* Dark Knight. Or *the* Man of Steel. Not the other ones."

Arash bumps my shoulder. "Thank you for the geekumentary version."

I guzzle more energy drink.

"But think about the grade I'll get if we catch him and I get to interview him," Arash adds excitedly.

His reasons for asking me, instead of our other friends, to execute this plan seemed fairly basic. One, our other friends wouldn't be caught dead in this neighborhood after the sun goes down. Two, everyone knows I'm a notorious night owl—though they don't know it's because of my extracurricular vigilante activities. Three, he knows I never turn down a challenge, even one as hazardous as this.

But I should have turned down this challenge. I should have had at least the most basic common sense to not put myself *closer* to the guy trying to track me down. And yet, I couldn't say no. I couldn't refuse the chance to spend time with Arash outside of Juniper Road High. My chest hurts with the amount of ifs and rules and secrets inside.

What if I just . . . told him?

"Why here?" I ask instead.

Arash rests his elbows between two energy drinks. He leans over the ledge but not too far. Only enough to get a proper view. "Because this is where he's been spotted the most. Around this neighborhood." He points in the direction of a structure almost opposite of us. "On the roof of that apartment building."

His finger moves to a smaller building nearby. "Around that pizza place. The dry cleaners next door." He points to a tower with sporadically lit windows crawling up the side like jagged teeth. "Those offices. All around this area."

He's right. I spend way too much time here.

The apartment building is where my nana—formerly known as Streamline—lives.

I eat pizza across the street. I watch over Mr. Chang's dry-cleaner shop.

The office building is where my dad used to work when he wasn't being Asteroid.

Before Mom—the recently retired Remedy—moved us out to the suburbs, I cut my teeth and shaped my bones in these streets.

But I mostly come here to visit Nana. I know she's lonely. Rule number one comes with consequences: No normal friends. No one outside of the small hero circle our family keeps can know who we are. And she refuses to leave the city behind.

"Here. Check it out."

Arash passes his phone to me, swiping through YouTube videos. Each clip is of me, all black costume and blue raven on my chest, feathers spread like fingers around the eyes of my mask. Me, on rooftops, jumping from ledges. Me, a blur as I run into alleys.

Me, being clumsy and careless and everything a sixteen-year-old rookie hero shouldn't be. I tug the zipper of my hoodie higher.

"You've put a lot of effort into this," I say. "Also, stalker much?"

Under the tinted lilac sky, Arash's blush is visible against his light brown skin, spreading rapidly like watercolor paint against a blank canvas. "Okay, so I think Raven's kind of boss."

A tiny surge of joy spreads through my throat at him using the correct name.

"Kind of?"

"A solid nine on the boss-level scale," he offers.

"Eh. I give him a hard five at best," I tease.

"He's better than that. He has all these cool powers."

I try not to make a face.

I'm only half as fast as Nana. I can leap a quarter of the height Dad can. Yeah, I heal quickly, but not as rapidly as Mom. I can't fly or smash through brick walls. There's no place for me in the Jackson hall of fame. Truthfully, I think I should just hang up my mask. Otherwise I might ruin my family's legacy.

"And he's just . . ." Arash's voice trails off into the gentle early March breeze.

"He's what?"

Arash's mouth puckers but he doesn't reply.

I want to know.

Raven is awesome?

Courageous?

Cute?

"Never mind," Arash mumbles.

Disappointment hits my chest like a fist, but I keep a poker face.

"Well," I say, looking around. "What do we do until he shows up? Besides wait and eat?"

Arash grins. "Homework!"

"What? Seriously? On a Friday night?"

It's not as if I'm that surprised. Arash is a great student. He maintains a superior grade point average while I try to stay awake in class. Mom's been talking a lot about college recently. I want to ask her what vigilante has time for college coursework? But Dad did it. And Nana managed to get a nursing degree while being Streamline. They also had no social life.

I'd like to have a community outside of other heroes. I want to go to college, play a sport, and go to parties. I want a boyfriend who doesn't have to worry about if I'll be home late—or *if* I'll make it home at all.

But I don't know how to tell my family that. I wish I could talk about it with someone. With someone like Arash.

I seal up the rice container to snack on later. The wings are already destroyed. "Okay," I finally say. "But how are we gonna study in the dark?"

Another smug grin shapes Arash's mouth. "Let me show you."

We pack up the untouched energy drinks, leftover rice, and sour candies before Arash leads me to another side of the rooftop.

A series of interconnecting steel poles creates a structure probably meant for hanging banners. Tangled around its metal bones are strings of colorful fairy lights. Maybe they were left over from the holidays. Maybe they've been here for years. I don't know. But I like the way they hang two feet above my head, like a small galaxy of mini stars and planets lighting this side of the rooftop under the cloak of a heavy blue-black sky.

Beneath the lights are two old lawn chairs and a wobbly iron table.

In all my nights around here, I don't think I've noticed this before.

"Wow," I say, my voice almost swallowed by another breeze. "Did you do this?"

"I did," confirms Arash as he drops one of those portable phone chargers onto the table. "I would've come over here first, but I wanted a clear view of the sunset."

"Genius."

"I prefer the title King, but Genius is acceptable." Arash laughs, this full noise that hits a sharp note at the end. At school, he's always laughing into his hands, trying to cover up the noise but out here, under an artificial galaxy and standing tall over a glowing city, Arash lets it loose. "Shall we get to work?"

We still have a decent perspective of Nana's apartment building and the pizza place. I can do my nightly surveillance from here. Not that Nana, even in her eighties, needs me to watch over her. She's still faster and stronger than an average human in their prime years. But it's part of the job—protecting people.

It's an adrenaline rush to save someone, a high that's hard to come down from, but the rulebook doesn't warn you of the repercussions when you fail to help them.

A year ago, when I was still new to doing this solo, I fell asleep in an alley while studying. I had an exam the next morning I couldn't afford to fail. Some guy decided that was the perfect time to carjack a Corvette from a nearby parking garage while I was napping. The police tailed him for five blocks before he lost control, jumping a curb and hitting pedestrians. One girl died.

Carla Santos. She was a year younger than me. And she'll never see another sunset because I dozed off.

I push away the images of her face on the news that night with a shaky breath and then dump my backpack on the ground. Carefully, I recline into a chair. It doesn't look sturdy, but it doesn't collapse under my weight either. Arash has already unpacked his messenger bag, laptop on his knees. I snatch my barely cracked copy of *The Great Gatsby* from my backpack. No disrespect Mr. Fitzgerald, but I'm bored out of my mind every time I open this book.

Why is this a classic? And what does it have to do with me, a sixteen-year-old Black teen in Atlanta?

I heard schools in other districts are reading books like *The Hate U Give*. The "economically blessed schools," as Nana calls them.

I stretch my legs out, trying to fit comfortably in the chair. The toe of my left shoe butts up against the sole of Arash's right foot.

"Careful of the kicks," he says, leaning over to wipe at an invisible smudge.

I'll admit it—Arash's shoe game is godly. He always has the freshest pair of anyone at Juniper Road High. On his phone, he has this app, LACES OUT, that alerts him to the newest kicks coming out and where to find them the cheapest. He's first in line for all the exclusive releases.

Tonight, he's wearing a rare pair of solid black AF1s with crimson stitching and red outlining the Nike swoosh. The soles are red too.

I glance at my own sneakers, the ones Nana bought for my birthday. They're still mostly white. *Grayish white.* There's not a rule in Nana's book about what shoes to wear while chasing criminals. These have held up pretty well, but I'm starting to outgrow them.

"You treat your sneakers like you're in a relationship with them," I say, almost laughing at the way Arash is still examining his shoe.

"So?" He shoots me an unpersuasive affronted expression. "Maybe I feel good in a clean pair of kicks? At least I know my shoes appreciate me. We chose each other."

"That's poetic. And a little weird."

"I feel like—" Arash pauses. His teeth pull at the corner of his lower lip, pinching so hard the skin turns white. "Nice shoes make me feel better about myself. About the way I look."

I tilt my head to one side. "The way you look?"

"Keep it real, Tris. No one's checking for a brown boy who isn't lean or tall." He shakes his head. "They're not really checking for a brown boy like me at all. Half the people we go to school with just look at me like I'm out of place."

I squint at him. I guess I never paid attention to the way anyone else stares at Arash. Probably because I'm too busy looking at him like . . . I don't know. Like he's incredible. Like he's beautiful, his laugh and soft shape and personality. The shoes are just a bonus.

I realize this is Arash letting me in. This is one of his secrets.

And it makes me warm, comfortable, like the city. It also makes me protective of him.

"These are the only things that make me feel . . . better than average?" he whispers, pointing to his shoes.

"You're not average," I try to argue.

"I am."

"Not to me."

"Oh?" He laughs, but it's not the one from earlier. It's hollow, scraped of all the joy. "Are you trying to compete with my shoes?"

I hesitate to respond. No one knows about my sexuality. It's another thing I haven't felt secure enough to trust anyone with yet. I don't know anything about Arash's sexuality either. But we're sixteen and it feels like, if we're anything but straight, we have to make an announcement about it in the next five years. We're supposed to disclose every piece of ourselves, so everyone else is aware. So they can decide whether they're comfortable with who we are.

People expect us to take off our masks and reveal our secret identities so they can decide if we're heroes or villains.

"Your shoes are aight," I finally say, smiling when his eyebrows zoom up his forehead. "But I kind of dig better-than-average Arshdeep, with or without the dope sneakers."

Arash tips his chin down, eyes on his keyboard. But the glow from the laptop's screen shines on his face.

He's blushing.

I nudge his foot again. He doesn't jerk away. He lets it sit there while he returns to typing. I pretend Nick Carraway is slightly more interesting than that tiny smile pushing Arash's cheeks up.

Yawning, I check my phone. It's one a.m.

I've long given up on my book, zoning in on some Algebra II sheets but it's not keeping me awake. And there's no real activity in the city, definitely not in this neighborhood, for once. Nothing other than a showdown between two angry cats in an alley nearby. A club's doors open randomly, exhaling reggae music into the streets.

No sign of Raven, obviously, though Arash has been scouting the rooftops from time to time.

Another yawn springs from my mouth into the crook of my elbow. That watery film from exhaustion sticks to my eyelashes.

"Here."

Arash nudges a can into my hand. It's a lukewarm, no-name brand of cola. For a second, I make a face at it. I hate cola but whatever reserve source of energy I have is tapped out from one too many late nights this week, so I crack the lid and sip slowly. Despite the taste, the caffeine sizzles through my cells pleasantly.

Arash chugs his own, mixing it with handfuls of sour gummy bears.

I almost gag watching him.

In the distance, rushing closer, sirens wail. Their red and white lights climb the sides of dark buildings.

I flinch hard, an unconscious reaction. Most nights, this is all I know. What are the sirens for this time? Could I be helping? Carla Santos's face flashes in my mind.

"Does the noise make you jumpy?" Arash asks.

All my breaths feel like they're on fire. I shake my head. "Nah," I lie. I hold up the cola. "I'm shocked at how gross this is."

Arash rolls his eyes. "Okay, hero."

I dream of those sirens. I dream of saving the day, and I dream of being too late to save the day, and I dream of not even being able to save myself. I want to tell Arash this, so I don't have to carry the weight on my own.

Eventually, the sirens fade as they draw closer to their destination. But their ghostly screams ring in my ears.

Should I be there?

Is it selfish to be with Arash instead?

"No more homework," he announces, tucking his laptop into his messenger bag. The metal legs of his lawn chair screech against the rooftop as he turns it to face me. "Let's play Kiss, Marry, Kill."

My eyebrows scrunch. "Wait, isn't it Fu—"

"Not in every version," Arash interrupts.

I snort. "It is in all the versions I've played."

"Not this one. Besides," he clears his throat, "kiss seems more appropriate, I'm guessing. Unless you have, you know."

"Unless I have . . . ?"

"You know."

"Arash, we're sixteen. You can say it. Teens are having sex in PG-rated movies now."

He sighs, shoulders deflating. "Unless you're not a virgin, Tris. I mean, I'm not saying that *isn't* true but."

"But what?"

"Have you?"

"I—" There isn't enough strength in my vocal cords to finish that sentence. I turn my head. My brown complexion has natural reddish undertones, so my blush isn't as noticeable as Arash's, but I'm still trying to hide the flames licking my cheeks. "Let's just play."

"Frequency, December, and Faze. Kiss, Marry, Kill."

I roll my eyes.

Arash is such a dork. Of course, he'd make this the heroes' version of Kiss, Marry, Kill. At least I'm not related to any of them.

"This is foul, Arash."

"What? You agreed to play."

"Yeah, but—"

"You can back out," he offers, but there's something sly in his voice. "If you're not up for the challenge, that is."

He knows I am. He knows I take any bet. A month ago I almost gave away the fact that I have metahuman genes running through my cells when Scott Perry challenged me to a slam dunk contest in gym. I tried to let him win, but Scott's a jerk and competition got the best of me, so I crushed him. It felt great until someone uploaded a video of me jumping over Scott's six-foot-one lanky body, doing a one-eighty before nailing a dunk.

I got offered a starting spot on the varsity team from the head coach and two weeks without TV and phone from Mom when I got home.

It was kind of worth it, though. That itch to be on the basketball team hasn't left since.

"Fine," I sigh. I consider my options. "Kiss December."

December lives in New York City. She can manipulate

moisture into ice, has an undercut and streaked blue hair, and freckles across her light brown skin.

"Because she's cool, literally," I explain.

Arash laughs, sharp squeak included.

"Kill Faze," I say without thinking.

Faze is my sworn enemy. He's more focused on patrolling the Atlanta suburbs, anything outside of the city's perimeter. Also known as the privileged and low-risk communities. The guy has TV-ready hair and even wears a letterman jacket over his costume. Plus, his superpower—creating massively destructive vibrations by touching things—is legit corny.

"Agreed," Arash says, nodding. "Superior loser."

I scratch my temple, then play with my hair. I need a trim. It's curling at the ends, standing up in all directions. The thickness is making my mask a snug fit. "So, I guess that means . . ."

"You're marrying Frequency?"

It's not the worst thing. Frequency resides in Florida. I'm not sure what heroes do in Florida. Wrestle alligators, fight hurricanes, and help maintain upkeep at retirement homes? Anyway, Frequency physically absorbs the wall of sound created by music to enhance his strength, which means if I'm sentenced to a life partnership with him, at least I'm guaranteed solid tunes.

"He's cute enough," I joke. "So, yeah. Marrying Frequency."

"Marrying a guy," Arash says, but it falls out almost like a question. The fairy lights reflect off his eyes, like a collision of constellations around a black hole.

"Marrying a guy," I confirm with a little less conviction.

Should I tell him?

Can I tell him?

It's Arash, which isn't the worst choice when it comes to coming out. Not after he's admitted he hates the way people analyze him. Not when something in his smile, his unrestrained laugh, the constant flush in his cheeks says something.

I hope it's saying something.

"It's just marriage," I eventually add, swerving my words before I confess too much. "We haven't outlined what that entails. It's not like I'm, you know, doing *other things* with him."

Arash shrugs. "Sure, I guess." He takes a sip of soda and changes the subject. "This is a poor substitute for a good espresso, but it does the job."

"Espresso?" My face pinches.

"Tris, espresso is life."

"You have so many problems, I don't know where to start."

Arash launches into a never-ending explanation of why espresso is vital. He breaks down the taste, the layers, the beans, everything. And I grin so hard, my mouth might not ever snap back.

This. This is why I want to shatter the glass I'm stuck behind. This is why I want to let Arash climb inside my world. Because I'll sit on a rooftop at nearly two a.m. and listen to him wax poetically about nonsense like the heart of an espresso shot and the importance of pulling it as close to thirty seconds as possible.

I'll remember these useless facts because they came from Arash.

He stops rambling. "What?"

Obviously, I haven't stopped grinning.

Tell him. Tell him. Tell him.

I whisper, "Nothing."

Maybe I daydream a little about what I wanted my answers to be.

Kill Faze. Marry Arash. Fu—I mean, Kiss Arash.

Kiss and kiss and kiss Arash.

Four a.m. stretches around us like gray clouds before a thunderstorm. Arash and I are elbow-to-elbow on the parapet. We're listening to tunes on his phone's speaker. He has respectable music taste with only a few questionable selections—like one too many tracks by Post Malone—but I can deal with his playlists. Shoulder to shoulder, we transfer body heat through our thin hoodies. But I keep our closeness light, not wanting him to feel the outline of my costume underneath.

I can pick out Nana's window in her apartment building by the potted plants sitting on the sill. I can imagine climbing those six flights of stairs, falling face-first onto the yellow futon in her living room to pass out.

Not right now, though.

I'm wide awake.

Energy assaults my nerves, fission dissolving Tristan from Raven, even though I know I'm both. Even though I know Arash is watching Nana's building, the pizza place, the alleys with hopes Raven will appear.

But, leaning next to him, I feel so much more like Tristan than the vigilante trying to carry on the legacy created by his parents, his nana, the three generations of heroes before her. I feel like Tristan, the teen who just happens to have a crush on a boy.

That's what I want to tell Arash—I'm Raven, but I'm also a boy with a crush who's scared to disappoint his family or end up alone like his nana. I'm slightly above average, but around Arash, I feel . . . limitless.

Occasionally, I steal glances at him. He blinks a lot, as if he's trying to stay awake. His lips part sporadically to whisper lyrics. The colorful glow from above falls over his face like spilled starlight.

He waits and waits for something that's right next to him.

Over his shoulder, Arash shoots me a soft, sleepy grin. Should I tell him? Should I risk him never looking at me like this again?

Soon. Not in this second, though.

I just want a few more minutes of Arash's smile and the music and being simply Tristan Jackson to him.

Sunrise blooms in rose and tangerine, sweeping the purple from the sky. A golden sun backlights all the buildings until they're only fuzzy, dark silhouettes. It's all a cruel reminder that morning is here.

My time with Arash is evaporating.

We pack up silently. Arash stuffs what's left of his sour candies into his messenger bag, along with the last untouched energy drink. I shove *The Great Gatsby* and my Algebra II book into my backpack. I demolished the rice an hour ago. We bag up the containers and empty cola cans to drop into an alley dumpster.

"I'm sorry." I rub the nape of my neck. My fingertips skim the collar of my costume. "Sorry that we didn't see Raven."

Arash rocks on his heels. "It's cool."

"Will you, uh—" My voice is pinched. "Are you still gonna try to catch him? For your assignment?"

I hate asking these questions. I hate wondering if the next time Arash and I will be alone is when he finally tracks me down on a roof or in an alley or outside Nana's building.

Tell him, you idiot.

"I'm not sure," he replies. "Thanks for sitting with me."

"No problem." I hold up our trash bag. "I got some bomb-ass food out of it."

"Maybe . . ."

There's a long breath and then we share a look. Somehow, sunrise and exhaustion make his eyes browner.

"Maybe we can hang again, you know, without all the waiting?" he offers.

Clear, clean oxygen fills my lungs. I beam. "I'd be down for that."

"Me too."

"But, like, after a good nap?" I suggest.

"A nap to defeat all regular naps."

We laugh in harmony, drowning out the cars and shops and birds waking up around the city.

Then Arash bites his lip, fiddles with the strap on his messenger bag. He's barely making eye contact. "Seriously, I'd like to hang with you." Shyly, he pushes away the curl on his forehead. He inhales sharply. "I like you. I'd want to . . ."

I cross my arms, smiling, watching him fidget and stumble.

"I hope I'm not reading this wrong. Because you're really awesome, Tris. So, maybe . . ."

Arash's face is redder than his hoodie.

I take a few steps closer. I shrink the gap where nerves vibrate between us. Nana's number one rule exists for a reason: to protect the regular humans in our lives. Heroes only date other heroes. Friendships are contained with strict limits.

It's for their safety. And ours too.

But I abandon the rulebook because life is filled with "what ifs." I'm not Streamline or Asteroid or Remedy. I'm not Nana or my parents.

I'm Tristan. I'm Raven.

I don't want to live my life behind a mask with no one to share who I am with.

My shoulders are tight. My stomach has constricted into four knots. But I push the words out before fear stops me.

"I'm Raven. I'm, uh, a hero. More like vigilante."

With shaking hands, I unzip my hoodie.

There it is. The top half of my costume. The blue-outlined raven on my chest.

Arash doesn't stare at me with wide, owlish eyes. He doesn't freak out. With a sheepish shrug, he says, "Yeah, kind of figured that out."

"You what?"

He laughs quietly. "Uh, have you not noticed my obsession with Raven? With you, I guess? The clues were there." He pushes his hair back. "I asked for your help because . . . I don't know. I wanted you to tell me. Or I wanted you to be okay with telling me."

My throat is dry. Arash knows. He knew all along. But he wanted me to say it.

"But *how* are you Raven?" he asks.

I can't wrap my brain around his question. Arash knows I'm Raven. Incredible.

"It's a long, long story. Like, a lot of science and family history and some real sketchy shit but, well." My lungs are exerting so much effort to keep up with my sprinting heart. "I didn't know how to tell you. Or how to come out because, I dunno. It's a lot."

"Well, you just did." Arash smirks.

Finally, my body remembers how to breathe and relax and process words.

"I'm Raven," I repeat, for confirmation.

He nods slowly. "I won't tell anyone. I *haven't* told anyone since I figured it out."

"Thanks," I exhale. A small part of me still worries my secret will escape, but a much larger part of me trusts Arash.

My next few words ease out of me. "And I'm gay."

Arash's eyes brighten. "That is . . ." Slowly, his expression begins to unwind. "I wasn't sure. I mean, earlier when I—"

"Dude," I say, laughing. "You're flailing."

"Sorry." He smiles. "You're gay. Cool."

"This isn't a big deal?" I ask, realizing I've just come out twice to him in less than three minutes.

"What? That you're my favorite hero?"

Heat rises up the back of my neck. "I'm not a hero. Just an above-average teenager."

"A friend of mine seems to think being better-than-average is pretty cool," Arash says.

"Yeah, yeah." I sigh. "But what about . . . the gay part?"

"What about it? You're Tristan Jackson. Just Tris," he says, inching a little closer. "The Raven part? So boss. The gay part? A major plus for the guy who's been casually trying to, I dunno, kiss you since last year."

"My dude." I smack a hand against my forehead. "We don't even hang out like that. How would I know?"

"You're the hero. Follow the clues."

"That's not even how that works." I chuckle, then my brain recycles all his words. "Wait. You want to kiss me?"

"Yes. But not now," he says. "Because I've kind of been up all night, drinking soda and eating sour candies and—"

"Stealing my basmati rice when you thought I wasn't looking?" I accuse with a smile.

"That too."

I nod. "That'd probably be bad. Not the kissing—our breaths thing."

"Yeah," he says quietly, looking at his feet. "So, we can wait on that."

"We do a lot of waiting, huh?"

"I think we're pretty good at it." Then Arash steps back, turns as if we've come to some agreed-upon resolution. Which I suppose we have but it's not enough for me.

With reflexes half as quick as Nana's, I grab Arash's arm and spin him back to me. I brush my fingers against his jaw, lifting it before bending down to kiss him.

There's a little hesitation, but he kisses back.

His cool palms hug my cheeks and he steps on my shoes to get closer. Our mouths open, his tongue teasing my teeth, and I almost lose it because this is happening. We're really kissing.

Arash is right. His breath tastes sour from candy and spicy from the rice but it's sweet with cola and not bad.

Definitely worth a repeat performance after we've brushed our teeth.

"Oh, Tris," he whispers against my mouth. "You taste like hot wings."

I think I've found another superpower—my cheeks catch fire in a blink, probably singeing the skin off Arash's hands.

He steps off my shoes, almost tripping as he moves back. "I'd really like to do that again, soonish," he says with a lopsided smile and squinted eyes.

"Same."

We stand there, painted gold and pink from the sunrise, watching each other. Eventually, I grab his hand. He squeezes back. We walk side by side toward the rooftop's exit.

"If you want," Arash says when we're downstairs on the street, "I can take you for that cup of espresso. Just to try it." We're not holding hands anymore but we're still standing close.

I snort, shaking my head. "That'd be nice. But first," I motion down the street toward Nana's building, "I need to check on my nana. Usually, I would've already but . . ."

Arash's eyebrows furrow, then it clicks. His eyes widen. "That's why you're—" he pauses, looking around. There's no one nearby; it's too early. "That's why Raven's always skulking—"

"Hold up. I don't skulk."

"You so skulk," he teases. "I get it. Why you spend so much time around here."

"Yeah. So."

"Later?" he offers.

We agree to meet at this coffee shop downtown. One that is far enough away from Juniper Road High, so we don't have familiar eyes on us. A place where we can stretch out, laugh, and talk without having to make any declarations. I'm glad I told Arash the truth, but for now, I don't want to share it with our classmates. I want to keep this warm, secure feeling between us.

I'm not like Nana. I'm not like my parents. I can share my secret. I have someone I can talk to about feeling like less than a hero. And I get to choose how and why. I don't need to peel my mask off for everyone.

We yawn in unison, blinking way too many times.

"I should go," he says.

"Me too."

Before Arash walks away, he shows me his own superpower: hyper-boldness. In the middle of the sidewalk, he kisses me one more time.

For the record—we need a lot of practice.

But there's time for that.

THE GHOST OF GOON CREEK
by Francesca Zappia

"I CAME TO ASK YOU FOR A FAVOR," GRACE SAID.

I set down my pen and my breadstick and closed my notebook. I was not the person who was approached in the cafeteria. I was not, generally, the person who was approached *anywhere*. When you know more about the local ghosts than you do about your classmates, people—especially the popular ones—learn to avoid you. Grace Chang, poster child for societal expectations, talking to me out of the blue was weird enough; Grace Chang asking me for a favor was downright concerning.

Grace always talked with her hands, and they were up now, moving fast. "The October issue of the newspaper is coming out in two weeks, and this year the feature section is completely Halloween-themed. We're reviewing haunted houses and horror movies, we've got a history of Halloween candy, and we're starting an annual two-page spread covering a local urban legend."

"Oh," I said.

"You know where I'm going with this?"

I did. I wished I didn't. "What do you want to know about?"

"The ghost."

"Which one?"

"The Ghost of Goon Creek. I heard that you go every year to find it."

I kept my expression even. Everyone in school knew Sydney Endrizzi collected local ghost stories, but usually no one brought it up except to make jokes. "Google knows as much about it as I do."

"Actually, I wasn't looking for information." Grace gave me a winning smile. "I was hoping you'd take me with you."

I paused sipping my chocolate milk, coughed lightly, and said, "Excuse me?"

"I'd love to come with you. I could interview you about it, if you'd be okay with that, and I could write about the experience and give the readers a sense of being there."

"I'm not going this year," I said stiffly. My brother, Tony, was in California now, so my days of physically hunting ghosts were over. Generally, it's not a great idea to go out alone late at night when you're a teenage girl, and my dad wouldn't let me unless I had someone along. Grace's smile faded. "Feel free to go yourself, though. No one will stop you. Just like, take a friend or two."

"Oh," Grace said, and she looked so crestfallen that I almost cared. "That's okay. I thought I'd ask because you're the resident expert on the paranormal, and it would be cool to showcase you as the experienced guide who's unraveling the mysteries of Goon Creek. You're kind of mysterious yourself. People would be interested."

My whole body went still, the tips of my fingers tingling, a knotted feeling in my gut.

"Mysterious?" I asked.

Grace nodded and shrugged.

People thought I was mysterious?

Mysterious, and not just weird? Sydney Endrizzi, friendless after her brother went to college, with her urban legends and her ghost hunts?

"And I'd seem mysterious in this article?" I asked. "Like, you wouldn't just tell the whole school all about my life?"

"No! Not if you don't want me to. Mysterious all the way."

I sat back, drumming my fingers on the edge of the lunch table. "There is no ghost, you know that, right?"

"The story exists, even if the ghost itself doesn't, and that's what the article is really about."

At least she wouldn't be asking me constantly if we were going to see something. "When I go, I stay out all night. That's part of the story. You have to stay until sunrise."

Grace's expression lit up. She nodded. "Yes, of course."

"Your parents would be fine with it?"

"If it's for the newspaper, yes."

"You have to bring your own snacks."

"No problem."

"And bug spray."

"Already got it."

"I get to read your article before it gets published, and you'll let me veto anything that makes me sound like a creep."

Grace held her hand over her heart. "I swear, I would never do anything to make you sound like a creep."

I stared at her.

"Yes," she said, "you can veto."

"Okay. This Friday. Meet me in the parking lot by the soccer field at ten."

Grace gasped and flapped her hands. "Oh my gosh, Sydney, *thank you*. I owe you so big. Friday at ten by the soccer field. Got it. Thank you!"

For a moment I thought she was going to rush around the table to hug me, but instead she hurried back to the other side of the cafeteria. A few people looked my way, probably wondering why newspaper feature editor Grace Chang was speaking to *me*, of all people, and what I could have possibly said to make her so happy.

I didn't know what she and I were going to talk about for hours in a cemetery at night, but if it made my classmates think I was eccentric instead of a loser, I'd figure it out.

Grace was waiting for me at the soccer field that Friday night. She leaned against the front of her car, backpack at her feet, typing on her phone. There were a concerning number of cars in the lot around her.

"I thought I could interview you while we walked." Grace had her phone out and waved it around. "Is that okay?"

I glanced at the phone camera, then back at her. "Sure." I'd never been interviewed before, and I had a bad feeling I would say something that would reveal how little I fit in. That was what usually happened. Having friends had been easy when I was little—the scarier or bloodier your stories were, the more other kids wanted to hear them—but middle school had changed everything. Scary stories lost their value to parties and fashion and kissing. Other girls weren't usually impressed by Bloody Pete, the murdered mascot rumored to run the football track on the full moon. What they really wanted to know was my celebrity crush. If only I could skip this part altogether—just have people *know* who I was.

We started across the field toward the woods, both of us with backpacks, me swinging my camping lantern. The lantern was more useful than a cell phone camera when looking for the ghost; it lasted longer, gave more light, and it didn't kill your battery. The trees stretched behind the high school, hiding the pond, the running trails, and the cemetery.

Grace started the recording on her phone. "Where are we going right now?"

I glanced at the phone, then back at the path before us. "We have to go to the old cemetery off Markel Road."

"Why didn't we drive there?"

"There's a specific set of rules you have to follow to get the ghost to appear. The first one is to walk through the woods until you reach the cemetery."

"How do you know these rules?"

I trailed my hand over the rusted sidebar of the soccer goal as we passed. There was a story about the soccer team dying in a bus crash in the sixties, but it wasn't true. "They're online. A lot of the story is well known. My brother was the one who told me."

"Your brother Tony?"

I bristled at the sound of someone else saying his name. She didn't know him, and that made it feel like she was trampling even farther into *our* thing, mine and his. "Yep."

Grace, to her credit, steered around that topic. "How long have you been looking for the ghost?"

"Since I was ten. So this'll be seven years."

"Have you ever seen any evidence of the Goon Creek Ghost?"

"My brother said he heard her speak once, but that was just my phone playing creepy noises behind a headstone."

Grace snorted. I decided she wasn't so bad. We reached the path into the woods, an inviting dirt trail that arced down to the pond and passed the dock. The moon was out, reflecting on the water and lighting our way. Laughter and voices floated on the air, and dark forms danced across the dock. That explained the other cars in the parking lot. I recognized a few letter jackets and one oversized alligator mascot head.

My insides knotted up with impending frustration.

"Yo, Gray-*SEE!*" The alligator's voice carried over the pond and the woods. Grace turned, already beaming. I went very still. A few others on the dock had turned to look. The alligator—the big cartoon head wobbled on top of a lanky teenage boy body—cut through the crowd to bound up the dock ramp toward us. "What are you doing here, newslady?"

"Are you allowed to have that head outside school property?" Grace asked.

The alligator reached up and pulled off his head. Inside was Sami Bitar, his shiny dark hair ruffled and a Cheshire Cat smile splitting his face. "It'll be back in the morning, don't worry. Oh, the phone's out. An interview?" He glanced at me. I stared back. Since grade school, Sami's voice had been a constant ice pick in my ear.

"I'm writing an article on the ghost, and Sydney agreed to be my guide," Grace said.

I shrugged by way of greeting.

"The Goon Creek Ghost?" Sami twisted around and called, "Hey, Allegra! Didn't you say you wanted to see the ghost?"

There is no ghost, I shouted in my head.

A girl split off from the group on the docks and my mood darkened. She wore black leggings and a Goon Creek crew neck, and her hair was up in a high ponytail. When she left the group, they lost their nucleus and had to shuffle around to re-form. They were all watching now.

Allegra Ferraro, voted Most Likely to Win Life, came up and leaned against Sami's side. "Hey, Grace. You're looking for the ghost?"

"With Sydney," Grace said, oblivious to the fact that I was in the midst of a slow and painful death, and the only way to save myself was to get away from these popular kids before I dissolved into a puddle of humiliation. "You want to come? It's going to be really fun. Overnighter."

I made a dying noise at the same time Allegra said, "Sure! My parents already think I'm spending the night at Kylie's." She turned back to the group. "You guys have fun without me, I'm going on an adventure."

Several people groaned. A few laughed. A large figure let out a startled cry and pushed his way from the group and toward us. Chris Maybank, in his custom-made letter jacket because the biggest size they made didn't fit him, stalked up the ramp.

"What the hell, Allegra," he said, combing his short hair into order. "You can't ditch me."

"Then come along," she said, hands on her hips. "Tell your parents where you're going, you know they'd be cool with it." Maybank—everyone called him Maybank, or Mabes, because he was one of nine Chrises in our class—scowled at her, but didn't retreat. Allegra said to us, "You don't mind, do you?"

"Not at all," Grace said. "Sydney?"

"Do I have a choice?"

Allegra and Sami laughed like it was a joke. But it was fine. They would all probably leave when they got bored, and while they were there, they could keep Grace occupied.

"You coming too, Sami?" Allegra asked.

Sami scoffed. "Hell no. I'm not stupid enough to hunt ghosts." He shoved the alligator head back on. "See you fools Monday." He pranced back down the dock.

"It's still a bit of a walk from here," I said, pointing down the trail and into the woods. "Are you both okay with that?"

"Walking's good for you." Allegra tightened her ponytail and started down the path. Maybank followed. Grace, looking ecstatic, restarted the recording on her phone and hurried along.

I crossed myself, pressed my hands together, and looked at the dark sky.

Grace was interviewing Allegra about her interest in the Goon Creek Ghost—she'd liked urban legends since she was little, and really loved scary movies, not something I would have attributed to the peppy track and field star—and while they walked ahead, I ended up next to Maybank. I wasn't a small person, but Maybank could've picked me up with one hand and rattled all the loose change out of me. His burly shoulders were hunched around his ears, his hands were jammed in his pockets, and his eyes darted from one side of the path to the other, watching the trees. Out of the three of them, he bothered me the least. He was quiet and he didn't seem to have any interest in me.

An October breeze rustled the leaves and cut through my long sleeves. It had been nearly eighty earlier in the day, and I hadn't thought a jacket would be necessary. I wrapped my arms around my middle.

"You cold?" Maybank said.

It took me a second to realize he was speaking to me. "I'll be fine."

Several minutes later, when the breeze hadn't let up and I felt my insides starting to shiver, Maybank shrugged off his letter jacket and held it out for me. He was only wearing a T-shirt underneath.

"I'm f-fine," I said.

Allegra looked over her shoulder. "Take the jacket. He's basically a human furnace."

"Yeah, I was sweating." Maybank offered the jacket again. Reluctantly, pretty sure they would think I was weirder if I didn't accept, I shed my backpack long enough to put on the jacket. Inside was toasty. Maybank stretched his arms over his head and yanked his T-shirt back down.

"Thanks, Chris."

"Call me Maybank."

"Okay."

I'd *known* he was called Maybank, but had never been invited to call him that myself. It was annoying that all three of them managed to make talking to people look so easy. I'd always thought popularity had more to do with how much money you had, or how good you were at being mean, but all they'd done was be chill. I was chill, wasn't I? I didn't judge people for what they said or did or looked like—

I'd done exactly that to all of them. Now that I thought of it, I'd done that to a lot of people. But that wasn't the reason people didn't like me. A lot of them judged me, too. *Ugh.* I bet none of them were analyzing every minute social interaction of their life right now. I flopped around trying to push up the sleeves of Maybank's letter jacket.

There was a soft *crack* in the trees to our right. Maybank stopped and said, "Did anyone else hear that?"

Then a dark form, misshapen and yelling, flew out of the underbrush. A shriek cut through the night as the shape crashed into Maybank, sending him to the ground in a tangle of limbs. Grace had her phone flashlight on them in the same instant Maybank shot up in victory, holding a cartoon alligator head in the air. Sprawled before him was Sami, cackling with laughter.

"Oh my god, you dick." Maybank turned away, scrubbing a hand over his head.

"You *screamed!*" Sami clapped his hands together and rolled up onto his knees. "I didn't know you had such a great falsetto, Mabes!"

Allegra swore under her breath. Grace lowered her phone with a sound of relief.

I was stuck between frustrated and rattled. Sami had to be so *loud*, and he had to do stupid stuff like *jump out* and interrupt us—

"I can't believe you all really thought I wasn't coming," Sami said. "Am I that good of a liar? I am, aren't I?"

"Get off the ground, you goob," Allegra said, helping him up. "It's not cool to scare someone like that. He could have hurt you."

"Nah, Mabes wouldn't do that." Sami brushed off his jacket and pants. Maybank threw the alligator head at Sami's chest so hard Sami lost his breath and stumbled backward. Then he laughed again. "You should go out for shotput, Mabes. Anyways, I changed my mind. I am coming with you."

My lips curled back. Grace immediately lit up. Maybank turned away, and Allegra put her hands on her hips. "No more scaring people," she said.

Sami put his hand over his heart. "Not on purpose. I swear it."

Allegra and Sami followed Maybank. Grace paused when she saw me standing there.

"You okay, Sydney? That was kind of scary."

"No, I'm not scared," I snapped. *Tony never messed around like this.* "I just—I don't like it when things get loud."

"Oh. Sami's pretty loud, isn't he?" She looked apologetic. "We should have asked if it was okay first for him to come. I'm sorry."

Grace did *look* genuinely sorry. How was it possible that everything she said sounded so honest? And how could she make me feel so bad about it? Anger drained out of me.

"Whatever," I said. "It's fine. Let's go."

"Hey!" Sami called from the bend in the path ahead. His voice carried twice as far in the night. "Hurry up, we have to get there *before* the sun comes up!"

Grace smiled and jogged to catch up. I plodded after her.

"Your brother is Tony Endrizzi, right?"

"I mean . . . do you know many other Endrizzis?" I asked.

Behind me, Allegra ignored the sarcasm and climbed over bubbled tree roots with a gymnast's ease. We'd left the path behind and now cut straight through the woods, a route Tony and I had taken every year, which meant I had to lead our little pack now. Unfortunately, I was the slowest of everyone, and the least in shape, and having the rest of them watching me from behind wasn't helping my coordination. I nearly pitched head-first over a large boulder hidden behind a root. There were lots of stories of people dying out here, and plenty were from bad falls. Yet another reason I didn't come here without Tony.

"Yeah, he's my brother," I said, putting all my attention into staying upright. "He graduated last year."

"He's so funny. He used to tell us about coming out here."

I glanced back at her, eyebrows shooting up. "You know him?"

"My sister was friends with him. He made this place sound so cool and mystical. I always wanted to go." She walked as if she was on level ground, hardly looking down. "Why didn't he come this year?"

Somewhere behind us, Sami cursed. "You all right?" Allegra called.

"Stupid alligator head," Sami called back, with no further explanation. I thought of Grace's sorry expression and counted backward from ten.

Allegra turned to me again.

"He's in school on the other side of the country," I said. One foot after the other.

Allegra rolled her eyes and nodded. "I know that feeling. My sister decided to go to school in London, and it's not like she has the money to come home. That bitch. I really miss her."

I slipped on a root. A big hand shot out to grab my right arm, and Allegra grabbed my left; together she and Maybank held me up while I found my footing again. "Ah, thanks, sorry." I scrambled back into place. My face burned, but neither of them laughed or teased me.

I cleared my throat and said loud enough for all of them to hear, "The ground is going to level out. Then we're going to get to the road on the hill. The hill is steep and the road is narrow, and we'll have to walk on the side of it so we don't get hit by any cars. They swing through fast. Then we'll come to a shoulder where the steps to the cemetery are."

They followed me across the last level patch of the forest before we met the cracked asphalt of the hill road. There were no streetlights here, and the trees rose tall and branchless above us. Phantom cars had been seen running off this road, only to vanish without any sign of a crash. The cemetery steps began at a tiny shoulder, only visible once I held my lantern over my head. The staircase was concrete, sunken into the side of the hill, cracked with weeds. Some of the steps had been completely overtaken.

"There are supposed to be fifty steps," I said, "but I've counted, and there are only thirty-five. We have to step on every one on the way up to be able to see the ghost, and we have to step on every one coming back down to stop her from following you home."

"Wait," Maybank said, "she *follows you home?*"

Sami clapped Maybank on the shoulder. "No skipping steps on this staircase, bud." Sami, who was known for bounding three steps at a time with his own lanky grasshopper legs, looked almost silly taking the narrow, densely packed stone staircase one step at a time. I went next—after swallowing a long sigh—so the lantern light led the way for the others.

We ascended slowly. Even Sami paced himself so he didn't leave the pool of light. Talk ceased so we could pay attention to our feet, to make sure we didn't miss the steps that had crumbled away or sunken into the hill until they were little more than a concrete face. Grace's breath fanned across the back of my neck. The trees twisted together overhead, blocking out the moonlight.

"Is there a reason for this?" Grace asked. Even though she whispered, the rest of us froze at her voice.

I shook myself out of it. "When you hit every stair, the ghost can hear your footsteps and knows you've arrived." I nudged Sami in the back to get him moving again. The stairs ended before we crested the hill, and the tangle of trees gave way. At the top, revealed by moonlight, was a cemetery twice the size of a basketball court, nestled in the woods. The headstones were worn as badly as the steps. No insects stirred in the darkness; the air hung still.

"Over here," I said, leading them to the center of the cemetery. A wrought-iron fence ringed what had once been a small paved circle where the paths through the cemetery met. In the circle's center was an overgrown flowerbed and a statue of an angel with her face in her hands, bearing a rusted plaque that read *Moss Hill Cemetery*. I set down my backpack and lantern by the angel. Grace dropped her bag with mine, and Sami set the alligator head beside them. "The first thing we do is circle up here, hold hands, and call the ghost."

They gathered with little fuss, but as we all joined hands, Sami said, "Is this like a Ouija board thing? Don't break the circle?"

"Yes," I said. "If you let go, the ghost climbs up your butt and moves you like a hand puppet."

Maybank spluttered, then cracked up. Sami, Grace, and Allegra all looked at me like they couldn't believe I'd said it. Apparently if you're a weirdo who likes ghosts too much, you can't also be funny.

When we were all ready, there was a long, uncertain pause. Tony had always been the one to recite the call when we'd come here. Now I was the only one who knew it. The others looked to me, waiting.

I cleared my throat.

"Winnifred Marsh," I said, "we summon you from your long sleep. Show yourself here before the hour of dawn and share the secrets of the afterlife."

Silence fell. Allegra, Maybank, and Sami looked around the cemetery as if expecting her to appear right there. Grace was the only one who watched me.

"How long do we have to stand like this?" Allegra asked.

"Until one of us feels a touch on the back of our neck," I said, and Maybank let out a very soft groan of discomfort.

After a few minutes of staring at each other, Allegra jumped and said, "I felt it! Oh my god, I felt it! On my neck! Four fingers and a thumb, like a little squeeze! Oh! Oh that was weird!"

"We can let go now," I said, and Allegra released me to clap a hand to her neck. She looked around at the rest of us with wonder. I'd had a hunch that one of them would feel something, or at least *think* they felt something. That was how it worked with spooky places: they made even the most unbelievable things real.

I couldn't help smiling. "That means she's here. There's a good chance she'll show herself to us before sunrise."

Grace went for her bag. "I did some research. I brought recorders to try to pick up sounds, and a video camera to see if we can catch anything." She glanced at me. "Just so I can say we did it for the story."

I shrugged. They could waste all the time they wanted.

"Now we wait?" Maybank said, shoulders hunched around his ears again. "All night here?"

"It's already midnight," Sami said.

"We would've been hanging out on the dock anyway," Allegra added, wandering off to look at the headstones. Maybank helped Grace with her equipment; Sami loped off to join Allegra.

I found my usual place against the wrought-iron fence, where a bed of moss and vines had grown over the stones and the bottom of the wrought iron. I dumped the snacks out of my bag, grabbed a package of Twizzlers, and took my phone from my pocket. No signal out here, of course, but it made me feel better to look at the screen. Until I saw the time. We had to sit out here for at least six more hours, and the others showed no signs of giving up early.

With Tony, filling time had never been a problem. We played cards, ate snacks, talked until sunrise. There was nothing wrong with Grace and Allegra and Maybank—and Sami too, I guess, though he could stand to shut up sometimes—but this just didn't seem like it would be the same.

"Are you okay, Syd?" Grace asked. We were already on a nickname basis, apparently, but I found it didn't bother me so much.

I started to respond, realized my throat was tight, and coughed to clear it. I waved the Twizzlers, as if that answered her question at all. "How's the setup?"

Grace had a recorder at the edge of the flowerbed and another in her hands. "I know we're not going to get anything, but it's fun to think we might. Makes things creepier, you know?" She sat next to me. Maybank had gone off to join Allegra and Sami at the north edge of the cemetery, where they'd found something on one of the headstones. "I hope them coming along didn't ruin your night. I know you didn't want to do this."

I glanced sideways at her and offered her a Twizzler. She took it.

"They're fine," I said.

She rolled her eyes. "Come on. Sami has been bugging the crap out of you all night. It's okay—he bugs me sometimes, too."

I raised my eyebrows. "Something *bugs* you? I thought you only had positive emotions."

I worried suddenly that she would take that the wrong way, but she laughed like I'd been joking with her instead of at her, which I had. "Hey, I can be mysterious, too! If Sami says or does something to annoy you, tell him to stop, and he will. It's kind of magic—you know how, when you tell boys to stop doing something, usually they'll do it more? Sami's not like that. *And* he thinks you're cool, so he'll do whatever you tell him."

"He thinks I'm cool?"

"He told me he saw you in the cafeteria line one time and was trying to think of things he could talk to you about. I guess he thought you would have been angry if he'd brought up ghosts."

He was right, I would have been angry. I would have thought he was making fun of me. I didn't need Sami Bitar to think I was cool, but the idea that someone was actively trying to get to know me was way more endearing than I expected it to be.

Sami, Allegra, and Maybank came trotting back to us then, Sami looking jazzed, Allegra wide awake, and Maybank on alert. They'd found a tombstone near the back that Sami swore had Winnifred Marsh's name on it. As Sami finished his story, he eyed my Twizzlers, and after a moment of deliberation, I held the package out for him. To his credit, he took only one.

"So, Sydney," he said, "does this mean you're going to talk to us at school now?"

I snorted. "Why would you want me to do that?"

I only realized how harsh it sounded after it was out of my mouth. They all fell into silence, expressions confused. I cleared my throat and said, "I—do—do I not talk to you often? I mean—you actually *want* me to talk to you?"

Grace, always the champion, waved her hands as if she could scrub out the conversation. "It's just that you're aloof, you know?" She looked to the others. "Mysterious, right?"

They nodded. "Like you're secretly a spy," Sami said.

"If I was a spy, I'd blend in better." A strange sort of numbness began in my feet and spread up my legs.

Allegra shrugged. "I don't know anyone who really knows you. I thought you didn't need friends."

"Didn't *need* friends?"

"Some people don't, at least not in school," she went on, as if it wasn't anything strange. "They have friends outside of school, in church or clubs or whatever. I'm not big on forcing myself on people who don't want more friends."

I rocked back and let their still-confused looks sink in. I hadn't had friends this whole time not because they thought I was weird and didn't want to be near me, but because I hadn't *put myself out there*? When I was little, it hadn't been like this; I'd had Tony, and kids on our street, and other kids in my class who either went to different schools or grew apart from me. No one had ever said one day I'd have to put in *work* to find friends—friends were supposed to show up and click with you and everything was supposed to make perfect sense.

"I'm sorry," I said, keeping my voice as level as I could, "I'm having a small existential crisis right now. I was convinced you all thought I was the weirdest person alive and wouldn't have touched me with a ten-foot pole."

Sami didn't even hesitate. "I've literally been trying to be friends with you since kindergarten."

"You were in my kindergarten class?"

"*Yes.* You had shoes that lit up when you walked." He was sitting on his knees now, holding out his hands as if he wanted to squeeze my head between them. "And you had the big box of crayons and you used *all of them.* You were so *cool.*"

"We didn't think you were weird," Grace said, cocking her head to the side and smiling, like I'd told a small joke. "Quiet, sure. You liked being alone."

Maybank grunted. "And you saved my biology grade freshman year."

I had to think about that one. "With the presentation on chromosomes? When we were in a group together?" I'd done most of the work because my group mates were all football players and had an important game at the end of that week.

Maybank nodded and looked embarrassed. "I've been meaning to make it up to you."

"Oh my *god!*" I yelled, loud enough that Maybank jumped and a few dark shapes fluttered out of the trees. "Am I clinically oblivious?"

Maybank scratched the back of his neck. "You're not oblivious."

Both he and Allegra flushed, looking the most ashamed I'd ever seen them. "You weren't completely wrong," Allegra said. "About—about the weirdness. But we didn't know you, and it's easy to make assumptions about a person when you don't know them. We're really sorry."

Maybank nodded.

"It's . . . okay," I said. I had already thought they found me weird; the apology was the surprising part. "Apologies accepted. As long as you don't start treating me like I'm weird again."

"I promise," Allegra said, holding up a hand. Maybank quickly copied her, and Sami and Grace followed, even though they hadn't had to apologize.

Then I laughed, because I couldn't think of what else to do, shook my head, and rubbed my eyes. "We're dumbasses."

"Yeah, kind of," Sami said.

Then we all laughed.

And like that, we were five friends hanging out in a graveyard.

While Grace dumped her protein bars and granola in the pile with the chips and candy, Allegra declared a round of blackjack using Skittles as currency. Maybank sat so close to me our knees were touching, like it wasn't anything weird to be sharing space. Sami promised he was going to take us for all we were worth, then proceeded to bust four times in a row.

The night passed. A few cars whispered by on the narrow road below the staircase, a few bats fluttered overhead, but no ghost appeared. The Ghost of Goon Creek became the excuse for us to haunt the graveyard until the early morning hours. Grace abandoned her notes and her recorders in favor of a game of speed against me, in which she beat me without breaking a sweat; Allegra found a bird skeleton behind one of the headstones and took pictures; Maybank sat around looking uncomfortable until Sami challenged him to sprints, and they took off from one end of the cemetery to the other. Maybank won; Sami tried to pants him as revenge; Maybank chased Sami up a tree, where Sami perched on a branch ten feet up and crowed at the sky.

When we sat around the lantern again, I unloaded all the local ghost stories I knew, every urban legend, every unsolved mystery. Everything Goon Creek and the surrounding towns had to offer. Things I'd looked into myself, nothing Tony had taught me.

"I collect them," I finally admitted. "I want to put them all in a book."

Sami snapped his fingers. "We should investigate them, and you and Gracie can write a book about it."

"You all actually want to do this again?"

"Yes," Allegra blurted out immediately, and no one argued with her, not even Maybank.

I shrugged, but I couldn't say I wasn't excited by the idea. I'd thought about going to seek out the other stories, but I'd never done it because Tony had never wanted to go.

Tony had been my only friend for too damn long. He'd moved on; maybe it was time for me to do the same thing.

Bleary-eyed and stuffed with junk food, we lay in the grass around the angel statue and watched the sky lighten over the treetops.

"Better head back," I said, dragging myself up. "It'll take a while."

"Oh god," Sami groaned from inside the alligator head. He'd been wearing it for the last half hour, swearing he wasn't falling asleep but occasionally snoring. "I forgot we have to walk all the way back."

"It's a shorter distance in the light."

One by one, we peeled ourselves off the ground and packed up our things. The cemetery was quiet; the dewy morning softened the overgrown foliage and cradled the worn headstones. We trudged back down the steps—every single one of them—to the narrow road.

The walk back through the woods was silent in a nice sort of way. My throat was sore from talking, my face tired from smiling. I'd sleep the rest of the day when I got home. The only one who didn't seem to feel the effects of staying up all night was Grace, who still looked fresh as a spring day.

Sami threw his arms into the air when the soccer field and the parking lot appeared. "Salvation!"

"Roll your window down while you're driving so the wind keeps you awake," Allegra said, pulling her ponytail out and wincing as she massaged her scalp. "Did you hear what I said? Drive safe."

"So we are doing this again, right?" Sami asked. "For Syd and Gracie's book?"

"Sounds good to me," Maybank replied, sounding surprised to hear himself say it. He held my backpack while I shrugged out of his letter jacket. "It was fun."

"I'm definitely in." Allegra yawned. "Mabes, you're driving me home. I'll see you all at school. Later."

"See you Gracie, see you Syd." Sami bounded off to his own car, buoyed by his second wind.

The three of them drove off. I had expected to feel hollow at their departure, like the night's openness around each

other had evaporated, but all I felt now was the light giddiness
that comes with too little sleep. They'd all started calling me
Syd. I had each of their phone numbers saved in my phone.
I knew things about them not many other people knew, and
they knew things about me. Too much for any of us to stay
mysterious.

"Do you have everything for your article?" I asked Grace as
she stuffed her bag and supplies into her car.

"Oh, definitely," she said. "It's going to be so great—I'll
send you a draft as soon as I have it typed up."

"That's okay, you don't have to. I trust you." I picked at my
backpack strap. "So . . . I figured Sami was joking about actually going around visiting all those places for the book."

Grace looked up at me, and for a horrible split second I
thought she was going to agree that it had been a joke, that of
course Sami hadn't meant it.

"No way," she said. "He was very serious. And I think it's
a great idea. It would be amazing to collaborate on it, and with
the others it could be so Scooby-Doo . . . oh my god, we should
give ourselves a name! Okay, I'm going to go home and think of
a group name, and you make a list of places we're going to go.
We could make a video series. We could make a *podcast*. This
is going to be *amazing*, I can't wait." Grace jumped into her car
and leaned out the window as she turned the ignition. "I'll text
you later with ideas!"

Then she was gone, too, and I was left alone. But I didn't feel
alone; I felt all of them still there, with shared memories of where
we went tonight, and the warmth of their numbers in my phone.

I took my phone out. The signal was strong here.

Went to see the ghost tonight, I typed. Then I paused, thought for a moment, deleted that text, and retyped.

My friends are doing a podcast of local ghost stories. Let me know if you want to be a guest.

I sent it. Tony didn't respond; he wouldn't wake up for hours.

ACKNOWLEDGMENTS

Mom and Dad, thank you for putting up with your insomniac child for years and for ignoring the flashlight under my covers as I stayed up (way) past my bedtime to read. I love you both more than anything in the world and am so grateful to have you as my parents.

Contributors, thank you for putting your hearts into these stories. I'm absolutely honored to be the editor of this anthology and am in love with every piece in this collection. You have my endless gratitude for making *Up All Night* even better than I'd imagined. It's magical and perfect.

Jim McCarthy, thank you for your continued guidance and support. We just passed our six-year anniversary as agent and client. I'm so grateful to have you at my side.

Algonquin, you have my endless thanks not only for publishing this anthology but also for packaging it so beautifully. Thank you to my lovely and insightful editor, Krestyna Lypen. Thank you to the brilliant Connie Gabbert for designing this absolutely gorgeous cover. And thank you to the entire Algonquin team, including but certainly not limited to Kelly Doyle, Megan Harley, and Ashley Mason.

My friends and family, thank you for your support. This past year has been difficult for all of us, but like the aim of this anthology, you've all brought a little magic to my life. Thank you to: Bubbie, Papa Bobby, Kayla Burson, Kiki Chatzopoulou, Alison Doherty, Brittany Kane, Deborah Kim, Katie King, Alex Kuntz, Elise LaPlante, Katherine Menezes, Anna Meriano, Christy Michell, Lauren Sandler Rose, Ariel Russ, Melissa Sandler, Amanda Saulsberry, Lauren Vassallo, and Kayla Whaley.

And lastly, thank you to readers, teachers, librarians, and booksellers. Without you, none of this would be possible. Thank you for taking a chance on this collection.

The middle of the night has always been a magical time for me. I hope these stories allow you to access all the wonderful, unique feelings that can be stumbled upon only in those odd hours.

Thank you for reading.

All my best,
Laura Silverman

ABOUT THE AUTHORS

BRANDY COLBERT is the author of several books for children and teens, including *The Voting Booth*, *The Only Black Girls in Town*, and Stonewall Book Award winner *Little & Lion*. She is co-writer of Misty Copeland's *Life in Motion* young readers edition, and her short fiction and essays have been published in a variety of anthologies. Her books have been chosen as Junior Library Guild Selections and have appeared on many best-of lists, including the American Library Association's Best Fiction for Young Adults and Quick Picks for Reluctant Young Adult Readers. She is on the faculty at Hamline University's MFA program in Writing for Children, and lives in Los Angeles.

KATHLEEN GLASGOW is the *New York Times* bestselling author of the young adult novels *Girl in Pieces* and *How to Make Friends with the Dark*. She lives in Arizona. You can find her online at kathleenglasgowbooks.com, on Twitter: @kathglasgow, and on Instagram: @misskathleenglasgow.

MAURENE GOO is the author of several critically acclaimed books for young adults, including *I Believe in a Thing Called Love*, *The Way You Make Me Feel*, and *Somewhere Only We Know*. She lives in Los Angeles with her husband and cat, Maeby.

TIFFANY D. JACKSON is the author of the Coretta Scott King–John Steptoe New Talent Award–winning *Monday's Not Coming*; the NAACP Image Award–nominated *Allegedly*; *Let Me Hear a Rhyme*; and *Grown*. She received her bachelor of arts in film from Howard University and her master of arts in media studies from the New School, and has over a decade of TV and film experience. The Brooklyn native is a lover of naps, cookie dough, and beaches, and is currently residing in the borough she loves, most likely multitasking.

AMANDA JOY is the author of *A River of Royal Blood*. She earned her MFA in Writing for Children at the New School. She lives in Chicago with her dog, Luna. You can find her online at amandajoywrites.com, and on Instagram and Twitter: @amandajoywrites.

NINA LaCOUR is the nationally bestselling and Michael L. Printz Award–winning author of *We Are Okay*, *Watch Over Me*, and several other novels for teenagers. She hosts a podcast called *Keeping a Notebook* and is the founder of the Slow Novel Lab. Nina also writes for young children and adults. You can find her online at ninalacour.com, and on Instagram and Twitter: @nina_lacour.

KAREN M. McMANUS is the #1 *New York Times, USA Today,* and internationally bestselling author of *One of Us Is Lying* and its sequel, *One of Us Is Next*; *Two Can Keep a Secret*; and *The Cousins.* Her work has been translated into more than forty languages worldwide. Karen lives in Massachusetts and holds a master's degree in journalism from Northeastern University, which she mostly uses to draft fake news stories for her novels. You can find her online at karenmcmanus.com, and on Instagram and Twitter: @writerkmc.

ANNA MERIANO is the author of the Love Sugar Magic series and *This Is How We Fly.* She graduated from Rice University and earned her MFA in Writing for Children from the New School. Anna works as a tutor and part-time teacher in her hometown of Houston. In her free time, she likes to knit and play full-contact quidditch. She stayed awake for thirty-six hours at her senior prom.

MARIEKE NIJKAMP is a #1 *New York Times* bestselling author of young adult novels, graphic novels, and comics. Her work includes *This Is Where It Ends, Even If We Break,* and *The Oracle Code.* She also edited the anthology *Unbroken: 13 Stories Starring Disabled Teens.* Marieke is a nonbinary, disabled storyteller, dreamer, and geek.

LAURA SILVERMAN is an author and freelance editor who currently lives in Brooklyn, NY. She earned her MFA in Writing for Children at the New School. Her books include *Girl Out of Water*, *You Asked for Perfect*, *It's a Whole Spiel*, *Recommended for You*, and the upcoming *Those Summer Nights*. *Girl Out of Water* was a Junior Library Guild Selection, and *You Asked for Perfect* was named to best teen fiction lists by YALSA, Chicago Public Library, and the Georgia Center for the Book. You can find her online at LauraSilvermanWrites.com, and on Twitter: @LJSilverman1.

KAYLA WHALEY lives outside of Atlanta, where she buys too many books and drinks too many lattes. Her work has appeared in the anthologies *Here We Are*, *Unbroken*, and *Vampires Never Get Old*, as well as in publications like *Bustle*, *Catapult*, and *Michigan Quarterly Review*. She holds an MFA from the University of Tampa and was formerly senior editor at *Disability in Kidlit*.

JULIAN WINTERS is the author of the IBPA Benjamin Franklin Gold Award–winning *Running with Lions*; the Junior Library Guild Selections *How to Be Remy Cameron* and *The Summer of Everything*; and the upcoming *Right Where I Left You*. A former management trainer, Julian currently lives outside of Atlanta, where he can be found reading, being a self-proclaimed comic book geek, or watching the only two sports he can follow—volleyball and soccer.

FRANCESCA ZAPPIA lives in Indiana and graduated from the University of Indianapolis with a degree in computer science and mathematics. When she's not writing, she's reading, cooking, or playing video games. She was chosen as the 2017 Emerging Author at the Indiana Authors Awards. Her second novel, *Eliza and Her Monsters*, was chosen as a *Kirkus* Best Teen Book of 2017 and a Junior Library Guild Selection, and was among the Top 10 of the YALSA 2018 Best Fiction for Young Adults list. You can find her online at francescazappia.com, and on Instagram and Twitter: @ChessieZappia.

KATIE KING

Laura Silverman is an author and freelance editor in Brooklyn, NY. She earned her MFA in Writing for Children at the New School. Her books include *Girl Out of Water, You Asked for Perfect, It's a Whole Spiel,* and *Recommended for You.* You can contact her online on Twitter @LJSilverman1 or through her website, LauraSilvermanWrites.com.